Like S In Heaven

Siobhan Dunmoore Book 3

Eric Thomson

Like Stars in Heaven
Copyright 2016 Eric Thomson
Third paperback printing February 2021

All rights reserved.
This book, or parts thereof, may not be reproduced in any form without permission.

This is a work of fiction. Names, characters, places and incidents either are the product of the author's imagination or are used fictitiously, and any resemblance to actual persons, living or dead, business establishments, events or locales is entirely coincidental.

Published in Canada
By Sanddiver Books
ISBN: 978-1-537294-70-4

— Lost —

War, now entering its seventh year, still raged across the stars. Humans and Shrehari kept dying as their admirals and generals struggled to find a weakness, a lever, anything that could break the stalemate.

The log buoy, a large, torpedo-shaped, unmanned spacecraft, did not care about the conflagration that had claimed so many lives already. Nothing actually concerned it. It had long since lost what little machine consciousness it might have had.

Centuries spent hurtling through interstellar space had completely drained its energy reserves, and its trajectory had not come close enough to any stars that might have helped recharge them.

Carrying the final message from colonists who had landed on a distant world after a long voyage, it had been aimed at what they guessed was the general direction of their home system. They had programmed the buoy to accelerate to a very high fraction of the speed of light over the course of many years before coasting to its destination.

The colonists did not believe that anyone would ever read the message it carried, let alone act on it, but since the buoy had one function and one only, it had cost nothing to launch it.

And so it sped on, for much longer than the brief centuries during which humanity had progressed from the first artificial satellite to a Commonwealth spanning more than fifty star systems, and now battling another sentient, space-faring empire.

It would have kept going until some natural phenomenon destroyed it, or until the universe eventually died. The course it followed would not have come close to its intended destination, but it would eventually enter human-controlled space and not that of the Commonwealth's deadly enemy.

The buoy did not notice. It had not noticed anything for a long, long time.

Even if the impossible happened and it reached the descendants of its makers, the craft would be unable to account for its voyage. Only the data etched into its memory circuits by those who launched it remained.

The buoy did not realize that had it slipped by a Shrehari patrol ship, unseen and undetected, years before the empire's feckless leadership planned a war while trade still crossed the nebulous boundary between the two future foes. Nor did it notice the abrupt end of a long peace followed by the plunge into killing on a galactic scale.

By then, it had reached the rim of human-controlled space. From there, it would coast across the Commonwealth for several centuries, still undetected, before vanishing into the Coalsack Sector.

A scavenger, one with sensors more finely tuned than most, and blessed with a hefty dose of good luck, was looking for opportunity far from the fighting. In due course, it detected a mass of cold metal traveling at something approaching relativistic speeds.

Sailing along the far edges of the frontier and with little to show for the voyage so far, its captain decided to tackle the tricky process that would slow the object down sufficiently so they could recover it.

The operation failed, but had the buoy's mind still been active, it would have noticed a distinct decrease in velocity.

A second try by the same ship a year later, after Nabhka and Cimmeria had fallen into Shrehari hands, reduced the little craft's speed even further. A third attempt, in the weeks before Siobhan Dunmoore, acting captain of the battleship *Victoria Regina*, made her last stand against Brakal, attracted the attention of a Navy survey cruiser, which took over from the scavenger.

It managed to bleed off the log buoy's remaining velocity and, upon inspection, claimed it for the government.

Against all hope and indeed against all probability, the log buoy had made it home, bearing a final message from a colonization ship launched centuries earlier, during humanity's first exodus to the stars, and believed lost without a trace.

Unfortunately, with a war raging, no one cared that the buoy's long voyage should have been impossible, that it defied humanity's understanding of space and time.

One

"It almost seems unfair," Lieutenant Commander Pushkin said, voice pitched low as he stared at the main screen.

"Why is that?" Siobhan Dunmoore's lips twisted with amusement at her first officer's comment.

"I feel like a schoolyard bully about to give the smallest kid in class a thorough thrashing."

"Would you rather feel like the smallest kid in class watching the bully come straight at you?"

"Of course not. I just seem to have had a brief moment of chivalry creep up on me for some reason."

"Fairness in war?" She snorted. "Please. If you're in a fair fight, you've screwed up somewhere along the way. Besides, we're not responsible for them having crappy sensor gear. We're not responsible for the war. Moreover, we're definitely not responsible for this one coming to snoop in a system we just happen to be picketing this week. The captain of that Shrehari corvette chose poorly."

"Shall we offer them the chance to surrender?"

"How many prisoners of war do we hold, Gregor?"

"None," he grudgingly admitted. "Or at least none the Admiralty will admit to."

Dunmoore nodded.

"Correct. Guns, how long until the enemy is in range?"

"Another five minutes for an optimal missile solution." Lieutenant Syten replied.

"I can't believe they haven't seen our maneuvering thrusters," Chief Guthren commented from his helm station. The coxswain, or Chief of the Ship, had taken the controls from the quartermaster of the watch the moment Dunmoore had called battle stations.

Though the ship was running silent, either all systems shut down or dampened to imitate the radiation signature of a mere asteroid, she had risked using thrusters to put them on a converging track with the badly shielded Shrehari corvette.

The enemy ship had attempted a covert run into the Alpha Cephei system, hoping to raid some of the mining colonies scattered among the moons of Amun, a massive gas giant. Unfortunately, even dampened, it leaked emissions to such an extent that it could not remain hidden from *Stingray's* more advanced sensors, especially not when those were under the keen eyes of Petty Officer Third Class 'Banger' Rownes, gunner's mate and fast becoming one of the best sensor techs on board.

"Probably blinded by their own reactors," the gray-haired petty officer remarked. "If they're on passive, as they should be, we'd have to light up like a Founder's Day party to register."

"True," Guthren nodded. "Mister Pushkin is right; it does seem a tad unsporting, but when it comes to the boneheaded bastards, I'll take any advantage without guilt, even if it feels like I'm beating up on a scrawny kid."

Lieutenant Kowalski, sitting at the signals station, snorted loudly.

"I fail to see how the Shrehari could be characterized as scrawny, cox'n. Their smallest look to be about your size, and you're not exactly tiny among humans."

"Okay then," he conceded, "it's more like the smart kid in class asking the village idiot to calculate the square root of infinity."

"Alright, alright," Dunmoore cut off the banter with hands raised in surrender. If she let it go on, Pushkin would jump in and when he and the coxswain got going, they did not stop until they had thoroughly derailed the discussion.

"Let's agree that the universe is unjust and because of that, we're about to send a crew of Shrehari to join their ancestors in the most expeditious way possible. Time, Mister Syten?"

"Two minutes." She tapped Penzara, her gunnery chief, on the shoulder. "Cycle the launchers and open the doors. Start the pre-ignition countdown."

"Aye," the grizzled, blocky non-com replied. Then a few moments later, he said, "All tubes are prepared to launch at your command."

"Ready to go 'up systems,' Number One?" Siobhan looked questioningly at the first officer.

"Ready."

"Let's ruin their day, then. It's been too long since we painted the last kill mark on our hull."

In fact, it had been over a year, in and around a system at the other end of the extended area of space that defined the almost seven-year-old war zone.

"Too bad reivers don't count as kills, sir," the blonde gunnery officer commented.

"Reiver marks are too ugly for our pristine hull," Pushkin replied with a dismissive shrug. "And anyway, we'd have to spend too much time sifting through the logs of the battle of Arietis to figure out which one of us nailed each bastard. As I recall, the mercenaries did pretty well in the eradication department."

"Time," Syten raised her hand.

"Up systems," Dunmoore ordered, the excitement of battle rising through her like a flush of heat.

Weeks of patrolling system after system, in case a long ranging Shrehari raider dared make an appearance, had not been quite as annoying as their service on the Coalsack frontier before the Arietis affair, but she still felt relief at finding a valid enemy target. There would be no second-guessing and no calculating the political fallout in this case. She merely had to engage the enemy and destroy him.

Around her, the ship came to life instantly when power surged through dormant systems. Even with passive sensors, the Shrehari had to spot them now. It would be interesting to see how the opposing commander would react.

"Do you think he'll keep trying to hide on the off chance that we might not have seen him?" Pushkin asked.

Dunmoore did not respond immediately. Instead, she nodded at Syten, ordering the gunnery officer to fire off a brace of anti-ship missiles. When the faint vibration of their launch had subsided, she smiled at Pushkin.

"If he thought he had a chance when we lit up, our birds screaming at him will soon extinguish that notion."

"He's gone active," Rownes reported. "His shields are up, and he's powering his guns. We're being painted by his targeting sensors."

"Quick little bugger, isn't he?" Guthren said with grudging admiration. "Though it won't do him much good."

"His point defense is opening fire." Penzara frowned at his screen. "All four birds are gone."

"What?" Dunmoore leaned forward in the command chair. "They must have improved their targeting systems since we last fought them. Another brace, if you please, then have the guns open up."

"He's fired at us. Six missiles," Rownes shook her head. "They've improved launchers as well it seems. I can't recall the *Ptar* class being able to shoot off more than four at a time."

"External tubes, maybe," Penzara scratched his chin. "I can't see how you could build extra ones inside the hull."

"Please tell me the missiles are still the old standard birds we're used to."

"Aye, Captain. Shouldn't be a problem for our calliopes."

The point defense guns were so named because of their multi-barrel configuration resembling nothing so much as an ancient steam organ with six tubes, but spitting superheated matter. They opened fire the moment the enemy missiles came into range and handily overwhelmed them.

"Crap," Rownes exclaimed. "He's spooling up his jump drives."

"A Shrehari running from a fight?" Pushkin sounded almost aggrieved.

"Maybe they got smarter during our absence, Number One. The commander of that *Ptar* knows he can't defeat us, no matter how many missiles his extra tubes can chuck out."

"That's rather unfair," the first officer replied plaintively. "Our first Shrehari target and we don't even get the —"

Penzara's jubilant shout cut him off.

"Two birds got through. His starboard shield is down."

"Firing now," Syten called out.

Large caliber plasma rounds sped away, leaving a broken trail of light that briefly connected the two ships. The Shrehari replied in kind, but having failed to breach *Stingray*'s shields, his smaller bore guns had no effect, though they created lovely blue and green auroras around the frigate as energies collided.

A patch on the corvette's hull began to blacken and buckle as shot after shot slammed home. Then, the image of the Shrehari vessel shimmered on the screen, and he vanished.

"One more round, dammit," Pushkin thumped his fist down on his console. "I could swear I saw the hull puncture and gasses erupt a fraction of a second before he jumped."

"Wishful thinking, sir?" Guthren asked with a hint of mischief at the first officer's disappointment.

"No, Mister Pushkin is right," Rownes said. "The logs show a hull puncture." She flashed a rather blurry image on the screen. "This is a nanosecond before he disappeared. If you look carefully, you can see a cloud of something on the hull."

"With any luck, he'll take too long to isolate the affected compartments and start having trouble maintaining his hyperspace bubble." The first officer shook his head. "Our luck that is."

"Shall we pursue, Captain?" The sailing master, though sounding dubious, seemed ready to plot a stern chase.

"No. By the time we reorient, our chances will be that much poorer, and there's no telling if there's another *Ptar* around, just waiting for the picket ship to hare off on a wild chase."

Though she sounded disappointed, no one mistook the gleam of satisfaction in her eyes. She had damaged the Shrehari, and that gave her more joy than anything else she had done in a long time.

"Probably for the best, Captain." Pushkin agreed. "Shall I release the ship from battle stations?"

"Sure." She stood and shook the tension from her shoulders. "Set us back to cruising stations and resume regular watch keeping. Mister Kowalski, I believe it's your turn?"

"Aye Captain." The thin signals officer locked her console and stepped across the bridge to take the command chair. "I relieve you."

"I stand relieved," Siobhan replied in the age-old formula. "I'll be in my quarters, drowning my sorrows in coffee as I compose an inconclusive contact report to HQ."

*

Dunmoore looked up from the chessboard, a predatory smile spreading across her lean, seamed face. The years of war had not been kind to her and under the shock of gray-tinged copper hair, she looked older than her real age. Her gray eyes, however, retained the hard gleam of vigorous youth.

She moved her knight and sat back, watching the expression on Pushkin's face. After a few moments, the first officer whistled softly and nodded.

"I've seen your self-control and ability to practice patience improve bit by bit ever since we got away from Arietis, Captain, but I didn't expect you to do so well, so soon."

"Checkmate, Gregor." The hungry grin widened, showing even, white teeth between thin lips while she savored her first victory over Pushkin, a rite of passage so to speak. The first officer had often accused her of being too rash, too impatient, and it had nearly cost the entire crew their lives. To atone for it, she had worked hard to master her temperament, using their daily chess games as one of many instruments to improve self-discipline.

"Indeed, sir. Congratulations. A hard-won victory, but a good one nonetheless." He looked up and met her eyes, his expression speaking of more than just one game of chess.

"Indeed." She rose and stretched her lean, almost thin body. "It's been thirty-six hours since the Shrehari *Ptar* jumped. If he had buddies with him, we would likely have spotted them by now."

"Do you think he'll come back?"

"Doubtful. We gave him a nasty hit, and he'll need some quiet time at a secure base to patch the hole. God knows what internal damage he suffered along with it. He's a tad far from his lines as it is."

"Then it's off to the Marengo system. At least we'll be able to dock at Valeux Station and stretch our legs."

Dunmoore snorted.

"I'm pretty sure the authorities there won't be thrilled at the thought of several hundred Navy spacers descending on their questionable bazaars. I'm also pretty sure that our chief engineer won't be wanting us to dock a ship this size on the kind of array Valeux sports, even if it's rated for our tonnage."

"Do you enjoy taking the fun out of things, Captain?" Pushkin asked in jest, as he stowed the chess pieces in their lined case. "Or did Arietis turn you into a grown-up?"

She stuck out her tongue at him, knowing he could not see the gesture, but felt oddly disheartened. Perhaps she had experienced a surge of maturity after the way she resolved the problem Admiral Corwin's madness had posed. It would certainly explain her greater caution of late. At least she could now boast of defeating the best chess player on the ship.

"Perhaps a mug of Shrehari ale might cheer you up," he suggested.

"Contraband?" Dunmoore affected a scandalized expression. "I thought you were supposed to be my conscience."

"Only in matters concerning *Stingray*." He snapped the case shut. A faint bell rang six times, making him smile. "Supper time. No wonder my stomach has been plaguing me. Perhaps my being distracted by hunger allowed you to win."

"Excuses, excuses, Gregor." She grinned. "Have no fear; I won't broadcast my victory to the wardroom. At least not tonight."

"The real trick," he replied, mischief twinkling in his hooded eyes, "is to repeat the feat."

The sound of a soft chime interrupted what would no doubt have been a tart reply.

"Bridge to the captain. We've received orders from Third Fleet HQ. I've had them piped to your console."

Pushkin's eyebrows shot up. "From Fleet HQ? A tad unusual, no? Usually, they send orders via the battle group."

"We're a bit out of the 39th's normal area of operations, thanks to Admiral Ryn hiding us on a patrol route as far away from civilization as she could. If higher headquarters has a mission for us that doesn't involve a return to Isabella Colony, it makes sense to transmit directly."

"True," he nodded. "I don't suppose that our next orders will see us vanish even deeper into space."

"Why not?" Dunmoore ran a gloved hand through her short hair. "We remain a liability for certain people until they act on their schemes."

"You'd think Admiral Nagira would keep them away from us."

Nagira, Siobhan's one-time commander, and mentor was the closest thing to a friend she had among flag officers. He had been responsible for her first command assignment, and for the current one. The fact that he had joined a cabal of senior officers opposed to the government did not erase the debt she owed him.

"Before we sink into idle speculation, why don't you let me read our orders." She sat down behind her desk and called up the recorded transmission.

"Oh dear," she said after a few minutes. "I guess we are vanishing deeper into space, but not in the way you meant it, Gregor."

The first officer gazed at her with barely restrained irritation, and she laughed gently at his expression.

"Are you taking on some of my impatience?" When he did not respond other than to narrow his eyes, she relented.

"We dock at Starbase 37 and pick up a Colonel Kalivan along with enough supplies for a very long-range mission, said mission being unspecified."

"I suppose I'll get the bosun to change one of the storerooms into a cabin." He sighed. "Having an officer senior in rank to you on board is going to be interesting, and not in a good way, even if he is a jarhead."

"Army, actually."

"Really?" Pushkin frowned. "Why are we about to carry a green grunt as a mission specialist for a trip into the galaxy's nether regions?"

"These orders don't say which means we'll likely find out from Colonel Kalivan himself when he comes aboard. In the meantime, let's eat and then get our sailing master to plot a least-time transit to our destination. Prepare a list of stores we need for an extended patrol mission. I'll add it to my acknowledgment message. Hopefully, the 37th won't balk at feeding a cuckoo from another battle group."

"Why should they? We're under orders from Fleet. If they complain, I'll just wave those instructions under their collective noses." Pushkin half-smiled.

"Just don't let Mister Kutora deal directly with their supply section for parts; otherwise, whatever goodwill we get from traveling under the aegis of high command will evaporate."

"No fear on that account. I think I've convinced our gentle chief engineer to control his temper and at least appear to be polite. You may recall that our last sojourn in port resulted in no complaints whatsoever."

"That almost deserves a commendation, Gregor."

"You simply have to know his weak spots." He brushed away the compliment. "Did you have any thoughts about captain's stores? I'm sure the colonel will expect you to entertain him."

Siobhan sighed.

"I suppose I should get that organized as well. Why do I suddenly feel less than enthusiastic about our new task?"

"Because you've been scalded in the recent past. Time to eat," he added, heading for the cabin door before they broached an uncomfortable philosophical discussion.

— Two —

Only a few of the beggars, whores and other assorted discards of society moved aside with any sort of alacrity at the passage of the powerfully-built Shrehari of the Warrior Caste. His well-worn civilian clothes contrasted with the green sash and long, curved dagger at his waist, marking him as a member of the Imperial Deep Space Fleet on half-pay, possibly discarded by the Admiralty for one failing or other.

The disreputable quarters of Shredar, by the spaceport, were home to so many half-pay and forcibly retired military personnel that one more, even though he carried the aura of a senior officer, seemed of no consequence.

As he passed from the shadows into the uncertain light of an old glow globe, those who cared to look would have seen an arrogant imperial of pure race, but one who had lived a hard life, unlike most aristocrats inhabiting the better parts of the capital.

He had shaved his head in the fashion of his caste, leaving a strip of black, stiff, bristling hair running from his forehead over the top his shiny, olive skull down to the back of his thick neck. The tonsure exposed a bony ridge and elongated predator's ears that twitched and moved as he unconsciously listened to his surroundings, always alert for threats. His face bore the cruel features common to his species, but the black eyes deeply recessed below thick eyebrows held a gleam of violence that eclipsed even the usual ferocity of the average fighter.

He looked too confident, too violent to be a member of the *Tai Kan*, the Shrehari governing council's secret police. His purposeful walk down unevenly paved alleys, ignoring the stench, filth, and apathy of the dispossessed, betrayed a vigor born of many victories.

Other half-pay warriors acknowledged his passing with polite nods or half-salutes, most knowing the warrior's name and what he represented. For some of the discarded fighters, he could be salvation, for others, the gateway to an even lower tier of hell.

Brakal did not care.

The only ones who mattered were those sworn to his service, his clan or his caste, in some cases all three. A Lord of the Empire and Clan Leader of the Makkar, the mantle falling on his shoulders after his older brother's death, he had carved a reputation for opposing the reckless council and its Admiralty sycophants. It made him a hero to many, be they on the front lines of a useless war or among his fellow lords. However, loyalty from those out of favor with the council meant little if it did not come with a command, and retiring to the Makkar estates, far from the maelstrom of war, would remove all ability to counter those drowning the empire in blood.

The roar of a lifting starship briefly drowned out the ever-present rumble of the slums, and when its sharp prow sliced through the low clouds, a fine rain began to fall, as if the freighter had torn through the sky's very fabric.

Brilliant droplets began to cover Brakal's head and shoulders, jewels in the uncertain light of the streets, but he felt none of them. After the day's events, he had one goal and one only.

He stopped in front of a stone building with a sagging roofline and quickly looked behind him to see if he had the *Tai Kan* on his tail. Little on Shrehari Prime, or anywhere else in the empire escaped them, especially those designated for a summary execution.

Brakal knew that his interview with Admiral Trage had likely placed him on the exclusive list of aristocrats living under a suspended death sentence. The only thing keeping the admiral from ordering his assassination was the threat of vengeance by those honorable members of Shredar's nobility who resented his conduct of the war.

He pushed his way past a thick wooden door and into a heady fog of smoke, ale vapors, and the raucous sound of many Shrehari males in their prime telling each other tales of honor, ribald jokes, or the latest satire aimed at the weakling emperor and his corrupt whore of a regent.

No *Tai Kan* intelligent enough to survive for more than a day on the streets would dare come here, or even report the treasonous words now spilling out onto the street. A cruel smile twisted Brakal's face, and he stepped in, scanning the room for the one he had come to see.

Urag, one-time gun master, and very briefly first officer of *Tol Vakash*, Brakal's last command, spotted him looming above the mostly sitting crowd and raised a jug brimming with ale over his head. He had replaced the loyal Jhar after the latter died thanks to that hell bitch Dunmoore.

Many of those in the tavern cast hungry glances at their former commander, anxious to divine the latest news from his expression.

After their defeat in the Cimmeria system, life on half-pay had become difficult. No captain wanted to take on a crewmember tainted by Brakal's rout at the hands of humans, much less an officer.

The Admiralty might have overlooked the stain, had it been another captain. However, his opposition to the council and his open contempt for the admirals who had mismanaged the war made anyone associated with Brakal as poisonous as *kroorath* vomit.

A few had found berths on privateers or commercial vessels, but most had moldered in the slums, taking their frustrations out in the many dojos catering to fighting men.

Brakal, Clan Lord of the Makkar and one of the few remaining proponents of the nobility's ancient customs, had made sure none of his former crew suffered deprivations, but it had taken a heavy toll on the family's remaining wealth. And since, in these times, money represented the gateway to power, its dwindling meant lean times ahead if he did not find a way to return his crew to service.

He dropped heavily into the wooden chair beside Urag and grabbed the jug, taking a deep draft of purple ale. After wiping his mouth with the back of his hand, he belched with satisfaction.

"A taste fit for the gods, Urag, not like the weak piss served at the Admiralty. But I forget," he thumped his second-in-command on the shoulder, "they're too feeble for the real stuff anyway."

"You seem in good humor, Commander. Either you strangled Trage with his own intestines or you had success."

"We have a ship, Urag," Brakal sat back with a self-satisfied smile, his sharp, yellow teeth glinting in the tavern's ancient lanterns, "a Tol class cruiser."

"How did you manage this?" Urag asked after he had recovered from his astonishment. "Surely they haven't forgiven you for losing to the flame-haired she-wolf."

"Siobhan Dunmoore?" Brakal rolled the unfamiliar name over his tongue. "Yes, a worthy adversary, that one. If we had a few like her in the imperial fleet, the war would be over. No, they haven't forgiven me. You remember my interest in the distribution of prize money in recent weeks?"

It had been yet another of Brakal's schemes to get enough leverage with the Admiralty so they would assign him a ship and, based on his previous attempts, Urag had expected no useful results.

"You found fire beneath the smoke, I gather?"

"And how." The smile took its remarkably cruel twist again. "That filth wearing admiral's robes and his equally stinking cronies have been skimming a large percentage of what should by rights have gone to officers and crew. They've become rich enough to buy their own starships while depriving our warriors, widows, and orphans of what is theirs by custom and law."

"You found proof?"

"I found enough to make sure Trage would give me anything I asked for."

"He'll give you a *Tai Kan* knife in the back as a bonus, Commander."

Brakal's derisive laugh filled the tavern, stilling the other voices for a few moments.

"I've ensured that my death in anything other than battle will bring the evidence to light and that *kroorath* dropping knows this."

"Still, Commander, he will find a way to rid himself of you."

"He's tried many times, and now, I'll be back on my own ship again, doing my duty to the empire. The cruiser *Tol Vehar* is due out of refit. They had earmarked it for one of Trage's favorites, but I've convinced the admiral that it would do better service under my command."

"So you've made an enemy of a fellow commander as well," Urag growled.

"Bah." Brakal waved the objection away with his usual sneer of contempt. "We're talking about Kretar, a congenital imbecile sired by an inbred moron. I've done the emperor a favor by delaying his elevation to a cruiser's bridge and giving these fine warriors around us a purpose other than rotting away when they could be fighting the humans."

"You discovered your evidence how?"

"By learning the lesson that discarded mistresses can be more dangerous than a whole fleet of human battleships. Trage made the mistake of telling the delightful Yonna of his arrangements, boasting no doubt, then throwing her aside for a younger woman. I subsequently made the wise choice of seducing Yonna for a night."

"Won't she betray you in turn?"

"No." A feral expression crept over his sharp features. "She understands that my ship is my true mistress, and declared herself more than happy to hand over the information as her vengeance on Trage. Though," he took another gulp of ale, "I now also have a playmate for the times we're back on the home world."

Urag shook his head in admiration. Brakal would never change.

"You scheme with the best of them, Commander."

"Hah. Insult me will you? Assemble the crew, miscreant, and find out how many we need to replace because they've gone elsewhere so I can start recruiting."

"You'll have no difficulties in finding men ready to pledge themselves to your service, Commander. The slums are full of unwanted warriors who've offended the regime."

"A system that lets prime material rot. It's a testament to our degenerate times under the current council, but a boon to us at this moment. Be about it then, you scoundrel. I've arranged the first shuttle to the orbital yards tomorrow at the midday hour."

Urag, the Shrehari equivalent of a grin on his face, stood up and raised his hands, shouting for silence.

"All former *Tol Vakash* crew will report to the commander of *Tol Vehar* at the shuttle docks tomorrow at midday for transportation to orbit so that they may resume their service to the emperor."

"We'd rather continue our service with a true warrior than a puling brat and his whorish mother," a rough voice called out from the far corner of the room. "Name *Tol Vehar*'s commander, Urag."

Brakal stood as well and searched for the heckler until he found his former chief engineer, a troll-like Shrehari covered in remarkably discolored skin patches. The engineer stared at him with a semi-feral leer, waiting for the expected if well-natured rebuke.

"You dare question *Tol Vehar*'s first officer, you pustule on an admiral's ass? I'll soon whip some discipline back into your stinking hide, now that you're back on full pay and serving on *my* ship, under *my* orders."

The cheers erupting from three dozen broad Shrehari chests almost brought the venerable tavern's roof down.

*

Brakal, trailed by his sworn man and bodyguard, Toralk, walked into the shuttle docks with an energy rarely seen since his defeat at Dunmoore's hands. He once again wore his uniform, as did the almost two hundred Shrehari milling about, many of them looking worse for wear.

The commander clapped his second on the shoulder in greeting.

"Does the tavern still have ale in store, or did this sorry lot of villains drink it all? It smells like a brewery in here."

"The result of your generosity." Urag scowled. "It's going to stink in the shuttle."

"But it will be good to go back to a ship, Lord," Toralk remarked in his raspy voice.

"It will and stop calling me lord," Brakal replied, sounding irritatingly cheerful to the many hung over spacers. "We're back in uniform, and not a second too soon."

Ever since Brakal became head of the Clan Makkar, Toralk had insisted on calling him lord instead of commander. He was the only one of the crew who dared do so, but then, Toralk and Brakal had grown up together on the family estates.

The former's family had served the latter's for more generations than either cared to remember and when Brakal joined the fleet, so did Toralk, the one as an officer, the other as a low caste spacer. Toralk had been watching Brakal's back for over twenty turns, and neither could imagine living without the other.

A tall Shrehari they had never seen before entered the building and, after scanning the assembled crew, walked straight toward Brakal. He stopped with military precision and saluted.

"I'm Lieutenant Regar, assigned to *Tol Vehar* as intelligence and political officer." The ironic smirk on the man's face drained Brakal's joy at leaving the surface of the home world behind.

"The *Tai Kan* graces me with a spy." He snarled, ignoring the salute. "You are aware that your predecessor died on my bridge, as will you if you dare interfere in my business."

"I know, Commander." His offensively cheerful expression remained unchanged, as did his voice, though it hinted at some private amusement. "I have my orders if you'd care to read them."

"I do not. Here are the only orders that matter: you will remember that you are not in *Tol Vehar*'s chain of command. You will obey all commands given by myself or Urag; you will not interfere in any way with the ship's business since you filthy insects have no notion of what it takes to operate in deep space."

"With all due respect, Commander," the private amusement became a bit more public, "this filthy insect has his watch keeping ticket, should you ever be in need of a relief officer. I served in the fleet before circumstances forced a change of career."

That admission brought Brakal up short, and he carefully examined Regar, trying to find any hint of falsehood or guile, but the man seemed infuriatingly open and relaxed.

"A forced change of career, eh? I shall take your qualifications under advisement, Lieutenant. Now leave us."

"As you wish, Commander." Regar bowed briefly, then walked away to stand by himself, looking out a scarred window at the tarmac.

"Regar doesn't exactly come across as *Tai Kan* does he?"

"No Toralk, he doesn't, which means he bears even more watching." Brakal shrugged. "Who ever heard of a filthy spy not oozing arrogance? It's almost like a finding an old whore who doesn't ooze disease from every pore."

*

Tol Vehar, like all those of its breed, including his previous ship, had a sleek beauty and a dangerous aura that Brakal loved.

Nestled in the shining spider's web of struts that sprouted from the orbital shipyards, the cruiser seemed like a hunter straining at its leash, impatient to taste blood.

"Let the gods not force me to threaten Yardmaster Hralk again," he muttered as the shuttle lined up to the station's gaping hangar doors in preparation for landing. "I don't wish to contaminate myself so quickly."

"You hadn't heard?"

"Heard what, Urag?"

"Hralk has been given an admiral's robes. He commands a strike force out on the far frontier."

"He what?" Brakal's shout turned heads throughout the large craft.

"Try not to break anything, Lord."

"I'll break whoever promoted that suppurating canker."

"Then you missed your chance, Commander. I hear Trage decided to reward Hralk for his years of bum licking. You were too busy entrapping the admiral to pay attention to gossip."

"Bah." Brakal turned back to the porthole and stared out into space, his pleasure at seeing *Tol Vehar* dimmed by the news his old enemy had bought his way to high rank.

"The moment he's faced with a fight, his incompetence will show, and with any luck, the *Tai Kan* cockroach attached to his fat arse will shoot him for treason. Though I wonder if he brought that delightful creature he had as a personal assistant with him. Maybe she remained here and is pining for a new protector."

"You'd take Hralk's leavings?"

"If you'd ever seen her, you wouldn't be so hasty to dismiss the idea. Handy with a blaster too, as I recall from my last visit to the yardmaster's office."

*

Two days later, while the crew finalized preparations to leave dry-dock, Urag rapped his knuckles on the bulkhead by the door to Brakal's cabin.

"Orders from the Admiralty, Commander. We've been given our assignment."

"An independent patrol in human space?" He looked up from his console, a hopeful glint in his dark eyes. Then he saw Urag's pained look.

"No. Tell me the infernal gods of the seven hells didn't play *that* joke on us."

"I fear so. We report to Admiral Hralk's command ship on the far frontier."

The thunderous roar of Brakal's reply echoed from stem to stern aboard *Tol Vehar*, and possibly even on the station itself. It took all of Urag's patience and willpower to calm him down again before he started throwing things at the bulkhead.

Regar, the *Tai Kan* man, had overheard the exchange from the shadows of the corridor. He smiled beatifically to himself as if enjoying Brakal's loss of composure, and wandered off in search of a cup of tea. This would prove to be a genuinely exciting assignment, under a commander who actually believed in things like honor and duty. They remained all too rare, even with the crucible of war winnowing out the weak and inept.

— Three —

"Message from the Starbase operation center, Captain," Petty Officer Pine called through the open door to Dunmoore's ready room. "Colonel Kalivan was on the liner that just docked and will be escorted to our airlock momentarily by a member of the staff."

"How kind of them," she muttered, looking up from her pad, "we've only been sitting here for three days after making one of the fastest passages ever recorded for a Type 203 frigate."

"Some things just are the way they are," Pushkin shrugged philosophically as he rose. "Hurry up and wait has been the bane of naval organizations since the days of galley slaves. Shall we?"

"I suppose so. It might be considered rude if I didn't greet an officer senior to me in rank."

A single petty officer third class in dress uniform stood by the airlock, tasked with controlling the ship's end of the long gangway. He snapped to attention and saluted.

"Sir."

"At ease, Pearkes." She smiled at him. The sharply turned out spacer made quite a contrast to the now long gone Petty Officer Zavaleta, who had had the airlock watch when she first came aboard what seemed like an eternity ago. "We should see Colonel Kalivan any minute now."

"Begging' your pardon, Captain," Pearkes replied, "but will there be a side party?"

She shook her head.

"He's not been made out as a commanding or a flag officer, or an envoy of ambassadorial rank. Therefore no formal courtesies are called for."

"I hope Colonel Kalivan shares that opinion, sir," Pushkin remarked, "else we might have a bit of a perceived insult to smooth over."

She shrugged, utterly unconcerned.

"I'm sure our passenger, having reached his lofty rank, has taken the time to study naval etiquette."

"Sir," Petty Officer Pearkes interrupted them, "the station-side sentry reports one civilian male approaching."

He pointed at the small screen set into the bulkhead by the door. Dunmoore examined her new passenger, as did the facial recognition subroutine in the ship's security computer. After a moment, a message scrolled up, confirming the identity.

"I guess the good colonel traveled in mufti. Open her up, Pearkes," Pushkin ordered with a nod.

The thick, armored hatch slid away with a sigh, revealing the full length of the gangway tube that connected starship and station. Crossing over was not for the faint of heart as the mostly transparent passage exposed the immensity of space.

When the new arrival had stepped over the coaming and into the ship, Dunmoore tried to smile pleasantly as she held out her hand in greeting.

"Welcome aboard, Colonel Kalivan."

He and Dunmoore were almost the same height, yet he managed to look down his long nose at her, after pointedly eying the empty airlock.

"Thank you, Captain."

His languid tone somehow irritated her, and she gave him a curt nod in reply.

Slender, with an aristocratic face and a neatly trimmed mustache, Kalivan appeared to be a few years older than Pushkin, his salt and pepper hair giving him a certain gravitas.

"This is Lieutenant Commander Gregor Pushkin, my first officer."

"Commander," Kalivan's nod seemed almost dismissive, but not quite enough to offend. "I don't wish to sound rude, but might I be taken to my quarters? The passage aboard *Listowel* proved to be somewhat hectic, especially the last day or so, and I could use some rest."

"Certainly, sir. If you'll follow me."

When they arrived at the cabin, Dunmoore touched a control pad, opening the door.

"Here we are, sir. A frigate doesn't have much private space, I'm afraid."

Kalivan entered the small compartment and looked around, a faint expression of distaste on his face, almost like that of a man who had just stepped into animal droppings but felt too tired to complain.

"This will be quite adequate, Captain. Thank you."

"You'll find the meal times posted by the console," she pointed at the far corner. "Of course, you'll be eating with my officers. The wardroom is toward the bow, right around the corner."

The colonel nodded once, his expression clearly wishing them away so that he could settle in and rest.

"Thank you for your courtesy, Commander Dunmoore." Then he closed the cabin door.

Alone once more in Siobhan's ready room, the first officer poured himself a mug of coffee, loading it with sugar and cream, to Dunmoore's general dismay.

"Wasn't that special?" He said, sitting down across from her. "He should get along great with Devall. They both seem cut from the same cloth, though young Trevane has learned how to interact with lesser beings."

"Maybe the Devalls and the Kalivans play variable gravity golf together. We should ask Trevane if they know each other." She took a sip. "I had intended to invite him for supper in my quarters, as a sort of welcome reception, but I suppose I'll pass, at least for now. He seemed miffed that we didn't provide a side party, judging by the way he looked around the airlock."

"The man certainly didn't care much for me."

"Yes, I noticed that. Perhaps he's all too rank conscious and doesn't know that the first officer of a warship actually matters most, especially when one needs favors."

"Or he's just naturally rude. I didn't see him smile at you either."

"Perhaps I'm just not his type." She winked at Pushkin, trying to steer the conversation away from complaints about their passenger. It could be a long trip in close quarters.

*

Later that evening, long after supper had come and gone without a sighting of Colonel Kalivan, the first officer did his final round of *Stingray* before turning in, profoundly lost in thought.

Living with Dunmoore, day in, day out, he had not really noticed the changes in her since the events at Arietis, yet with a newcomer in their midst, she seemed strangely skittish. He felt a bit uneasy now, wondering whether she had indeed lost some of the fire that had burned brightly within her before their encounter with Admiral Corwin.

"You look like you have indigestion, Commander," Lieutenant Devall commented as Pushkin entered the wardroom for a quick glass of water.

"Just going through the list of things I have to check before I can safely go to bed. You'll be doing the same soon enough, mark my words."

"Our passenger's making you uneasy?"

"And what if he is?" Pushkin countered irritably, betraying his disquiet. "Ours not to reason why and all that stuff. They call this the Navy for a reason."

"I'm not surprised," Devall nodded soberly. "I watched him come aboard on the bridge monitors, and he's one of the people my own family call stuck up aristos."

"A bit of respect for your seniors, Lieutenant."

"Why?" Devall shrugged. "Colonel Kalivan isn't Navy. He isn't a nice man either if I'm any judge of my own species."

Pushkin shook his head, a sad smile briefly relaxing his tense features.

"So young and yet so cynical."

"When you come from a family like mine, it's bred into the genes."

"True." The first officer drained his glass. He glanced at Devall's pad. "The computer will have you mated in two moves, Trevane. You shouldn't have castled."

The ship's bell softly rang six times.

"I'd better get going if I want to be in bed by the time midnight rolls around."

"Good night, sir."

*

For the first time in weeks, if not months, Siobhan had a restless night, chased by dreams of exploding starships, dying crewmembers and sinister admirals. She woke with a start and, as she fought to calm her jangled nerves and breathe normally, her eyes found the old ship's clock with the image of an emaciated knight on its face, sitting alone on a narrow shelf.

A gift from the crew of her first ship, the scout *Don Quixote*, it now served as a reminder of her many weaknesses, including her tendency to tilt at windmills, something that often cost the people around her dearly.

Five bells in the night watch rang before she could fall asleep again. This time, her dreams included terrifying creatures whose sole ambition was rending her limb from limb.

*

"The ship is ready to depart at your command," Pushkin announced when Dunmoore took the captain's chair after a restless night.

She heard the door whoosh open behind her and turned to face the new arrival, correctly deducing that it might be their passenger.

"Good morning, sir," she nodded amiably at the stern-faced man, now wearing the army's rifle green uniform, adorned with the oak leaves and three four-pointed stars of his rank on the collar. "I trust you slept well."

"Tolerably." He remained on the threshold, and Siobhan understood Kalivan waited for the invitation to enter. It spoke well for the acerbic colonel's respect of naval protocol.

"Would you like to watch our departure from the bridge?"

"I would indeed, Captain, thank you." Kalivan took a determined step in and stopped, looking around until

Pushkin directed him toward an unoccupied seat behind Siobhan.

"Incoming from Starbase control," Kowalski said, bringing Dunmoore back to her immediate task. "The gangway has been retracted and secured. We are cleared to release moorings and depart."

"Acknowledged. Whose turn is it to take her out, Mister Pushkin?"

The first officer looked at Siobhan with a merry twinkle in his dark eyes, though he jutted out his chin stubbornly.

"Having consulted the roster just now, I believe that it's yours, sir."

She bit back a sarcastic retort, remembering all too clearly a conversation they had some time ago about the need for a captain to demonstrate her ship handling skills every so often.

"In that case, it must be Mister Guthren's turn to helm her out."

"Indeed," Pushkin replied, still standing at the parade rest position, his hands joined in the small of his back.

She nodded tightly and turned toward the main screen, noting that her coxswain had almost lost the battle with his suppressed mirth.

"Navigation lights on, Mister Tours."

"Navigation lights on, aye," the sailing master replied, touching his console. Immediately, red and green lights sprang to life on the upper and lower sides of the hyperdrive nacelles and the hull, with red indicating the port side of the ship and green the starboard side. Simultaneously, white strobes began flashing, one on the top of the upper superstructure and one on the bottom of the lowermost keel tier, below the missile launchers.

"Hull illumination on."

"Hull illumination on, aye."

Powerful projectors, strategically positioned along the ship's exterior, turned on, lighting up *Stingray*'s name, registration number and, most importantly for the crew, the kill marks that they had earned at so much cost during the wild running battle near Cimmeria.

"Would you like to see how we look from the station, sir?" She asked Kalivan.

"Why not. It may prove instructive. The last of the Type 203s leaving port and all that."

Dunmoore felt irritation stiffen her spine at his dismissive tone.

"Can we get a feed from Starbase control, Mister Kowalski?"

"On the port screen, Captain," she immediately replied, having anticipated Siobhan's request.

Siobhan felt a sudden rush of pride push away her irritation at Kalivan when she saw the magnificent sight of her ship, lit up as if for a naval review.

One of the few remaining vessels from a bygone age of peace, when shipwrights had the time to produce elegant designs, *Stingray* was the last of her breed and not destined for service much longer. The Wyvern shipyards had almost completed construction of the first of the newest frigate design, the Voivode class, and Dunmoore had no doubt that once they launched *Jan Sobieski*, her ship would be decommissioned.

"Release mechanical moorings," she ordered, face once more directed toward the main screen. Faint thuds reverberated through the hull as the station's grappling arms broke free.

"We are on tractor beams only," Tours reported once the sounds had faded away.

"Helm, stand by thrusters, sublight drive active."

"Stand by thrusters, sublight drives ready, aye," Chief Guthren replied.

"Make to Starbase control: ready to be pushed out."

Slowly the aspect of the station changed as the separation between it and the ship increased, until they floated a thousand meters away, orbiting the planet in parallel to their erstwhile port of call.

"Thrusters, set for one-third ahead, twenty degrees to port. Wait for my mark."

Guthren repeated the order hand hovering over the controls.

"Make to Starbase control: release energy moorings."

"We're floating free," Tours reported seconds later.

"Helm, engage. Give us a departing view."

They watched, entranced, while the station became a mere toy, then a pinprick as the frigate spiraled away from the planet, breaking out of its embrace, headed for the hyperlimit, where they could safely jump to faster-than-light speed.

"Sublight drives on."

Their view of the planet suddenly shrank when the ship accelerated at a rate that would have turned the humans aboard into red jam, were it not for inertial dampeners.

"Secure from departure stations, Mister Pushkin."

Then, with a sardonic grin, she asked, "I trust you'll rate my performance as satisfactory?"

"Quite, sir. Mister Tours, I believe you have the watch."

"That I do." The sailing master rose from his console after slaving it to the command chair. "I relieve you, sir."

"I stand relieved," Dunmoore replied. She glanced at Kalivan. "Would you care for a coffee, Colonel? Perhaps we can discuss the mission in some more detail, now that we're underway. My sailing master would prefer some coordinates to aim at if he's to plan our journey with any hope of precision."

No one on the bridge missed the very reasonable sweetness of her tone, except the one man who did not know yet that it signaled danger ahead. *Stingray*'s captain wanted answers, and she would get them.

Kowalski and Pushkin exchanged amused glances behind Kalivan's back when the man followed Siobhan to her ready room.

— Four —

"How do you take your coffee, Colonel?"

"Black is fine."

Kalivan took a seat, managing to look like he had entered an admiral's salon or a general's perhaps. He gave Pushkin an irritated glance but understood that Dunmoore would not send him away. The first officer handed out full mugs and took the other chair, trying hard *not* to look like he was in a salon.

"What do you know about the pre-FTL era, Captain? Say circa 2075 to 2115?"

Surprised by the question, Siobhan sat back and rummaged through her memory, eyes on the far bulkhead.

"Earth sent out a fair number of colony ships able to approach the speed of light to stars with identified planetary systems, their passengers in cryo for the trip. Several hundred as I recall, each carrying tens of thousands."

"Correct." A polite nod of approval. "You'll also remember that when the first FTL ships headed out from Earth in the late twenty-second century, we discovered that many of the colony ships never made it to their intended destinations and had, in fact, vanished without a trace."

"Indeed, sir." Fully alert now, she felt the first real stirrings of interest, beyond a mere concern for her orders. A glance at Pushkin confirmed that he also seemed intensely curious.

"Shortly after the outbreak of the war, a scavenger operating on the far edges of explored space detected a mass of cold metal traveling at something approaching relativistic speed. He tried to tackle the tricky process to slow the object down sufficiently for recovery. The first attempt failed, but the scavenger managed to decrease its velocity. He tried again a year later, with the same lack of success, then a third time two years after that, but on this occasion, a Navy survey cruiser appeared on the scene. Your brethren managed to bleed off the object's remaining excess velocity and, upon inspection, claimed it for the government."

"Did he? That must have pleased the salvager to no end."

Kalivan gave Pushkin a dirty look.

"Perhaps, but that's beside the point." He put his half-empty mug on Dunmoore's desk. Now where was I? Yes — it turned out to be a log buoy, an enormous one, hence the claim. Brought back to port, it sat in a station's hangar deck for a few months, likely forgotten due to the exigencies of war, until a passing intelligence analyst noticed it and let his curiosity take over. He had the thing shipped to the Fleet laboratory on Dordogne where they managed to revive its systems."

He paused as if to build the suspense, something Dunmoore found unreasonably irksome.

"It apparently came from the cryo-colony ship *Tempest*, launched in 2103, one of those early explorers who vanished from the historical record once it left Earth's solar system. This makes it the first log buoy from a lost ship to ever be recovered."

Pushkin's low whistle mirrored her own astonishment. Before she could comment, Kalivan raised a perfectly manicured hand to still her.

"The colonists launched it after they arrived in a system with a habitable world, but not the one they'd planned on colonizing, needless to say. They hoped the buoy would eventually make its way back home and let the rest of humanity know what had happened, which is a bit curious in itself."

"How so?"

"*Tempest* was a privately chartered affair, carrying twenty thousand people with the goal of establishing a new civilization that would leave the ills of the old far behind them. Utopian, from what records we have of the era. History describes Earth as an unpleasant place in those days, before the FTL exodus, and more than one colonization consortium crystallized around the desire to try something new, or in this case, something old, meaning a society built around shared ownership, low levels of industrialization, with most colonists living an agrarian lifestyle. They intended to deliberately turn their backs on space travel and drop a few centuries down the technology ladder, to some sort of utopia without the bad aspects of the society they'd left behind."

"Really?" Pushkin snorted. "They sound like the idiots running my ancestors' *Rodina* just before the first spaceflights. It didn't turn out well back then."

"Yes." Kalivan sniffed. "Strange notions indeed, but people will have ideals and try to live by them, or at least some will, while others will exploit them."

He paused as if gathering his thoughts.

"However, the fact that they wished to let Earth know where they'd ended up seemed a little curious. Perhaps the notion of cutting all contact with the rest of our kind overrode those ideals, once they realized that they'd ended up far from our home system. It could well be that they realized the chances of more colonists arriving at some point when FTL finally became a reality, were close to nil. Of course, the hyperdrive was still a few decades in the future when *Tempest* sailed, but many technical kinks had already been ironed out."

"So we're going to go pay them a visit, is that it?" Despite herself, Dunmoore felt an intense fascination with the story.

"Indeed we are." Kalivan smiled at her apparent eagerness. "You're probably wondering where I come in. As you may know, the army trains some of its officers and troops as civil affairs specialists, though we're also well versed in other matters dealing with influence activities, and that happens to be my branch."

"Influence activities?" Pushkin frowned. "I'm not sure I've encountered that term before."

A cold smile appeared on Kalivan's lips.

"We try not to advertise. Some people would find what we do a little disturbing. The army's book definition calls it the integration of designated information-related capabilities in order to synchronize themes, messages, and actions with operations to inform Commonwealth audiences, influence alien and hostile audiences, and affect adversary and enemy decision-making. In other words, stripped of the bullshit, we do psychological operations and propaganda."

Pushkin's eyebrows rose, and he nodded.

"Okay. Bullshit artists, then."

"Just so, if you wish to be crude." Kalivan turned his attention back to Dunmoore. "I'm stationed on Dordogne, so I naturally gravitated to the research surrounding the log buoy's origins, and when the matter of finding the colonists came up, I lobbied to get the mission. For my sins, they turned me into a one-man operation and assigned your ship as my conveyance."

He dug a data wafer out of his tunic pocket and held it out to Dunmoore.

"All of the known details are on here. Of course, the colonists didn't send us galactic coordinates, since they weren't in use at that time, but with the information about the star they reached, the bright boys in intelligence tracked its general area down quickly. Your sailing master will find the approximate coordinates included."

She placed the wafer on her console screen, uploading the data into the ship's memory banks, and then quickly scrolled through to find their destination. Pushkin, feeling rather impatient, glanced at Kalivan and noticed an air of amused expectancy about him as he watched Siobhan read. His thin lips twisted into an amused smile when her eyes widened.

"That can't be right."

"What can't be right?"

"The coordinates, Gregor." She called up a holographic map of the Orion Arm and touched her screen, causing a particular star to pulsate. "There's the destination, and here," another touch and a red icon appeared, "is where our unnamed trader first tried to pick up the buoy. It may have been traveling at a respectable fraction of cee, but it was still only a small fraction in relativistic terms if this information is correct. And that being the case, the data doesn't make sense."

"The information is correct, Captain." Kalivan's didactic, almost pedantic manner made him sound like a professor overly enamored by his own learning. "And the data does make sense."

"That means either the buoy encountered a wormhole shortcut, or someone launched it centuries before *Tempest* left Earth, or your intelligence boffins got it wrong."

"I assure you, Captain, everything is entirely correct. The buoy's AI doesn't report transiting a wormhole before it lost all power, and it shows wear consistent with well more than four centuries in space. Two millennia actually, give or take. What in fact happened is..."

"*Tempest* encountered a wormhole that projected it well away from its destination, not just in distance, but also in time." Dunmoore completed the statement.

The first officer's incredulous snort caused Kalivan's face to tighten for a few seconds.

"You are aware, Mister Pushkin, aren't you, that wormhole theory has always included a temporal element? It hasn't been proved up to now, but this might be it."

"Time travel forward, perhaps, sir," he replied, feeling stung by the colonel's words, if not his tone, "but going backward would violate God knows how many universal laws."

"Perhaps so," Dunmoore rose to her full height, intending to stop the debate before her usually stoic first officer could talk himself into trouble with Kalivan. "But one of the lessons of history, as we found when our ancestors perfected FTL travel, is that what we thought to be universal constants often apply only to this version of the universe. The only way to find out if *Tempest* did indeed travel back in time is to find this colony and hope the descendants of the original colonists have managed to hang on, if not thrive."

"Indeed." Kalivan nodded, acknowledging Dunmoore's attempt to prevent a rift between him and Pushkin, though the gesture fell short of an apology. "All of the facts we obtained from the log buoy tell us that there might be a human world out there, colonized well before humanity left Earth; indeed, before our entire ancestral planet had even been fully mapped."

"And if they've indeed achieved what they wanted, they might have forgotten their origins, which would make it a first contact kind of scenario." Siobhan refilled her coffee mug. "Why didn't the Admiralty send a full team instead of one army colonel and a clapped-out frigate?"

"Because," this time his smile held an edge of bitterness, "we are not required for the war effort, and in the grand scheme of things, tracking down a ship that vanished over four hundred years ago is at the bottom of the priority list."

Pushkin's laugh sounded like the bark of a mad seal.

"Story of our lives, Colonel. Welcome aboard *Stingray*. I'll reserve my judgment about the time travel angle until we get there. The mad scientists have screwed up royally before. There can be any number of plausible explanations that don't involve the fourth dimension."

Under Dunmoore's hard stare, Kalivan found the grace to concede the point.

"As you say, Mister Pushkin. We shall see."

"I'll post this on the ship's net so that everyone can familiarize themselves with the reason for our mission. If that's all for now, Colonel, I'd like to confer with my sailing master on the navigation plan. I expect you'll wish us to get there by the most expeditious route, and since we're heading into the unknown, we'll have to be very careful."

*

"What do you think of our passenger, Viv?" Kathryn Kowalski sat down across from her roommate with a loaded lunch tray.

Vivan Luttrell, the ship's surgeon, chewed thoughtfully and after swallowing her food said, "I wouldn't play poker with him, even for bragging rights instead of money."

"Why? You're as close to a professional card sharp as we have aboard."

"The eyes, young Kathryn. Look at his eyes. He can see right through people, and it makes some of us uncomfortable."

"Whose eyes?" Lieutenant Trevane Devall asked as he dropped down beside Luttrell. "Or let me guess: Colonel Wes Kalivan."

"Don't you agree he has strange eyes?"

The second officer shrugged.

"Simple: don't look into them and you won't be hypnotized by his manly wiles. He's just another aristo like me, nothing else."

"You've always got an easy answer, don't you?" Kowalski snorted.

"Life is easy. We just tend to make it hard on ourselves. For example, the other day, Able Spacer Teller decided he would rather not inventory the loose ammunition and guesstimated the quantity instead. When he admitted his dastardly deed to the bosun, his life became hard, not because Chief Foste is hard to please but because Teller decided that it should be so."

"How very Buddhist of you," Luttrell commented around a mouthful of bread. "I didn't know aristocrats went for the spiritual stuff."

"What can I say," he shrugged languidly, "once you've amassed a fortune, all that remains is feeding the spirit."

"If I don't get the ammunition inventory report by the end of the watch," a gruff voice said behind them, "I'll be feeding your spirit some professional development."

Devall grinned at the first officer.

"Funny you should mention that. I'm regaling my comrades here with a life lesson involving said inventory."

"Do tell," Pushkin replied, "or better, don't tell. I only have twenty minutes to eat, and I'd rather not listen to a long, involved, and probably pointless story."

"We were discussing the colonel," Luttrell offered.

"Surprise, surprise," the first officer muttered over his shoulder as he served himself.

"And what, pray tell," he asked sitting down with the others, "were your conclusions."

"Don't play poker with him," Kowalski said with a straight face.

Pushkin took a bite of food and chewed contemplatively while looking up at the deckhead as if pondering the matter.

"I'd say that it would be a wise choice," he replied after swallowing. "Not only is he a psychological operations and propaganda artist by trade, something the army calls 'influence activities,' but from what I've seen so far, Colonel Kalivan is smart, driven and outranks everyone else on board. Besides, this mission is his baby, one that the

Admiralty doesn't love as much as he thinks it should, so beware, my children."

"Always a fount of good cheer, aren't you, Commander." Luttrell's rueful tone drew the expected chuckles.

"I try, Viv, I try. It comes with the job. I have no doubt the good colonel will treat us all with proper respect, but let's not tempt fate. At least not until we've discovered the danger signs."

"You mean like when the skipper goes all sweet? Gotcha." Kowalski nodded. "We'll keep our eyes open. By the way, what do you think about this lost colony stuff? You were in on the briefing?"

"I think it's interesting," Pushkin's cautious tone wasn't lost on the perceptive signals officer, "though I have my doubts about data that can only be explained by a wormhole that operates in four or more dimensions."

"Ockham's razor?" Devall cocked an eyebrow in question.

"It's always something to consider when facts seem out of kilter, yes. The laws of the universe tend to be a bit more rigid than some of our less scientifically inclined fiction scribes would like. By the way, speaking of universal laws, including those of faulty maintenance, you'll want to have someone check the hatch leading to the environmental scrubbers down on deck three once we're FTL. It seems to be sticking."

The public address system interrupted any further banter.

"All hands, now hear this: jump stations in ten minutes."

"Okay," the first officer swallowed the last morsel of his lunch. "We seem to have reached the hyperlimit. Let's wrap this up and secure the wardroom. We've got work to do."

They nodded and, without further comment, rose to stow their trays.

Watching from the open door, unnoticed in the shadows of the passageway, Siobhan smiled. Gregor Pushkin's easy manner with the senior officers spoke of a man ready for his own command. With any luck, it would be soon. He had paid a hard price to get where he was and deserved it.

"Lost in thought, Captain?" Startled, she turned around to see Kalivan's sardonic smile. "I confess that I did give you a lot to digest. I hope you didn't feel offended at my implying that your ship is useless to the war effort?"

"You're not the first to make a comment of that sort, sir." She bit back a more choice reply. It would not do to let him push her buttons so quickly.

"No, I suppose not. Last of her class and all that. I wouldn't be surprised if this were her last mission, you know." He fell in beside Siobhan as she walked aft, leaving her to wonder whether Kalivan suffered from tone-deafness when it came to others or merely enjoyed being rude.

"Oh?"

"New frigates are coming on line soon. It stands to reason that when the Admiralty has a fresh hull to take *Stingray*'s place, they'll retire her." That didactic tone again. She felt a sudden urge to scream overtake her.

"I'm well aware of that, Colonel." She stopped in front of her quarters and eyed him coldly. "If you'll excuse me, I have to pick something up."

Once the door had shut behind her, she took a deep breath. They could debate ad nauseam whether *Stingray* was surplus to the war effort, but she would gladly concede that he got the mission because no one needed him.

How the man ever made colonel in one of the regular services defied belief. She hoped the descendants of *Tempest*'s colonists had actually founded a colony based on faith in unicorn farts and pixie dust, as Guthren so pungently put it when he read through the data, otherwise, Kalivan, as official Commonwealth Envoy, could very well start the next intra-human war.

— Five —

"This is to be our new home?" Urag's disgust sounded so heartfelt that even Brakal could find no words of remonstrance. "I'd like to meet the idiot who thought it a great idea to cobble together a dozen of the biggest freighters he could find, placed the resulting abortion in orbit around a dead planet in the ass-end of nowhere and call it an Imperial Deep Space Fleet station."

"Perhaps it's not the finest thing we've ever seen." Brakal felt philosophical for once, he and his second-in-command having briefly changed roles. He rubbed his bony chin. "But from here, we can send raiders to harass the humans on a part of their frontier they thought safe."

"At this range? It'll be in dribs and drabs. What use is that to the war effort? No, if they sent Hralk to command and you to serve him, the Admiralty considers this strike force of little use other than to keep an eye out for whatever could emerge from the black depths of uncharted space."

The communications officer interrupted Brakal's retort.

"Sir, we've been ordered to dock immediately. The admiral commands you to attend him at the earliest opportunity."

"I suppose I'm about to find out if he brought his delicious aide with him. Please inform the station that I shall go make obeisance to Hralk's regal ass forthwith."

"Not in those words," Urag added with a warning glance at the under-officer operating the signals.

An hour later, he stood in front of his old adversary, whose feral smile clearly showed that he remembered their last encounter. Hralk had lost none of his bulk, and his arrogance had grown with the size of his fief.

"Brakal." Yellow teeth gleamed dimly beneath deep-set eyes the color of dead stone. "I finally get my just due and immediately the Lords of the Admiralty saddle me with your unwanted presence. The gods have a very strange sense of humor."

"For once, we are in agreement." He smiled back with the same predatory expression on his face. Looking around at the unadorned command suite, mostly bare metal bulkheads and basic furnishings, he grunted. "Not quite the whorehouse luxury of your former office, but you have been given command of an afterthought."

"I intend to correct that state of affairs." Hralk leaned back in his chair and picked his teeth with a long, claw-like fingernail. "We are within reach of human trade routes and space they have so far failed to patrol in any strength. Your ship and the others of my strike force will raid what you can and give the damn insects enough heartburn to dissolve their innards. You'll have your orders within the hour."

"What, no meal to celebrate the renewal of our relationship and cement our oath to take the fight to the foe?"

Hralk laughed, the sound a deep rumble that came from deep within.

"You haven't lost your questionable wit. Good. You'll need it."

He waved a pudgy hand toward the door.

"As I said, your orders will come shortly."

"You could have told me that over the comlink, Hralk. Why have my ship dock and me walk all the way through this pestilent contraption?"

"Because I wanted you to see my face in person, Brakal, so that you might remember I am now your commanding officer." The admiral waved dismissively toward the exit. "You may go."

When he left the command suite, Brakal saw the *Tai Kan* spy chatting up Borunna, Hralk's personal assistant. He could feel Regar's mocking smile follow him out the door and into the passageway, and wondered what new devilry might hatch aboard his ship.

Once Brakal's footsteps had faded into the distance, Borunna pointed at the door.

"The admiral will see you now, Regar."

Although a civilian, her tone, and gesture very much reflected the rank held by her superior. Regar had no doubt she did double duty, in and out of bed. She had that look about her, considering Hralk's reputation. He dipped his head with exaggerated respect and then obeyed her gesture.

"So you're the *Tai Kan*'s operative aboard *Tol Vehar*." The admiral examined Regar with malicious eyes.

"I have that honor, Lord." The reply and accompanying bow were suitably unctuous, designed to flatter Hralk's over-inflated sense of self. Hralk did not belong to one of the noble families, like Brakal's Clan Makkar, and Regar knew, from his *Tai Kan* file, that this had always rankled the newly minted admiral.

"You will report to me as well as your superiors. Brakal is known for harboring disturbing ideas, and I cannot afford a reckless commander in my strike force."

"As you wish, Lord." Regar's expression shed some of its obsequiousness.

"You are also authorized to kill Brakal if he oversteps his bounds."

"May I point out that my own life would then be forfeit? His crew is loyal to a fault. My predecessor aboard *Tol Vakash* died at their hands when he attempted what you just suggested, Lord."

Hralk grunted dismissively.

"You have your orders, Regar. How you carry them out is your affair. We're all expendable in the service of the emperor."

Some are more so than others, the *Tai Kan* agent thought, wondering anew how men like Hralk obtained promotion without a single day's service on the human frontiers.

"As you command."

"Then be about your business."

Once back aboard the ship, he joined the other officers on the bridge only to be met by Brakal's suspicious glare.

"What business would a spy have with the admiral?"

"Hralk summoned me to receive orders, Commander." That mocking smile returned.

"And they were?"

"To kill you if you overstepped your bounds." The smile turned into a toothy grin.

"Tell me, spy, what would you consider me overstepping my bounds?"

"I truly have no idea. Admiral Hralk believes he can command a *Tai Kan* officer, and I prefer to let him keep that belief. It serves my purposes. As to the matter of assassinating you, let me just say that I enjoy my life and the amusements it offers. I would not do anything to change that."

Brakal laughed.

"I think I may begin to like you, spy. It would be a shame if your blood had to flow over my decks. If there are no more distractions, let us be away from this place before its stench befouls our air. Urag, ready the ship for undocking maneuvers. I believe I shall test my bounds by hunting humans."

*

"It seems almost unfair, Commander," Urag murmured, a barely repressed laugh rumbling deep in his chest. He stood beside Brakal's command chair, eyes fixed on the screen, watching their prey as they hurtled toward it. "He cannot have guessed that we would range so far from our known bases and so deep into space they claim as neutral."

"Fairness is for children or choosing your concubine for the night, Urag. The humans have not fought fairly. Why should we?" A rictus twisted Brakal's bony, olive-skinned face, highlighting his ridged brows and sharp cheekbones. "I think I may enjoy our orders to do as we wish, so long as we stay out of Hralk's way. Prepare to activate all systems."

"He still hasn't detected us," the gun master reported, "but he's a non-standard model, what the humans call a sloop, so perhaps his sensors aren't as good."

"Or maybe our shipyards have finally mastered the art of cloaking emissions, now that the Lords of the Fleet understand we must adapt our doctrine," Brakal replied, with more than a hint of disgust in his voice. "If they'd opened their poxed eyes earlier and stopped listening to the brainless councilors surrounding that harlot of a regent, we might have ended this war a long time ago."

"Treasonous words, Commander," Urag cautioned. "You still live on sufferance and every utterance of yours will be scrutinized by your enemies."

"Let Regar report me. This crew is loyal and won't stand for *Tai Kan* chicanery." He pounded the arm of his chair with a meaty fist encased in a hard gauntlet. "If he becomes too much of a problem I'll have him spaced."

"I merely counsel caution, as per my duty."

"We are nearing optimum missile range," the gun master interrupted a repartee he had heard many times before. The crew of *Tol Vehar* had been together for a long time, shifting from ship to ship at the whim of the High Command, more often than not because their commander offended someone powerful but then gained the support of someone equally powerful.

It helped that he had become a hereditary clan lord after his elder brother's death, one of the four hundred who, in better times, constituted the closest the empire had to a legislature. Even now, with the council wielding emergency powers, the lords retained sufficient influence to keep some of the worst excesses in check. Otherwise, his enemies would have had him killed a long time ago, and probably many of his officers as well.

"Activate."

The cruiser came to life in a flash, appearing on the hapless sloop's sensors like a nightmare become reality. It had but seconds to raise shields and prepare for battle; seconds the Shrehari would deny them.

"Launch missiles; get ready to follow up with all guns."

Five minutes later, nothing more than wreckage remained of the Commonwealth Navy sloop *Cyane*, its crew dead. Though the Shrehari cruiser's approach had been masterful and supported, for once, by technological advances that erased some of the gaps between the two enemies' capabilities, ultimately, the sloop's captain bore much of the blame.

After all, she had taken her ship into unpatrolled space without orders and had failed to keep an adequate sensor watch at all times. *Cyane*'s loss would remain a mystery for a long, long time and after being overdue for two weeks, the Admiralty would officially list her as missing, presumed destroyed.

For Commander Brakal, the scourge of the fleet, it became the first in what he hoped would be a string of victories that would restore a reputation shattered by the flame-haired she-wolf.

"Report this kill to the admiral," he ordered, a cruel smile splitting his sharp features, "and let him see we haven't been sitting on our fat arses like the rear-echelon fornicators surrounding his august person."

"May I use your exact words, Lord?" The signals under-officer asked with a glint of mischief in eyes hooded by a broad, bony brow.

"You may not," Urag snapped before Brakal could reply. "Report one sloop ambushed and destroyed with no damage to *Tol Vehar*. Add the time and coordinates, nothing more."

"Spoilsport," Brakal grumbled. Then, more loudly, "Find me another prey, Gun Master. This one has merely whetted my appetite."

*

Stingray emerged from FTL well beyond the Commonwealth's acknowledged sphere of influence, which, mostly meant space the Navy did not bother patrolling.

Once ship and crew had shaken off the transition, Dunmoore ordered systems down, to limit their emissions while the drives spooled up and Mister Tours recalculated the next jump. They had come out close to a star with nothing more than debris instead of planets circling it and therefore of no interest to either humans or Shrehari.

No more than a few minutes later, Chief Penzara raised his hand to attract Siobhan's attention.

"I've got an emergence signature ahead of us, sir, on a course that approximates ours. Probably Shrehari, possibly a Ptar class corvette. He's gone silent."

"Really?" Dunmoore's eyebrows shot up. "What's he doing out here?"

"Looking for imprudent civilian shipping?" Syten suggested.

"A bit of a coincidence that he'd be dropping out of hyperspace so close to us, no?"

"Indeed, Mister Pushkin," the gunnery chief nodded. "I don't think he's seen us yet."

"Then we'd better make sure that state of affairs continues," the first officer replied, scanning his console to make doubly sure *Stingray* seemed like nothing more than a dark spot against the backdrop of stars.

"On tactical, Chief," Dunmoore ordered.

After studying the display for a few moments, she nodded.

"A burst from the drives should accelerate us enough to catch up with him and still keep our signature unobtrusive."

"You intend to attack?" Pushkin managed to hide his disapproval, but Siobhan caught it nonetheless. "Though it might be a Ptar, he could still get lucky and cause us enough grief to force a return home before we can tackle our long run across the black."

"If he caught our scent a few jumps back and we've only now detected him, that means he's a brilliant tactician, and he's curious about what we might be doing on this heading. Either way, I think it would be prudent to end his little hunt now, while we have him in our sights. The gods of war seem to have decided that we see him before he sees us on this tack, and that means they wish us to seize the advantage."

"Colonel Kalivan might disagree, sir," Pushkin whispered into her ear, so only she could hear. "Our mission isn't to seek and destroy."

"Bugger Kalivan," she whispered back. "The orders didn't explicitly forbid me from engaging the enemy. Therefore, since it's my ship, it'll be my rules of engagement. We fight."

— Six —

"It's definitely a Ptar class," Penzara said a few hours later, squinting at the new data scrolling across his screen. "Has to be, with that kind of power curve, though his emissions are a lot cleaner than what I'd expect. Must be fresh out of refit. On the other hand, the buggers could have found a way to improve their shielding as well. If he had been a few seconds faster going silent, I'd likely not have been able to home in and keep a lock. I'll bet you're right that he's been shadowing us for a few jumps, wondering what we're doing, Captain. There's no other reason for him to be here."

"True. He is a bit far from home, but then so are we." Pushkin frowned. "Mind you, perhaps the Shrehari quietly annexed this sector without intelligence finding out."

"I doubt intelligence would be that inept, all joking aside, though it might explain a lot of things." Dunmoore examined the three-dimensional schematic, index finger tracing the scar on her jawline. Then she smiled cruelly. "Helm, nudge us five degrees to port, zee plus ten, on a very wide arc, with short thruster bursts. With his sensors in passive mode and a little luck, he won't notice until it's too late."

"Five degrees to port, zee plus ten, short bursts, aye," Petty Officer Takash replied, fingers dancing. "Laid in and ready."

"Engage."

"Shall I put the ship at battle stations?" Pushkin asked.

"Not yet. We still have a good half hour to go before we're in range. Do it in twenty minutes or so." She knew that fidgeting on the bridge would not do her any good, but it would irritate the crew, and therefore nodded at Tours to take the command chair. "Coffee, Mister Pushkin?"

"Are you intending to switch on our IFF when we attack?" He asked, pouring two mugs from the small urn in her ready room. *Stingray* had been sailing with running lights off and her IFF silent, turning the ship into a visual and electronic mystery. Moreover, because she had not been close to the Shrehari frontier since her refit after Cimmeria, the enemy would not have her new emissions fingerprint either.

"That's the dilemma, isn't it? Strictly speaking, the rules of war say I have to, but if we don't destroy him before he can transmit a report, or even worse, he gets away, the Shrehari will know a solitary frigate is heading into the black and wonder why. Since there's no one to tell that we didn't actually follow the formalities, we'll open fire under false colors as it were."

When Pushkin did not respond or even show any sign of disagreement, she smiled.

"What happened to the first officer as his captain's conscience? Isn't your job reminding me of the folly of my decisions?"

He shrugged.

"While I subscribe to the notion that a genuine measure of someone's honesty is what they'd do when no one's watching, I also don't think we need to follow chapter and verse of the Aldebaran Convention when it comes to the Shrehari. At least not on matters that don't deal with actual war crimes. If they can't figure out we're Navy once we've fired off our first salvo, then that's their problem."

"Spoken like a real rogue of the star lanes." She raised her coffee cup in salute. "We seem to be rubbing off on each other."

"And would that be so bad?" He grinned shyly.

"I suppose not." She glanced at the tactical schematic on her ready room screen. "He hasn't bolted yet. I wonder if we can get close enough to use guns only."

"He'd have to be a complete optimist to think he's hidden from a Commonwealth-built starship at short range and, as I recall, the Shrehari aren't known for their lack of realism. He'll bolt before we're near. We'll have to expend a few missiles."

"Pessimist."

"All part of a first officer's duties."

They sipped their coffee in companionable silence for a few minutes.

"How much more time do you think we have left aboard the old girl?" Pushkin asked, touching the nearest bulkhead.

"What brought that thought to mind?"

"I'm not sure. Something is telling me this might be our last cruise. That they chose us for the mission in part because, with the first of the Voivode class frigates coming off the slipways soon, *Stingray*'s reaching the point where she's expendable."

"Cheerful this morning, aren't you? Colonel Kalivan made the same comment a few days ago, just before we jumped on the first leg." Siobhan scowled. "I hope you're wrong. After this commission, I'm likely to end up in a shore billet, possibly for good."

"Why wouldn't you get another ship?"

A bitter laugh escaped her throat.

"This is my third command, Gregor. I doubt they'll give me a fourth after everything that's happened, and definitely not as a post captain."

"That would be a shame. The Admiralty could do a lot worse than put you on the bridge of a cruiser."

"Flattery will get you nowhere," she replied with a sad smile, "though I'll try my best to get all of you decent billets on the newer starships when we're decommissioned. Truth be told, I've already sent my recommendations to the personnel directorate in case you're right about this being our last outing."

Pushkin inclined his head in thanks.

"It doesn't' mean they'll listen to me, though," she cautioned.

The intercom beeped and Tours' voice came on.

"We're ten minutes from engagement range, Captain. He still hasn't gone up systems. I'm about to call battle stations."

"Thank you. Go ahead."

The sailing master must have had a finger hovering over his call screen because the siren went off a fraction of a second later, sending the crew to their guns, launchers or damage control teams, pulling on their personal protective equipment along the way. Dunmoore grabbed her survival bag and followed Pushkin onto the bridge.

"All divisions report ready," the first officer said a few minutes later, "and all systems are green. The ship is ready for action."

"Thank you, Number One."

"I'm impressed," Chief Penzara remarked, "we're almost on top of him, and he's still a faint ghost on my sensors. They've definitely improved something while we were off keeping the Coalsack frontier safe from democracy."

Dunmoore glanced at Pushkin.

"Perhaps we can sneak up to gun range after all. Overconfidence has spelled the end for more ships than anything else."

"Too late," Penzara called out. "He lit up and is accelerating."

"Damn." Siobhan shook her head. "We were so close. Systems up, Mister Pushkin. Guns, raise shields, go to active targeting and fire a spread of missiles when ready. Helm, accelerate to full. He'll try running, and we can't have him go FTL before we've put in our licks."

Power coursed through the ship while the shield generators formed a protective bubble around her hull, transforming *Stingray* from the hole in space she had been moments earlier into a warship ready for action.

"Missiles away!"

"He'll not escape those." The chief's excitement was palpable. "His hyperdrives are still spooling up, and he can't jump for a few minutes."

Defensive fire began to blossom on the Ptar's hull as the Shrehari captain desperately tried to shoot *Stingray*'s birds down before they could explode against his shields and collapse them.

Two missiles vanished, but the others kept accelerating, and soon, the Shrehari fire control systems could no longer react fast enough. A pair of greenish-blue auroras erupted around the Ptar when the missiles struck.

"Shields are holding, but just," Penzara reported.

"We'll finish it off with guns. You can fire at will, Mister Syten."

Plasma bolts erupted from *Stingray*'s main guns as she closed the distance with the Ptar. The Shrehari had finally gotten around to firing missiles, but at this range, they had no chance to accelerate and Penzara's guns quickly swatted them aside.

Dunmoore leaned forward in the command chair, willing her ship to close the distance even faster so she could finally take her prey before it escaped. The Shrehari corvette desperately tried to keep her at bay, but its sublight drives just could not generate enough thrust to open the distance between the two starships.

Chief Penzara let out a whoop of joy.

"Shields have collapsed."

The first black streaks materialized on the Ptar when *Stingray*'s plasma, unhindered now, splashed against its hull.

Then, the corvette shimmered when its hyperdrives kicked in.

"No!" Siobhan shouted, her fist hammering the chair's arm. "Sailing master, plot a pursuit course. We're not going to let this one get away."

"Course plotted and laid in. Helm has reoriented the ship. We are ready to follow."

"Sound emergency jump stations." Dunmoore, frustrated, sat back and prepared herself for the momentary wrench of leaving normal space. Ten seconds after the last klaxon died down, the frigate went FTL.

Once the ship and their stomachs had settled down, she asked, "Do we have his wake yet?"

"Negative." Penzara shook his head.

"Mister Syten, get the torpedo room ready, just hold off on fueling the warheads for now."

"Aye, aye, Captain."

Time ticked by much too slowly for Dunmoore's taut nerves and she caught her fingers drumming on her thigh more than once. Pushkin thought about suggesting a quiet coffee in her ready room, but he knew that she wanted to be in her chair the moment Penzara picked up the Ptar's trail. Fortunately, they got their first reading of a disturbance 'ahead' within half an hour.

"I have something," Penzara raised his hand to attract her attention, "slightly to port. It's on screen."

"Got you," Siobhan's low, breathy whisper almost sounded like arousal and a predatory smile spread across her face. Anyone who did not know her might well have wondered what kind of woman sat in the frigate's command chair.

"Fuel the torpedoes and fire when ready."

Down in the bow, both senior gunners waited patiently, tracking the target's wake on their fire control screens. Dressed in full armor, the better to survive should the frigate take a bad hit, the isolation it provided helped them concentrate. Sitting in their individual launch tubes beneath the firing station, the torpedoes waited for the signal to launch.

Massive weapons without the sort of AI brain that controlled missiles, they consisted mainly of a miniaturized jump drive topped by a small antimatter warhead. Torpedoes had no guidance system since, under the laws of hyperspace, they could only travel in the direction they had been launched. Giving them anything more would have been useless.

However, it made the gunners' job a difficult one. Without the sophisticated fire control computer to help, the senior torpedo gunner aimed and fired entirely on instinct.

For this reason, torpedo specialists such as Petty Officer Lako were reckoned the best in the business, and those who topped the usual thirty percent success rate became minor legends. Petty Officer Lako did not consider herself a legend, but she knew her business. Yet that still did not calm the butterflies in her stomach.

The board showed all systems green, indicating that the antimatter warhead was stable, the jump drive warm, and the tube ready.

Now that the target's wake signature was growing ever clearer, Lako could patiently feel her way to a firing solution, adjusting the aim as the frigate closed in.

"Torp, this is the bridge," Syten's voice sounded unusually loud in her ears. "Are you ready?"

"Aye, sir," she replied through clenched teeth, eyes still glued to the screen.

"Then you may fire tube one at your leisure."

Lako's eyes narrowed to a slit, and she took one deep breath before releasing it halfway. Then, she fired.

The torpedo's signature flickered for a microsecond as it almost returned to normal space before its hyperdrive kicked in. However, the small jump engine worked perfectly. Her screen now tracked the torpedo's tiny wake as it sped away from the frigate, heading straight toward the massive, pulsing turbulence that marked the target.

And missed.

The dumb weapon sped past the Ptar, its wake vanishing into the depths of hyperspace. It would drop out of FTL once all of the drive's fuel had been exhausted, and then self-destruct.

Lako swore quietly, but she readied the next one. If she missed with that one as well, her average would drop below fifty percent, and that would earn her a lot of ribbing in the chiefs' and petty officers' mess.

She felt her way toward a firing solution again, happy that Syten refrained from riding her, and ejected a second one. It too tried to drop out of FTL for a tiny fraction of a second before its drive lit up and propelled it toward the Ptar.

Petty Officer Lako's aim proved truer this time. The torpedo entered the broad area of turbulence created by the corvette's hyperdrives and vanished from all screens. Aboard *Stingray*, the crew waited for signs of a hit, no one more so than Guthren. His hand hovered over the drive cutout to ensure they did not overshoot the Shrehari ship by too big a margin once the torpedo had thrown it back into normal space.

Then, without warning, the Ptar vanished from the tactical plot and Guthren cut out the hyperdrives before Siobhan even had time to issue the order. Momentary nausea overcame them, but it faded quickly.

"Shields up. Track the target. Helm, come about one eighty, emergency turn." Siobhan's voice held a ferocity that belied her earlier forced calm.

"Shall we offer them the chance to surrender?"

"Getting soft in your old age, Gregor?"

Siobhan bit her lip impatiently while Guthren brought *Stingray* around on an intercept course to finish the Ptar off, shedding as much forward momentum as he could, their bow thrusters pushing hard.

"They wouldn't accept it anyway."

As if to underline her words, the Shrehari ship, in a desperate attempt to salvage at least a Pyrrhic victory, opened fire at extreme range with everything they had left. It was not enough.

Stingray's shields easily deflected the plasma rounds, showing no more than a bright green shimmer at the edges.

"You may open fire at will, Mister Syten."

As the frigate's main guns hammered out round after round, they could see black marks distorting the Ptar's hull, eating through armor and breaching compartment after compartment. Geysers of rapidly crystallizing gasses erupted in the wake of the broadside, testament to the dying starship's final moments of agony.

Then, with the suddenness that always caught a victorious crew by surprise, the Shrehari blew apart, sending chunks of metal spinning out of control in all directions. Awed silence descended on the bridge when the realization that they had just killed eighty odd Shrehari dawned on them.

"Wow." Penzara shook his head. "Seeing that never gets old."

Dunmoore turned to Kowalski.

"Do we know if he got a message off? He's bound to have friends nearby. Ptar's don't roam by themselves this far from their home base."

The signals officer studied her log.

"He emitted a coherent subspace burst shortly after dropping out of FTL, while we were turning, but I have no way of uncompressing and decoding it. Shrehari tech might lag ours, but there's nothing wrong with their cryptography."

"So we can assume a distress call, warning of a big, bad, unidentified attacker, has gone out. Let's not stick around to discover if it's been received. Mister Tours, get us back on course."

*

"Commander, a message from the admiral." Urag stuck his head into Brakal's cabin.

"And what does he want now?"

"The *Ptar Kash* has been destroyed."

Brakal's head snapped up. "Where?"

"Not far. Less than a fraction of a parsec."

"Did he identify his destroyer?"

"No. All we have is an indistinct visual. The enemy did not emit a signal he could track."

"Show me." Brakal stood up to follow Urag back out onto the bridge.

At the first officer's orders, the image of a shadowy starship appeared on the main screen.

"This was taken in the moments before the *Kash* transmitted its final report."

Brakal stroked his chin, eyes narrowed, as he examined the eerily familiar silhouette.

"Human. Definitely human and I'm convinced that we've met this one before, or one of its like." He turned around. "We will hunt him down. Get us to the *Kash*'s last position at best speed."

"As you command."

*

"Scan for the beacon." Brakal's ill humor hung over his crew like a shroud.

"It no longer sends, Commander." The gun master shrugged. "The humans may have taken the time to destroy it."

"Fah." Brakal brushed the objection away. "Find the thing, wretch. Without it, we have no chance of tracking down this impudent maggot who dares destroy our shipping this far from its bases."

"Commander?" Urag sounded puzzled.

"If we're lucky, *Ptar Kash* will have been equipped with one of the new recording beacons, with its own basic sensor suite. It may give us the direction in which the human went. With him no longer visible on long-range scans, it's the only chance we have."

"Finding a small object in this debris cloud?" *Tol Vehar*'s first officer snorted softly. "Has unjustified optimism finally overtaken reason, or are you relieving your anger at the crew's expense? It'll take days to sift through the mess."

"If you have no useful comment to make, be still and obey my orders."

Urag straightened his back at the harsh tone, wondering what was eating at Brakal. Ever since the news of the *Kash*'s destruction, he had been like a wounded *kroorath*, lashing out at the slightest provocation. The stoic sub-commander had not yet realized that Brakal had come to a decision concerning their shadowy prey. Otherwise, the argument against pursuit would have become acrimonious enough to make some wonder at the wisdom of signing on to the cruiser.

It took many hours of sifting before they found a heavily armored block, the size of a full-grown man, inside a sliver of hull spinning out of control. Retrieving the beacon took many hours more, but finally, a satisfied Brakal stood before it on his hangar deck with a feral smile of satisfaction splitting his dark, bony face.

"So this is the magic object that will show us where the human went?"

"You sound unconvinced, Urag. Those hairless apes aren't the only ones able to make leaps in technology. Once the Admiralty got tired of taking savage hits without a means of retaliation, they ordered the development of a tracking beacon to replace the older locating units. This beautiful object is one of those. All we need to do is hook it up to a power cell and download its memory. It will show us the way."

Less than an hour later, after studying the results, Brakal sat back and rubbed his chin, lost in thought.

"Why is the poxed whoreson heading *away* from both our and human space? There is nothing but interstellar dust in that direction. We can barely even see stars through it."

"Will you follow?" Regar wore his habitual insubordinate expression.

"If I do, will you report me to that diseased mass of fat who calls himself our strike force commander?"

A low rumble of laughter deep in the *Tai Kan* spy's chest signaled his amusement at the question.

"How you interpret your orders isn't my concern."

"Really? I'm surprised. Spies usually scrutinize my every thought, let alone my every action, as if I were a laboratory specimen. Tell me, Regar, what is your concern?"

"Winning this war, of course, so I can enjoy some peace and quiet at my family's estates instead of spending my life aboard warships."

"You're a very strange man for someone employed by the codpiece lickers of the *Tai Kan*." Brakal dismissed the Regar with a shrug. "Plot a course, Urag. We follow his last known track. Perhaps we may discover why he's heading into the uncharted depths of dark space."

— Seven —

"Didn't you think indulging in an attack on Shrehari shipping to be at odds with our mission?" Kalivan sounded more disappointed than angry, though it came across as irritatingly paternalistic.

"Perhaps." Dunmoore shrugged and took a bite from her sandwich, chewing slowly while she fought back the temptation to lecture him about the Navy's job of destroying the enemy wherever they found him.

"Mind you," she continued, "if he'd been so inclined, the bastard could have followed us to see where we were going, and I can't see that as being healthy for the mission either."

"You believe a ship that size would have the autonomy?"

A real question, without the usual sarcastic undertone. Siobhan allowed herself a faint smile.

"The Shrehari idea of austere conditions would make even our toughest special ops folks weep, which means they can pack more supplies in a hull of a comparable size. It wouldn't have been fun for the crew, but that corvette could have made it to the target star system and back without a problem, provided they'd kept their maintenance up to date."

"I see." Kalivan nodded. "And if there's one in the vicinity, there may be others."

"That's pretty much a given, but space is vast, starships tiny and sensor gear has its limitations, not least because of the time lag issues at sublight speeds. It takes good techs and a lot of luck to find a ship, which is why most battles are fought within or near star systems that are of use to us or the enemy."

A stiff nod. "That does make sense. Well, let's hope this one's friends won't be able to sniff us out."

"I doubt it. We're sticking to deep space. The best place for a Shrehari to wait for us would be at the end of the trip, provided he knew where we were going, which he doesn't."

"To change the subject somewhat, Captain, but staying in the realm of strategies and tactics, do you perchance play chess?"

Siobhan laughed.

"I do. My first officer, who's a master at the game, has been trying to turn me into a useful opponent."

"And is he succeeding?" Kalivan's sardonic expression had returned, but this time, it felt less patronizing.

"I can't tell. You'll have to ask him. He just keeps beating me."

"Perhaps you'd consent to a game when you have some time. I could make up my own mind as to your skills. You have somewhat of a reputation as a tactician, you know."

She snorted.

"Perhaps, but as Gregor keeps telling me, I don't have the patience of a chess player. You're on, Colonel. Shall we say at two bells in the dog watch, before supper?"

"Certainly. As the leading idler on this trip, I'm available whenever is convenient for you." That polite nod again, this time with the ghost of a self-deprecating grin. "Until five then, Captain."

He stood, picked up his empty plate, and left Dunmoore to enjoy the remains of her meal.

"Am I mistaken, or did our good colonel just crack a smile?" Pushkin dropped into the vacated seat.

"Your eyes didn't lie, Gregor. We've got a chess game planned later today."

"Really? Is he finally showing some signs of sociability? He's been acting pretty aloof since we left Starbase 37, to the point where even Devall is finding him somewhat strange for a member of his social class."

"Perhaps he's thawing." She shrugged. "I'll do what I can to encourage him. We have a long trip ahead of us."

"Perhaps it's finally time for supper in your quarters. This is the longest you've gone without inviting a passenger to sample your wine locker."

"I fear that my plebeian vintages might disappoint him."

"Bugger his disappointment."

"You'll share the table with us, Gregor. I don't feel in the mood to entertain Kalivan by myself."

"Invite Kutora as well. That should provide the colonel with plenty of entertainment."

"The pedant and the grouch? That's probably too much of an explosive combination."

"Devall, then, or Kowalski."

"I'll think about it." She glanced at the time. "I believe Syten wants to discuss some training ideas. She's probably waiting for me already, so we'll discuss this later."

*

"I believe that's a check for me." He released his bishop and sat back.

The smug look on Kalivan's face annoyed Siobhan more than it should have. He had proved to be a decent player, not as good as Pushkin, but still able to out-think her by at least two moves. If he could just show a little humility, his style would not be so aggravating, but each move came with such an air of condescending superiority that it drove her mad.

She had hoped to crack a little of the self-satisfied facade by sharing one of the few diversions she allowed herself on patrol, but if this first game gave any indication, it would do the opposite.

"Not for long." She moved a knight to block him, and then realized she had fallen into his trap.

Looking up at him, she saw not the previous smugness or even so much as a hint of triumph, but his eyes shone with suppressed amusement.

"I see what Mister Pushkin means when he chides you for lack of patience."

At that moment, she realized that he had deliberately provoked her into a rash move, that she had let her annoyance at his mannerisms overtake tactical prudence. Unsurprisingly, it exasperated her even more, and it must have shown in her expression because his amusement only seemed to increase, though he carefully kept from smiling openly.

"Well played, Colonel," she replied between clenched teeth.

"I'm a bit surprised at being able to goad you like that, Captain. Your reputation as a tactician had led me to believe that you could place yourself inside an opponent's decision-making loop and be the one doing the goading."

"Evidently not when it comes to chess, sir."

She forced herself to relax. It was just a game, and her defeat at his hands lay squarely on her shoulders: she had let him get inside her head too easily. It gave her a whole new appreciation of the man, and of his less well-known military specialty.

"I feel I should apologize." He reached for his coffee mug and took a sip of the lukewarm brew. "It wasn't fair of me to play mind games in such a pure pursuit as chess. I suppose it's a combination of natural inclination and professional deformation. That's by way of explanation, not an excuse, mind you. Growing up as I did, you either became superb at manipulating others, or you perished."

"Hence the specialization in influence activities."

"Indeed, though I did start off as an infantryman, like every other army officer. I suppose I could have gone into public affairs or the judge advocate general, but I don't have an affinity for parroting the party line or for the tedium of military law. Would you like another match?"

"I'll pass. Licking my wounds is something I prefer doing in private." She glanced at the time. "I've also got a few things to sort out before supper."

"In that case, thank you for the match, Captain."

He rose and bowed briefly, the gesture polished like that of a courtier, before leaving Siobhan to her solitude. It did not last long.

The door to the bridge opened.

"How did it go?"

"Hi, Gregor. Please, have a seat, Gregor. Would you like some coffee, Gregor?"

"My, my. That bad?" Pushkin smiled at her grouchy greeting.

"Don't ever play poker with that man."

"Yes. Viv Luttrell said as much the other day. Not where he could hear, thankfully. Your officers have been very correct in his presence, even if they all find him a tad overbearing."

"Let's just say that his choice of military specialty is all too apt." She scowled. "The bastard got into my head."

"I'm sure he's of legitimate birth, Captain." The first officer sat down across from her, still smiling. "But for some reason, I'm not surprised. I get the feeling Colonel Kalivan has been playing with us from the start. Devall said as much. Apparently, skill at manipulation is a prerequisite for our higher castes."

"So he said. And yet they send him to track down a lost colony ship."

"Why not? If we find something, he'll make a name for himself and if he's a younger son, as Devall believes, it may be his big opportunity to shine."

"Younger son?" She shook her head. "Sometimes I think we're two separate civilizations, Earth and the inner systems, and the rest of us."

"You and me both. Still going forward with tonight's supper *en famille*?"

"It would look a little churlish if I canceled because he beat me at chess by messing with my head." She stared at the star map on the wall. "You know, he actually did me a favor."

"How so?"

"He showed me that I'm much more susceptible to emotional manipulation than I believed. By irritating me with his superior mannerisms, he tricked me into acting rashly and losing. It won't happen again, that I can guarantee you."

"You think?" Pushkin cocked a skeptical eyebrow. "You're as human as the rest of us. Pushed far enough..."

"Always the voice of cheerful reason, aren't you."

"I may have said this before but yes – first officer's union rules."

*

The chime's soft sound wrenched Siobhan from her contemplation of the holographic projection depicting their immediate surroundings, with its shadowy section, where interstellar dust blocked her view of the stars beyond their current position — in the visible spectrum, that is. *The black...*

"Come."

Siobhan turned toward the door and tried to put on a welcoming expression. Perhaps she should have postponed the private supper in her quarters, but having gained some insight into Kalivan and faced with a long voyage, she had finally come to the conclusion that the sooner, the better.

"Good evening, Captain." Devall's relaxed smile gave her a measure of ease, as did the genuine pleasure at the invitation to dine she saw reflected in his eyes.

"Come in Trevane." Her stiff smile softened just enough for the second officer to notice, but he knew better than to comment on it.

Pushkin appeared behind Devall before the cabin door could close again. By contrast, his face showed keen anticipation at finally having their passenger in a confined environment. Kalivan had mostly stayed aloof from the others in the wardroom, though he had been polite enough, and therefore had remained somewhat of a mystery to the frigate's officers.

He glanced at the old ship's clock with the silhouette of the gaunt knight on its face.

"I guess we're a minute early."

"I would expect no less." She gestured toward the cooler holding an open bottle of white wine. "Serve yourselves, gentlemen. We won't stand on ceremony tonight."

Just then, the chime sounded again.

"Our guest of honor has arrived." With Pushkin and Devall to stiffen her resolve, the smile pulling her mouth up by the corners seemed and felt much more natural.

The door opened again, this time admitting Kalivan. He had changed into his more formal service dress, a black-trimmed, rifle green version of the midnight blue uniforms worn by the others.

"Welcome, Colonel."

"Captain." He nodded. "Commander Pushkin, Lieutenant Devall. Thank you for the invitation. I understand from what I've read of naval customs that dinner in the captain's quarters is a rare and extraordinary occasion."

"Perhaps not unusual, Colonel, but I do try to arrange things so that that it's a real change from the wardroom. It also allows us to speak more freely than we otherwise would in front of the more junior officers."

"Just so." He nodded again.

"Has Vincenzo prepared something special?" Devall asked.

"But of course." She saw the question in Kalivan's eyes and gave a half shrug. "My steward, really one of the bosun's mates who volunteered for additional duties, is a bit of a gourmet with some unique culinary skills. He's the closest thing we might have to an executive chef on board. I think you'll be pleased with tonight's menu."

"I look forward to it. Might I inquire what we'll be served?"

Pushkin chuckled.

"We'll find out when it's brought in. Vincenzo likes to surprise us with his creations."

"Some wine?" Siobhan held up the light green bottle, shiny with moisture from the cooler.

Kalivan squinted at the label.

"A tolerable vintage. I'll gladly take some."

Pushkin and Devall exchanged a glance at the army officer's off-hand characterization of the wine, the second officer shrugging minutely as if to say they should not take the foibles of the high-born too seriously.

When all held a filled glass, Dunmoore raised hers.

"Gentlemen, to our mission and to this ship. May she take us there and back again."

"To the mission and the ship," they replied dutifully, before taking a sip of the chilled liquid.

"Definitely tolerable." Kalivan's smile showed an unexpected hint of warmth. "My compliments for your wine cellar."

"I trust you'll find my red just as satisfactory, Colonel." Siobhan gestured at the small table surrounded by chairs raided from the wardroom. "Shall we sit?"

As if Vincenzo had been waiting for that very moment, the cabin door opened to admit the bosun's mate and a wardroom steward, each carrying a tray with the appetizers.

"What's on the menu?" Dunmoore asked, shaking a napkin out over her lap.

"For starters, we have smoked blue troutling, Captain" he replied, placing a plate in front of Kalivan with a small flourish, "followed by leek and opalberry soup. The main dish tonight is roast boar with mushrooms. And to finish, a cheese plate and the chef's surprise for desert."

"Sounds impressive." Kalivan nodded.

"It's less so when you know that the wardroom, chiefs and petty officers' mess, as well as the rating's mess, will all be served some variation on this theme. I do take on some stores of my own, but food-wise, we eat what the rest of the ship eats."

"A very commendable notion." Kalivan's brief, seated bow, no doubt meant sincerely, seemed to irk Pushkin. Siobhan flashed him a warning glance.

"A delicious looking one as well," Devall offered after examining his plate.

"Please eat." She picked up her utensils and looked at them expectantly.

"Tasty indeed," Kalivan said after swallowing his first bite. "My compliments to your kitchen."

"Galley, Colonel. Aboard ship, we call it a galley and I'll be happy to pass along your compliments."

"Pardon me. I've studied your naval particularities, but apparently not to a sufficient degree. I shall strive to do better."

"You know," he continued around a bit of fish, "service lingo is a funny thing."

"How so?" Siobhan took a sip of wine and let its tart coolness wash over her tongue.

"We're all part of the Commonwealth Armed Services, yet we often don't speak the same language, even though we're all engaged in the same overall task. I suppose it's an atavistic leftover from the days when we, as a species, were confined to a single planet, fighting among ourselves for resources, supremacy, or silly ideological beliefs."

"And now, we're combating non-human species while we're still fighting among ourselves for power, ideology, or just plain old greed." The first officer's eyes shone with distaste. "Some things never change."

"A very dim view of humanity, Mister Pushkin," Kalivan nodded again, "but one which I tend to share when I'm feeling less than sanguine about things. As you might imagine, in my specialty, I tend to see some of the baser human instincts when it comes to money and politics."

The three naval officers stared at him, curiosity writ plainly in their eyes. He smiled, pleased that he had captured their attention.

"My specialty has been called civil affairs since back in the old days before humans found ways of using FTL travel to beat up on each other, also known as the Migration Wars. That innocuous title covers many sins, such as propaganda, psychological operations, and other things in that vein, as well as the better-known civil-military cooperation work. We're just more honest nowadays in calling part of it influence activities. Trust me when I tell you that I've met some slimy individuals in my work of preventing human on human brush wars or patching things up afterward. The Shrehari might have been spanking us regularly for the last six years, but the capacity for human stupidity, or rather cupidity, remains unfathomable."

Dunmoore nodded, a faint smile twisting her lips.

"We've also run across those slimy individuals, Colonel. I don't know if you army folks get to count coup, but my crew and I have derived some satisfaction from using our meager naval might to end their depredations."

"Have you now, Captain?" He raised his glass. "Then you and I aren't so different after all."

Siobhan gave Pushkin a warning glance, to forestall the inevitable snort of disbelief. She did not have to warn Devall. He was well bred enough to control his reactions and show only what he wanted to show which, at this point, seemed to be his usual smile.

"Perhaps." She spun her glass idly, locking eyes with Kalivan. "Though our backgrounds must vary significantly."

"Ah yes." He carefully set his fork down on the plate and wiped his lips with a napkin. "You refer to my being born and bred on Earth, a member of the so-called aristocracy, while you're an Outworlder. I do think the differences between the systems colonized during the first wave of expansion and those of the second wave are exaggerated."

"And yet we still managed to fight two civil wars over planetary rights." Pushkin's almost aggressive tone drew another warning glance from Siobhan.

"True. Human nature, such as it is, hasn't changed much over the centuries, no matter what the social engineers have tried."

"Tried and failed, since well before we conquered space," Dunmoore smiled at his wistful tone, the first unaffected emotion he had shown.

"Hundreds of millions dying in the process – billions, if you count the Migration Wars – and yet we keep repeating the same mistakes." Kalivan shook his head ruefully. "If we do find a human colony at the end of our journey, we might well observe how a microcosm of our species has dealt with the inherent human urge to control others through means fair and foul."

Devall's lips twitched.

"Hearing you speak, Colonel, one would almost assume you to be a raving revolutionary, at least where other members of your social class are concerned."

"Your social class as well, Lieutenant."

The second officer nodded, conceding the point.

"I'll note however that my particular sub-species tends to be less hypocritical about asserting power and influence. We don't have any so-called progressive politicians on Pacifica keeping the masses docile with the promise of a comfortable life, unlike some of the inner systems I can think of. Brute force works better and is a lot cheaper."

"Touché." Kalivan's smile broadened. "I find politics tiresome, much to my family's dismay. The army provides a more peaceful life by comparison and a more honest living at that."

"Why not the Marines or the Navy?"

Dunmoore's genuine curiosity elicited a self-deprecating grimace.

"Politics again, I'm afraid."

He broke off as Vincenzo and the steward entered to remove the empty plates and serve the next course. This time, the wine selection, a red from Dordogne, met with Kalivan's more enthusiastic approval.

"You were asking why the army," Kalivan said, once the ratings had left. "It's rather simple. With a last name like mine, they would have assigned me to one of the Earth-centric formations had I joined the Navy or the Marines, and I wanted to escape the isolated bubble of inner system society."

Siobhan studied him with renewed interest. He did not give much of a good initial impression, but she could see depths to the man that intrigued her, especially when it came to dispelling her preconceived notions about Earthers.

Pushkin caught the expression in his captain's eyes, and his jaw tightened, though he remained courteous and polite throughout the rest of the meal.

— Eight —

"Good morning, Captain."

Kalivan straightened his back with a long stretch, hands raised above his head. Even though the morning watch had not quite ended yet, he was far from alone in the improvised gym taking up most of the open space on the shuttle hangar deck.

"Colonel." She nodded politely, and then took an empty mat to begin her own stretching exercises. "I trust you enjoyed your meal last night."

"Immensely." A faint smile creased his solemn face. "The dishes were well executed and the conversation interesting, though I fear my contributions to it weren't necessarily always to your first officer's liking."

Siobhan chuckled.

"Gregor tends to view anyone not born on an Outworld with suspicion. You'll find a lot of that among my crew."

"And Lieutenant Devall?"

"He's another oddity, Colonel. His family has enough influence to prevent his being used as an ornament in some admiral's salon and is more than happy to have him serve on the frontiers, honing his killer instincts."

"Yes," Kalivan smiled again. "I've heard that said about the Devalls. He certainly strikes me as a competent officer."

"Trevane is that. He'll no doubt be a lieutenant commander by this time next year and first officer on another frigate if I have anything to say about it."

"Good for him." He stopped stretching and shook his limbs as if to loosen them. "Do you spar, Captain?"

"Minimal contact only," she replied after recovering from her momentary confusion at the question. "I can't afford to visit Luttrell's dungeon of cures on a regular basis. It wouldn't be good for morale."

Kalivan laughed.

"Understood. Do you have a preference, or would you be agreeable to freestyle?"

"Freestyle is okay."

For the next ten minutes, they danced around each other, lashing out at unexpected moments, their hands and feet stopping just millimeters short of inflicting a crippling strike.

Siobhan had not experienced a workout as intense as this in a long time and the sweat plastering her copper hair to her skull bore ample witness to the demands of the match. Kalivan possessed her suppleness and speed, lean muscles rippling beneath the tight-fitting exercise singlet.

Neither saw Pushkin's thoughtful face through the hangar control room's polarized window.

*

"Did you enjoy last night?" Kowalski sat down beside Devall in the otherwise empty wardroom, holding a breakfast sandwich in one hand and a cup of coffee in the other.

"Aren't you on watch in ten minutes?"

"Grumpy, much?" She took a bite and chewed slowly, watching the second officer from the corner of her eyes. "Was it so terrible?"

"Vincenzo served us splendidly prepared dishes, the captain offered up fine wines from her private stores and the conversation scintillated. Anything else you want to know?"

"Colonel Kalivan?"

"Ah." He drained his cup and sat back. "Now we get to the nub of the question. Forget what you think about his standoffish behavior and his somewhat superior attitude. He knows what he is and where he comes from, and I'm sure, he knows precisely where he's going. The asshole act is just that, an act, to fool people into dropping their guard."

"Oh." She mulled over that statement for a few moments. "And how's the captain reacting to all that?"

"With more fascination than I'd have thought. Turns out the bugger can lay on charm if he wants to." Devall glanced at the time display. "You'd better eat up. If you're late taking over as officer of the watch, Pushkin will give you an earful."

"Aye." She swallowed the last bit of her sandwich and washed it down with the rest of the coffee. "Speaking of which, how did our first officer take it?"

"I haven't seen him glower that much since the day our Siobhan took command of *Stingray*."

She snorted.

"Stands to reason, I'd say."

"Why is that?"

"Think about it, Trevane."

Then, with a wiggle of the fingers in the guise of salute, she left the second officer to his thoughts.

*

"I find it curious," Kalivan said, settling into the chair opposite Siobhan, "that the Survey Service never went deep into this area of the galaxy."

"My guess is that they had enough room to explore well away from the Shrehari Empire and not bother with a sector where fewer stars boast a planetary system – at least within a reasonable distance of the Commonwealth. Had the war not come about, I'm sure they'd have eventually turned their ships into this direction. I've heard that some pundits consider this to be our next frontier."

"Which makes us real explorers, then." He smiled. "How exciting."

"I doubt we're the first, be it human, Shrehari or other to come this way, though we may well be the first who'll return with a full report, if not a full survey."

"And if we find a lost colony, we'll be famous. Not a single one has been found in over two hundred years."

"I can do without fame."

Kalivan seemed surprised at her dry tone.

"I'd have thought it helped come promotion time. Getting noticed isn't easy."

"It doesn't when you've already been noticed more than you wanted, and not in a good way." Seeing his quizzical expression, she shook her head. "I guess you didn't research my history before embarking, did you, Colonel?"

"I studied what's public knowledge, and I know that Admiral Nagira thinks highly of you. As I understand, he chose your ship for this mission."

Siobhan laughed bitterly.

"We're most likely on this mission because we're expendable, Colonel, not because Admiral Nagira holds me in high esteem. No, I've tangled with too many people who hold grudges to wish any sort of fame."

Too many people who dread my revealing their involvement in Operation Valkyrie, she thought, thanking whatever miracle had kept her in command of *Stingray*.

"I get the feeling that I shouldn't pry, so I won't."

Siobhan realized that she had let her mask slip for a second, showing a hint of the inner turmoil that seemed to be part of her nature.

"I appreciate that, sir."

"Why don't you call me Wes? It'll be a long trip, and I'm only a passenger, not your superior officer. Would that suit you, Siobhan?"

She nodded, though she felt strangely hesitant at taking the proffered olive branch. Kalivan sounded genuine, so the unexpected reaction surprised her. Forcing back the feeling, Dunmoore smiled.

"It would, Wes."

"Can I interest you in a game of chess later, when you can take a break from ship's business? I promise I won't use my psy ops wiles on you this time."

"Perhaps."

A voice behind her cut off whatever she wanted to say next.

"Captain, the sailing master is waiting for us in the conference room. He's got the navigation plan for the remainder of the trip plotted out, as you requested."

She turned to see Pushkin's solemn face staring back at her, wondering if he had overheard any of the conversation with Kalivan.

"I'm coming, Gregor. Would you care to join us, Wes?"

Pushkin's surprised look at her use of Kalivan's first name briefly gave her pause.

"I'd like that."

Then, as if on cue, the surprised look took on a deeply thoughtful cast, but she was already on her feet and headed for the door, and thus failed to notice.

*

Pushkin poked his head into the ready room a few days later, shortly after *Stingray* jumped on a long reach through the dark expanse.

"Chess game after supper, Captain?"

Siobhan glanced up from the engineering report, feeling unexpected irritation at the interruption.

"I'm afraid not. Colonel Kalivan and I will be dining in my quarters and discussing possible mission parameters for when we arrive at our destination."

He seemed taken aback at the notion.

"May I respectfully inquire why I'm not invited to join such a discussion, seeing as how it may have a direct bearing on this ship's welfare?"

She sighed, pinching the bridge of her nose.

"All in good time, Gregor. All in good time. If truth be told, I want to draw more confidences out of Wes – Colonel Kalivan – and try to divine any hidden intentions that may affect our future. That'll be better done in private."

"Understood." Though his tone seemed grudging, he nodded.

Studying her taciturn second-in-command, she decided it might not be politic to mention she had started to enjoy Wes' company.

Dunmoore could relax with him in a way she could not with any other member of her crew, Pushkin included. A starship captain's life was solitary, and she found that she actually relished the chance to talk to someone who did not fall under her command, with all that implied.

Without a further word, Pushkin retreated onto the bridge, leaving her to stare, lost in thought, through the open door at the quiet efficiency of the duty watch.

Like Stars in Heaven

*

"You're a fan of pre-spaceflight era music." Kalivan gestured with his wine glass toward the gentle sounds that seemed to emanate from the bulkhead.

"And you must be as well if you recognize it."

She smiled at him and raised her own glass in a silent toast.

"Musical appreciation is hammered into children from a young age where I come from, the older, the better, and all in service to the snobbery of my kind, though I confess that I do enjoy nineteenth-century opera to a greater extent than more recent works. As much as I love Bizet or Puccini, I can't stand Wyeland and could never figure out why his *Farhaven* still gets so much top billing."

"Probably because it depicts the massacre at Fort Wagner in such gory detail."

"Probably. It does speak to regrettable contemporary tastes, doesn't it?"

Siobhan walked over to the computer screen by her bed and touched it briefly. A pair of strong male voices replaced Mahler.

"Now that is pure music," Kalivan said after listening for a few minutes, immersed in the harmony. "*Au Fond du Temple Saint* always gives me goose bumps. Bizet's best composition, I'd say. You?"

She turned back to the screen without answering when the Pearl Fishers duet tapered off and touched it again.

"This," she replied in a throaty almost-whisper, "is my favorite."

Their eyes met as the strains of *Nessun Dorma* filled the cabin with a soaring voice evoking a magical world far from the war and a frigate headed into the black.

"*Turandot*, Puccini's finest work. You truly are a woman of taste and refinement," he murmured, as if afraid to ruin the moment.

"A five-hundred-year-old recording of Anders Bellatti, one of the greatest tenors of the pre-FTL era."

"What a voice." Kalivan shook his head in wonder. "What sentiment."

He fell silent, letting the music wash over him like a tidal wave, savoring the words, the tonalities and the harmonies of the chorus, reveling in the amazing sounds.

"Not a bad selection for an uncultured Outworlder, eh," she said when the player fell silent, leaving behind an indelible auditory mark that still resonated within.

Her wry grin made him laugh with delight, and she felt an odd warmth spread across her cheeks. Kalivan made as if to lean toward Siobhan when the door chime rang, announcing the arrival of Vincenzo with their meal.

It seemed like a small thing, but it broke the moment. Once seated in front of a simple supper, no different than what the galley would serve the remainder of the crew, they turned to business. Siobhan felt a wholly unexpected and melancholic sense of regret.

"What exactly," she asked, eying him over the rim of her wine glass, "do you expect to find?"

"Vindication?" He shrugged. "Few people back home believe we'll find a lost colony. The fact that the log buoy seems to have traveled for much longer than one would expect, considering when *Tempest* left Earth, doesn't intrigue our superiors. They gave me the file because no one else at HQ wanted it and because, frankly, no one at HQ wanted me around. Apparently, judging by my last efficiency report, I've become too fond of speaking my mind and making others uncomfortable."

"I've been accused of the same thing. Perhaps we were matched up for this mission because neither of us is wanted anywhere near our respective flag officers."

Although, in *Stingray*'s case, she knew it to be more than just a disagreeably frank commanding officer annoying her superiors. Perhaps Kalivan had also pried into matters best left alone.

"Perhaps." He took a sip of wine, eyes roaming over the star map on the bulkhead. "Tell about that sensor ghost your Lieutenant Syten discussed at lunch?"

His sudden change of subject, from something personal to a technical matter, startled her, and she had to pause before replying.

"We picked up a weak reading far behind us just before going FTL. It could be a passing ship, a cloud of ionized gasses or even the reflection of a more distant ship bouncing off a cloud of gasses. The sensors couldn't resolve it."

"Could it be a Shrehari following us?"

"Anything is possible, though if we saw him as a faint blip, he wouldn't be able to pick us up at all. Their electronics just aren't as good as ours are. Space is vast and *Stingray* tiny; tracking us down would be quite a feat."

"If the ship you destroyed managed to get off a warning, perhaps one of its siblings managed to pick up our scent."

"Possible, but unlikely. As I said, the Imperials just don't have the gear for long-range detection. Now that we're FTL on a very long jump, even if it was a Shrehari looking to avenge the Ptar, he'll be hard-pressed to figure out where we're going, other than deeper into the black. They haven't surveyed this part of space either, to my knowledge."

"To your knowledge, perhaps, but we don't know all that much about their ambitions away from our dear Commonwealth."

She nodded, conceding the point. "Agreed. All that to say, I doubt we need to worry about Syten's sensor ghost."

"If you say so."

He refilled both their wine glasses and turned the conversation to more light-hearted subjects. As the evening wore on, they barely noticed Vincenzo when he cleared the table and served coffee. The chiming of the ship's bell, proclaiming the change over from the dog watch to the evening watch did not register either, nor did the subsequent tolling of the hours.

Six bells in the evening watch had passed by the time Kalivan finally stepped out into the passageway, smiling over his shoulder at a relaxed and contented Siobhan. When the door closed, he turned aft, toward his cabin and came face-to-face with Gregor Pushkin.

"A word in private, Colonel?"

Kalivan studied the first officer's expression, but it betrayed nothing.

"Certainly, Commander. If you follow me to my quarters, we should be at ease there."

"I'd offer you a seat," Kalivan said, waving around the spartan compartment once the door had closed behind them, "but as you see, I have only one chair, and I'll be taking it."

"I'll remain standing for what I have to say."

"My, my, you sound so serious Mister Pushkin." Kalivan repressed a smile when he saw a flash of anger at his amused tone. "Tell me what it is that has you here so late in the day."

"The captain's welfare, Colonel."

Kalivan's eyebrows shot up in mock astonishment. "Whatever do you mean?"

"Please. You know perfectly well what I mean."

"Do I, now?" The mocking smile grew.

Pushkin's face tightened, but he maintained his stoic facade and continued in an even tone.

"The captain hasn't had an easy time of the last few years, and she's had no companionship whatsoever. No one aboard will thank you for taking advantage of that, least of all me. Take care that you don't hurt her because if you do, you may not find your time with us very pleasant."

"And now threats." The smile vanished, replaced by a look of concern. "If I didn't know any better, Commander, I'd think you were suffering under the spell of the green-eyed monster."

When Pushkin's jaw muscles visibly twitched, Kalivan raised his hands, palms facing outward, in a sign of surrender.

"I apologize for ascribing your concern for your captain to jealousy. Your devotion to her welfare is commendable, and you may consider me warned. I will take care not to give her any reason to believe that I'm interested in anything more than friendship. Does that satisfy you?"

The first officer's jaw muscles continued to work in silence for a little while longer.

"It does," he finally replied. "This ship and its crew cannot afford a distracted captain. Mistakes in deep space tend to cost lives."

"Understood." Kalivan nodded once. "Was there anything else you wished to discuss?"

"No." Pushkin, his temper once more under control, tapped the panel beside the door. "Have a good night, Colonel."

Alone once more, Kalivan spent a long time staring at the space Pushkin had occupied. The first officer might have taken offense at the notion of jealousy, but to a man well versed in psychology, it seemed plain enough he carried suppressed feelings for Dunmoore, feelings he could never acknowledge lest he lose his effectiveness as the frigate's second-in-command.

Kalivan would have to tread more carefully around her from now on.

*

Devall looked up from his pad when Pushkin entered the wardroom.

"Doing your rounds?"

"Yeah." The first officer poured himself a coffee, all the while avoiding the other man's eyes.

"Something eating at you, Gregor?"

"Nothing to concern yourself about." Pushkin dumped his usual load of sweetener into the black liquid and stirred the resulting syrupy mess.

"I'd say as the spare, I have everything to worry about when the heir isn't his usual stoic self." Devall put the tablet down and leaned back in his chair. "Want to talk about it?"

"Not particularly, no."

"But you will anyway. Keeping it bottled up inside isn't healthy for you or for the rest of us. The captain and the ship can't afford a distracted first officer."

Hearing his own words thrown back at him by a man he had come to consider not only his invaluable right hand but a friend as well, Pushkin's anger melted away, and he sat down with a heavy sigh.

"I think I've made a bit of an ass of myself lately, especially just now."

"Kalivan?"

Pushkin nodded. "How did you guess?"

"Those of us who know and love you have come to the conclusion that you're concerned about the amount of time he spends with the captain. You *are* aware of how it is aboard a starship, don't you?" Devall smiled briefly. "Nothing remains hidden for long."

"And is the general consensus that I'm acting like a jealous cretin?"

Devall snorted.

"Did he accuse you of that?"

"In so many words, yes. How did you know I've just come from speaking with him?"

"Kathryn saw you enter his cabin. She dropped by the wardroom just now, on her way to the bridge."

"Keeping tabs on me?"

"We do like to know what you and the captain are up to. It saves us from unpleasant surprises. However, back to your question, Kalivan hasn't exactly endeared himself to the rest of us, so your concern for the captain is understandable. Seeing him muscle in on the close relationship you two have doesn't exactly fill anyone with high confidence, especially in light of his specialty."

"Trevane, I threatened an officer senior in rank to me. It wasn't precisely the high point of my professional career."

"So? You did your job as first officer. The last thing we need is someone messing with the captain's feelings, especially if Syten's sensor ghost is a Shrehari ship shadowing us. That Ptar may well have been in touch with its fellow patrol vessels. We get into a bad fight where we're going, and the ship might not make it home this time."

Pushkin drained his mug and set it down.

"You have a really annoying habit of being right and that means you'll make a good first officer. I suppose I should finish my tour of the ship before turning in." As he stood, he leaned over to look at Devall's pad. "The AI has you mated in three moves. You're improving, but you've still got a long way to go."

— Nine —

Dunmoore swiveled her command chair to face the door upon hearing it slide open. Colonel Kalivan stood at the threshold, almost at attention, a faint smile on his face.

He had been nothing but correct in public since his conversation with Pushkin, though his continued familiarity with Siobhan in private would not have thrilled the first officer.

"Might I come in, Captain? I understand we're about to emerge, and I'm rather excited to see what we find."

"By all means," she nodded toward an empty station, "though you'll likely find things underwhelming. We'll still be a light year or so away from the most likely target star, and absent radio emissions on a frequency we can monitor, there probably won't be anything exciting. I brought the ship to battle stations as a precautionary measure."

"Nevertheless." Kalivan sat down and examined the tactical schematic on the main screen, avoiding Siobhan's gaze with studied professionalism. "I'll take my entertainment when I can."

The klaxon sounded, warning all hands that their universe was about to shift in a most unpleasant fashion and that those most prone to transition nausea should sit or lie down to avoid a fall. A minute later, human guts twisted while artificial systems briefly surged and dipped as the frigate dropped out of FTL.

An alarm siren replaced the klaxon as the shields came up automatically and feedback howled through the ship's systems. Even the artificial gravity flickered just enough to throw crewmembers off balance.

"We emerged right in the middle of an ion storm," the sailing master shouted. "Category three, by all appearances."

"Our shields are keeping the worst of it away from us," Pushkin chimed in, "but we don't have long before the generators begin to feel the strain. We need to jump out soon."

Dunmoore touched her communicator.

"Engineering, this is the bridge, how quickly can we do an emergency transition to FTL?"

"It's been a long reach, Captain, and we need tuning," Kutora responded after a moment, "but I can feel the ion storm just like anyone else. Stand by."

"Mister Tours," she said, ignoring the chief engineer's habit of cutting her off, "I trust you've got something plotted."

"Aye, but without letting the drives spool through a full cycle after this last jump, we might emerge somewhere unexpected."

"We don't seem to have much choice unless you can see the edge of the storm within sublight range."

"Negative." He shook his head. "It's a big one. I'm planning on a jump of at least six light months."

"Let's try not to win the lottery by coming out of FTL in the middle of something solid. As soon as Mister Kutora gives us the go, we go." She glanced over her shoulder at Kalivan. "Are you entertained yet, Colonel?"

Face ashen, he shook his head briefly and swallowed.

"Not particularly. Do these events happen often?"

"More often than you'd think, though we usually get some warning thanks to advisories from whoever spots one on his long-range sensors. Out here?" She shrugged. "We're on our own. More than one starship has vanished thanks to ion storms, usually without leaving a trace. If you're interested in that kind of space tale, ask Lieutenant Devall. He's got quite a fund of stories to chill the blood."

"I'll pass, I think."

She gave him a quick smile, meant to be reassuring, then turned to her first officer.

"Status?"

"The shields are holding, but if you listen carefully, you can hear the generators howl in pain. We're also showing increasing stress on the hull and frames, which aren't *Stingray*'s strongest points since Cimmeria. I'll have Mister Kutora and his crew do a full survey of the ship once we're in calmer space. We shouldn't proceed any further with exploration until we're sure she can take it."

"Definitely." Siobhan nodded, fighting back her increasing anxiety at the feeling of helplessness while they remained within the storm.

"Engineering has the drives back online," Tours announced.

"Sound the emergency jump warning, fifteen seconds, and then go."

The klaxon's insistent wail rang in their ears, seeming like an appropriate counterpoint to the savagery of nature unleashed battering *Stingray*. Then, the universe shifted again.

"Get the survey going, Number One," Dunmoore said once she had swallowed her stomach. "If something has broken loose, we need to get it fixed before emerging again. With things this unsettled around here, who knows what new challenges await wherever this emergency jump is taking us."

"Hopefully not into the heart of a star," Pushkin muttered, though not in a low enough voice because Tours chimed in.

"That's why I went for six light months," he said. "The nearest star, our target, by the way, is one full light year away."

"Glad to hear it. I'm not sure our shields could have handled fifteen million degrees Celsius."

"Or the environmental systems," Guthren added, "and there's not enough beer on board to help out with the heat."

"The two of you do understand that with a pressure of over two-hundred sixty billion bars at the core of a G-class star, we wouldn't live long enough to realize we were screwed, right?" Tours' beatific smile made Siobhan laugh and the anxiety of the previous minutes drained away.

"Of course," he continued, "we wouldn't even make it that far, hyperspace physics and all. Besides, consider yourselves lucky that as a category three ion storm, it didn't extend beyond Newtonian space. Otherwise, I'd have no idea where this jump might take us. Thankfully, I can guarantee we won't come out anywhere near a gravity source powerful enough to give us grief."

"And if your guarantee fails, sir?" The coxswain asked.

"Then you can sue me for damages, provided you're able to find lawyers in heaven."

"Alright people." Dunmoore raised her right hand to end the back and forth. "Survey, then any repairs. We'll try again after this jump."

She rose from the chair and nodded at Kowalski.

"Stand down from battle stations. I'll be in my ready room."

"Aye, sir. I relieve you."

"And I stand relieved." Siobhan glanced at Kalivan. "Coffee, Colonel?"

"I'd like that." Some color had returned to his cheeks, but he still looked like a man who had seen his own impending death up close.

Once away from the bustle of the bridge, Dunmoore asked, "Are you alright, Wes?"

"I am now." A weak smile briefly played on his lips. "This has been a first for me."

She chuckled. "Don't think we end up in the middle of ion storms all the time either. We've merely been trained how to react. Thankfully, we shouldn't have suffered much from it. A category four or higher, now that could have caused real trouble, especially so far from the closest Starbase."

He stared at the holographic projection by the bulkhead, now showing them to be on the other side of the dark expanse, jaw muscles working.

"Doesn't the sense of isolation and distance give you the willies, especially when faced with the fury of a nature that cares little for us puny humans?"

"Whether we're fifty light years away or five hundred, the end result of a catastrophic failure is the same. You get used to thinking in terms of recovery distance, and we passed that well before crossing the black expanse, so really, it doesn't factor into any of our thoughts."

"I suppose I should admire the naval mind for being able to remain calm and collected in the face of such immense distances." A weak smile tugged at his lips. "If you can't get a subspace message to the nearest relay station from here, then a distress signal via conventional radio waves is all that remains. And it wouldn't be received until long after we'd all died, provided that it didn't dissipate completely."

"You're correct. Anything we try to send, be it subspace or normal, has little to no chance of making it where someone could pick it up. Our log buoy would be the only means to tell humanity of our fate, and even that's dependent on how long its antimatter fuel lasts."

"Since it can travel FTL, I daresay that ours would get back quicker than *Tempest*'s."

"Likely." She smiled at his use of the possessive. He seemed to have begun taking a very proprietary interest in the frigate. "But to answer the question you're really asking, yes we do sometimes get overwhelmed by the idea that we're an infinitesimally small speck of humanity that might never see home again, but those who can't cope with the idea end up leaving the service, sometimes involuntarily."

"Space madness?" He cocked an amused eyebrow.

"Something like that."

"Have you ever had it?"

She snorted.

"I'm generally too busy thinking of other things to marvel at my stupidity in choosing a life that has me living in a metal cocoon surrounded by cold vacuum."

"How do others cope with it?"

"In whatever way they can, be it compulsive exercising, immersion in VR games, sex, or the bottle. As long as they can function to my standards when they're on-duty and don't bother anyone with their private pursuits, I don't really care."

"And your pursuit is doing your duty?"

"Starship commanders have precious free time, Wes. We make love to our ships, immerse ourselves in combat simulations, and try to keep drinking to a minimum. The stereotype of the superannuated, alcoholic captain who saves the day is merely a product of bad fiction."

"It sounds like a very lonely existence."

"Maybe to someone who's not lived his life in the Navy, but my crew is my family. I'm never really alone."

"And yet you're apart from them. Not physically, of course, but because you hold the responsibility for all of their lives in your hands. How can one experience the intimacy of real companionship with such a burden?"

"You've never been in that situation? I find it hard to believe."

"Things are different for an army officer. We don't spend our lives in deep space, where a single mistake can kill an entire crew. Though I've commanded a battalion, I've never been alone, as you are alone. I've always had a brigade commander nearby, civilians around me with whom I could interact and, God help me, I've had loving family members as well. In contrast, you are quite alone, no?"

She nodded thoughtfully.

"I suppose so. Being a starship captain does have its drawbacks, but it's the life I'm living, for good or ill, until the Admiralty sees fit to relieve me, and I do mostly enjoy it."

She bit her lip, eyes betraying uncharacteristic indecisiveness. It had been years since she had opened up to anyone on matters beyond duty. Perhaps the time had come to break that rule with an outsider like Wes Kalivan.

"But it can be lonely. I've not had a close relationship since before the war started. Spending most of my time in space, and much of that as captain or first officer doesn't leave room for another person and definitely not someone from among my crew."

He smiled sadly.

"I get that. No one wants emotional entanglements in one's own chain of command. It quickly poisons any unit's morale."

"How about you? Any entanglements?"

"In my chain of command? No. Outside of it, at times yes, but nothing of late. Like you, I'm somewhat too deeply immersed in my duties, especially since this little mystery surfaced."

Siobhan, disconcerted by the very personal nature of the question she had so impulsively asked, and fearful she might have given him cause to suspect interest on her part, shifted her eyes to the star map. She raised her coffee cup to cover the lower part of her face.

The amused twinkle in Kalivan's eyes bore testimony to the fact that he had noticed her sudden, if well-hidden embarrassment. Dunmoore's simplicity and directness delighted him, a welcome change from the schemers, connivers, and assorted manipulators he usually dealt with, especially those in his own family.

"You did know that your first officer is very protective of you, right?"

Dunmoore's eyes snapped back to Kalivan, and she lowered the protective mug until it hovered over her lap.

"What exactly do you mean?" Suspicion tainted her voice. "It's part of his job to ensure his captain's welfare, lest he finds himself forced to take command under the most inauspicious circumstances."

"I mean his concern for you goes deeper than that, Siobhan."

"How do you know, and more to the point, why tell me?"

Yes, he wondered, why did I mention it? Kalivan studied her face, unsure about his own motivations. It had to be something beyond his natural tendency to play mind games with all and sundry.

"He advised me, quite politely, mind you, that he'd not take kindly to my causing you personal distress."

"I see. This is why you've been acting more distant in public in the last while?"

"Indeed."

She bit her lower lip again.

"Let's not go down that path, Wes."

"Then I'm sorry I mentioned it."

"So am I."

He rose and put his cup down.

"Thank you for the coffee. Always a pleasure. My apologies if I overstepped my bounds. It won't happen again. I wish you a good day, Siobhan."

She stared at the closed compartment door for a long time after his departure, until a soft chime broke through her reverie. Unexpected irritation at the interruption bubbled up, and she angrily stabbed the console with a stiff finger.

"Dunmoore."

"Captain, engineering's done the initial damage survey. We're in the conference room."

"I'm on my way."

Immersion in work remained the only cure she knew for the doubts that gnawed at her.

*

"We were lucky." Kutora's low rumble matched his somber expression. "The shields came up quickly enough to prevent any significant damage to the hull, though I've no doubt when we scan the frames one by one, we'll find some additional microscopic fissures. Some of the circuitry will need replacing, however. Artificial gravity, as well as both long and short range sensor suites, are operating on secondary networks, the primaries having given up the ghost. I'm not surprised, mind you, a ship this old. Our biggest issues are with the shield generators themselves. They did sterling service in preventing further damage, but that came at a cost. I can fix most of them with what we carry, but some parts I can't fabricate, so I'd suggest you avoid getting into any fights because they'll fail a lot faster than you'd expect. In fact, the aft starboard generator might go adios on us if a Shrehari so much as sneezes on it."

"Then we'd better hope there are no boneheads with a bad cold on our tail," Devall said, smiling.

"Aye." Kutora gave the second officer a dark look, unimpressed by his flippant humor.

"How long for the shield repairs?"

"Four days, if we don't find anything worse when we take the generators apart." The chief engineer shrugged. "Otherwise, your guess is as good as mine."

"During which time we really want to avoid storms, battles and plunging into asteroid fields." Dunmoore nodded. "Priority on the shields, but monitor the artificial gravity generators. Operating on backups isn't going to feel comfortable. Once we can protect ourselves again, we'll tackle the rest. Any other issues from the storm?"

"Those were the biggest problems," Kutora replied. "There will assuredly be others once we finish the in-depth survey. I have no doubt some additional failures are going to crop up in the next few weeks, but that shouldn't be anything we can't handle. But, at the risk of sounding tiresome, I'd like to note once again that we should avoid combat if at all possible."

"I'll take that under advisement." She gave the chief engineer a tight smile. "We've come this far, and I'd hate to turn around before even taking a peek at where *Tempest* supposedly ended up."

When he did not reply, Dunmoore asked, "Anything else?"

"No, sir." Pushkin shook his head. "Repairs will be under way within the hour, starting with the aft starboard shield generator, in case we meet someone prone to sneezing fits when we emerge from this jump."

Kutora glowered at the first officer but nodded nonetheless.

"Aye."

"Thank you." With a last nod, she left them to go wallow once more in the privacy of her ready room.

The ion storm had been a piece of bad luck, but all things considered, *Stingray* had pulled out of it in better shape than she had any right to expect, especially for a ship that still carried the scars of her previous battles, left only partially treated because her days were numbered.

With a sigh, she plunged into the long list of reports queued up for her attention.

— Ten —

The transition back to normal space felt as wrenching as always, but they had cleared the storm by a wide margin.

"There you go, Chief," Tours grinned at the coxswain. "We're nowhere near a nasty gravity source, let alone in the heart of a star."

"Or we are, and this is the afterlife, with us condemned to sail through the universe forever." Guthren shrugged. "I don't know how we'd tell the difference."

"True." The sailing master nodded with a philosophical expression on his round face. "But then, life may be an illusion, and death the reality."

"If you're done with the chief, Mister Tours, could I have a quick moment of your attention and find out where we actually are?" Dunmoore caught Pushkin's eye and made a face.

"We are where I'd hoped we would be," Tours replied. "Half a light year from the storm and not much further from the target star than before. Just at a different angle."

"As emergency jumps go, that went well. Plot a course to bring us within ten light hours of the system. We'll jump again once engineering is happy. I'm sure Mister Kutora will want some extra time."

"If you ask him for an opinion, Captain," Pushkin said, "we'll be here for the rest of the week."

She shrugged.

"Then so be it. We took a long time getting here, so there's no point in rushing with repairs. In the meantime, we can watch and wait, see if anything followed us out here or better yet, see if anything is traveling unknown star lanes near where *Tempest* seems to have landed."

"Sensors are already doing their damnedest, sir," Penzara said, "but until engineering gets to them, I'm afraid we can't fully trust what they show. But so far, there doesn't seem to be anything within detection range."

"Then I think we can cancel battle stations."

And I can get back to administrivia, she thought, sliding out of the command chair.

"I'll be in my ready room."

Tours stood.

"I have the watch, Captain."

"Then I stand relieved."

But not faced with relief. No sooner had she retreated into privacy that Wes Kalivan showed up, still bouncing with impatience and at loose ends while the crew made repairs to the frigate.

"Chess, Siobhan?"

She dropped her tablet and repressed a sigh.

"Sure, why not."

*

Three days later, *Stingray* finally resumed her journey, and after a jump had brought her within ten light hours of the star, everyone waited impatiently for the first signs that they had reached the right destination.

"Nothing on any frequency, Captain."

Kathryn Kowalski shook her head after completing a survey of all communications bands used by humanity since the invention of the radio six hundred years earlier.

"If someone's in this system," she continued, "they're under very tight emcon or their signals are so weak, they've already dissipated."

"And yet it's the only star in the region that corresponds to the parameters listed in *Tempest*'s log."

"Aye, Mister Tours." Siobhan studied the schematic of the system, wondering whether it had all been for nothing. "Perhaps the colonists didn't survive, or they've lost the use of anything that can broadcast radio waves."

"We'll still head inward to look, won't we, Captain?"

Kalivan had taken a spare seat at the back a few minutes before *Stingray* dropped out of FTL, and had so far remained silent. Though he had acted like any good passenger given the privilege of the bridge, his impatience felt like a ghostly presence hovering over them.

"Of course." She fought to contain a faint smile of amusement. "Keep in mind we're under tight emcon ourselves. When we switch to active scanning, we may well see things the passive sensors can't pick up."

"Will you remain in this state for long?"

"No, Colonel." She swiveled the command chair to face him. "I'll be going 'up systems' shortly, but I will also keep the ship at battle stations, just in case we missed something that might bite us the moment we stop acting like an electronic hole in space."

He nodded once, face tight with anticipation. "Understood."

"Chief Penzara, what say the sensors?" Dunmoore asked, her attention back on the tactical schematic.

"Not much, sir, though Rownes swears she can make out small objects moving on their own power around the inner system. I don't see it myself, but she does have a talent for sniffing up trouble."

"Wishful thinking?"

The gunnery chief shrugged.

"The only way we find out is by getting closer or going active."

"Captain?"

"Yes, Mister Pushkin?"

"Might I suggest that since we have some leeway, especially when it comes to time, we head in-system running silent, just as we did at Arietis? One burst from the sublight drives and then we coast. If Rownes' sensor ghosts are real, it might be better that we figure them out before they see us."

"It didn't work all that well back then."

"Different circumstances, sir."

She nodded slowly, observing Kalivan's reaction out of the corner of her eyes. He would not be pleased by an additional delay in getting answers that might vindicate what she knew had become his obsession.

As she expected, he seemed put out by the suggestion. His jaw muscles worked for a moment as if he were deciding whether to speak up or not. Then his gaze swept over the bridge, and he realized many pairs of eyes watched for his reaction.

"If you think it best, Captain, then by all means. I can wait a few days longer at this point." A tight smile belied his words.

"Very well. Mister Tours, plot a course to take us as close to the hyperlimit as possible in FTL so we emerge in the shadow of one of the gas giants, hidden from any planets in the Goldilocks zone. From there, we will head in-system under full emcon. If we find nothing worthwhile to see, we'll accelerate out. If we find something, we'll decelerate and decide whether we want to say hello."

"Shall I make it so we can slingshot out?"

"By all means, Mister Tours."

Within minutes, the sailing master had sent *Stingray* on her way and, with nothing else to do but wait, Siobhan invited Kalivan to join her in her ready room rather than sit on the bridge and fidget.

"The last bit is always the most agonizing." Dunmoore nodded at a smaller version of the bridge's tactical schematic before raising her coffee mug to her lips. "Especially if we want to check things out under stealth conditions."

"I've heard it said that warfare in space is light years of boredom interspersed with a few thousand kilometers of sheer terror," Wes Kalivan replied, sitting down across from her. "I'll assume that we're in for a long wait with precious little else to do."

"Pretty much. Mind you, if we were actually sailing into an enemy-held system, the boredom would be spiced up with an edge of tension that takes some getting used to. I've known a few who eventually felt overwhelmed by it and cut short their careers with a permanent shore billet."

"About my comments a few days ago, concerning your first officer…"

She cut him off with a wave of the hand.

"Let's leave that be, Wes. We're all professionals aboard this ship and know the score."

He nodded gravely, hoping his expression seemed sufficiently contrite. He could sense a hard streak beneath the calm, composed, officer-like image Dunmoore projected, one that corresponded to her reputation within the Navy.

"If we're to wait, may I suggest a game of chess?"

"Sure." She smiled. "I suppose getting whipped by an army officer will remind me that I'm not infallible."

*

The intercom chime woke Dunmoore from a light sleep, and she reached over to touch the screen.

"Dunmoore."

"Captain, it's Devall. We're coming within passive sensor range of the fifth planet, the one with the lovely rings. I think you're going to want to see this."

The second officer, who evidently had the watch, sounded as calm and collected as if he were ordering steak tartare in his favorite restaurant.

Finally, she thought, pulling on her boots and tunic. The last few days had been nothing but a whirlwind of ship's business, chess, and light reading. They could all use a change of pace from the boredom.

"Rouse Colonel Kalivan. I'm sure he'll be interested."

"Already done, sir." This time, Devall managed to sound smug enough that she could picture his faint ironic smile. "He'll likely beat you to the bridge."

The second officer had been right. Kalivan had already settled into what he now thought of as his chair at the back of the bridge when Dunmoore came in.

She looked at the sensor station and saw Petty Officer Rownes staring with intense concentration into the depths of her console screen. Taking the command chair from Devall with a quick nod of thanks, she smiled at seeing Kalivan bite back his impatience. Rownes would report once she had collected her thoughts about the data she saw.

After a few moments of complete silence on the bridge, the middle-aged former merchant spacer raised her hand to attract the captain's attention.

"Sir, as early scans established, the fifth planet has five moons and Mister Tours called when he said that the tidal forces would turn the surface into something less than pleasant, even without considering the toxic atmosphere."

"The widespread volcanic activity makes it a pretty nasty soup," Lieutenant Sanghvi, the junior navigator interjected, earning a tolerant shake of the head from Rownes.

"Sorry, please continue PO."

She nodded.

"Thank you, sir. Notwithstanding the nastiness, I'm detecting non-natural radiation sources, in other words, coherent emissions from the planet in widely dispersed locations, indicating some sort of artificial power sources. The moons, on the other hand, definitely have artificial installations dotting their surfaces. We'll be within reasonable visual range shortly. I've already fed targeting information into the computer so it can start recording the moment we're close enough. The one thing that puzzles me right now concerns the emission signatures I'm tracking. They seem to be heavily dampened somehow. I can't tell you why or how. It's just a feeling I have. Once we can match the coherent radiation with the visuals, we'll know for sure."

Dunmoore nodded slowly, her fingertips playing over the scar running down her jaw line. Rownes has turned out to be an even better sensor witch than the gun captain she had been before her promotion into the chiefs and petty officers' mess. Her feelings tended to become fact rather more often than could be explained by mere chance.

"So someone is occupying this system, someone with at least the technology for in-system space travel."

"The descendants of *Tempest* colonists?" Kalivan sounded as excited as she had ever heard him. "Can you imagine? Centuries without contact and now we appear in an FTL-capable starship to welcome them back into the human family."

"Let's not get ahead of ourselves, Colonel." She turned and smiled at him. "This may not be a human civilization at all. Perhaps it'll be a case of first contact, which could be just as thrilling."

"Or it could be a Shrehari outpost," Devall said, shrugging. "We're far from the empire, but I'm sure even they sent out colony ships, perhaps even sublight ones before their current civilization rediscovered FTL travel."

"And that's why we're running silent."

A brief smile crossed Dunmoore's tired features.

"Aye," Rownes turned back to her readout, "but if they're Shrehari, I think I'd pick up on it. Their emissions have a pretty distinct signature."

"So they're of human origin?" Kalivan leaned forward in his seat.

"I didn't say that, sir." The petty officer shook her head. "I meant that I didn't get the feeling we're looking at Shrehari technology. But whatever it is, I still say the folks down on the planet and on the moons are doing their best to avoid broadcasting. No radio transmissions to be found across the spectrum. The only reason I picked anything up is that we got the sensor upgrade when we went into refit after Cimmeria. And because Mister Kutora's gang fixed the buggering system yesterday, of course. Otherwise, I might not have found anything until we were right on top of them."

"And our current course doesn't take us that close to that planet," Sanghvi said.

"Of course not. We were aiming at the one with the most chances of sustaining our kind of life." Dunmoore caught her fingers drumming impatiently on her thigh and forcefully stilled them. "No signs of spacecraft traffic?"

"None, sir. At least not near the fifth planet."

"And your sensor ghosts near the fourth planet?"

"Nothing definite yet either, sir, though I dare say there's less of them than when I first looked."

"Do you think they could have picked us up and are hunkering down hoping we'll just pass through and be on our way?" Devall studied the sensor data scrolling by on a side screen.

"Perhaps." Dunmoore frowned. "It's tempting to send out a ping just so we can see what'll happen, but we won't do that."

"We're getting the first long-range visuals on the nearest moon-based installation," Rownes called out.

"Put them on the main screen."

When the picture stabilized, Devall let out a low whistle.

"Not what I was expecting, Captain."

"Me neither. But with the moon tidally locked, it does make sense."

"What in the name of all that's holy are we looking at?" Kalivan's tone sounded almost plaintive.

— Eleven —

"Unless I'm greatly mistaken," Devall, jerked his chin at the screen, "that's a mass driver array, and it doesn't look like it's designed to sling cargo. Very similar to late twenty-first century designs I've seen, except somehow more menacing, if I may use that word."

"Mass driver array?" Now Kalivan sounded puzzled.

"Yes, sir. I'd wager that it's an electromagnetically driven weapon designed to sling rocks or warheads or beer bottles for that matter, at very high rates of acceleration toward some target or other."

"Which, once again, would make sense." Dunmoore nodded her approval. "That moon, and likely its four siblings, is made of rock, thus providing a nearly inexhaustible source of ammunition. In a sense, that array is a gigantic scatter gun."

"You've seen the like before, Lieutenant?" Kalivan asked.

"Only in theory, sir. I'm a gunnery officer by training, and we had to study all forms of space-based weaponry, including the stuff made obsolete by the advent of plasma ammunition."

Pushkin, who had joined them moments before Rownes called up the video of the mass driver, chimed in.

"Considering the theoretical rate of fire and range, it can't be anything other than defensive."

"I still wouldn't try to get too close, sir." Devall went over to Rownes' console and had the computer overlay a grid on the image.

"Look at the number of tubes and rings. That thing can put a lot of stuff up in a single salvo. If it's just as good as the drivers we used in the last decades before we switched to plasma weapons, it'll be able to pump them out every ten to twenty seconds and throw up a relatively dense screen of stuff."

"Are we at risk?"

"No, Colonel." The second officer shook his head. "We're much too far away for one thing. For another, those rocks would make easy target practice for the close-in defense calliopes because we'd see them coming. There's a limit to how much acceleration they can put on their ammunition without booster assistance, and if you're going to put a drive on a warhead, it becomes a missile so you might as well launch without the expense of something like that."

"It could still throw some rather big and nasty nuclear mines across our way," Pushkin remarked with his usual gloomy frown. "We did play some dirty tricks with ours, both in the Cimmeria system and at Arietis."

"In any case," Dunmoore held up a hand to forestall what could quickly to become a lengthy discussion between her first and second officers, "we'll have gunnery keep an eye on that array and any others we find. Let's make sure whoever owns them doesn't shoot something indigestible across our bow, notwithstanding that we're likely well out of range."

She turned to Rownes.

"Now that we have more data on the emissions source, what do you think PO?"

"Something that large needs a massive power plant, Captain, but I'm not picking up anything stronger than say, a small stationary fusion reactor. Or to be more precise several small stationary fusion reactors. There appear to be a dozen or so mass driver arrays spread out over the moon's surface."

"So they're masking them somehow."

"Looks that way, sir."

"Who'd want to mask static installations?" Devall shook his head in puzzlement. "It's not like they're going anywhere."

"More to the point," Pushkin asked, "what is it that's happening in the soupy atmosphere and needs a ring of massive defenses, assuming the other four moons are equally well provided with mass drivers? Judging by what

Rownes has picked up, the coverage given by the multiple arrays seems rather comprehensive."

Since no one had an answer to his question, silence fell over the bridge.

"Well," Siobhan finally said, "at least we now know that there's a space-faring civilization occupying this system, one that likes to build massive weapons, primitive as they may seem to us at first glance."

"Even primitive weapons can hurt, Captain."

"Yes they can, Mister Devall, and since it's probably a good idea we remain in stealth mode, we'll have to forego the chance to probe more deeply in this area for now. The fourth planet remains our target. If there's a sentient race whose idea of a fresh breath of air resembles the atmospheric mixture on number five, we'll not bother them."

"Captain." Rownes' hand shot up.

"What is it?"

"I think they just launched something." A pause. "On screen now."

One of the ringed tubes forming the mass driver array on the nearest moon lit up briefly then fell dark again.

"That energy surge just registered, sir, like they had to unmask," the petty officer said, "though I'll bet if I weren't looking straight at the thing, I'd likely have missed it."

"Can you pick up whatever they just shot?"

"I'll try, sir, but it's going to be a tough one. Without emissions to give it away, it'd have to come straight at us for me to have a chance."

"Do your best, PO. You're a genius with that sensor, so if anyone on this ship can find it, that'll be you."

The older woman nodded once, and then got busy communing with her electronics.

"Do you think they might have just sent out a probe of some sort?" Pushkin asked, one arm cradled by the other, fingers tapping his chin as the gears in his brain spun at high speed. "Our recon drones tend to be invisible as well."

"You think they might have caught wind of an intruder in their system? Namely us?" Dunmoore's eyes narrowed as she stared at the screen. "Wouldn't be the first time we sailed close enough to a masked sensor buoy for it to pick up what little emissions we might be leaking. They might have had days to triangulate on us."

"No, it wouldn't," the first officer replied, thinking back at their attempt to infiltrate the Arietis system, and how that bit of curiosity had almost cost them everything.

"If it is a probe, it'll not come near until we're well away," Sanghvi offered, calling up the tactical schematic, "unless it lights up a drive of some sort, at which point Rownes will have no problems seeing it. There's no way that array could accelerate it hard enough to catch up."

"Should we launch a recon drone?" Pushkin asked.

"Not yet." Dunmoore shook her head. "The folks on that moon could simply have tossed the day's garbage into space, so there's no point in getting excited right away. I'd like to get a closer look at the next planet before risking anything that might give us away."

"You're getting a bad feeling about this, Captain?" Kalivan asked.

"No, not exactly. I just don't want to find out too late that one of those moons is actually a massive battle station. Anyone who builds that many electromagnetic mass drivers and then tries to hide their emissions might well have something nastier than centuries old technology hidden away."

Her calm tone did not fool Pushkin. Siobhan Dunmoore had something nagging at her subconscious. He glanced at her with a raised eyebrow, but she gave him a minute shake of the head.

"We'll stick to the plan and continue on our present course and under the current conditions unless things change dramatically."

"Sir," Rownes raised her hand again. "The sensors have a visual on the next moon and have picked up what I think is another launch of the kind we just saw."

"Mister Sanghvi, plot a possible intercept, just like you did with the first one."

"Already on it, Captain." The young navigator feverishly tapped commands into the astrogation system.

"There," he said a few moments later. "If it's been fired in the general direction of our current course, it could come close enough that, if it were one of our recon drones, it might very well see something, if only *Stingray* occluding the background stars."

"Perhaps it's just another garbage evacuation launch," Kalivan said.

"Perhaps." Dunmoore's lips twitched and this time, she did not quite realize that her fingers had begun slowly drumming against her thigh again.

*

"I'm sorry, sir." Chief Penzara shook his head an hour later. "Neither Rownes nor I can find any trace of whatever the mass drivers on those moons pumped out."

Dunmoore frowned with irritation, but mostly at her own impatience. The temptation to break out of stealth mode never quite left her. They had detected more launch activity from the other moons, each as quickly done as the first, and each sending out something unknown and undetectable by the passive sensors.

Guthren snorted.

"If that was their daily garbage evacuation, it's probably just as well. I've seen the inside of a station's waste bins and trust me, they make the environmental sludge vats look good."

"We're about to sail past the planet anyhow," she replied, rising from the command chair. "Which means it's becoming less material, though if the fourth planet, which seems to have a breathable atmosphere, is equally surrounded by installations like the ones we've left behind, it would have been nice to know more."

"Can't be helped, sir," Penzara replied. "We can have stealth, or we can poke into everyone's secrets. Until the boffins at Fleet R&D come up with some stealth active scanning, we're half blind."

"If it were possible, I think that after six years of fighting the Shrehari, they'd have found something."

"Aye, sir." The old gunnery chief shook his head. "Well, at least the new frigates coming off the slipways this year should have a lot of fancy gear we can only dream about in our old girl."

He patted his console gently.

"Though I'll miss her when we dock for the last time."

"Me too, Chief. Me too." Dunmoore turned to Lieutenant Syten. "I believe you have the watch."

"Yes, sir." The gunnery officer rose from her station and took the command chair. "I relieve you."

"I stand relieved."

Pushkin joined her in the ready room and, under her amused gaze, made himself a cup of what she privately thought of as his sugar sludge.

"Since we know this system's inhabited, and there's enough activity around the fourth planet to indicate it is as well, we're going to have to begin braking soon," he said, slumping into the chair across from her. "Otherwise, we're in for a long set of tacks to retrace our course."

"I know." She shrugged. "It's a damned if you do, damned if you don't kind of scenario. We unmask and they're hostile, it might get too hot. This time, there's no way we make it back to a Starbase on a single hyperdrive like we did from Cimmeria. The distance is much too great. We don't unmask, sail by and don't find what we've come all this way for, we'll have wasted months of travel. Or we do both, as in sail by, see enough to warrant a longer stay and unmask while we turn, giving a potentially hostile force time to track us."

"Or they may already know we're here. Remember, Rownes' comment about activity decreasing since shortly after we dropped out of FTL. As funny as it may be to think they've been shooting their junk into space, the probability that we've disturbed something that warrants over half a dozen probes is much higher."

"We've left the fog of war far behind us, and yet it still makes things hard to see." She ran her fingertips along the scar on her jawline, eyes staring at the star map without actually seeing anything. "I'm afraid Colonel Kalivan will want us to scan more energetically in the next few hours or days at most, and since that comes under the heading of 'mission' and not 'ship,' I might find myself with few arguments to the contrary. We are a warship, after all, not a lightly armed survey cruiser."

At the mention of the colonial officer's name, she saw his jaw tighten briefly. Though Kalivan had been more than proper in public, they had spent a lot of time in her ready room or quarters playing chess, listening to music and talking.

Siobhan not only saw it as her duty to play the good host to a senior ranking guest aboard her ship but she also thoroughly enjoyed spending time with someone who did not belong to her ship's company.

"When it comes to the safety of the ship and crew, Captain, the mission can fling itself into a black hole. We're not actively engaging the enemy, and there's no pressing need to solve the mystery of *Tempest*'s log buoy."

"And yet…" she let her voice drift off. After a few moments of silence, broken only by the faint sounds of Pushkin slurping his coffee, she shook herself.

"I suppose I'm as keen as Wes to uncover the fate of the colonists, and seeing evidence of a space-faring civilization, albeit one without apparent FTL capability, and using the technology we abandoned some time ago, only reinforces my interest."

"In that case, you'll need to decide about decelerating soon, Captain." He drained his coffee and rose. "If you'll excuse me, I'll go rouse Mister Tours and set him to prepare some options for you."

"Thanks, Gregor. I don't know what I'd do without you."

"All part of the job."

"First officers' union rules?"

"I wouldn't do it any other way." He briefly came to attention before pivoting on his heels and leaving Siobhan to her thoughts.

With a sigh, she turned to the computer screen and dialed in a three-dimensional view of the inner star system. Something nagged at her subconscious, but it refused to make itself known, leaving her to figure out the next move based on a gut feeling, something she did well — in combat.

However, this was not combat. It was not even chess, and she could not begin to fathom what they faced.

The intercom's chime broke through her concentration, and she repressed an unaccustomed surge of irritation.

"Captain, we've just been pinged by something or someone," Lieutenant Syten said when she acknowledged the call.

Her head snapped up.

"What?" Then, "I'm on my way."

*

"That had to be the most miserable passage yet. At least we managed to emerge on the very edge of that demon storm. I shudder to think what might have been if the gods had dropped us in the middle."

Brakal drained his mug of ale, scowling at the off-duty officers enjoying what few amenities the wardroom of *Tol Vehar* had to offer.

"Ironically, it seems the Imperial Deep Space Fleet isn't built for deep space exploration." Regar, the *Tai Kan* spy, chuckled.

"You have a very annoying talent for stating the obvious," Brakal grumbled.

"One of many, Commander." Regar raised his mug in mock salute. "Annoying those I'm ordered to watch has its uses. You do remember that we'll have to embark on a return voyage just as long and stultifying once you've satisfied your curiosity and bloodlust upon that human frigate you believe we're trailing."

"I believe nothing, Regar." Brakal slapped the metallic tabletop with an outstretched hand. A fierce smile split his hard, bony face. "I know that a ship disturbed the black. My sensor technician has found the traces. If this is indeed the flame-haired she-wolf who bested me at Cimmeria, the empire would be well served if we discover what has taken one of the human's best tacticians this far from the war. If I cannot fight, I can at least find."

"Indeed. Moreover, it gets you well away from Hralk for many months. Perhaps long enough for him to trip over his fat belly and lose his command." Regar's ironic grin made the spy seem almost sympathetic, though it would be dangerous to forget he stood apart from the loyal crew.

"The gods of the underworld may grant me such a boon, yes." He stared into his mug as if expecting to see *Stingray*'s silhouette outlined in the dregs. "His like are what keeps us fighting the humans with no honorable end in sight. A plague on all admirals and their sycophants."

"And on the generals running the *Tai Kan*."

"Hah! A spy who speaks treason. Will wonders never cease? Perhaps passing through the black has affected your thought processes."

"My thought processes changed many years ago when, as a youngling, I first experienced the filth of the *Tai Kan* politics. You think your Admiralty is a place of utter perdition? You know nothing, Commander." A cruel smile took the sting out of the political officer's words.

"Though," he continued, "I suppose I owe my *Tai Kan* career to those in the fleet who desperately need killing. Perhaps there is little to choose from either service."

"Oh?" Brakal's eyes lit up with curiosity.

"An admiral with a love for money and the power it could buy. I still had notions of honor and duty swirling in my head so I reported him. Sadly, he had enough friends to get me out of the fleet while covering his fat arse, but my family also had enough connections to keep me in uniform."

"And the *Tai Kan* offered a better career than any other." Brakal nodded. "I'm surprised a man so free with his opinions has thrived."

"My superiors seem to think highly of me. But then, none are easier to fool than those who devote their lives to lies."

"No doubt." Brakal raised his hand for a refill when the intercom chimed.

"Commander, this is Urag. We've calculated the most probable destinations for the human ship lying within a few light years and have an itinerary to propose."

Brakal pushed his mug away and rose.

"On my way," he jerked his hard chin at Regar and said, "You might as well come. A *Tai Kan* spy who holds such contempt for his superiors might have enough of a brain to contribute intelligent thoughts."

Regar inclined his head respectfully, acknowledging the backhanded compliment.

"Perhaps."

When they entered the bridge, a three-dimensional star chart projection twinkled merrily by the navigation console.

"Speak," he ordered, dropping into his raised command chair.

Mtak, *Tol Vehar*'s astrogator, bowed his head briefly.

"Lord. The star I'm currently outlining is not the nearest to where we believe the humans emerged from the black, but it is of a type we know they prefer for their colonies. Long-range scans indicate it possesses some planets so I consider it the most likely candidate."

"You do, do you." Brakal rubbed the stiff crest of hair running across his skull. "I suppose it's as likely an idea as any other. Who knows what the poxed humans are after?"

"They might not be after anything at all now," Urag pointed out. "If they emerged in the middle of the storm, we'll be chasing a ghost."

Brakal shook his head. No. The storm didn't get them. I'm convinced of that. Plot a course toward the proposed star. Make our jumps short. I don't wish to stumble on anything that can prevent us from returning to the great Admiral Hralk's stinking abode."

"As you command, Lord." The astrogator snapped to attention.

"And cease calling me lord, you miscreant. It's bad enough that Toralk gets away with it. At least he has the feeble excuse of being a clan retainer."

"Yes, Commander. My apologies. It's just that since you've found us a ship to serve on, we feel as if we too belong in some fashion to Clan Makkar."

"Take care that you don't make that feeling too well known. The Makkar aren't exactly on the Admiralty's most favored list." Brakal bared his sharp teeth in a cruel smile. "Though I suppose our resident *Tai Kan* spy will report your loyalties and those of the crew the moment we return."

"Loyalties?" Regar feigned not to understand. "I'm sure *Tol Vehar*'s crew members have splendid loyalties."

Brakal eyed him with suspicion, Urag with outright disbelief.

"Less talk, more action," the former finally said. "Get this ship on its way before we start simpering like the feeble-minded geriatric idiots of the imperial court. I need to fire my guns at something, and there's no adequate target in interstellar space."

"Yes, Commander." Mtak and Urag both dipped their heads, the latter giving Regar a warning glance.

— Twelve —

Syten stepped aside to take the gunnery console while Dunmoore sank into the command chair, eyes locked on a side screen showing what little they knew about the contact.

"What's your take on this, Chief?"

Penzara, eyes narrowed while he chewed on his lower lip, did not immediately answer.

"If I were a betting man..."

"Which you aren't, you cheap bugger," Guthren interjected.

"...then based on the direction of the scan, I'd say whatever those mass drivers fired is indeed some kind of stealth probe and one of them has come close enough for us to pick up its scan signature."

"Or the thing has found us."

"We haven't picked up a repeat ping." Penzara shook his head. "Just the one and nothing more. If it's locked on, we'd surely be getting a steady signal."

"If it got a return signal from our hull, then perhaps it has all it needs: confirmation that something is here," Dunmoore said.

"In which case, we could reasonably expect more probing."

"No doubt, Chief." Siobhan nodded. "But we're getting out of range, so unless these probes have engines of some sort, they'll be losing us, if they haven't lost us already. I can't see the mass drivers having imparted enough delta-vee to keep up with the ship."

"Speaking of which," the sailing master interjected, "Mister Pushkin asked me to prepare options, seeing as how it's a given the fourth planet shows evidence of intelligent life."

"Technological life at any rate," the coxswain said. "We'll be seeing in due course if it's intelligent."

"Cynical, aren't you, Mister Guthren?" Tours replied, chuckling.

"I've done my fair share of living, sir, and so-called sentient beings have disappointed me more often than not."

"The options, please, Mister Tours." Dunmoore injected just a touch of asperity in her tone.

She heard the soft whisper of the bridge door opening behind her and suppressed a sigh. Without turning, she knew Kalivan had come for the newest developments.

A headache threatened to erupt and she pinched the bridge of her nose between thumb and forefinger. Guthren caught the gesture and briefly shook his head at the army officer. Nodding, Kalivan took the empty station at the back of the bridge and hid his impatience as best he could.

"Okay," Dunmoore said, after contemplating the three possible navigation solutions. "It's time to stop pussyfooting around. We'll take your first option and brake just enough to allow us the choice between entering into orbit around the fourth planet and accelerating away if things go sideways. Good suggestion, Mister Tours, by the way. A compromise will leave few genuinely happy, which is always a good sign. We'll maintain maximum emcon and hope that they won't be looking straight at us when we brake."

"Aye, aye, Captain." The sailing master nodded once and turned back to his screen, entering the command string that would fire the frigate's braking thrusters at the appropriate times. "Done."

She swiveled the command chair aft.

"As you can see, Colonel, you'll be getting your wish, although we'll have to make the leave or stay decision from a greater distance, which isn't going to give our passive sensors the chance to develop a fully detailed picture."

He inclined his head politely.

"I shall, as always, defer to your better judgment, Captain, and stifle the explorer in me screaming to make first contact."

"From what I've read, Colonel," Guthren said, half-smirking, "first contact can just as well end up being last contact."

"Indeed, cox'n, indeed. Our experience with the Shrehari being a case in point."

"Heh. If we could have made it last contact, I'm sure things would be better than now, when we just can't shake the bastards loose."

"I think *Stingray*'s likely to be as close to having shown the Imperials a clean pair of heels as it gets in this war," Dunmoore said. "We're as far away from their sphere as we are from ours."

"Don't jinx it, Captain," Guthren grimaced. "The boneheaded bastards have a way of showing up when it's the least convenient."

"Noted," she replied with a wry smile, then turned back to Kalivan. "Since we'll be a while before anything else happens, Colonel, might I offer you a cup of coffee?"

"With pleasure."

His smile seemed about as warm as the coxswain had ever seen on a man speaking with the captain, and though he could not see Dunmoore's face, he instinctively knew she had reciprocated.

"I must confess that I'm feeling an unseemly amount of impatience," Kalivan said a few moments later, behind closed doors.

"We can tell, Wes," she replied with a wink. "But I can't make it go any faster now. I may be sole master aboard after God, but even I can't overrule the laws of physics. A game of chess to pass the time?"

*

"Captain," Devall stuck his head through the open door to Dunmoore's ready room, "we've been pinged again, this time from the vicinity of the fourth planet."

Siobhan looked up from her pad, grateful at the interruption. After three bouts of chess, supper and a lengthy discussion with her officers around the wardroom table, she felt as impatient as Kalivan, who had been working it off in the improvised gym on the hangar deck for the last few hours.

"I suppose that can only mean they know we're here, if not exactly who we are. It makes me wonder if running silent is slowly going the way of mass drivers in modern warfare."

"Or the folks who own the local real estate have pretty good sensors," he replied with a small shrug. "Nothing says the Commonwealth has a monopoly on bleeding edge technology."

"True. Just as long as the Shrehari don't catch up to us, I suppose."

Devall's head suddenly turned back toward the bridge when he spied Rownes' arm shoot up to catch his attention.

"The pings are now steady, sir," the petty officer announced in a tone loud enough for Dunmoore to hear. "They're probing us."

"Wonderful." Dunmoore grimaced as she met Devall's eyes. "What do you think? Should we abandon silent running?"

The second officer glanced at the sensor readout on the main screen and shook his head.

"The signals are still faint. I say we should keep them guessing. It'll only take about ninety seconds to go live and get the shields up in any case, and there's no way they can lock on, fire and hit us in that amount of time."

Dunmoore nodded.

"Agreed. Pass the word to the crew that we're being probed and to be ready for battle stations."

It took less than two minutes after Devall's announcement for both Pushkin and Kalivan, the latter still in his sweat-stained gym clothes, to appear on the bridge.

The first officer turned a critical eye on the ship's status board, catching Devall's attention with a raised eyebrow. The second officer shook his head, tilting it toward the captain to indicate that she had decided against changing the alert level.

Pushkin's lips twitched, making it clear he knew on whose advice that had been. The gunnery officer and sometime prize captain in Devall still had a tendency to color his opinions, though it spoke well for him that he tried more and more to act like a first officer.

"A thought, Captain," Pushkin said, coming to stand by the command chair. "If we go live now, Penzara can start scanning the planet and its surroundings in detail well before *Stingray* gets in range of any defensive weaponry, even assuming their tech level is comparable to ours, notwithstanding the outmoded mass driver arrays we saw on the fifth planet's moons. It might save us getting too close to anything we may not like. After all, they know we're here and giving them a better view of *Stingray* at this point probably won't make much of a difference."

Dunmoore smiled, eyes darting between Pushkin and Devall. The two of them would make a good pairing as captain and first officer, just as she and Pushkin did. Siobhan firmly believed in the old adage that when everyone thought alike, someone was not thinking.

She had no need to inquire about Kalivan's opinion. He radiated the urge to turn every sensing device to full power. He also, now that she noticed it, emitted the scent of a man in need of a shower. It did not seem as unpleasant as she might have figured, but it was out of place on her bridge, if only because of her unexpected reaction.

"Captain," Rownes called out from the sensor console, "I've picked up multiple energy surges on all three of the fourth planet's moons and from several of the Lagrangian points."

Devall went to look over her shoulder at the readout.

"The ones on the moons could be the same kind of mass drivers we've seen before, but those coming from the Lagrangian points likely aren't. Large scale mass drivers on artificial satellites don't make much sense."

"Something powered then." She nodded. "I guess they took the decision for me. Let's see what just happened over there. Mister Pushkin, up systems, up shields. PO Rownes, you may scan at full power."

She heard a faint voice behind her say 'finally' but ignored Kalivan's sigh. An excitement akin to that of going into battle had taken hold of her, complete with the intensity of focus that combined the analytical and her gut instincts.

Pushkin, recognizing the look on her face, caught the army officer's eye and then nodded toward the door, signaling that he should get back into uniform. Kalivan pivoted on his heels without a further word and left.

Chief Penzara joined Rownes at the sensor console and began organizing the mass of information that threatened to overwhelm the petty officer, aware that Dunmoore waited with growing impatience for data that could inform her next move.

"Well," Penzara said after almost half an hour, "the earlier probing has now become a much more coherent signal, which means they're beginning to get an idea of what we are."

"And what are they?" Dunmoore asked.

"Hard to tell at this distance. Whatever they launched is definitely under power, small if you compare it to a starship, but larger than our missiles or shuttles. The acceleration rates are pretty steep for all of them, meaning if they're manned, they've got inertial dampeners of some sort."

"I thought inertial dampeners were an offshoot of FTL technology," Kalivan, who'd rejoined them moments earlier, said, "and we've seen no evidence of jump capable ships."

"Technically they are, Colonel," Pushkin replied, "because the ability to generate the power to form a hyperspace bubble is similar but not the same as that needed to prevent the crew of a ship from turning into pink goo. We just figured that out at roughly the same time. One doesn't actually require the other, so they could have stumbled upon dampeners without figuring out FTL travel."

"Ah," Kalivan nodded, "I see. Thank you, Number One."

Pushkin scowled at his use of the familiarity, but only Kowalski, who had taken the signals station from her petty officer, noticed.

Dunmoore however, turned the command chair back and, smiling slightly, whispered, "Point of naval protocol, Wes. Only the captain gets to call him that."

"Got it," he whispered back, feeling slightly embarrassed by Siobhan's correction, even if she had pitched her voice so only he could hear.

"My apologies, Mister Pushkin," he said in a louder voice. "We ground pounders don't always know when to shut up."

"No need to apologize, Colonel," the first officer replied, his square face devoid of emotion.

"You're very gracious, Commander."

Fortunately, before Pushkin could wonder whether Kalivan had indulged in some gentle mockery at his expense, Penzara raised his hand to indicate he had something to report.

"I've detected two more large scale launches from all of the previously identified points of origin, for a total of one-hundred and fifty objects heading toward us in three waves."

"Something tells me these aren't local entrepreneurs trying to get at us with their wares before we dock." Kowalski's sarcastic comment drew at least one appreciative chuckle.

"Not at the rate they're accelerating, sir, no." Penzara shook his head. "They'd not have time to decelerate to match velocities with us so they can show us their crap. Not that anyone aboard would be interested in alien baubles."

"The more important question, Chief," Dunmoore cut through the banter, "is whether or not those baubles are carrying something that could scratch the paint job."

"Make it four waves," Rownes interjected. "Another fifty on the way for a total of two hundred. Projected time to intercept for the first wave is on the main screen."

"I'm designating targets," Lieutenant Syten said, "but we'll have to begin engaging at long range."

"Assuming they're carrying warheads that can, as the captain said, scratch the paint." Pushkin nodded.

"I'd really like to figure out if any of those are manned. Destroying unmanned craft or missiles is one thing; killing people we've never met can pretty much guarantee we'll never meet them in any way other than over the barrel of a gun." Dunmoore grimaced at the thought. "We're a little too far from home to start another war."

"They fired first," Guthren pointed out.

"Aye, but perhaps only on general principles because we're something that looks like a threat."

"Then perhaps we might wish to indulge in a bit of gunboat diplomacy to calm down agitated spirits."

"Correct, Colonel." Siobhan nodded. "Which is why I'd like to make sure we don't take first blood."

"I think I might have your answer, Captain," Penzara said. "The objects launched from the Lagrangian points have stopped accelerating and are dropping behind the objects fired from the moons."

"Can we get even a hint of whatever's there?"

"No, sir. The things might well have remained undetected if we hadn't caught those successive launches. It's sure to be a station of some kind, but our sensors can't make anything out at this range."

"It seems that the locals have developed some pretty good stealth technology." Siobhan tapped her chin with a gloved finger. "Okay. Priority targeting on the objects still accelerating. We should be able to take out the first wave handily enough, now that we've excluded the Lagrangian objects."

"Aye, Captain," Syten replied. "Laid in and ready at your command."

"You may fire once you have the optimum targeting solution."

"I have it. Salvo away."

Two dozen small defensive missiles streaked out of their launchers, the drives glowing brightly on the main screen for a few seconds before they accelerated out of sight, on a heading to meet the incoming objects head-on at high speed. Designed to disrupt rather than destroy, the anti-anti-ship missiles had a small warhead and little more than a very stubborn and persistent onboard computer that would pursue its pre-programmed target until it died, the target died, or something caused it to seek a new target.

Tense minutes passed as the two flights converged on each other, and then a series of very distant flares briefly joined the star-filled darkness on the main screen.

Penzara whistled softly as he scanned his readout.

"Whatever those things were, the explosions registered in the gigaton range."

"Nuclear?"

"Most likely. It didn't have any antimatter signature that I could see. We've not fielded anything fissionable that powerful in a long time, Captain."

"And with good reason," Pushkin grimaced. "Too big, costs too much to accelerate and too easy to shoot down, though if one of those explodes against the shields, the radiation will be enough to give us serious heartburn."

"The first wave is gone, though," Rownes reported. "And the objects launched from the Lagrangian points are decelerating rather dramatically."

"Hah!" Guthren barked. "We've got their attention."

"And another six dozen gigaton range warheads coming toward us, plus whatever the probably manned objects intend to do," Syten pointed out.

"This could easily get boring," Dunmoore remarked, sitting back in her chair, an idle smile on her lips, "not to mention eating up a fair chunk of our ammunition supply."

Pushkin visibly paled as he correctly interpreted his captain's intentions by the tone of her voice.

"They're gigaton range warheads, sir. A few of them get through, and the ammo supply will be the least of our worries."

"And shooting them down with our main guns will be even more impressive; don't you think so, Number One?"

"If we start engaging at extreme range," Syten said, sounding more dubious than usual, "we might be able to take them all."

"Provided they're not programmed to evade direct fire," Pushkin replied.

"What are the odds they're nimble enough at their current velocity, keeping in mind that plasma shot expands dramatically at extreme range? We only need to graze the thing to set it off, let alone throw it off course."

"I still consider your optimism to be at bit too — optimistic, sir."

"Noted, Mister Pushkin. We'll try it on the second wave and see how good Mister Syten and her gunners are."

Ignored by the bridge crew, Kalivan had been observing the interplay with apparent fascination. He had always held the picture of an autocratic captain in battle, whom no one dared gainsay, especially one as spirited as Dunmoore, but he could see the sense in having her officers voice their concerns when time permitted.

"I've assigned targets to the main guns, sir."

"Fire when they enter extreme range. We can afford sustained fire, so keep at it until they're destroyed."

Pushkin's fears proved exaggerated, not that anyone blamed him for voicing them. Counterbalancing his captain's reckless streak came with the job, and the other officers agreed he did it splendidly.

"I guess there's truth to the old saw that the bigger and heavier the missile, the less sophisticated the technology," he said after twenty-four multi-gigaton warheads blew up in succession.

"Brute force rather than finesse and sophistication." Dunmoore nodded. "What's the status on the ones we think are manned?"

"Peeling away, Captain," Penzara said, chuckling softly. "They got the message that we're bigger and badder."

"Glad to hear it. Perhaps now we can figure out what the hell is going on around here without shouting at each other over a pile of charred corpses. That never works out well."

"If they want to talk," Pushkin said.

"Always the realist, aren't you." She grinned at him.

"Always, Captain. First officers have to be realists, and speaking of which, I'll point out that the closer we get to the planet, the more they can throw at us in closer succession. At some point, they may get lucky."

"True." She nodded. "Mister Kowalski, have you managed to pick up anything that looks like a carrier wave we can hook into and see if they want to jaw-jaw instead of war-war."

"No." The signals officer shook her head. "No radio at all. I wouldn't be surprised if they're doing everything via tight beam, perhaps optical only."

"It is the best emcon solution for someone with that kind of stealth technology," Pushkin said.

"But not terribly flexible." Siobhan bit her lower lip in frustration. "I don't see that we have many options. Getting any closer, as you said, would give them more chances to hit us and even a glancing blow on the shields can cause a lot of grief after our brush with the ion storm. Mister Kowalski, please send out a message on all radio frequencies identifying us as the Commonwealth Starship

Stingray with the usual blather about being explorers who are coming in peace."

"If I may suggest," Kalivan interjected, "perhaps identify us as an Earth starship rather than a Commonwealth one. If those are the descendants of *Tempest*'s colonists, they'll not have heard of the Commonwealth since it didn't exist when their ancestors left the home system."

"A sound idea." Dunmoore nodded.

"I have an additional thought, sir," Kowalski said. "Our current Anglic has drifted from the Standard English spoken at the time of *Tempest*'s launch. Perhaps we should use words and expressions that were current three or four hundred years ago."

"Of course," Siobhan grinned. "Well done, Kathryn. Let us see the message before it goes out. I trust you're conversant with old English, Colonel?"

"I had to become so, Captain. The log buoy, remember?"

"Indeed." Words flashed up on the main screen, many of them seeming distorted to their twenty-fifth-century eyes.

"Has language really changed that much?" Pushkin sounded skeptical.

"You'd be amazed at what social pressures and the conceit of correctness can do to ideas and the meaning of words," Kalivan replied. "In some of the cases I've studied, wholesale perversion of language has often resulted from the desire to impose strictures on thought, followed invariably by radical political change, and never for the better."

"Lovely." The first officer shook his head.

"I suppose we've got a good enough message," Siobhan said. "Short of sending it through five rounds of word polishing involving a couple of admirals with strange ideas on grammar, I'd say we're ready to go."

"Agreed, Captain." Kalivan nodded.

"Fire it off, Mister Kowalski. If they're in space, they have to know about radio, and with any luck, they'll be monitoring something. If not, we can try painting one of their artificial satellites with our laser transmitter once we're in range."

"Done," Kowalski reported moments later. "The time lag to the fourth planet is small at this distance."

A palpable sense of frustration descended on the bridge as the minutes, and then the hours ticked by while *Stingray* hurtled on a course that would take it past the planet and back out toward the hyperlimit.

The manned craft had long since vanished, no doubt swallowed up by stealthy battle stations sitting in darkness at the Lagrangian points. They could not detect any other space traffic, and it almost seemed as if an entire civilization had dropped into a hidden bunker and shut all hatches behind them.

Colonel Kalivan could hardly contain his impatience and Dunmoore took him first to the wardroom for a meal, then to her ready room for a few distracted rounds of chess.

"What will you do if you get no reply whatsoever?" He asked, moving his king's bishop. "Check."

"I don't know. We've still got to get close enough for a fix on something orbital we can paint with a laser, and that won't be for a few hours yet." She countered with her queen's knight. "They're masters of stealth. We can't get a useful lock on their stations at this range."

"Do you think they can hear us either way?"

"If I were running that place, I'd be listening very hard to try and figure out who could be powerful enough to appear in my system, coming from interstellar space, and swat away my multiple missile barrages without much effort. For a civilization that apparently hasn't progressed to FTL travel, we have to be a fascinating apparition."

"So their government is probably even now conferring in panicked tones about how to deal with us."

"I don't know about panicked, Wes, but I'd say that scenario is likely, provided they're human or a species that's not too dissimilar from us." She moved her queen. "Check."

He stared at the board, looking for a way out. Before he could move a piece, the intercom chimed.

"We've got a reply." Kowalski sounded as calm as always, but Siobhan could sense an undercurrent of excitement in her tone.

"Audio only, or video as well?"

"Data." Kowalski sounded puzzled. "A single sentence in old English: *lend me your ears.*"

Kalivan jumped up with excitement.

"It's them; it's the descendants of *Tempest*'s colonists. That's a line from an ancient play by the same author from whom they borrowed the colony ship's name."

"Indeed," the signals officer confirmed after searching her database, "from a piece called *Julius Caesar*."

Siobhan rose with a final glance at the chessmen.

"I'd have had you in two more moves, Wes."

"Perhaps," he replied, his mind already elsewhere as he stepped onto the bridge without waiting to let Siobhan pass first, as courtesy would have dictated. His unconsciously crowding out the captain earned him a frown from the first officer who had risen from the command chair when the door opened.

"Rather obscure as a means of introduction, Colonel," Pushkin said.

"No, it's perfect." The colonial officer sounded giddy. "Who but the humans we purport to be in our greeting message would know about a play written almost a thousand years ago."

"What do we reply?" Dunmoore asked, briefly nonplussed by the turn of events.

"Easy," the colonel grinned broadly. "Send *I come to bury Caesar, not to praise him*."

"And that'll tell them we're human and not say, nasty critters like the Shrehari?" Pushkin frowned with disbelief.

"I doubt anyone outside the Commonwealth has ever heard about the Bard of Avon."

"Who now?"

"William Shakespeare, Mister Pushkin. And you've just made my point if a well-educated officer such as you doesn't recognize his nickname."

"Then, by all means, send the suggested reply, Mister Kowalski," Dunmoore ordered. "I certainly have no better idea at the moment."

"Make sure you send it in the same English they've used. After all, they have been cut off from human civilization for a few centuries."

"Will do, Colonel."

After a few tense moments during which Dunmoore caught her fingers drumming on her thigh more than once, the signals officer raised her hand to get her attention.

"We've received a reply, sir: *why are you here?*"

— Thirteen —

Dunmoore and Kalivan looked at each other, the one astonished, and the other puzzled.

"Of all the possible questions, that's one I did not expect," he finally said. "Why are we here? You'd think they'd be happy to hear from other humans after all this time. Or want to know how we got here, especially if we're right, and they don't have FTL technology."

"What do we answer?"

"We tell them that *Tempest*'s log buoy made it back to human space, and we were sent to find them, to see if they survived."

"Make it so, Mister Kowalski."

Dunmoore stared at the tactical schematic showing the fourth planet, its moons, and all known and suspected artificial off-world constructs. Something still rankled. Then, her eyes narrowed as an idea wormed its way out into the open.

"What is it, sir?" Pushkin asked, noticing the look on her face.

"Where are their ships? I don't mean the small craft they sent behind their missiles. If they've populated two planets, they have big ships, even if they don't have FTL technology. We're close enough now that our sensors should be able to pick up significant reactor emissions."

"We know there's something at the Lagrangian points, and we're still not seeing that. Assuming those objects are station-sized, meaning bigger than ships, why would we pick up something smaller?"

"You're probably right, but it still bothers me. We saw their missiles and small craft because they were boosting.

For all we know, there could be some large sublight cruisers coasting in our direction."

The minutes ticked by without a reply to *Stingray*'s last transmission and Dunmoore began to wonder whether they had triggered a crisis among the colonists.

"Captain, your intuition may have been right." Chief Penzara raised his hand, drawing the avid interest of everyone on the bridge. "Our sensors picked up one of their ships on visual when it passed between us and their sun, giving us an excellent silhouette. Its emissions are almost at background radiation levels, but now that we have a fix, we're able to track it. If you'll look at the starboard tactical screen."

All eyes snapped to the right, hungry for a look at what Penzara had found.

"It reminds me of a monitor that had an uncontrolled growth spurt," Pushkin said. "Can we get a scale, Chief?"

"Working on it."

Dimensional data began to appear next to the slightly blurry image of a strangely constructed spacecraft. Pushkin let out a low whistle.

"How about a sublight battleship with uncontrolled growth?" Dunmoore asked. "Are those rail guns?"

"Looks like it, sir." Penzara nodded. "And what I'd say is a whole whack of missile pods. The thing seems to pack a serious punch, but the rail guns make it more of a short range combatant. We've already seen their missiles and had no problems picking them off. I'd have expected lasers as well, but until they fire, we might not be able to distinguish them from the rest of their ordnance."

"Then we'll make sure to keep our distance." Dunmoore ran a gloved finger over the scar along her jaw line, deep in thought. "Now that you have a baseline, can you find any others?"

"I've had the sensors tackling that problem from the moment I found the first one, but it'll take a bit of time, sir. With their tight emcon, we'll be down to looking for dark spots where they occlude the background." Penzara broke off as new data flashed up on his screen. "A ship just lit up fifty thousand kilometers from our port bow, Captain. Looks like they're firing with whatever their railguns usually pump out. Based on the signature, it seems to have some sort of guidance mechanism."

Dunmoore groaned with annoyance.

"Why do we always have to do things the hard way? Take out whatever they've just flung at us, Chief."

"Aye, aye, sir."

Stingray's close-in defense guns fired in rapid succession and a string of nuclear explosions washed-out the background stars.

"Mister Kowalski, please transmit on all frequencies that we'd like to talk to whoever might be the designated grown-up in this system. Advise them that I'm tired of this posturing and if they'd like me to demonstrate the awesomeness of *Stingray*, they're welcome to designate a sacrificial ship. I'll even let the crew evacuate before I turn it into tiny bits of random wreckage, but someone will speak with us. We didn't come all this way to be shown out of the system without so much as a hello."

Pushkin stared at his captain in surprise.

"Are you feeling alright, sir?"

"At some point, I simply get tired of the bullshit, Number One. If they're playing games, I'll make them understand that months in hyperspace on a wild goose chase, or a lost *Tempest* chase if you want to be more precise, does not put me in the best of moods."

"Shall I target the ship that fired on us?" Syten asked.

"Oh yes Lieutenant, and if we don't get a reply to our message of friendship and interstellar love, I'll even let you see how close you can shoot without touching the target."

"Captain!" Kalivan's voice, strangled by outrage, drew a grim smile from the first officer. "Do you really think that being aggressive in return will help matters?"

"Perhaps not." She stroked her chin, eyes on the tactical display. "Mister Syten, use our communications laser at full power to target the ship that just fired, and then any other ship within range that Chief Penzara happens to find. Wait for my command."

She turned a tight grin on Kalivan.

"They'll not know it's a communications laser rather than a weapon and may well assume that we're giving them a little warning nudge." She raised her hand to forestall his next objection. "I'll give them time to consider my last message before I escalate, Colonel. Have no fear."

Kalivan nodded once and sat back, fighting to control his impatience while Penzara and his sensor crew found ship after ship, now that they knew what to look for.

"Massive fleet," Pushkin commented, scanning the growing list, "made up of huge ships."

"And none display any of the characteristics identifying them as FTL-capable under the technology in use by every space-faring species we've encountered," Syten pointed out. "But, they do seem to know what they're doing. Based on the estimated range of their weapons and our present course, they've got a screen between us and the planet, just not an effective one, since we could likely sweep it aside."

"Until we run out of ammunition," Pushkin replied, an eyebrow cocked in amusement. "That's a lot of metal to turn into scrap."

"We're not turning anything into scrap. At least not yet," Dunmoore said. "I'll forgive them the stuff they fired at us since it hasn't come anywhere near scratching the paint on our hull."

"Sir." Kowalski lifted a hand. "Incoming transmission. Data only again."

"I guess my fit of temper got their attention. What do they say?"

"They say, and I quote, this system does not have a designated grown-up, and we do not wish to sacrifice a ship. Please select a representative to meet with us. Further instructions will be provided shortly."

Dunmoore's eyebrows shot up.

"Sounds like someone's got a sense of humor over there."

"Then they're likely not aboard the ships converging on us. They've lit up and are painting us with laser-based targeting designators." Penzara refreshed the tactical display.

"Any sign they're about to fire?"

"No, but then we're only starting to dissect the scans, Captain."

"We're getting navigation instructions," Kowalski said. "I'm feeding them straight to Mister Tours."

"I assume I'll be the designated representative?" Kalivan asked while the sailing master digested rather unfamiliar spatial coordinates.

"Of course." Dunmoore nodded. "You know, if I recall the historical records correctly, first contact with the Shrehari wasn't nearly as complicated as this little family reunion with fellow sentients from Earth."

"Probably because when the Shrehari shot first, they didn't miss," Pushkin replied, deadpan. "It set the tone for a refreshingly uncomplicated long-term relationship rather quickly, the current war excepted. Besides, this is family business."

Siobhan looked at her first officer with the growing suspicion that he was amusing himself at someone's expense.

"I do believe you have a point," Kalivan said. "Considering the two Migration Wars were all human affairs, and the ancestors of the folks out there left before the first one, they may not have developed our innate aversion for civil war."

"Considering the amount of sublight warships they've put out into space, I'd say they have as good an appreciation of war and its effects as any of us."

Dunmoore's dry tone signaled her first officer that this particular discussion had ended.

Pushkin nodded his understanding and turned his eyes back to the tactical display.

"Sir," Tours raised his hand. "I've deciphered their instructions. We're to decelerate on an arc toward the fourth planet and, once there, establish an orbit between the inner and middle of the three moons."

"Escorted by battlecruisers on steroids the entire way, no doubt."

"No doubt, Number One. Chief, have they done anything more than just paint us with their target designators?"

"Negative, Captain. I'll leave Mister Tours to confirm it, but I'm guessing the nearest half-dozen are getting set to box us in."

"That's only to be expected." Dunmoore shrugged. "In any case, between our close-in defense guns and the shields, they'll be hard-pressed to cause us much grief before we can accelerate out of range."

"Based on what we've seen, Captain," Pushkin cautioned. "They may still have something that might just overwhelm us."

"Noted." Dunmoore nodded. "We'll not relax our vigilance anytime soon."

"Course programmed," Tours announced. "We'll reach orbit in just under three hours at the current rate of deceleration."

"Very well. Helm, execute. Let's see what they've got waiting for us." She rose and tugged her tunic down. "Mister Syten, I believe you have the watch."

"Yes, Captain."

"The bridge is yours." She glanced at Pushkin and Kalivan. "Coffee in my ready room, gentlemen? We should discuss the matter of representation."

When the door closed behind them, the first officer looked at his captain with overt suspicion. Dunmoore raised an eyebrow and smiled crookedly.

"I know you're wondering whether I'm about to add myself to Colonel Kalivan's delegation, Gregor, and I also know that if I even so much as hint at it, you'll be on me in a flash, so let's get that out of the way. Captains do make first contact and have made first contact on numerous occasions. We have first officers to take over if something nasty happens."

"Sir..."

She cut him off with a raised hand.

"I know. It's your job to argue with decisions you find questionable, but this is very much a diplomatic mission and as the military commander of said mission, I believe it's my duty to accompany the Commonwealth Envoy." She smiled at Kalivan. "As I'm sure you'll agree, Colonel."

He shook his head ruefully.

"Captain, with all due respect, I don't wish to get between Commander Pushkin and you on this matter, so I'll reserve my opinion."

Dunmoore laughed with unfeigned delight.

"A wise man indeed. Mister Pushkin can be a bit overwhelming when he puts his mind to it." She winked at her first officer. "And that has kept us out of trouble more than once. Have no fear, Gregor, I won't leave the ship without Vincenzo and a squad of his mates, nor would I let Colonel Kalivan leave without making sure that the situation is safe for all of us."

"With all due respect," Pushkin said a scowl still firmly affixed to his saturnine features, "the stories of captains making first contact is balderdash served up by low brow fiction that would see landing parties made up solely of department heads. Add in the inevitable deaths of whichever poor bosun's mates were detailed as security, and you have what has passed as standard operating procedures in fairy tales for much too long."

"I must confess that he has you there, Captain," Kalivan said, a mischievous smile twisting his lips, "but since this isn't exactly first contact, I suppose the point could be considered moot."

"Is that what you call reserving your opinion, sir?" Pushkin asked, straightening his back and staring at him through hooded eyes.

"Perhaps it was more in the way of hedging my opinion, Commander." He inclined his head briefly. "I hesitate to engage in a contest of wills with your captain, as you'll no doubt understand. If she wishes to join me as the head of the naval component of our mission, I'd be loath to gainsay her. In fact, I'd feel reassured if truth be told."

Dunmoore quickly pressed a mug of overly sugared coffee into her first officer's hand and one without additives into Kalivan's and raised the third one as if in salute.

"There's nothing wrong with a healthy discussion. We'll make the final decision once our hosts indicate how they wish to meet our envoy and what the environment will look like. Does that meet with your approval, Number One?"

Pushkin held her eyes for a few moments and then nodded.

"It does. Provisionally."

When she saw the set of his shoulders lose its intensity, she knew she had won a temporary reprieve.

They war-gamed some possible assumptions while emptying the coffee urn until Pushkin excused himself to take care of ship's business, leaving Dunmoore and Kalivan alone in the ready room.

"He's splendid at teasing out the worst-case scenarios, isn't he?" Kalivan asked, nodding toward the closed door.

"Yes, among many other things," she replied in a thoughtful tone. "Gregor's also excellent at sailing close to the line between legitimate argument and insubordination. It bodes well for him when he gets his first frigate command."

"A chip off the old Dunmoore block?" Kalivan smiled at her, one eyebrow raised.

"Hopefully without all the career killers I've had the displeasure of meeting."

"Come now, surely you've done well for yourself."

"In spite of some people who wanted to bring me down a few pegs. Admiral Nagira had a lot to do with my continued survival."

Sensing that he had touched what still seemed like a raw nerve, Kalivan fell silent, eyes on the tactical schematic showing their approach to the fourth planet, and he began to feel a rising surge of anticipation. It would not be long now before they met the descendants of the *Tempest* colonists and perhaps found an answer to the mystery of the log buoy that had plagued him for so long.

The intercom pinged.

"Captain, we have an incoming transmission, audio, and video from the largest of the planet's moons."

Kalivan and Dunmoore glanced at each other, and then with a growing smile, she asked, "Does the Envoy wish to take the call?"

"Is vacuum cold?"

He looked almost giddy at the prospect.

"Perhaps we should go next door to the conference room. You can sit at the head of the table and look ambassadorial."

She stood and waved toward the door.

"I'll have the bridge pipe the transmission through once you're ready."

When Kalivan had taken Siobhan's usual chair moments later, flanked by a Commonwealth flag on his right and an armed forces flag on his left, she sat to one side and with the touch of a finger, linked the room to *Stingray*'s communications array.

The main screen came to life instantly, and they found themselves staring at a sharp-faced human female whose society, whose entire civilization, in fact, had evolved apart from the remainder of the species. Though not quite a first contact in the strictest sense, it might as well have been.

"On behalf of the Dominion of Miranda," the woman said, "welcome."

— Fourteen —

"I am Samila Rano," the woman continued, "the officer designated to greet you."

She spoke a language that both knew came from pre-spaceflight English, but it and Rano's accent sounded just strange enough to briefly confuse them.

The army officer smiled.

"I am Colonel Wes Kalivan, envoy from the human Commonwealth to our brothers and sisters on Miranda. This," he nodded toward Siobhan, "is Commander Dunmoore. She is the captain of our ship, which is called *Stingray*."

Rano's eyes flickered between the two officers, but her dour expression did not show as much as a shred of warmth.

Her angular features, dominated by short, dark hair and deep-set blue eyes seemed like a perfect match for the sober, almost somber black uniform.

Insignia glinted on both sides of her chest, none of them looking even remotely like something derived from the Earth they had left behind. She did not speak for almost a minute, leading Dunmoore to suspect that she might be running Kalivan's reply through an Anglic to Mirandan translator.

"Colonel and commander are rank designations?" Rano finally asked. It took Kalivan a few seconds to make out the words, and then he nodded.

"They are. I am a senior officer in the Commonwealth ground forces while Commander Dunmoore is a senior officer in our space forces. A colonel usually commands a unit of between two thousand and four thousand soldiers, while a commander is typically the officer in charge of a sizable warship like *Stingray*."

The Mirandan considered them for a few seconds and then nodded once.

"I have so noted. Officials of suitable rank will meet you. Once I have arranged this, you will be contacted again. In the meantime, we will transmit instructions for your ship to observe once it reaches orbit."

The screen went blank with a suddenness that startled Siobhan. She blinked a few times and then turned to Kalivan.

"Not much for small talk, our Mirandan cousins, are they?"

"Probably just cautious." He shrugged. "I'm sure we would all behave in a similar manner after being out of contact with the rest of our species for so long."

"True." She rose and worked an unexpected knot of tension from her shoulders. "Though I would have paid money to hear you say the immortal first contact phrase."

"Which one: take me to your leaders?" Kalivan chuckled. "Considering that Samila Rano doesn't seem like the type to crack a smile at anything, I'd say the joke would have been wasted, if not counterproductive. You noticed a certain rank consciousness thing going on there, didn't you?"

"Indeed. I seem to recall the original colonists belonged to an egalitarian movement that didn't believe in things like military force." She led the way back to her ready room and slumped into her chair. "My cox'n used the terms belief in unicorns and pixie dust after reading the briefing you prepared if I recall correctly."

"You do, and yet here we are." He glanced at the urn. "It's just as well that your man hasn't refilled it. My bladder is suddenly indicating that I have an urgent appointment in the heads. Please excuse me."

Alone once more, she called up the latest analysis from Chief Penzara's sensor crew and found few surprises when it came to the three moons. Heavy mass driver arrays on all of them, installations that might indicate mining and, of course, habitats dug into cliff and crater sides. The largest moon boasted what could only be a sizable, heavily defended military outpost, complete with guns on the heights surrounding an immense, flat landing space at the bottom of a deep crater whose slopes seemed covered with blocky metallic modules.

For a brief moment, she pictured a Starbase dismantled into its individual rings and decks, then dropped on the surface and could appreciate the sheer size of the facility.

The objects they knew orbited at the Lagrangian points remained indistinct as if covered by some sort of stealth field, yet if they matched the lunar base in size and power, they would be formidable defenses against any unwanted intruder.

She studied the projected orbit they had assigned *Stingray* and quickly understood that they would be covered by Mirandan ordnance at all times, be it from the moons or from large orbital platforms only now becoming visible to their sensors.

With those on one side and the sublight battleships on the other, her aging frigate would be the object of constant scrutiny and the thought made her uncomfortable to a degree she had not anticipated.

Where Kalivan felt nothing but excitement at meeting the descendants of colonists thought lost centuries earlier, she had begun to feel more ambivalent, especially after the hard to decipher Rano.

When the intercom chimed, she rose and crossed over to the bridge instead of answering. Lieutenant Syten swiveled the command chair around.

"We're about to enter orbit as indicated, sir. The Mirandans have stated that they expect us at their military outpost on the largest moon, which they call Iris, the one in the big crater. They'll let us know the exact time momentarily."

Chief Penzara called up an image of the area Siobhan had admired moments earlier.

She nodded.

"As I surmised. Have a shuttle prepared. Perhaps Lieutenant Kowalski could be spared to fly it, and ask the second officer for a security detail. Six bosun's mates should do. Sidearms only, no armor."

Dunmoore thought for a few moments.

"Let me make a slight amendment. Landing party to be in service dress uniform, ribbons only, no medals. I'll let Colonel Kalivan know."

"Aye, aye, sir."

*

Dunmoore, looking painfully formal in her dress blues, met Kalivan, now attired in army rifle green, at the door to the hangar deck.

Pushkin, a frown of disapproval still creasing his forehead, was inspecting the landing party, accompanied by Lieutenant Devall. Chief Petty Officer Foste, the bosun, had appointed herself in charge of the envoys, or to be more precise, her captain's security and headed the contingent of smartly turned out spacers, Vincenzo most prominent among them.

Each wore a large, unmistakably aggressive blaster at the hip, in a cut-away holster that might have looked formal but was perfectly functional. Foste even carried a short, silver-topped rosewood cane, the symbol of a chief's authority, tucked under her left arm.

Footsteps sounded behind them, and Lieutenant Kowalski came around the corner, slightly out of breath and still doing up the top of her high-collared tunic.

"I flight-checked the shuttle before changing, sir," she said, skidding to a halt, "so we're ready to go whenever you give the word. Sorry for my lateness. I had a brain flash and needed to raid Mister Kutora's spare parts locker."

She pulled two small, flat devices, no bigger than a playing card from her pocket and handed one each to the two senior officers.

"Data spools for engineering bots. I thought that you could carry them and make a record of every conversation you have, without our hosts being the wiser. It'll help analyze the linguistic drift and start building a picture of their society."

Dunmoore turned the object over in her hand. Neither its shape nor its color gave any hint as to its function. She nodded once and tucked it into her right breast pocket. Kalivan followed suit wordlessly, though she felt a hesitation born of anxiousness at not offending the Mirandans.

"Good thinking, Kathryn." She jerked her chin toward the little parade beside the boxy craft. "When Mister Pushkin is satisfied, we'll leave. The Mirandans are waiting for us."

When Siobhan saw Chief Foste raise her hand to her brow in salute, she knew her first officer had finished.

"Shall we?" She headed straight for Pushkin, knowing he would have some parting words for her while the others climbed aboard.

"I presume General Order Eighty-One is in force, sir?" He asked by way of greeting.

"Of course." She gave him a smile meant to be reassuring, but it did not break through a scowl that seemed permanently etched on his features. "If the Mirandans play false and take us prisoner, you're to act in the best interests of the ship and crew first and only, and that interest is to get them home. Our lives become forfeit."

"The needs of the many." He nodded. "Take care, sir. They might be human, but until proved otherwise, they're not the same as us."

"Oh, I wouldn't worry too much, Gregor. The fact that they *are* human means they'll be intensely curious about us and about what happened to humanity since their forebears left Earth. Shooting first doesn't leave much room for asking questions later, no?"

"They did try," he reminded her. "Even after we identified ourselves."

"Miscommunication error, no doubt. It's been known to happen in our Navy as well."

"Or some of them aren't happy to see us and decided to take matters into their own hands until someone with enough clout slapped them down. In any case, I urge you to take care, Captain." He leaned toward her and dropped his voice to a whisper. "And keep an eye on friend Kalivan. His enthusiasm might drag you to places you'd rather avoid. He might outrank you by one step, but you're still the mission commander."

"I will."

Pushkin snapped to attention and saluted.

"Godspeed. We'll keep tabs on you as much as feasible, but the orbital period they've forced on us will mean *Stingray* is going to be on the other side of Miranda from Iris for part of the time."

Kalivan's head popped through the shuttle's starboard hatch.

"We're all raring to go, Captain."

"Coming."

She gripped Pushkin's arm and squeezed briefly.

"I'll tell you all about it at supper tonight."

"Seeing as how you're taking an overnight bag, I'm not going to hold you to that promise."

"Fair enough. I'll tell you all about it when I get back. Take good care of my ship, Gregor."

"I will, sir."

Then, she turned and quickly climbed aboard. Moments later, with Pushkin safely on the other side of the airlock and the hangar deck depressurized, the space doors opened, framing the Mirandan moon Iris. Its airless, pockmarked surface shined brightly against the velvety black of space, reminding her of the one time she had seen Earth's moon from orbit. Kowalski nudged the shuttle through the opening and out into space, lighting her thrusters as soon as they had cleared *Stingray*.

"I have the beacon they want us to monitor," she told Siobhan. "It leads straight to the crater with the vast tarmac."

"As expected."

They closed the distance with Iris in silence and soon, the massive base filled the view screen.

Up close and in person, it seemed even more overwhelming to Dunmoore's eyes, a monument to primitive military power of a kind the Commonwealth had not seen in centuries.

The few ships sitting on the dusty tarmac seemed larger than her frigate and exuded that same brute strength. Even the markings, in recognizable letters and numbers, looked out-sized and blocky.

A set of red lights, outlining a square mark, began to flash urgently at the edge of the crater's flat bottom, and Kowalski brought them to a hover above the mark before gently landing dead center. Almost immediately, they dropped beneath the surface, their landing spot transformed into an elevating platform.

It came to a halt twenty meters down, in a small hangar, while above them, a large hatch slammed shut, cutting them off from the shaft. Lights came on, and Kowalski reported growing air pressure outside. When the pressure reached one atmosphere, a green light came on over the metal door cut into the rock beside a blank window.

It opened inward with a smooth movement and a human female wearing what looked like a dark uniform stepped through, followed by half a dozen individuals whose battle armor, visored helmets and heavy rifles gave no doubt as to their function.

The troopers took up positions on either side of the door, their weapons at a high port while the woman approached *Stingray*'s shuttle.

"I guess Samila Rano has been detailed to greet us in person as well," Dunmoore remarked, releasing her seat restraints and climbing to her feet. "Let's not keep her waiting."

"Sir," Kowalski ventured, "may I suggest that I be the first off. I'm probably closest in rank to Rano, based on her comment about finding Mirandan representatives of the appropriate rank, and I'm willing to bet they have a heavy enough dose of hierarchy mania around here that she'll take either you or the Colonel stepping out first to be — well, weird."

Siobhan considered the offer for a few seconds and then nodded.

"Cogent analysis, as always, Kathryn. I'll have Chief Foste and her detail follow you out to secure the shuttle, and then I'll get off. Colonel Kalivan, as the most important member of our party, will exit last."

"That would seem appropriate, sir."

"Then let's make it so." Dunmoore glanced at Kalivan, who nodded, knowing that his opinion on the matter carried little weight.

Kowalski straightened her uniform and made sure her beret sat at the right angle. Satisfied, she opened the port hatch and stepped out.

Rano raised her right fist to her chest and briefly dipped her head.

"Welcome. I am Senior Leader Samila Rano."

"Lieutenant Kathryn Kowalski," the signals officer replied, saluting. "I'm *Stingray*'s communications specialist and the envoy's pilot."

"It is a rank designator, this word 'lieutenant'?"

"Yes. I'm in charge of one of our ship's departments."

Rano's eyes widened when Foste and her six mates filed off the shuttle and took up positions on either side of the hatch, standing at the parade rest position. At the bosun's command, they snapped to attention. Kowalski followed suit and saluted, along with Foste, when Dunmoore emerged.

The Mirandan raised her fist to her chest again, dipping her head.

"Commander Dunmoore. I am pleased to greet you in person."

"Likewise."

Before Rano could speak again, Kalivan stepped through the hatch and straightened his long frame. He looked very dignified, very ambassadorial, as he returned his escort's and the Mirandan's salutes.

"Envoy Kalivan. On behalf of Cyrus Hames, Protector of the Dominion of Miranda, welcome to Ariel Base."

*

Rano led the way down a bare passage lit at intervals by encased globes. Half of the Mirandan troops accompanied them, the rest having stayed inside the underground hangar.

Equally, half of Chief Foste's crew had remained with the shuttle, including the bosun herself while the remainder, as well as Kathryn Kowalski, accompanied Dunmoore and Kalivan.

They passed through several massive, armored airlocks before emerging into a broad perpendicular corridor. Unlike the previous one, however, its surfaces shone with smooth, light shades of yellow, making it felt much warmer to the eye.

Conduits ran along the ceiling, color-coded for maintenance and images of ships, troops, and military equipment hung here and there on the walls. Armored and armed Mirandan soldiers stood on either side of the passageway at regular intervals, their expressionless eyes examining the newcomers with all the curiosity of machines.

Just before they reached yet another airlock, the Mirandan officer stopped and, with an outstretched arm, invited them to enter a large room where a cluster of men and women, wearing the same type of uniform as Rano, waited beside a table.

"Group Leader Trask," she announced, her fist against the chest in salute, "may I present Colonel Kalivan of Earth and Commander Dunmoore of the Earth ship *Stingray*."

A stocky, middle-aged man detached himself from the group and raised his fist in the Mirandan way, nodding at Kalivan. For the first time, they could see how the insignia on Rano's chest differed from those of the reception committee.

Trask, for example, wore something that resembled three silver fern leaves joined at the stem within a rectangle of silver thread where Rano wore three silver lozenges in a vertical row.

Kalivan returned the greeting with a flourish that would have done the SecGen's guard proud.

"I am pleased to make your acquaintance, Group Leader Trask."

"And I yours, Colonel Kalivan," the Mirandan replied in a low, gravelly voice, his accent thick, the words sounding distorted enough to challenge Dunmoore's concentration. "We are astonished at receiving visitors from a place that has almost faded into myth after such a long, long time."

A puzzled smile briefly lit up Kalivan's formal expression.

"Surely you haven't lost the memory of your ancestors' provenance in just four centuries?"

Trask emitted a sound that seemed half-bark, half-laugh.

"Four centuries? The envoy from Earth jests. You've contemplated our works in this system, yes? We know you've passed Sycorax close enough to see the bases on its moons, and now that you've been in orbit around Miranda for a few hours, you know the extent of what we've built here as well. Do you think four centuries would have been enough? That the original twenty-thousand would have multiplied fast enough to populate two planets and all of their moons?"

The Mirandan laughed again.

"If you're indeed from Earth, you know as well as I do that the twenty-thousand left our ancestral star in *Tempest* two thousand of your years ago."

— Fifteen —

Cyrus Hames, Protector of the Dominion, turned away from the thick, armored window overlooking the government precinct at the heart of Sanctum when he heard the door to his office open with a click. He remained standing, hands clasped together in the small of his back, looking every millimeter the soldier he had been before the Two Hundred had called on him to serve one last time.

The man who entered the office seemed hewn from the same granite as the system's dictator: stocky, gray-haired, face creased by decades of toil and worry, and deep-set eyes that missed nothing.

"Sir." Geoff Martell, the commander in chief of the Defenders, as the Mirandans called their military forces, briefly came to attention on the threshold.

Hames nodded once to acknowledge the formality, then waved his old friend to one of the chairs facing his desk.

"I'd have been content to see these Earthers arrive after my term ended," he said, dropping wearily into what he privately derided as his throne. "Another three months and the problem would have belonged to the next Protector."

"Have the Two Hundred designated your successor yet?"

"No, and this little twist will make negotiations between the factions that much more acrimonious. Things are bad enough as is."

He shook his head.

"After twenty centuries of isolation and struggle, give or take a few decades," Hames continued, "the descendants of those left behind show up in a ship that presumably goes faster-than-light, armed with weapons we can't match and protected by means we can't even begin to comprehend. And it had to happen on the eve of my retirement."

"And yet, it's the opportunity of a lifetime — several lifetimes, Cyrus. Imagine getting a hold of their technology. We'd never again need fear any xeno incursions."

"Assuming they're inclined to share." The Protector shrugged. "Better yet, presuming our scientists and engineers can even grasp the principles behind it, let alone replicate what Earth has developed over all this time. Who have you assigned to meet with their envoy?"

"Jodan Trask. He's one of the few group leaders who wasn't clamoring loudly to either greet the Earthers with open arms or destroy them so they don't report our existence to their superiors. As neutrality goes, he's the closest I could find."

"I'm not surprised. Trask always had an uncanny ability to hedge his bets. He served on the general staff as a bannerman during my last years in the job you're now enjoying so much. A good go-between when the senior leaders were at each other's throats over some triviality or other."

Martell examined his old friend critically, noting the fatigue deeply etched into his face. Few wanted the Protector's job. In fact, most candidates had to be drafted. It had a tendency to chew the incumbents up and spit them out at the end of ten years looking a century older.

That the Two Hundred still had not settled on a nominee came as no surprise. Many of those able to fill the Protector's boots managed to avoid an offer that they might not be able to refuse.

"Perhaps these Earthers can help us with the xenos Mira Dalian's people are holding. They're of a different sort than the last few who invaded the Dominion."

The head of Miranda's military forces grimaced at the name.

"If they can, it had better be soon. Dear Mira seems to be going through this new species at an alarming rate."

"She's entirely too keen on dissecting xeno threats," Hames replied in a tone that betrayed his own distaste for a woman he neither liked nor could dismiss without the consent of the Two Hundred.

As head of the Custodians, the organization responsible for internal security, she served not at the Protector's pleasure but at that of Miranda's hereditary legislature.

"Sometimes I wonder if she doesn't take things too far. One hears things coming from Custodian headquarters these days, especially when her hunters get their hands on some feral Skraeling. By the way, you knew she opposed our opening discussions with the Earthers and is far from pleased that you overrode the opinion of so many senior leaders within both the Defenders and the Custodians."

"Mira and that half of the Two Hundred who refuse to sanction my dismissing her, actually." Hames shrugged again. "Like I said, I'd have been more than happy for my successor to deal with this tearful reunion or those new xenos. I've grown much too weary of the Protector's responsibilities to care for Dalian's opinion or that of her supporters."

He stared down at the richly inlaid surface of his desk and released a long breath.

"When do we hear from Trask?"

"We'll get the first report within the hour, I'd say. The Earther envoy and his retinue landed on Iris just as I left Defender headquarters."

"And their ship?"

"Under constant surveillance. I have no doubt that it can defend itself if those opposed to contact try something dire."

"I'm more concerned that they might try something stupid with the envoy and his people." Hames grimaced. "There are enough hot-heads in your ranks who'd see it as their duty to the Dominion."

"If something like that happens, we can expect retaliation from their ship, and after the display of power, I doubt my hot-heads, as you call them, would be stupid enough to trigger something that might cause us irreparable harm."

"Never underestimate the power of idiocy. Please tell me that news of the Earthers' arrival is at least still being kept tightly held. The last thing I need is unrest among the population, especially from the various fundamentalist groups. They've been enough of a thorn in my side over the years."

"I'd have no fear on that front, Cyrus. Mira's minions will do their jobs with accustomed vigor, particularly when it involves the more extreme xeno-lovers and Earth haters. Besides, those who know about the Earthers also know that blabbing would be dangerous for their continued health."

"When it comes to the point where I'm actually glad at Dalian's efficiency, it's well past time I retire." He sighed.

"You really are tired, aren't you?" Martell examined his friend with unfeigned concern.

"More than you can imagine. I daresay our ancestors set the Protector's time in office at ten years with the idea that no one would wish another term and prolong the agony, both for the man in this chair and for the Two Hundred."

"Not everyone would agree. Recall Yora Krant. According to the records, Defenders and Custodians fought each other to the death when he refused to step down."

"I recall, Geoff and now that you've planted that idea in my mind, I also seem to remember the Custodians fought on Krant's side."

"It did them little good in the end. Krant's head adorned a pike in Founders' Plaza, along with those of the senior leaders who supported him."

"Perhaps." Hames stared down at the desktop again. "I wonder if Mira's on the shortlist to replace me."

"You *are* cheerful this morning, aren't you?" Martell grinned. "If she's chosen, she'll have my lot to contend with. There's little love for her among the Defenders."

"There are always people willing to show love in return for favors and your lot, as you call them, aren't immune."

"For sure, but I do know who most of those are."

The men fell silent, lost in thought.

"Why did the Earthers have to show up just as we're trying to work through an orderly succession?" Hames asked after a minute or so.

Geoff Martell had no answer to the question either, and he merely shrugged.

*

Kalivan gave Dunmoore a triumphant glance.

"I knew it," he said, awe in his voice. "*Tempest* went through a wormhole that had a temporal component. We finally have proof that they exist. The ancestors of these folks here landed on Miranda at around the time the Western Roman Empire collapsed."

"Pardon me?" Trask sounded puzzled. "What would this wormhole be and why would it have a temporal component?"

"A wormhole," Dunmoore said, "is pretty much like a tunnel in space with two ends, each at separate points in space-time. They instantly connect places that can be hundreds, thousands, or even hundreds of thousands of light years apart. We've known for some time now that they exist but we simply never had proof that they also connected different points in time. What Colonel Kalivan means is that *Tempest* went through such a phenomenon by accident and ended up here, sixteen hundred years before it left."

An expression of alarm replaced Trask's earlier incomprehension. The other Mirandan officers began whispering among themselves.

"Group Leader," Kalivan's tone had become noticeably gentler, "the year in which we find ourselves is 2467 according to the standard calendar. *Tempest* left Earth in 2103, three-hundred and sixty-four years ago. You might have been on Miranda for two thousand years, but for the rest of humanity, only a little under four centuries has passed. This is extraordinary."

He looked at Dunmoore again, awe mixed with exultation radiating from his eyes.

"A living laboratory of societal evolution. Commonwealth scientists will be fighting each other to study Miranda."

Siobhan shrugged, still not wholly convinced of the temporal aspect. However, she had no convincing explanation how a population base of twenty-thousand could have built up what they had seen so far. Not in the space of three-hundred and sixty years. Therefore, she decided to let it ride until confronted with tangible evidence.

Trask, still stunned by the revelation, weakly waved them toward chairs and then sat, staring at the visitors in disbelief. The whispering among the others rose to a crescendo.

"That would explain," he finally said, in a strangled tone, "why we never heard from Earth until now. We were the only humans not living on our species' planet of origin for most of our existence here."

"It gets better," Dunmoore said, privately amused at the Mirandans' reaction, "humanity has spread to more than fifty star systems grouped together under a government we call the Commonwealth. In doing so, we've encountered many non-human sentient species. In fact, we're at war with one of the larger non-human polities right now."

"How..." Trask shook his head, unable to digest what he heard.

"The first workable faster-than-light propulsion system was successfully tested less than twenty years after *Tempest* left, making cryo-ships like it obsolete. After that," she smiled, "we humans did what we've always done, we expanded as far and as fast as we could. No one knew what had happened to your ancestors — distant ancestors, as we now know — until *Tempest*'s log buoy showed up on the edge of Commonwealth space after a two thousand year voyage that, by all rights, it shouldn't have survived. Because it presented such a puzzle, our government sent us to find out what had happened. It's been a long voyage to get here, even at many times the speed of light. We're glad you finally decided to talk."

*

"Interesting." Chief Penzara glanced over at Petty Officer Rownes. "Are you seeing the same thing?"

"If you mean their cities seem to be partially or wholly dug in and appear fortified, then yes," she replied. "If what I'm seeing around most of them are gun emplacements, then it's like they've hunkered down in preparation for a massive invasion."

"Not surprising, considering how they've developed the moons of the two planets they occupy," Pushkin said, looking over Penzara's shoulder.

"And that's without even counting the stuff in orbit," Tours added, "and there's a lot of it. No wonder they're keeping us in such a high orbit."

"Perhaps this is a nasty neighborhood. They didn't build those over-sized battleships for fun."

"But is it bad enough that they have to partially bury their settlements? It can't be because of ugly weather. The vegetation patterns don't show evidence of nature playing hardball." The sailing master sounded skeptical.

"What I wonder about, sir," Penzara said, "is how they were able to do so much in three hundred years, starting from scratch, with twenty-thousand people and no backup from Earth. Even the home worlds, which we began to colonize not long after *Tempest* left Earth, don't look that built up and they had plenty more folks coming in after first landing."

"Hopefully, Colonel Kalivan and the captain will find some answers." Pushkin took the command chair again and settled back, eyes on the image of Miranda dominating the main screen. "I'm more concerned about what we know is there and can't see, even with sensors that should be centuries ahead of what the Mirandans have."

"Working on it, sir," the gunnery chief replied. "But it'll take some time. We already have proof they have excellent emcon and physical stealth capabilities. Finding their ships turned out to be relatively easy because of the size. Smaller stuff, not so much. They might not have FTL, but they seem to have my sensors beat right now."

He shrugged.

"Case in point, we lost our landing party's signal the moment their shuttle dropped below the moon's surface."

Pushkin's fingers began tapping the command chair's arm.

"I'm not sure I like that part." He grimaced. "Let's leave the surface scans for later, Chief. Concentrate on the moons and whatever is near us we haven't noticed yet."

"Feeling paranoid, sir?" The sailing master smiled briefly.

"All part of the job, Mister Tours. First officers are required to display appropriate levels of paranoia when the captain has left the ship to meet with the natives, especially since we're so far from home. There's something about this place that makes me feel uneasy."

"I know what you mean, sir," Rownes said, grimacing. "The feeling is getting to me as well. Maybe it's because those are humans out there, and nothing about them seems familiar."

"You've never been to Nabhka then, I gather?"

"Not as such, Mister Tours," the petty officer replied. "Docked at their orbital station a few times when I served on merchant ships before the war, but they didn't let us off. Poor buggers must be having a grand old time under the Shrehari."

"Well, if you ever visit there once the war is over, provided the boneheads give back that system, you'll get a pretty similar feeling, and they've not been cut off from humanity for centuries. Different strokes for different folks, as it were. The original Nabhka colonists had as many weird beliefs as Colonel Kalivan's briefing would have us believe the *Tempest* colonists had."

"True." Pushkin nodded. "But I've actually set foot on Nabhka, and I can tell you it didn't feel as strange as this place does."

*

"Commander."

Brakal looked up from his bowl of *hrach*, a snarl twisting his raw features. Fresh food had become scarce aboard *Tol Vehar,* and though he hated the bland porridge, every crew member would be eating it this midday, and so the officers would eat it as well. There would be no favoritism or special treatment on his ship, but my, did he ever hate *hrach*.

"What is it, Urag?"

The first officer glared at Regar, who was sharing Brakal's table as he frequently had over the past few days. Regar returned Urag's hostility with a mocking stare before returning to his dish.

"Mtak confirms a habitable planet in this system, the fourth. He also detected traces of massive nuclear explosions between it and the fifth planet."

"Nuclear explosions, eh?" Brakal dropped his spoon into the much-hated broth and scratched his bony chin. "Has our human quarry met with a new foe? As I recall, we've never found evidence that any sentient species inhabits this wasted part of the galaxy."

"Actually," Regar said, leaning back in his chair, "we haven't explored the area much. The Admiralty's attention is, understandably, on achieving final victory against the humans. However, I understand that a *Ziq* class survey ship or two may have penetrated this far. Perhaps our quarry met up with one of them?"

"You might have told us before this," Urag growled.

"Why? It didn't seem relevant until now. You know how we *Tai Kan* spies work — no information given before its time." This time, a feral smile replaced the derisive expression. "Or given at all, if it suits us."

Upon seeing the rage in Urag's eyes, Brakal raised his hand.

"Enough."

Both officers had the good sense to abort yet another argument. The commander's temper had frayed along with that of everyone else aboard *Tol Vehar*, but he was the only one who could exercise it on others with impunity and given sufficient reason, he did.

"We will reduce our signature and enter this system under complete stealth. Have the navigator aim us at the fourth planet. Whatever has happened there will become apparent in due time."

Urag nodded.

"It will be done, Commander." He glanced at the bowl of *hrach*. "Though I fear by the time we've caught up with the human ship, you'll long even for that mush. It'll be hard rations once we've shut down all non-essential systems."

Brakal barked a laugh.

"Bad food makes for evil tempers, and that means the crew will fight so much harder. Make it so, Urag. Make it so."

— Sixteen —

"Fantastic." Trask shook his head once Kalivan and Dunmoore had fallen silent. "Simply amazing. You've accomplished more in three-hundred and sixty years than we've been able to do in two thousand."

"Perhaps they've not had the sort of destructive xeno problems we've experienced, Group Leader," one of the officers in Trask's retinue said in a distinctly unpleasant tone.

"And you are?" Kalivan smiled at him.

"Bannerman Rudden. I'm the group leader's chief of staff."

The silver hair and beard framing a pink, slightly round face, might have given him a kindly cast, but the distaste visible in his pinched expression reminded Siobhan of an eccentric admiral she had known before the war and who had lectured her at length about what he deemed her rebellious streak.

"Would you care to elaborate, Bannerman? We're strangers in a strange land, so to speak, and I'd be fascinated to hear about your history."

Trask seemed to be recovering from his astonishment, and he waved Rudden's reply away.

"Perhaps later." He bowed his head toward Kalivan by way of apology. "My orders don't give me leeway to discuss matters concerning our security without further authorization."

"Understood," he replied with a pleasant flourish of the hand. "We all answer to higher commands. I shall strive to restrain my intense curiosity about your history until your leaders feel ready to share. In the meantime, we will be pleased to answer your questions."

Dunmoore gave Kalivan a warning glance, to remind him of their sometimes-heated discussion before leaving *Stingray*. She had forcefully sided with Pushkin in setting a limit to how much they would tell the Mirandans.

After all, these long lost colonists had fired first and would have gleefully wrecked the frigate if it had not been so much more advanced than their best technology could muster.

"I'm sure we will have many questions, Colonel Kalivan, but those too are subject to higher command's direction," Trask replied, ignoring a pointed glare from Rudden. "At this point, I have to report back to my superiors and await instructions. If you follow Senior Leader Rano, she will provide refreshments while you wait."

The group leader rose, along with his retinue and the Mirandans, save for Rano, filed out of the room.

Kalivan and Dunmoore looked at each other, the former shrugging, and the latter grimacing.

"When in Rome, I suppose," he murmured. Then he smiled at Rano.

"Please lead the way, Senior Leader."

"Are we in contact with *Stingray* or the shuttle?" He asked Siobhan in a low tone as they followed the Mirandan through yet another door, trailed by Kowalski and the bosun's mates.

She leaned back toward Kowalski. "Kathryn, are we linked to anyone?"

"Not even with Chief Foste, Captain," she replied after surreptitiously glancing at a small hand-held sensor. "This place is a heck of a good Faraday cage. The Mirandans seem to have the kind of emcon a signals gal like me can only dream of."

"That and a lot of other stuff I'd like to figure out," Dunmoore replied.

When Rano turned back with a quizzical look on her square face, Siobhan smiled.

"We're quite impressed with the facilities. It must have taken a lot of effort to develop this base."

"What the Protector and the Two Hundred decree for the greater good of the Dominion becomes reality very quickly, Commander."

With that sibylline statement still hanging in the air, she gestured toward a table laden with various drinks and small plates of food.

"Please avail yourselves of anything you desire. I shall return momentarily."

Once they were alone, Dunmoore raised her hand to get everyone's attention.

"We will enjoy the hospitality and take this time out to speak of lighter things, understood?"

She looked at each of them in turn until they nodded. It would not do to discuss either their hosts or the situation where unseen ears could hear. In fact, she suspected the Mirandans hoped for exactly that, an unfiltered discussion among the newcomers.

These lost colonists seemed intensely secretive, but the big question hanging over the landing party and indeed over everyone aboard *Stingray* was why. Granted, twenty centuries of isolation, if one believed their assertions, would have lessened any feelings of attachment for those humans who had remained on Earth, but she still found the suspicious atmosphere to be curious.

"A bite, Commander?" Kalivan proffered a plate with a small, delicate morsel that had an enticing aroma.

*

The three most senior Mirandan leaders rose when Cyrus Hames entered the spare, utilitarian conference room.

"Protector." Gano Marant, Speaker for the Two Hundred and consummate politician, bowed his head politely, the gesture masking his impatience at seeing Hames shuffle off into retirement.

"Speaker." Hames did not bother trying on a smile. He knew the upcoming discussion would make their previous disagreements seem like minor spats.

He nodded at Geoff Martell, the only friend he could count on, then locked eyes with a hard-faced, middle-aged woman. She had deep-set blue eyes, raven black hair and a uniform that molded the kind of muscular body that only drugs and extensive weight training could produce.

The head of the Mirandan state security apparatus hated both Hames and Martell in equal measures, and she did not bother hiding it anymore. There seemed to be no point in polite dissimulation, not when her discussions with the Speaker about the succession were going so well.

"Custodian Dalian."

A small, predatory smile briefly twisted her lips.

"Bad luck that this happened on the tail end of your mandate."

"Nothing ever occurs when we wish it to," he replied, sitting down at the head of the oval table. "Thank you for making yourselves available on such short notice. Chief Defender Martell has received a preliminary report from Group Leader Trask concerning his meeting with the Earthers on Ariel Base and we must now make some decisions regarding our dealings with the visitors. Geoff?"

Martell leaned forward, hands clasped, elbows resting on the shiny surface. A grim expression replaced the studied neutrality he had worn while they waited for Hames.

"You've all seen the recordings of what happened when my ships tried to neutralize theirs, so I won't bother picking through that particular after-action report. Suffice to remember that they appear technologically formidable, more so than the last batch of xenos."

None of them demurred, and he continued.

"The visitors are indeed human, indistinguishable from us in all ways, and they have provided evidence that they do indeed come on behalf of the planet the twenty-thousand left behind two millennia ago. Except, in their accounting of the timeline, on Earth the year is 2467. Only three-hundred and sixty odd years separate them from the time *Tempest* set out."

"How is that possible?" Dalian demanded. "Time travel is a myth."

"Not even they know for sure, but it appears the log buoy our ancestors wrote about truly existed and did make it to human-controlled space. According to the Earthers, it seemed to have shown the wear of twenty centuries and had lost every last bit of power."

"And that proves what? Nothing." The Custodian sneered. "They lie and have their own reasons to do so."

"I've seen a recording of their meeting with Trask. Either the envoy, Kalivan, is an excellent actor, or they're telling the truth."

"You're too trusting, Geoff," she replied with a dismissive wave of the hand.

"And you're too paranoid, Mira," he shot back. "I can't figure out a reason why they'd lie about this, but then I suppose I don't have your twisted mind. In any case, the visitors believe that the wormhole some of our histories claim sucked *Tempest* into this area of the galaxy had a temporal component that shot our forebears back into what was the fifth century on Earth. At this point, without any evidence either way, I propose that we keep it as the operating theory, although it's fair to note that the other senior officer, Dunmoore, seemed to be skeptical of the idea, but she did not contradict Kalivan. This date discrepancy isn't why I asked the Protector to convene the Inner Council, though I believe it's necessary to the discussion we must have before things proceed any further."

When Dalian declined to pursue the argument, Martell composed himself before speaking again.

"What we really need to discuss revolves around the fact that these Earthers — they call the polity governing their cluster of fifty-odd colonized systems the Commonwealth — have the ability to travel through space at speeds that are faster-than-light. This is something our scientists have never been able to perfect, even though we've known xenos have the same capability. By the words of this Dunmoore, the Earthers discovered it within two decades of *Tempest* departing on her voyage, so it is possible to do on a human scientific and technological base. They showed us where to find Earth's star in the firmament and by our own scientists' calculations, it is indeed hundreds of light years away."

He glanced at Dalian as if daring her to doubt his latest declaration, but she remained silent although he could see a distinct look of calculation in her hard eyes.

"Yes, Mira, the star's spectral signature corresponds to that which the archives tell us is the home star of our species."

"To enable this long-range FTL ability," Hames said, eyes narrowed in thought, "they must necessarily have access to an immensely powerful source of energy. Moreover, it must be one they carry in a ship much smaller than our standard-pattern cruisers, one that even the xenos who've attacked our world didn't seem to have in the same measure. Since it must also power their weapons and defenses, which we've already seen are well beyond ours, it makes them much more formidable than anyone we've fought off. Obtaining FTL technology is less important to us than finding the secret of that energy source. Imagine how well we could protect our homes if we had access to such. The next xeno incursion might just be the last one once word gets around that Miranda and Sycorax are impregnable."

"Better yet, if we obtain human FTL technology, something we can understand and replicate," Dalian said, "we could root out xenos where they live and expand the Dominion beyond this system, ensuring once and for all that our species survives no matter what."

"It already survives around many stars, if the tale is true," Marant pointed out, chuckling. "Surely you mean our civilization, which by necessity has evolved differently from theirs."

"The Speaker brings up an important point," Martell said. "They claim to have made contact with xeno species and in some cases they even carry out trade with them, though they are presently at war with a xeno empire that rivals their Commonwealth in power and size."

A grimace of disgust twisted Dalian's face.

"A difference in civilization indeed," the Speaker said, sounding as repelled as the Custodian looked. "Consorting with xenos."

Hames shrugged.

"A polity powerful enough to spread over such a vast area of the galaxy has more options than we do."

"And if we had their technology," Dalian said, "we could give ourselves those options too. Since their Commonwealth is too far away to be of any use to us, even with their faster-than-light technology, I would say our duty is to become its equal."

"And that would necessarily begin with acquiring their technology…" Marant's voice trailed off, and he smiled. "Imagine if we could leave this system. Imagine if we could track down the home planet of the newest xenos now stewing in the Custodians' dungeon and make sure they never bother us again. By the way, Mira, have you had any luck extracting something, anything from the disgusting creatures?"

"No." She shook her head.

"Perhaps the visitors will know their species and show us how to communicate with them," Marant suggested.

Hames frowned.

"A bad idea, I think," he said. "If it's a species they've befriended, they might take offense at our treatment."

"Or it could be an enemy species and the Earthers could be treating those in the same way we do."

The Protector raised his hand.

"Let's not go off on a tangent, my friends. The xenos can wait. We still have a lengthy discussion ahead of us. Geoff's report only set the scene. I'm sure we all agree that obtaining access to our visitors' technology is of paramount importance to the Dominion's future well-being."

"There's a very easy way to ensure we get everything we want," Dalian said, her predatory smile returning, "and no danger of these visitors ever going back to tell the rest of them we exist. It will buy us the time we need to become as powerful as their Commonwealth."

"Why must you always go for the jugular first, Mira?" Martell asked, visibly disgusted.

"Because I serve the Dominion to the best of my ability, dear Geoff," she purred, not at all offended.

"Perhaps someday I should take the time to remind you of techniques that yield the same result for less bloodshed."

"Where would be the fun in that?"

Hames sighed. This discussion could become acrimonious indeed, but he worried more that Mira Dalian might be on the shortlist to replace him and thus already enjoy Marant's tacit support.

If she obtained formal control of the Dominion's ultimate levers of power once he stepped down, the Creator help them all, especially the growing number of dissenters tired of living in a constant state of emergency.

As if she had read his thoughts, Dalian smiled and said, "Besides, expansion to new worlds would quickly take care of misguided energies now devoted to opposing the regime. Think of how that would help bring back the political stability we enjoyed in the early days of the Dominion, once we'd shed our unrealistic ideals in the face of off-world aggression."

*

The Mirandans left their guests alone in the reception room for almost two hours, during which Dunmoore and the others demolished most of the food offerings.

Rano had reappeared at one point and had politely directed those in need to the washroom facilities but remained otherwise unhelpful when it came to their curiosity about Mirandan history.

An examination of the facilities had yielded little other than the impression that their hosts had stagnated at the level of Earth in the years immediately before the discovery of FTL travel, and the subsequent explosion into Sol's stellar neighborhood.

What they had experienced of Ariel Base so far felt like it had a patina of long use that reminded Dunmoore of her previous, albeit temporary command, the battleship *Victoria Regina,* launched a long time before her own birth.

Finally, Trask, followed by the eternally disapproving Rudden, who still looked like he had smelled something rebelliously offensive, rejoined them.

"Cyrus Hames, Protector of the Dominion, has requested that you join him in Sanctum, our capital on Miranda," the group leader announced. Unlike the choleric chief of staff, he kept his personal opinion of the invitation from showing.

Kalivan inclined his head.

"How very gracious of him. Of course, we accept. When would we go?"

"Immediately."

Dunmoore turned to Kowalski just as Trask continued.

"We will convey you and Commander Dunmoore, Colonel Kalivan. You may return your shuttle and escort to your ship."

A moment of awkward silence descended on them and the pinched expression on Rudden's face hardened at the visible dismay on Dunmoore's face.

"With all due respect, Group Leader, we would consider it impolite to the Protector if we didn't bring a suitable retinue." The words rolled smoothly off Kalivan's tongue, and Dunmoore had to repress a pleased smile, lest she gives the choleric bannerman a stroke. "At the very least, the commander and I require one aide each to accompany us."

"Very well," Trask said after considering whether the request needed confirmation from his unseen superiors. "One apiece. I'm sure that won't present any problems."

Before Kalivan could delve into the details, Siobhan jerked her chin at Kowalski.

"Kathryn, I'll keep Vincenzo as my retainer. Take the rest back to the shuttle and have Chief Foste join us. She'll be of suitable rank for the envoy. Have her bring our overnight bags and give my best to the first officer."

Kowalski nodded once and then turned to Rano.

"If you'll lead the way please, Senior Leader."

After a last glance at Dunmoore, she and the landing party, minus Leading Spacer Vincenzo, vanished into the corridor, flanked by armed Mirandan troopers.

"It's a signal honor to be received by Protector Hames, Colonel," Trask said by way of small talk while they waited. "I suppose you'll also be introduced to Speaker for the Two Hundred Marant as well as Chief Defender Martell and Custodian Dalian, who form the Inner Council advising the Protector."

"Speaker for the Two Hundred?" Kalivan cocked a curious eyebrow. "May I infer that the Two Hundred constitute your legislature? We have a person called the Speaker of the Senate, our own legislature on Earth, which funnily enough, also has around two hundred members."

Ignoring Rudden's warning glance, Trask nodded.

"The Two Hundred started off representing the original family groupings who came to Miranda in *Tempest,* but with our expansion across Miranda and then to Sycorax and the moons, they now stand for geographical areas. The Speaker is the Two Hundred's delegate to the Protector's Inner Council."

"Fascinating."

Kalivan's wistful tone sounded comical to Dunmoore's finely attuned ears, and she could sense the questions crowding each other in his fertile brain. Hopefully, the Protector would put his curiosity out of its misery.

"Is Chief Defender Martell your military's highest ranking commander?" Siobhan asked in the ensuing silence.

Trask nodded.

"And as you may have surmised, Custodian Dalian is the head of the Dominion's Security Office."

She had not but the title made sense, as did the inclusion of such a person on the Inner Council. Their arrangement seemed to be one step further than the Commonwealth had taken, thank God. Having the SecGen, the Grand Admiral, the Speaker of the Senate *and* the head of the Special Security Bureau sitting at the same table, deciding the fate of humanity, would have been disastrous. Certainly more so than the government's current management of the Shrehari War.

Foste arrived at that moment, carrying four small bags.

"Good to go, Captain," she announced. "When I left, they were buttoning up the hangar while the lieutenant warmed up her engines."

"Thank you, Chief." Dunmoore relieved Foste of the extra packs and handed Kalivan and Vincenzo theirs before smiling at Trask. "We can head to Miranda's surface at your convenience, Group Leader."

"Indeed." He nodded at Rano. "She will guide you to the ship designated for the transit to Sanctum. It has been a pleasure meeting you, Colonel, and you, Commander. Please enjoy an uneventful trip."

Trask and Rudden watched them leave, each wondering in his own way how things would unfold. Though the group leader held no definite opinions, he considered himself a pragmatist, and would support whatever could be achieved for the Dominion at minimal cost.

Rano placed Kalivan, Dunmoore and their personal aides, Chief Foste and Leading Spacer Vincenzo, into the care of a six-member armed detail that accompanied them aboard a winged craft showing black streaks from many atmospheric reentries.

Siobhan found the fact that it carried no markings other than a lengthy alphanumerical sequence on the tail fin unusual.

Commonwealth craft wore roundels, squadron insignia, or regimental badges very openly, to better identify their home unit. Even *Stingray*'s shuttles wore the gray and blue of their mothership's emblem along with the eight-pointed starburst and anchor of the Commonwealth Navy.

Blisters along its hull might have concealed weapons but in all other respects, it looked as harmless as its design seemed ancient.

The interior turned out to be as spare and drab as she expected, with several rows of deep, well-padded seats stuck behind the cockpit. After they and the Mirandan troops had strapped themselves in, the platform on which the craft rested rose up through a rocky shaft and out into the brilliant light of the system's primary.

It lifted off moments later to the vibration of powerful thrusters, breaking free of Ariel Base's crater, and headed for Miranda, a beautiful blue-green orb wrapped in shreds of white cloud.

They spent the trip down to Sanctum mostly in silence. Kalivan and Dunmoore could not discuss much of anything within earshot of the Mirandans, and even Vincenzo remained uncharacteristically quiet, though he examined their escort with as much painstaking attention as he could muster.

After an uncomfortable crossing from Iris, followed by a descent that sometimes felt like they rode the crest of a category five ion storm, they touched down at the military spaceport serving the Dominion's capital.

When she rose from her seat to disembark, Dunmoore felt the subtly stronger pull of Miranda's gravity, which explained why so many of them seemed to have a wider and shorter build than her people.

The air that greeted them, the first they had breathed in months that had not come from a recycler, carried a heady mix of scents. Of course, she could taste the usual metal, ozone, and lubricant common to spaceports across the galaxy, but she also inhaled the aroma of plant life utterly alien to a human nose newly arrived on the planet.

The warmth of the sun felt surprisingly good on her pale face, though an undercurrent of humidity would quickly turn that small pleasure into an annoyance once she began to perspire.

The tarmac, onto which they stepped, boxed in by their escort, lay at the bottom of a narrow valley and seemed to lose itself against the horizon in either direction. Cut into the gray cliff walls on both sides, blank windows and doors seemed to glower in the bright light of Miranda's star while high above, gun and missile emplacements watched over them.

"A bit heavy on the fortifications," Kalivan murmured as they watched a cluster of individuals, all in the same dark Mirandan uniform, emerge from the nearest door and head their way.

"Very similar to their lunar base, I'd say," Dunmoore replied.

"Agreed."

Six of the seven newcomers, three men, and three women, stopped a few meters from the shuttle while the seventh approached them. An older man, he wore the silver insignia with the three fern leaf cluster that Kalivan had provisionally classified as marking the Mirandan equivalent of a general officer, except with an extra four-pointed star at its base, likely making him senior in rank to Trask.

"Colonel Kalivan, Commander Dunmoore." He dipped his head briefly while striking his chest with a closed fist. "I'm Senior Group Leader Borik Nan, chief aide to the Protector of the Dominion."

"Pleased to make your acquaintance, Senior Group Leader," Kalivan replied after returning the salute

Commonwealth-style. "We're honored that someone of your importance has come to greet us."

Butter would not melt in the army officer's mouth, Dunmoore thought, repressing an amused smile.

"Protector Hames is anxious that you be treated with all due honors, Colonel."

Nan sounded equally smooth, a necessary talent when one worked directly for the ruler of two planets, if not yet the entire system.

Dunmoore heard the Ariel Base troopers climb back aboard the shuttle at an unseen signal, their mission accomplished. The well-armed sextet standing patiently behind Nan had taken over.

"If you'll follow me."

He gestured toward the open door at the base of the cliff and then turned on his heel to face the way he would come.

Their new escort fell into step on either side of them, and they quickly left the outdoor warmth behind, stepping into a cool, artificially lit room furnished with nothing more than uncomfortable-looking plastic chairs and tables. It was empty, as were the corridors taking them deeper into the stone rampart.

They came to what Dunmoore thought of as a transport tube station, and she felt gratified to be proved right when automatic doors opened on the flank of a shiny pod sitting hard up against the concrete platform.

"This is part of our protected underground transportation system, Colonel," Nan said once they had followed the guards aboard and the pod began moving. "It connects all parts of Sanctum and is impervious from aerial attack."

"Is aerial attack a frequent problem, Senior Group Leader?" Dunmoore asked in an entirely innocent tone.

Nan hesitated before answering.

"Less so in recent decades. The orbital and lunar defenses protecting Miranda and Sycorax have been quite effective, but xenos who haven't yet learned to keep their distance will appear from time to time and can cause some damage before they're destroyed."

"We've indeed noticed the strength of those defenses." Kalivan nodded. "It would take a foolhardy intruder to risk coming close to your worlds."

"And yet, they come." Nan shrugged. "There's no accounting for how xenos think if they do so at all."

"Have there been any recently? I mean other than us?" She still sounded perfectly innocent.

Nan stared at her, half-surprised, half-suspicious.

"I would hardly qualify you as xenos, Commander. After all, you're human. Your people came from the same original planet as mine, not some alien hellhole."

He frowned as if wondering what Dunmoore meant.

"It's just that we have met many non-human species during our expansion and exploration, and I'm curious as to whether any of those might have come this far." She smiled at him. "As you might have heard, we've been locked into a lengthy interstellar war with a species we call the Shrehari."

"Group Leader Trask has reported this fact to Protector Hames."

Sensing that Nan wanted to avoid answering the question, she motioned at the guards.

"Are your military forces part of a single service comprising both ground and space elements? I notice that uniforms and insignia are the same here as on Ariel Base."

"The Defenders are indeed a single service."

"Trask mentioned something about a Custodian Dalian. Is her service separate from the Defenders?"

"Indeed." Nan nodded. "The Custodians protect from within while the Defenders protect from without."

They felt the pod slow down and Nan, visibly relieved that Dunmoore's attempt at small talk was about to end, rose from his seat.

"We've arrived at the station serving the government precinct."

Still boxed in by their guards, they walked through what seemed endless security stations and down neat, well-lit, but undecorated corridors before climbing a granite staircase. Other than stone-faced sentries, they did not meet anyone, even though Dunmoore had the impression that there were hundreds, if not thousands nearby.

"We've arrived at the Protector's Palace," Nan said when they emerged into a large, high-ceilinged lobby.

Its walls held the first evidence of interior decoration they had seen, mostly images of battles past and people famous enough to have been immortalized.

The marble floor was inlaid with a silver design, a circle enclosing a sword and fern leaf device, the latter similar to the insignia worn by Nan and Trask. Dunmoore had but a few moments to examine the pictures before the aide led them up a winding staircase. Many of the images showed heroic human shapes in battle armor defeating and in some cases beheading non-human creatures of species she could not identify. Charming.

When they reached an equally large lobby on the upper floor, their escort peeled away wordlessly, leaving them alone with the Mirandan officer.

"Please wait here. I will inform Protector Hames that you've arrived." Nan vanished through a large wooden door bearing a replica of the seal she had seen below.

"I'm going to hazard that we're not just under surveillance," Kalivan whispered, leaning over so his lips almost touched her ear, "but that we have hidden weapons trained on us at this very moment."

"No doubt," she replied. "Otherwise, they wouldn't have left the human xenos alone."

"Ah." His eyebrows shot up. "You picked up on their frequent use of that ancient Greek word."

"I'm going to hazard," she said, half mockingly, "that the offspring of *Tempest*'s idealists don't much like strangers, especially those whose ancestors aren't from Mother Earth."

"And not even those very much," he replied before straightening his back when the door opened again.

"The Protector will receive you now. Your aides may stay there." Nan pointed at a settee group at the far end of the landing.

Dunmoore caught Foste's gaze and nodded toward the seats.

"Take a load off, Chief. Shoot the breeze with Vincenzo."

"Sir." The spacers snapped to attention, saluted and did a perfect about turn before marching off.

Siobhan and Kalivan looked at each other, and then the latter shrugged.

"Ready or not, we're on deck, Commander."

The two officers stepped into the most sacred office on Miranda to meet with the man who ruled over this strange and distant offshoot of humanity. Hopefully, they would now get answers to questions that had so far been ignored.

— Seventeen —

Gregor Pushkin, ensconced behind Dunmoore's desk in the privacy of her ready room, glowered at Kowalski, his jaw muscles working in silence. He knew she was not at fault, but he did not feel like hiding his annoyance at the captain's foolhardiness.

"Well," he finally said, "at least she took escorts."

"Vincenzo wouldn't have let her go without him in any case, sir."

The first officer snorted.

"Ain't that the truth? However, we now have our two senior officers on the surface of Miranda, or damn near there, and well beyond our ability to ensure their safety. Brilliant."

"I don't know that they're in any danger, sir. Granted, they shot at us when we first showed up, but that could have been on general principles. They treated us well down on that lunar base, though I'll say they have an obvious paranoid streak. No one wanted to talk about anything more than the weather without permission from HQ. And their reaction to what we told them? Very bizarre."

"How so?" Curiosity replaced Pushkin's earlier annoyance, and he waved at a chair. "Sit, for heaven's sake. This isn't a chewing out by the first officer."

"A couple of things struck me, other than the obvious one concerning the discrepancy between their timeline and ours. First among them being the looks on their faces when we told them we'd made peaceful contact with some non-human species. Although we did mention that the Shrehari aren't on our most favored alien list these days. I got the feeling that this isn't a safe part of the galaxy from their point of view, hence the impressive defenses. The other big thing is how some of them, including one senior guy, seemed to be displeased with our presence as if they have a faction that isn't keen on a family reunion."

"Which would explain the bunch still shooting after we'd open communications." The first officer nodded.

"But the one thing that I found a little disconcerting concerned technology. The greed in their eyes when we described FTL travel, the general principles behind antimatter reactors and the rest of it almost gave me the willies. They've stagnated for a long time, even though they must have received the visit of FTL-capable civilizations to warrant this kind of military buildup. I got the feeling that they'll want us to share everything so they can bootstrap themselves into an interstellar civilization."

"Which we can't, by law, do without permission from the Grand Admiral, even though these folks are human and not technobarbarian aliens."

Kowalski nodded.

"It'll be an interesting diplomatic problem for Kalivan and the captain. The one area where they have us beat is emcon, which would fit in with a civilization susceptible to off-world predation. When I think of how Earth used to broadcast far and wide back in the day, waving a big 'we're here' flag, not realizing the dangers..."

"Hindsight is a beautiful thing." Pushkin chuckled. "Lucky for us, the only FTL civilization within reach happened to be the Shrehari, and they were too busy rebuilding an empire after their latest crash into the long, dark night of barbarism."

"The Mirandans might not have been so lucky."

"That seems pretty likely, all things considered. Short of having a big enough power source to go forth, they developed extreme stealth." He sighed. "That being said, I guess I should have figured the captain would go along with the Mirandan invitation to meet with their leader, but I'd be a lot happier if we were in contact with the landing party. We had a few tense moments when you vanished from our sensors after you dropped below that moon's surface."

"Well," Kowalski tried an innocent look that did not fool Pushkin, "I may have semi-inadvertently given us a means to track the Captain and Colonel Kalivan."

"Semi-inadvertently? Kathryn, you never do anything by accident."

"Okay. On purpose then." She smiled.

She explained about the data recorders taken from engineering bots.

"The things have a tracking module as well. I didn't think we'd need to use that functionality and didn't tell the captain because I figured she or the colonel might take exception, seeing as how this is a diplomatic mission. As long as they're not in a Faraday cage or deep underground, we should be able to find them with active scanning, though that might trigger Mirandan sensors. In passive mode, they should show up as long as they're on the surface."

"It's better than nothing. Well done."

"Of course, it would help if we were allowed to occupy a lower orbit."

"At this point, I'm more comfortable with what they gave us. There's too much we still don't know and the more maneuvering room, the better."

Kowalski's eyebrows shot up.

"You're expecting trouble?"

"Always." A wry smile relaxed Pushkin's face. "A good first officer looks for it everywhere."

He was about to elaborate when the intercom chimed.

"Speaking of which." He touched the controls. "First officer here."

"Sir, it's Chief Penzara. Rownes has picked up something you might want to know about sooner rather than later."

"On my way." He chuckled as he cut the link and stood. "Trouble showing up on cue again."

Once on the bridge, he made his way to the sensor station and looked over Petty Officer Rownes' shoulder.

"What have you got?"

"I was purging the sensor log when I came across a ghost just beyond the orbit of the outermost planet." She called up the data. "If I were a betting woman, I'd call that a starship dropping out of FTL."

"What Rownes calls ghosts," Penzara said, "invariably end up being the real deal. I think we may have company."

"Nothing else, of course, or you'd have mentioned it," Pushkin said in a thoughtful tone, "which means it might be someone running silent. I wish we could ask the Mirandans if they often get that kind of intruder, but I'm afraid we'll get their version of no comment. Ask navigation to plot a most likely course for something heading toward us and then concentrate some of our resources on that area of space."

"Shall I warn our hosts?" Kowalski asked.

"No." Pushkin shook his head. "Not yet. For one thing, I don't want them to know we can detect things that far out and for another…"

His voice trailed off with uncertainty.

"And for another?" Kowalski prompted.

"I don't know." The first officer shook his head. "Let's just keep an eye outward and see what happens."

He slowly walked over to the command chair and sat, still lost in thought.

"And continue looking for whatever the Mirandans are keeping quiet in our vicinity."

"Don't trust 'em, do you, Mister Pushkin?" Penzara grinned over his shoulder at the first officer. "Can't say I blame you. Folks that deeply into stealth have stuff to hide from honest spacers like us."

*

The gray-haired man who rose from behind a large, bare desk to greet them wore the dark uniform they had begun to recognize as Mirandan standard, but his seemed wholly unadorned. No silver fern leaves or other devices relieved its sobriety. He examined Kalivan and Dunmoore silently for a few seconds, then essayed a brief smile.

"Welcome to Miranda. I'm Protector Cyrus Hames."

"Thank you for receiving us, sir. I'm Wes Kalivan, Commonwealth envoy, and this is Siobhan Dunmoore, captain of the Commonwealth frigate *Stingray*."

Hames came out from behind the polished marble slab and gestured toward a cluster of chairs to one side.

"I think we'll be more comfortable there."

He saw Dunmoore's eyes widen slightly in surprise as she gauged the thickness of the windows and walls, and his smile returned.

"It seems somewhat formidable, doesn't it?"

"That would be an understatement, sir. We've noticed that Miranda is remarkably well defended."

Hames sighed as they sat.

"We have a rather complicated history and parts of it are somewhat obscure even to us after all this time."

He seemed to search for his next words with great care.

"As you would know from your own history, our forebears did not intend to set up their colony in this system or anywhere in this area of the galaxy, for that matter. At first, the colony thrived, but then, after many centuries of peaceful existence, the first xenos appeared above Miranda and attacked. There's not much in the records describing the incident. Apparently, we suffered widespread destruction at the time, but it left a lasting scar on our society, one that deepened with each new attack over the following centuries. Many died, some were taken, never to be seen again, and the xenos damaged our technological base to the point where our survival came into doubt. By then, we'd abandoned all notion of space travel, being content with the bounty Miranda offered and had settled happily into an agrarian society with only enough technology to allow a decent life for all."

"It's not an unknown course of events for early colonies, sir."

"Perhaps, Colonel." A wry expression softened Hames' tired features. "But we were alone here, forgotten and isolated. I daresay the colonists who reached their appointed destinations enjoyed some support from Earth, especially once faster-than-light travel became possible."

"You are, of course, correct." Kalivan inclined his head.

"So much we know," Hames continued. "Our records get clearer after we abandoned our founding ideals four centuries ago and concentrated on survival in what we now perceived to be a very hostile universe. The xeno incursions didn't abate, but as we gained cunning and strength, they became less fatal for us and more lethal for them. We abandoned the pastoral underpinnings of our ancestors and ruthlessly modernized, regaining much of what our forebears had left back on the mother world: industry, high technology, armaments, and the idea of military defenses.

Much of our vital infrastructure went underground, to protect it, while we reinforced what remained above ground. You've noticed this office's windows. They're built to withstand anything short of a direct nuclear strike on the Protector's Palace. So it is around Miranda and our outposts on Sycorax and the moons."

"Your defenses are impressive, as are your ships."

"And yet yours is even more impressive, Commander. My advisers tell me you could likely have inflicted a lot of damage on our forces had you been minded to do so. I must thank you for your restraint in the face of the aggression shown by some of our more zealous commanders. Rest assured their animus came purely from the desire to ensure no Mirandan suffers what our ancestors suffered. We entered into a considerable debate as to whether or not we open communications with you, a debate still far from over. History has shown us the need for utter self-reliance and complete distrust of outsiders."

"Understood, sir."

"The one thing that tipped the scales in favor of meeting with you stems from your use of FTL technology, something we knew existed based on the xeno vessels that trespassed into our system. We've never been able to duplicate the capability. Not that we captured many intact enough to study in any case."

"Though the theory for FTL travel had already been enunciated by the time *Tempest* left," Dunmoore said, "we weren't yet able to do anything with it. Someone had to come up with a portable source of energy powerful enough to warp space-time and create the hyperspace bubble which allows a starship to travel many times the speed of light."

"So our scientists have surmised." Hames nodded. "Your vessel indeed appears to ride on an immense reservoir of power, much bigger than most, if not quite all xenos who've intruded into our space."

Neither Kalivan nor Dunmoore missed the acquisitive spark that had appeared deep within Hames' eyes, matching that of Trask's officers on Ariel Base, though he had schooled his face to remain conspicuously bland.

"We can certainly share knowledge," Kalivan said, "but we don't have any scientists aboard who could explain the underlying principles of our reactors and drives. As you may have surmised, we're on a voyage of exploration."

A brief spark of irritation tightened the Mirandan's face, extinguished the moment it appeared. Dunmoore suppressed a smile, privately cheering Kalivan's smooth equivocation.

"Surely the little you might provide would still be an enormous step forward for us, Colonel."

"Of course. We would be happy to share what we can. After all, we cannot leave fellow humans at the mercy of aggressive species."

Hames seemed to relax just a bit at his reply and Dunmoore's earlier pleasure at her companion's diplomacy vanished. Many things concerning *Stingray* could not and would not be shared with anyone outside the Navy, not even humans in need of a technological leg up.

History had recorded too many instances where giving societies without FTL technology access to the stars had ended badly. The Mirandans were not as backward as some of the non-humans who went from barbarism to interstellar space without the intervening step of civilization. However, something about the pervasive, if not oppressive militarism and naked aggression she sensed disturbed her.

However, that discussion would have to wait until she and Kalivan could speak without being overheard.

The latter must have sensed her sudden unease because he nodded toward her and said, "I'm sure there will be restrictions as you'll understand. Commander Dunmoore is at the mercy of our Navy's orders as well, but once we establish permanent relations between Miranda and the Commonwealth, I'm sure our government will be happy to offer all the expertise you need."

"Yes." Hames nodded. "Of course."

They heard a knock at the door, and Nan's face briefly appeared.

"Protector, the others have arrived."

"Excellent. Colonel, Commander, in a moment you'll meet the three people who form my Inner Council."

"Group Leader Trask mentioned them," Kalivan replied. "The heads of your armed forces, your security forces, and your legislature."

"Indeed and here they are."

Hames climbed to his feet, followed swiftly by his guests when a man in uniform, with four silver leaves on his chest entered. He and Hames seemed hewn from the same granite, and Dunmoore guessed the Protector had probably come to his current job via the military.

A middle-aged woman with deep-set blue eyes, a square, strong-jawed face, and raven black hair entered hard on his heels. She wore a gray uniform with black insignia, but it resembled the black version in all other respects.

The last to enter, a man whose apparent softness contrasted with his steely gaze, wore civilian clothes, but even they seemed vaguely military.

"Colonel Kalivan, Commander Dunmoore may I introduce Chief Defender Martell, Chief Custodian Dalian, and Speaker Marant."

Both officers snapped to attention, and Kalivan briefly dipped his head.

"Honored to meet you."

Dunmoore looked up to see Mira Dalian eying her intently, almost hungrily, and repressed a shiver.

"So these are the envoys of an Earth that aged three and a half centuries to our twenty," Dalian mused, "and in that short time, they've outstripped us by such a wide margin. Hopefully, we'll be able to rectify that little problem very quickly."

"Don't be so impatient, Mira," Marant chided. "They've only just arrived."

"Who knows when the next xeno incursion will come?"

"Already bored with the last one?" Geoff Martell asked as Hames bade them sit around a table while his aide served something that reminded Siobhan of herbal tea.

"You've had a recent attack?" Dunmoore asked.

"Not an attack as such," Dalian replied. "They didn't get a chance to wreak any damage. The Defenders seized them by surprise and very quickly, but they managed to destroy the innards of their ship. A new species. Thoroughly ugly and unable to speak in anything more than loud grunts."

Siobhan noticed that Hames and Marant seemed less than pleased at Dalian's revelations and wondered why. The woman's expression, however, had not changed. She still examined Siobhan with interest that bordered on the uncomfortable.

"Perhaps Commander Dunmoore knows the species and how to deal with it," she added.

"I thought we'd decided not to bore our visitors with our xeno problems, Mira." Hames' tone caught Dalian short.

"Has the Protector given you an overview of our history?" Martell asked. "Otherwise, our aversion to outsiders would not make much sense to those who haven't fought to survive on Miranda these last centuries."

"A very brief one," Kalivan replied. "Perhaps not enough to seize the full import of your past vulnerability to aggressive outsiders."

Martell chuckled.

"Protector Hames always strove to be a master of understatement. It's a trait a lot of us will miss when his term is over."

"Oh?"

"My ten years end in a few months, Colonel."

Dunmoore sensed, from his tone, that he ardently wished for that day to come soon.

"Then another will shoulder the burden of keeping the Dominion and its people safe."

"Has that individual been identified?" Kalivan asked.

"No." Marant shook his head. "The Two Hundred are still deliberating."

"Back to our history," Martell said. "I think our guests won't understand who we are now unless they know how we got to where we are."

"The xeno attacks," Dunmoore said.

"Just so." Hames nodded. "Vulnerability is what defined us once xenos shattered the illusion of a peaceful, pastoral existence, never to recover. It defines us politically, militarily, security-wise, architecturally, socially — in every domain imaginable. In fact, our fear and distrust of outsiders are so deeply ingrained that even you, fellow humans, would be considered xenos by a large proportion of Mirandans. You are not of us and thus strangers to be kept at bay."

"Hence Protector Hames' earlier remark that the debate about opening communications with us remains unresolved."

"Indeed." Mira Dalian said. "And if the general public were to find out that off-worlders, even human ones, had been received by the Protector and his government, we might experience severe social problems, perhaps even riots. You and your crew certainly wouldn't be safe. If not for the iron discipline among Defenders when it comes to keeping military secrets, I daresay we'd already hear crowds baying outside. We do have fringe elements whose views are rather extreme."

"Our Custodian is exaggerating just a bit," Marant interjected.

"A lot even." Martell stared at his internal security counterpart with hard eyes.

"But she has a point," the Speaker continued. "News that the humanity our ancestors left behind has reached out to gather us back into the fold will be disturbing. It will be especially disruptive for those where the myth of our ancestors escaping an Earth gone to perdition remains very much alive. Worse yet, the news that this humanity has developed the power and technology to straddle the stars with impunity, whereas we've suffered again and again under the onslaught of semi-feral creatures, will cause strong resentment."

Dunmoore could sense the man's barely suppressed hunger for knowledge that would bootstrap the Mirandans to interstellar power status. It seemed as powerful as Dalian's soul-searching stare.

She felt a sudden pang of longing for her ship and the familiar faces of her crew rather than these strangers who wanted — wanted what? Reunification with humanity? The means to become a second interstellar power in their own right?

"We would be more than pleased to share our scientific advances with our Mirandan brothers and sisters."

Kalivan's tone remained as smooth and soothing as ever.

"And as soon as we get home, we'll arrange for a delegation of qualified people to come here and teach you all we know. It would please my government to welcome

Miranda back into the embrace of humanity among the stars."

"With the caution that since we're at war with the Shrehari Empire these days, resources are, as you'll understand, mostly committed to the fight," Dunmoore added.

"You have your own xeno problems then?" Dalian seemed to perk up.

"Very much so. The Shrehari are a tenacious species. Very warlike and aggressive. It came as a surprise because we'd been at peace for a long time after the initial clash when we first made contact. However, they're the most advanced and largest non-human polity in this part of the galaxy. Most of the others are small enough to keep the peace, either out of trade interest, disinterest in other species or," Siobhan smiled, "because they don't wish to feel the weight of our Navy's guns."

"You tolerate peaceful contact, trade even, with non-humans?" Marant sounded surprised. "Now there's something that we must make sure doesn't become general knowledge. It's considered a capital crime on Miranda."

Kalivan's smile seemed to freeze in place. Dunmoore had no such diplomatic qualms. Her eyebrows shot up in disbelief, but she refrained from speaking long enough for her common sense to catch up with her mouth.

"I'm sure our historians will find your past fascinating," the colonel said after carefully parsing every possible response that flitted through his mind. "You say you didn't come upon non-human sentient lifeforms until you were brutally assaulted by off-worlders several centuries after your arrival?"

An awkward moment of silence followed Kalivan's question.

"Indeed." Hames finally nodded. "The first few raids made off with several hundred, if not thousands of ours, taken captive. The Creator only knows what became of them."

"Slavers." Dunmoore made an exaggerated grimace. "We've got standing orders to kill those on sight, and yet some still think it worth the risk to capture humans."

"Proper rules," Hames approved. "Perhaps you're not so different from us, merely powerful enough to keep the xeno rabble in its place."

"And yet we're at war with one of them and not winning anytime soon. Neither are they, but there you have it." Siobhan shrugged. "Keeping the Shrehari in their place isn't about to happen, big, bony, snarly brutes that they are. I've fought some of them, and they're good warriors, some excellent even. They even have a sense of honor we humans can appreciate."

"Xenos with a sense of honor?" Marant shook his head. "Wondrous things happen in your part of the galaxy, Commander."

"Describe these Shrehari, please," Dalian asked, her eyes narrowing in thought.

"Humanoid in most respects, larger than average humans, very bony features, leathery, olive skin..." Dunmoore went on to describe them in detail, both physically and what she knew of their behavioral patterns.

"They sound positively dreadful," the Custodian said when Siobhan fell silent. "It's no wonder you're fighting them."

"I'd rather have them agree to an armistice and pull back into their own sphere. Too many have died for no reason."

"Surely fighting xenos who wish you harm isn't for nothing?" Martell asked.

Dunmoore decided to concede the point. The discussion and their obsession with off-worlders had begun to grate on her nerves.

"Granted, Chief Defender."

"Perhaps we should ask our guests to give us an overview of Earth history," Hames suggested, equally desirous to change the subject, "especially the time after our ancestors left."

"Certainly," Kalivan's smile relaxed. Then, without waiting for any further inducements, he launched through the turbulent decades of the first mass exodus to what had become the core systems, the First Migration War that ended Earth's domination over its colonies and the subsequent creation of the Commonwealth. He described the second wave of colonization and the ensuing war of independence fought between the younger colonies and their mother worlds, the older colonies. Then came the first contact with non-human species and the first Shrehari War. He ended with a description of the government structure while Dunmoore gave an overview of the Armed Services.

When they fell silent, what seemed like hours later, the four Mirandans appeared overwhelmed by the information.

"My thanks, Envoy Kalivan. You've certainly given us a lot to consider."

"My pleasure, Protector."

"Would it be possible to get a copy of your historical database?" Martell asked.

"If you could point Commander Dunmoore at something she can use to talk to her ship, she'll be happy to satisfy your curiosity."

"Perhaps later." Hames rose, swiftly followed by the others. "For now, it would be only right to offer you the chance to rest. You'll be staying in the palace of course. I've convened a small reception for the evening meal in a few hours, to include some of our senior officials from the Defenders and Custodians, as well as the Deputy Speaker."

"Very kind of you, Protector." Kalivan inclined his head. When he looked up again, Borik Nan had entered the room.

"If you'll follow me," he said, "I will lead you to your quarters."

"Until later," Hames smiled briefly.

"Until then, sir."

*

When the door had closed behind the visitors, Hames invited his inner circle to sit again.

"That was ... illuminating is one way to describe it," he said.

"They seem entirely too tolerant of xenos," Dalian made a disgusted face, "except for those Shrehari, which, I suspect is what I have in my cells right now."

"The thought had occurred to me, but I still think it wise to keep the Earthers away from them for the moment."

"As you wish." Her tone skirted insubordination, but her nod showed sufficient respect, if not for the man, then for the office he held.

"Is it just me," Martell asked, "or are they reluctant to discuss technology with us? They seemed free enough with words when it came to other subjects."

"Why should they trip over themselves with offers of riches?" The Speaker shrugged. "We're a speck in space compared to the might of their Commonwealth."

"And that, my dear Gano is precisely why we need to attain their level as fast as possible," Dalian said. "If their leaders decide to send a fleet of ships like *Stingray* to reattach us to a humanity that has developed values diametrically opposed to ours, it would be the end of the Dominion. That is the one thing we cannot allow."

"Considering the distance, why should they bother?" Martell asked.

"Perhaps Mira is worried that the Earthers might take away her chance at serving the Dominion as its next Protector, or perhaps the one after that," Marant replied, a mischievous grin taking the sting out of his words.

She snorted derisively.

"That would be the very least of my worries. No, what I fear is the loss of our ability to dictate whatever terms we want to the universe at large and deal in whatever way we wish with all those who dare trespass into our space. You heard them speak about their two civil wars, both designed to keep independence-minded worlds shackled to their central government. We cannot afford to share that fate, and without their technology…"

"It always strikes me as wrong when I have to say this," Martell sighed, "but Mira has a point."

"Then the question is what do we do about it?" Hames suddenly seemed exhausted.

"I've got a few suggestions," Dalian replied, "but they'll take us down a path from which there will likely be no return."

"As long as we preserve the Dominion."

— Eighteen —

Foste and Vincenzo sprang to their feet the moment Kalivan and Dunmoore emerged from Protector Hames' office.

Nan glanced over his shoulder at the two officers. "We've of course provided adjacent quarters for your aides."

"Very gracious of you, sir." Dunmoore essayed a quick smile at the dour Mirandan and then nodded at her crewmembers. "We're staying here at least overnight, folks. There's a reception later where the colonel and I will meet some more of this planet's movers and shakers."

"Very good, sir." Foste took the new situation in stride. "Will someone be communicating this back to Mister Pushkin?"

"I'm sure the good senior group leader can point me at a commo unit, Chief. Besides, we've promised our hosts a download of the historical database."

"I shall inquire, Commander," Nan replied, leading the way down the winding staircase.

Once back in the vast lobby, Dunmoore stopped at an image that showed a yellowish-green creature being hacked to death by peasants armed with nothing more than farm tools. Something about it struck her as odd. She glanced at the neighboring pictures and saw variations on the same theme.

"May I ask what manner of creature this species is?"

Nan stopped and turned to stare at her.

"We call those Skraeling. They've not bothered us in a long time, Commander. Now if you'll please follow me."

Kalivan and Dunmoore exchanged a glance, the former's eyes promising questions the moment they were alone.

They took one of the corridors radiating outward like the spokes of a wheel and soon enough, Nan ushered them through a door into a simply furnished, windowless sitting room.

"This suite shall be yours for the duration of your visit." He pointed at a pair of closed doors to the right. "The quarters reserved for you are to that side, Colonel and yours, Commander are the ones beside it. Your aides have the ones opposite. One of the junior officers will collect you for the reception in three hours. If you require anything, use the communications panel set into the side table. Please remain here, for your own safety. I will inquire about updating your ship of your status."

With a final nod, he vanished, the door slamming shut with the kind of finality that spoke of a heavy and very secure lock.

Dunmoore gave her companions a warning glance, and then stared significantly at Foste. The bosun pulled a small hand-held sensor from her pocket and thumbed the screen, keeping it as well hidden as she could in the palm of her large hand.

After a moment, she nodded and tugged on her left earlobe. A scowl twisted Vincenzo's bushy mustache but he took his petty officer's warning to heart and swallowed whatever questions he might have had.

"I'll unpack your things, Captain," he said instead, holding up her overnight bag. "If you'll slip out of your uniform for a few minutes, I'll set it to rights for a reception."

"Thank you." She smiled at him and unfastened her tunic before disappearing into one of the two VIP bedrooms.

Kalivan winked at Foste when she handed him his valise. "I'll sort myself out like the ground pounder I am, Chief. No need to trouble the lad."

Then he left the bosun standing in the middle of the thick rug, wondering what fresh devilment awaited them. After a few moments, she shrugged soundlessly and inspected the quarters set aside for her and Vincenzo.

When Kalivan emerged from his room, looking refreshed, Siobhan glanced up from her tablet and met his gaze. She then looked up at the ceiling and tugged her earlobe once, to remind him the walls had ears. He nodded.

"Rather fancy digs."

"It is the residence of their head of state," she replied, smiling. "One would expect a modicum of luxury, even on a planet that seems to have made militarism a virtue."

"By necessity, as we must always remember." He dropped into one of the plush chairs. "You seemed quite taken by some of the images in the lobby."

"Not so much taken as intrigued."

"Oh?"

"Compared to some of the others, I'd venture those represent the very earliest days of the colony's xeno problems."

He thought about that statement for a few moments.

Foste, who had heard Dunmoore's last few words as she appeared on the other side of the common area, said, "That's what I figured as well, Captain. Shovels and hoes aren't exactly high-tech weaponry. Those creatures, I think Mister Nan called them Skraeling, didn't exactly look like they were better armed. Worse, likely. Can't wrap my head around them coming off FTL starships to raid for slaves."

A look of understanding lit up Kalivan's eyes and Siobhan nodded.

"I had the same thought, Wes."

"Puts yet another slant on all we've heard and seen so far. Of course, like all such iconography, it could be allegorical."

"If it were allegorical, I think we might have seen heroic colonists fighting off well-armed Skraeling," Foste suggested.

"I think your bosun's nailed it, Siobhan, though I suggest that it might be something we don't discuss with our hosts at this point."

"Why not? They make no bones about their aversion to non-humans."

"Still, let's not broach the subject," he said in a mild tone, though Dunmoore and Foste knew an order from the senior Commonwealth officer on Miranda when they heard it.

"Changing the subject," Kalivan continued, "did you speak to your first officer yet?"

"The ever helpful Nan assured me that Defender HQ had passed the word of our extended stay to *Stingray*."

His eyebrows shot up, but since Siobhan seemed quite sanguine about the situation, he let the matter pass.

"Where's the youngest of our party," he asked Foste.

"Sleeping. He's thoroughly internalized the old bosun's rule that you catch your winks whenever you have a few minutes to spare."

"Wise practice. We have the same in the army, but I find myself too old for catnaps these days."

Dunmoore pointed at a stack of tablets on the low table.

"Help yourselves. A young lady with no silver on her uniform came by while the two of you were otherwise busy and dropped off some entertainment, as well as a few drinks and nibblies."

"Anything good?" Kalivan reached over and took one of the large portable computers.

"If you mean the catering, I don't know. There's nothing alcoholic that I could tell, and I'm not particularly hungry right now. The water's nice and cold, though."

"I meant the entertainment."

"Well-curated is the term I'd use. There's little here to give us an in-depth glimpse into their society, at least not overtly, though I'm sure someone like Kathryn Kowalski could tease out many disconnected elements and assemble them into a useful intelligence precis. The articles on geography and nature seem more in-depth, but no mention of the planet Sycorax. Nor is there any mention of a native species that might be linked to these Skraeling," she added, forestalling the inevitable question.

"Why would they hide stuff from us, Captain?" Foste also picked up a tablet and absently turned it over in her hands.

"We're xenos of a sort as well, from their point of view, and thus not to be trusted, I'd say. It can't be easy for them to absorb the notion that there are billions of other humans out there, who have more advanced tech and who don't consider non-humans as automatic foes."

The bosun snorted. "Good thing we didn't grow horns or tails in the time since *Tempest* left Earth."

She wandered over to the food table and picked up a bottle, passing its opening under her nose.

"Juice of some sort." Foste did the same with the remainder and turned back toward the officers. "Captain's right. Nothing with ethanol."

A glimmer of unexpected mischief shone in Kalivan's eyes. "Disappointed?"

"Bosun's tradition, Colonel. Come to a new port, you taste what the locals brew or distill."

"Perhaps the Mirandans are teetotalers."

"God forbid, sir. It'll be a long visit down here if that's the case."

*

"How kind of them to tell us the envoy and his party would be enjoying the Protector's hospitality for a few days," Pushkin murmured when the transmission ended.

The officer who had contacted them, a senior group leader by the name of Nan, had been most correct but had stalled any effort on their part when it came to speaking with Dunmoore directly.

"I hope they brought a few changes of underwear," Devall remarked from the first officer's station. "I doubt they'll allow us to send a resupply run to the surface."

Pushkin ignored the second officer and, fingers drumming impatiently on the arm of the command chair, turned to Kowalski.

"Have you tracked their signal yet?"

"Negative. I've had nothing since they landed and vanished into another Faraday cage. Those Mirandans are experts when it comes to emcon. The sensors will pick the trackers up the moment they emerge out in the open again, but until then, unless you want to go active..."

The first officer stared at the image of Miranda filling one of the side screens and frowned. If something happened to Dunmoore and the others, it would be the devil's own work to extract them, or would be if she had not invoked General Order Eighty-One. Not that he would obey if he saw the slightest chance. When he looked back at the main tactical display, the coxswain caught his eye.

"Sir, if you're thinking what I figure you're thinking, maybe you can authorize me to prepare a few things. That is if Mister Kowalski is available as well." He kept his voice low, pitched only at Pushkin.

Guthren had spent a few years in special operations before returning to a line ship, specially sent aboard *Stingray* to watch Dunmoore's back when she first took command. If anyone on the frigate knew about extractions, he would.

"If you're proposing to disobey the captain, then you have my authorization."

"Getting nervous in the service?" Devall had overheard the byplay, but when Pushkin and Guthren glanced at him, they did not see the slightest hint of mockery in his eyes. "If so, welcome to the club. In the last day or so, I've been feeling like the main course at an all you can eat buffet on Shrehari Prime."

"Glad I'm not the only one with latent paranoia, Trevane. Let's prepare for the worst and hope for the best. For all we know the Mirandans could be the sweetest, most peaceful folks in the universe."

Kowalski snorted softly.

"Having met those sweet, peaceful folks, I'd say prepare for a fight but hope that they'll stay scared of our guns. Something has been bothering me about their rank nomenclature from the get-go, so I ran a few searches through the historical database. Guess what I came up with?"

"Do tell." The faintly amused smile that usually adorned Devall's refined, aristocratic features had returned.

"They're very similar to those used by an extremely nasty pre-spaceflight Earth dictatorship."

"I think I know the one you mean," Pushkin said, shaking his head. "Early to mid-twentieth century Europe. I hope that was coincidental, something a bunch of former pacifists came up with to describe functions for what must have been a complete novelty to them, a defense force built from scratch, and not as an intentional way to emulate that particular bit of history."

"If I recall the history of that era, it didn't turn out well for the folks in question."

"It didn't turn out well for a pretty big chunk of humanity."

"I did get a pretty strong whiff of xenophobia from the Mirandans," Kowalski pointed out. "Coincidence? Perhaps. But I'm more inclined to pull out Ockham's razor."

"Among competing hypotheses, the one with the fewest assumptions should be selected?" Devall asked. "I'd say that maybe you're making more assumptions than a simpler answer requires."

"In this particular game, it all depends on which square you begin," she retorted, "and I'm standing on the one that says 'firsthand knowledge.' How about you?"

Devall waved at the tactical schematic.

"Considering we're all but boxed in by their defenses…"

"And that's only what we can find." Pushkin's glum expression reflected all of their views.

*

The main door to the common room opened to reveal a splendidly attired female officer whose dark uniform dripped with decorations, including an intricately knotted cord dangling from the right shoulder. She raised her closed fist to her chest.

"I'm Bannerman Jhain, junior aide to the Protector," she announced. "I've been given the honor of escorting you to the reception hall."

"If I've got the general gist of their system," Kalivan whispered in Dunmoore's ear, "it sounds like the lady's at your rank." Then, more loudly, "Please lead the way, Bannerman."

She stepped aside to let them out of the room but held up her hand when Foste and Vincenzo attempted to follow.

"Your aides may remain here. There will be no need for their services tonight."

Dunmoore looked back at the bosun and Vincenzo, having correctly guessed that the order would annoy them. The latter's face already reflected an intent to argue with Jhain when Foste put a hand on his shoulder.

"Easy, lad. The captain and Mister Kalivan will be all right."

Though the words seemed directed at Vincenzo, her eyes locked with the Mirandan officer's until she nodded.

"Of course. The Protector's Palace is the safest enclosure on the planet."

"We'll see you later," Dunmoore said before following Jhain and Kalivan down the silent hallway, aware of her crew's stare following them until she heard the door to the suite slam shut.

Jhain remained silent throughout their trek back to the lobby and down a different corridor. Both Dunmoore and Kalivan briefly examined the pictures adorning the walls as they passed through, this time in light of their earlier discussion.

Foste's words still rang in her ears, as they did in his, judging by the expression on his face when their eyes met. She saw something uncanny in those images, something that disturbed her deeply.

A murmur of voices replaced the stillness of the palace when Jhain led them around a corner. There, in full splendor, they found what seemed to be the entire Mirandan general staff, dark uniforms spangled with silver and gray uniforms decorated in black, and not a single civilian suit to be seen. Even Speaker Marant wore a uniform of sorts. At their appearance, a hush fell over the large, windowless hall and almost a hundred pairs of eyes turned on the newcomers.

"Colonel Wes Kalivan, of the Commonwealth Army, Envoy to Miranda," Jhain announced in a clear alto, "and Commander Siobhan Dunmoore, of the Commonwealth Navy ship *Stingray*."

Protector Hames broke away from a knot of senior officers and waved them over.

"Welcome." He nodded politely. "May I introduce you to our most senior Defenders and Custodians?"

Dunmoore hoped Kowalski's recorder worked because she would not be able to remember all the names to save her life.

Kalivan seemed to be in his element, however, a pleasant smile on his even features, eyes twinkling, gestures controlled. When they had gone around the room, a soldier in a white tunic approached them with a tray holding long-stemmed glasses filled with some dark liquid. It turned out to be wine with a particular ethanol content and fullness that stimulated all too many taste buds.

"I think Chief Foste will be glad when we tell her about this," Kalivan remarked in an aside to Siobhan.

"Your aide, Envoy?" Martell asked.

"Indeed, sir."

The head of the Defenders chuckled softly.

"Under-officers are the same no matter where, aren't they?"

"We call them petty officers," Dunmoore smiled at him, "but yes, they are. How did you know she's an under-officer?"

"One can tell, Commander. One can always tell." He gestured around the room with his glass. "Don't let this assemblage of all that glitters in the Dominion impress you. Though some would have it otherwise, there are only four who really count, and you've already met them in a smaller setting. A little hold-over from the years of darkness when we struggled to survive and our ancestors' vision for Miranda died."

"What about the Two Hundred?" Kalivan asked.

Martell shrugged.

"Other than the power to name the four, they have little to do with the day-to-day management of our government institutions, although even that power is often contested."

"And your people don't seek a greater say in who runs things?"

"Some. We've always had dissenters. Most understand that the ponderous democracy of our ancestors can't keep them safe in a hostile galaxy. Some even believe it almost led to our extinction. Professional politicians arguing while xenos pillage and plunder isn't something we wish to contemplate ever again."

"It seems to me we could use some of that thinking to ream out the sewers on Earth," Dunmoore muttered, loud enough only for Kalivan to hear.

"I beg your pardon?" Martell asked.

"Commander Dunmoore was lamenting the fact that our institutions lacked the decisiveness and unity of command yours seem to have in the face of existential threats," he replied with a small, deprecating smile.

"Ah yes, your war against these Shrehari." The Chief Defender nodded knowingly. "It's not a perfect system by any means, but it has served us well enough. Miranda has been essentially xeno-free for generations."

"Even of Skraeling?" Dunmoore's innocent expression almost made Kalivan choke on a sip of the heady Mirandan wine.

Martell contemplated her for a few moments, his jaw muscles working, and then he shrugged.

"We've never been able to eradicate all of them, I fear," he replied. "Some feral groups still roam the less accessible parts of the planet, but they've not been a threat for a long time. I suppose you saw the images in the lobby."

When she nodded, he continued.

"I keep telling Cyrus that it's time to put them in storage. There's something faintly obscene in their portrayal of our ancestors."

Siobhan wanted to ask a follow-on question but caught Kalivan's warning glance.

"You mentioned recently captured xenos earlier," she said instead. "Would it be possible to see them? I'd be interested to find out if we know them. If an unfriendly species is venturing into unclaimed space between Miranda and the Commonwealth, my superiors would surely like to know, as you might appreciate."

"Indeed." Martell stared into his glass for a second or two before looking up again. "Xeno affairs are in the remit of Mira Dalian and her Custodians. She would have to ask permission from the Protector."

"I understand," Kalivan replied, giving Dunmoore an unmistakable if non-verbal order to stop pursuing the xeno angle.

She felt her old rebellious streak rise up at his caution, but Protector Hames forestalled her imminent disobedience by inviting them to follow him into the dining room.

"How did it go, Captain?" Foste asked, looking up from her tablet when Dunmoore and Kalivan entered the suite hours later.

"Like any formal dinner full of flag and general officers in resplendent finery." She unfastened her tunic and shrugged it off. Vincenzo wordlessly took the garment to her bedroom. "I found the food interesting, but I suspect that for Mirandan palates, it was the usual officer's mess chow. They have potent potables, by the way. Not bad either."

"I know," the bosun replied, pointing at a table by the door. "The palace flunkies left us some bottles along with our supper, so I can cross that item off my list. Any good tidbits fall into your ears?"

"We now know that the Skraeling, those yellow-green creatures getting hacked to death by hoes and axes in the lobby pictures are, or rather were a species native to Miranda," Kalivan said. "Although my dinner companion didn't come out and say it in so many words, I gather they were sentient or at least semi-sentient. When the first off-world xeno incursions happened, something triggered a change in the colonists' policy toward them, and they're no more than perhaps a few isolated packs in the darkest corners of the planet."

Dunmoore snorted loudly.

"Oh, so it's fine for you to pursue the matter, but not me?"

"My dear Siobhan," he smiled at her, "it's all a matter of waiting for the right time and the right person. Chief Group Leader Harels seems rather fond of wine, and the wine appears to be fond of releasing his usually suppressed desire to speak at length."

"Well," she grinned, "you're not the only one who suborned his native guide. I had the pleasure of sitting beside a Custodian panjandrum with a whole bouquet of black leaves on her breast, and she described their latest xeno captures in detail. Hold on to your berets, folks, because I think they've got themselves a passel of Shrehari traders or surveyors."

"This place is as far from the empire as it is from the Commonwealth, no?" Foste asked.

"Why should that stop the boneheads?" Vincenzo shot over his shoulder as he walked over to the improvised bar. "Hasn't stopped us and we have more sense. A glass of their vino, Captain?"

"If you would, please. In the interests of good diplomacy, I followed the rule of tasting the booze, not drinking it during supper. Otherwise, Colonel Kalivan would have felt I'd let our side down."

"Never," he exclaimed.

"That's not what your evil eye told me when I pestered poor Martell with questions during the reception."

"Time and place, my dear, time and place."

"In that case, the place will be Custodian headquarters, the time to be determined."

"What?"

"I convinced the lovely Custodian Senior Group Leader Yarvik, my dining companion, that it might profit Mirandan security to show us their captives. Yarvik heads the Custodians' xeno division, which is probably why they detailed her to entertain me." Siobhan took a sip of wine and then smiled at him over the rim of her glass. "She put it to Dalian who then went off to speak with Hames after we rose from the table."

"You do realize Dalian heads their version of the Special Security Bureau."

"Sure. And our SSB is full of folks rejected by the Armed Services for having sociopathic tendencies. That doesn't mean a militaristic society like Miranda has the same recruiting policies."

"A little harsh on the SSB, no?"

"Have you ever dealt with their operatives in person, Wes?"

He shook his head. "No."

"I have, several times, hence my pungent description. That being said, I think it's important to confirm whether the Shrehari made it this far beyond the black, even if it's the only thing we bring home. Command won't be happy with the notion of them expanding into what some visionaries see as our next frontier. Did you get a similar invitation to visit Defender HQ?"

"Sorry. As a lowly senior bannerman — colonel in their system — I don't have enough prestige to get into Miranda's holy of holies right now. However, they will arrange for me to meet leading members of the Two Hundred, their legislature, so it'll be interesting. Sadly, it doesn't help me get proof they've been thrown back into the past by a rogue wormhole, and I really do need it after I spent so much time convincing command there was something very odd and old about *Tempest*'s log buoy."

"We still need to get a copy of our historical database sent down," she reminded him. "Perhaps the quid will attract a pro quo."

"Indeed."

"Of course, that would mean letting me talk to my ship directly. Gregor Pushkin won't part with a single piece of data absent my direct authorization."

"And you expect this to be a problem?"

"After they so kindly told my crew about our stay here instead of allowing me to do so, you'll permit me to wonder."

Kalivan nodded.

"I believe I will." He accepted a glass of wine from Vincenzo and took a sip before continuing. "On a related subject, I got the idea that this isn't the monolithic society it appears to be at first glance. My dinner companion spoke of splinter factions at odds with the administration, some of which would be more likely to massacre us 'Earthers' than offer a fond embrace."

"Really?" Dunmoore raised a skeptical eyebrow. "What a lovely civilization they have."

"I get the idea there's more going on beneath the surface than any of them would like to admit. This may not necessarily be a happy place."

"Few dictatorships are, or at least can keep the ordinary people happy for long." She shrugged. "I wonder if the original colonists would recognize what their children have become."

"They'd be horrified." A grim laugh escaped Kalivan's lips. "Their children have become everything they fled from."

"Proving once again that we humans always revert to the long-term historical mean."

"Authoritarian?"

"Something like that." She drained her wine glass and set it down on the table. "I could use some more pungent terms, but..."

She tugged on her earlobe and glanced at the ceiling.

"It might cheer you to know that the one splinter faction who wouldn't expel us on sight is clamoring for a return to the earlier days of the colony, now that xeno attacks have waned thanks to the powerful military shield around Miranda and Sycorax."

"Your dinner companion *was* talkative," Dunmoore smiled.

"Don't forget that I'm well trained when it comes to influence activities."

His self-satisfied smirk drew a delighted peal of laughter from Siobhan.

"I'm sure that some of our hosts will wonder whether your parents were married to each other," she replied.

"Who needs parents when one can afford the best in gestation pods?" He raised his wine glass in salute and winked, then emptied it in one gulp. "Not bad. Now if you'll excuse me, keeping a smile painted on my face all evening has been rather tiring. I never could pass for a courtier, hence the army career." Kalivan stood, nodded at his companions, and sauntered off to the room set aside for him.

"I do believe the colonel is right." A wan smile briefly softened her face. "Diplomatic parties can be tiring." Then, with a flourish, she too emptied her wine glass. "Enjoy the rest of the evening, but try to avoid a hangover. We have no idea what Mirandan hooch can do to someone not weaned on it."

"No worries, sir." Foste nodded. "Neither the lad nor I are big drinkers. We'll turn in as well."

That night, bad dreams plagued Siobhan, leaving her lying awake in the darkness, wondering why she could find no rest, even after an eventful and tiring day, and wishing she lay in her quarters aboard *Stingray*, amid the familiar scents and sounds of the only home she had.

— Nineteen —

When Dunmoore emerged from her room the next day, feeling like she had spent the night battling demons, the others had already made a sizable dent in the breakfast spread delivered, as Foste put it, by the house elves before anyone woke up.

"The ever helpful Nan called," Kalivan said by way of greeting. "He's arranged to let you talk to the ship this morning. They're chomping at the bit to get a copy of our historical database. Well, that and of course our technical one as well."

"Which I can't hand over without authorization," she replied, helping herself to a plate of fruit. "Though the medical database is fair game, for obvious humanitarian reasons, seeing as we're the same species. The database on non-human species might be in a bit of a gray area, on the other hand, especially when it comes to the Shrehari."

Kalivan caught her eye, and then glanced up at the ceiling, reminding her their hosts had to be listening in. She shrugged in response, concentrating on her meal and thereby ending the conversation.

An hour later, Senior Group Leader Nan showed up in person and invited Dunmoore to follow him.

"I have arranged for the Protector's communications staff to link with your ship via Defender headquarters," he said, leading the way down yet another corridor radiating from the lobby with the bizarre imagery. "Thus you needn't make the trip across Sanctum to use the HQ facilities directly."

"Very kind," she murmured, glad to find no trace of sarcasm in her tone, then in a louder voice she asked, "Will we eventually be shown around the capital?"

"In due time," Nan replied. "As you've been informed, we have factions who see all off-worlders, including those of our species as enemies, and the Protector wishes to keep his honored guests safe."

"Not to mention keep the restive part of the population from getting even more unruly, right?"

Nan did not see the scornful smile on her face, but something in her tone caused him to grunt.

"Anti-social elements are kept under proper control by the Custodians, Commander. Surely it must be the same in your Commonwealth."

"I suppose it depends on what you and I understand by the term anti-social. We allow dissenters to hold and even publicly expose their points of view, as long as they do it in a non-violent manner and in full respect of the law."

"Really?"

Though he sounded incredulous, she sensed that Nan would have liked to pursue the matter, but he muttered something unintelligible, and then fell silent for the rest of their trek to the communications room.

There, she found equipment that would not have seemed out of place on some of the Commonwealth's older facilities, with the notable absence of a subspace terminal. A serious young man in the ubiquitous black uniform offered her a chair in front of a terminal, then touched some controls. They waited for almost a minute before she heard Kowalski's voice.

"This is the Commonwealth Starship *Stingray*. We understand you have Captain Dunmoore on the link?"

"I'm here Kathryn." The video component stabilized, and she found herself looking straight at the signals officer. "Is Mister Pushkin available?"

"He will be, in a moment, sir. It's his down time right now, but he left orders to be roused the moment we heard from you."

The image on the screen split in two, Pushkin joining the call from his quarters, looking just a bit bleary-eyed.

"Captain. It's good to see you. We were a bit puzzled by the transmission from the Mirandans yesterday, telling us you were extending your stay. Are things going well?"

"As well as could be expected, under the circumstances." She gave him a tight smile. "Our hosts are understandably curious about the Commonwealth and the progress we've made since the year *Tempest* left on its voyage and have asked us to share what we can from our database."

When Dunmoore saw Pushkin's jaw harden, she caught his eyes and held them for a few moments.

"At this time, what I'd like is to have Kathryn prepare a copy of the historical database for transmission to the Mirandans, so they can catch up to events on Earth since their ancestors' departure."

"Yes, Captain." He nodded once, a wary expression on his face. "Would this be all, or will there be more at another time?"

"I'm considering the medical database as well, but please discuss the matter with Doctor Luttrell."

"Will do. How long do you plan on staying down there?"

"At least another day or two. The colonel and I both have meetings lined up, but I doubt they'll happen today. How's the ship?"

"Same old, same old. Mister Kutora assures me all of the items on his list will be crossed off within the next day."

She saw, by his expression, that he would have liked to say more, but felt he could not.

"Excellent. I'm sure we'll speak again before our return. Kathryn can discuss the transmission of the data with her Mirandan counterparts. If there's nothing else, get back to sleep, Gregor. Acting captains need their rest."

"Aye. Until later, sir."

Dunmoore turned to Nan.

"That's it for now, Senior Group Leader."

The Mirandan nodded once, and then issued orders concerning the receipt of the historical database to the duty under-officer, before leading Dunmoore back through the maze of corridors.

"What now?" She asked.

"Protector Hames has directed you be given an overview of our history, in return for you graciously giving us a copy of yours, so you may understand why we need your assistance to join the rest of humanity in traveling across the stars."

So, she thought, a grim smile pulling at the corners of her mouth, the schmoozing is about to start.

*

"We have a term for this in my line of business," Kalivan whispered in Dunmoore's ear after ninety minutes of video extolling the Mirandans' struggle against a hostile galaxy.

"Horse shit?" She whispered back.

"I prefer the technical term, propaganda, but your pungent characterization is likely apter."

Romin Cesta, Senior Director of Information and their host of the moment, perked up and asked, "You have questions, Envoy?"

"More than you can imagine." He graced the dour Mirandan with a suave diplomat's smile. "You surely didn't put this together just for us. Is this used in your schools?"

"Of course. The production you're watching right now is used to introduce our children to history, so that they can correctly understand the ideals of our Dominion and why they're so important in the face of xeno danger. We have many more that delve into the details and are shown as the children get older."

Cesta's air of paternal pride seemed absurd to the two officers after they had endured an hour and a half of pretentious jingoism.

"Our office also produces highly entertaining historically-based stories to keep the memory of our past alive among the adult population."

"Do the children also get an overview of Miranda's earlier days; say from before your ancestors formed the Dominion in response to xeno incursions?" Dunmoore asked, out of mischief as much as out of curiosity.

With Cesta's attention on Siobhan, Kalivan gave her a sharp jab in the ribs with his elbow.

"That era is covered later, once the little ones have thoroughly assimilated the Dominion's history so that they can fully understand the folly of our forebears in colonizing Miranda without a thought to the evils that lurk among the stars."

"Yet, if I understand things right," Kalivan said, "Miranda had a peaceful, agrarian existence for well over a thousand years before non-human species found it. In the course of human history, that's quite an accomplishment."

"Perhaps." A dubious frown creased Cesta's forehead. "But during those centuries, we were weak, vulnerable, and contemptible even. It would be folly to extol those days as a lost ideal, now that we're strong and able to throw off those who wish to prey on the Dominion."

Kalivan nodded.

"I think I understand, senior director. The galaxy can indeed be hostile to those not adequately prepared. We've had our own moments."

"A thought just struck me," Dunmoore turned in the plush auditorium chair to look at him. "Xeno incursions started about four hundred years ago, around the same time we developed FTL technology, give or take a few decades. We know the Shrehari regained it a century or two before that and neither of us have so far met another civilization that made the same leap to interstellar travel independently."

"I think I see what you mean," Kalivan replied. "Either the Shrehari inadvertently gave that tech to species we've never met and who became the Mirandans' xenos..."

"Or there's another interstellar civilization on the far side of the Mirandan system that we haven't encountered yet." Siobhan nodded. "That's vital intelligence."

"Agreed." When he saw Cesta's puzzled expression, Kalivan smiled. "Apologies for the tangent, Senior Director, but Commander Dunmoore has raised an interesting point."

"I'm sure, though what that might be escapes me at the moment. Xenos are xenos, no matter their origin, are they not?"

"Some are more dangerous than others." Dunmoore shrugged. "It pays to know which is which."

"We made it simple and treat all of them in the same manner." He gestured toward the frozen image on the matte screen dominating them. "Shall we continue?"

Dunmoore leaned toward Kalivan until her lips brushed his ear.

"Do we have to?"

Instead of replying, he waved regally at Cesta and said, "By all means, Senior Director. We find your educational videos absolutely fascinating."

Dunmoore jabbed him in the ribs when Cesta had turned back to the video controls.

They broke for lunch, relieved at escaping the auditorium, but still had to endure Cesta's constant nattering. Siobhan privately dubbed him the Senior Director of Too Much Information but managed to keep a polite, interested expression on her face, in deference to Kalivan's well-oiled diplomacy.

"Could we get copies of your historical teachings sent to my ship, and by that I mean the videos as well as your records?" She asked when they sat at a large table in what Cesta called the Protector's dining lounge. "A fair exchange for us providing you with a copy of ours, as it were?"

"I'm sure that can be arranged. When we see Senior Group Leader Nan, I'll make the necessary inquiries."

Cyrus Hames' senior aide proved to be both agreeable and helpful when he joined them shortly after that, but when he announced that the Two Hundred, or to be precise, a Select Committee, would host a reception in their honor that evening, Dunmoore felt hard-pressed to keep up the pretense of diplomacy.

After a mostly sleepless night, she would have been happier spending a few quiet hours shooting the breeze with Wes and her two spacers before an early bedtime. Tomorrow, she had an appointment with the Custodians and wanted to be alert, not dulled by fatigue, but Kalivan seemed pleased with the invitation.

Later, when they had returned to their suite to prepare for the reception, she grimaced at Kalivan.

"A day of propaganda and now an evening with this world's version of senators?"

"They desperately hope we'll understand them," he replied with a somewhat undiplomatic but very wry smile. "We're being courted if you like."

"I get that."

She handed her tunic to Vincenzo for a quick cleaning, and then leaned over to place her lips near Kalivan's ear.

"What worries me," she whispered, "is their plan when they find out we're not keen on taking the proffered engagement ring, or at least not without top cover from the Admiralty."

"Let's see where this goes, shall we?" He murmured.

"Yes. Let's."

*

"My new friend Under-Officer First Class Geyer, the man to whom I spoke earlier today, is proposing to send us a massive historical data dump," Kowalski announced when Pushkin bade her enter the captain's ready room.

"And by the twinkle in your eyes, may I assume that you'll be diving into it the moment your watch ends?"

"Of course."

She mimed being taken aback that he would even ask the question.

"Then I'll issue two orders." He leaned forward, forearms on the desktop. "One, remember to sleep. Research is not an exemption from taking your regular turn on the bridge. And two, make sure their data dump goes straight into the quarantine box and doesn't leave it. Do your reading via a segregated connection."

"Viv will make sure of item one, and I've already set up things to cover item two. All I need is your permission to receive the data."

"You have it. If you can prepare a digest or a short briefing for the department heads, say by the end of the next forenoon watch, I'm sure we would all find it very useful. These are strange people, for all that we have matching DNA sequences. If there's nothing else, go commune with Under-Officer Geyer."

"Will do, sir."

She briefly came to attention, before leaving Pushkin to his thoughts.

Four hours later, after coming off watch, Kowalski sat on her bunk in the cabin she shared with the ship's surgeon, watching the first of the educational videos when Viv Luttrell came in, her tunic already half unfastened.

"Hitting the entertainment files early today?" She kicked off her boots and dropped into the opposite bunk. "Or did you intercept some Mirandan code or other you're desperate to decipher?"

"It is work, but not in the cryptographic realm." Kowalski stopped the playback and looked up at her roommate. "Our Mirandan cousins sent up some videos covering Miranda's history or at least the history of the last few centuries."

"Interesting?"

"Fascinating, if you can get past the turgid propaganda layer. Reminds me of the horse crap produced during the last Migration War in an attempt to extol the virtues of colonial government. They made us watch it in one of our psychology classes at the Academy. How to manipulate the masses."

"That bad, eh?" Luttrell smirked. "And I suppose our Gregor expects a precis sometime tomorrow?"

"Yep." The signals officer nodded. "You'll be glad to know he did tell me to make sure I got enough sleep."

"Because he knows working straight through will dull your brain, which he can't afford. Not with the captain down on the planet and us floating in the middle of the most heavily armed chunk of space I've ever seen. He may be hiding it well, but our first officer's been on edge since the moment our skipper decided to go off with her buddy Kalivan."

"There's a lot of that going around and this stuff," she held up her tablet, "isn't going to help."

"Really?" Luttrell crossed the cabin and sat down next to Kowalski. "Let me see a sample of your homework assignment before I hit the showers."

"Oh my," *Stingray*'s surgeon said, an hour later, "these people seem severely dysfunctional, at least to my eyes. Our historians and social scientists will have a ball studying their society. Talk about turning *Tempest*'s idealistic colonization charter on its head."

"They're not the first human grouping to have gone down that road, Viv."

"No," Luttrell shook her head, "I suppose not, now that you mention it. It's amazing what fear can do to otherwise rational, sensible beings."

"What was it a wise man once said? If you give up freedom for security, you deserve neither?"

"Or in this case, give up your humanity for security." A weak, almost sad smile briefly twisted the surgeon's lips. "I don't envy the Captain or Colonel Kalivan."

*

Gano Marant waited for them by the entrance to the same reception room used for the Protector's meet and greet the previous evening, a welcoming smile plastered on his face.

"Commander Dunmoore, Colonel Kalivan," he dipped his head by way of greeting, "most gracious of you to accept our invitation at such short notice. The Select Committee, once I apprised them of your arrival, wanted to meet you as soon as possible."

"Select Committee?" Kalivan politely raised his eyebrows.

"The leading twenty, who head the Two Hundred's subcommittees. Our most senior members, so to speak, the most influential among us."

"*Primus inter pares.*"

Marant shot Dunmoore a puzzled look so she elaborated.

"First among equals."

"Ah." The Mirandan smiled. "Very apt indeed. What is its origin?"

"Latin. The basis for Earth's Romance languages. It's no longer spoken as such."

"The Commonwealth uses many different tongues?"

Kalivan smiled.

"Indeed, though only a few are considered universal enough to be spoken by most citizens."

"How interesting. You must tell me more about your various forms of speech someday."

He made a sweeping arm gesture toward the room where a small knot of men and women in splendid civilian clothing waited, staring at them with undisguised curiosity.

"Shall we?"

"Members of the Select Committee," Marant announced once they had entered the room, "may I present Colonel Wes Kalivan, Envoy of the Commonwealth and Commander Siobhan Dunmoore, captain of the

Commonwealth Starship *Stingray*, now in orbit around Miranda. They have crossed the interstellar void between Earth and Miranda to establish contact between the Dominion and the rest of our species."

Polite applause greeted the Speaker's declaration, and the two officers briefly came to attention and nodded.

"We are honored by the reception we've enjoyed since arriving in the Dominion," Kalivan said.

White-jacketed waiters appeared out of nowhere with trays bearing full wine glasses. Once they had been passed out, Marant raised his.

"I would like to propose a toast, to friendship and open collaboration between our peoples."

"To friendship."

Marant then introduced his colleagues one at a time and by the end, Dunmoore felt her fixed smile turning into a rictus of pain.

The waiters reappeared with plates of finger food and began to circulate while the members of the Select Committee split into smaller groups, one surrounding Kalivan, another corralling Dunmoore, and a third monopolizing Marant's attention.

"How do you like Miranda so far?" A woman who had introduced herself as Sarina Atreus asked Siobhan.

"I haven't seen enough of it to form an opinion," she answered. "We haven't left this palace since arriving, but if the rest of Sanctum is as splendid as this place, I'm sure it will be very pleasant."

"Trust Cyrus to monopolize you." Atreus giggled. "Well, I certainly hope you'll be able to see more of the extraordinary work we've done here, under some very trying conditions."

"Indeed. Senior Director Cesta showed us documentary videos of your history earlier today. Your society lived through traumatic times."

"And so many of us were lost," another Select Committee member said. "Thankfully, we're now strong enough to stop the xenos, but still at a cost. If we were able to go out into the galaxy and end the threat to our children and grandchildren forever, we could secure the Dominion's legacy for all times."

"Yes," Atreus chimed in, "and, of course, we could maintain contact with our Commonwealth cousins."

Dunmoore smiled, not sure how to answer diplomatically, but another politician saved her from having to try.

"You say you haven't been out of the palace yet," a middle-aged man by the name of Linc Lam, said. "Perhaps Speaker Marant can prevail upon Cyrus to let you visit with some of us. I do understand his desire to keep your arrival from becoming widely known, for Dominion security reasons, but surely, if he permitted us to meet with you..."

"I will be leaving the palace to visit one of the Custodian facilities tomorrow," Dunmoore replied, "so it's not like the Protector is holding us prisoner."

"Mira Dalian's taken an interest in you, has she?" Lam's expression betrayed his dislike of the Chief Custodian. "That's not always a good thing."

"Please, Linc. She may become the next Protector," Atreus protested. "Don't give our guest the wrong impression."

"Many pardons." Lam inclined his head. "I should not have dragged you into Mirandan political matters. Just be aware that among the Two Hundred, and indeed within the wider population, many hold differing opinions as to the future of our institutions, now that we've secured our planets and been without serious threat for several decades."

"Understood." Dunmoore nodded as politely as she could, wondering whether these politicians knew about the recent capture of xenos and the destruction of their ship.

"And Linc is one of them." An insincere smile tugged at the third Mirandan's lips. "If you'll let him bend your ear after a few drinks, he'll even express reservations concerning our policy toward xenos. We've learned to tolerate his foibles."

Lam ignored his colleague's jibe and asked, "May I infer that your visit tomorrow will be to the Custodian's Xeno Division?"

"Indeed."

"Then please, Commander, do not judge Miranda by what you'll see and hear there." Lam's tone had remained light, but his eyes implored her to listen.

"It didn't even take a few drinks this time," Atreus said, shaking her head. "Linc, you're a wonder."

"At least I take the time to wonder about things, Sarina." He took a sip of his wine and then speared Siobhan with his eyes again.

"Did you know that under Dominion Law, you and yours are classified as xenos?"

Atreus' crude snort drew a disapproving glare from Gano Marant, standing a few meters away, conversing with a few colleagues.

"Surely you of all people, Linc, understand that our ancestors never expected to see other humans and thus wrote the laws as simply as they could."

"Yet if we were to apply that law to our guests as rigorously as Mira Dalian and her cronies enjoy enforcing all of our laws," he glared at Marant for a few seconds, "then these *humans* not born of our people would have no rights within the Dominion."

"I'm sure Protector Hames will amend the law in question soon enough, now that we know we have kin across the stars," the other Mirandan said. "In the interests of friendship and mutual cooperation."

"Probably," Lam conceded. "Cyrus is a pragmatist after all, unlike some, but I thought it only fair Commander Dunmoore knows who we are, warts and all. In the interests of friendship and cooperation. That being said, Commander, do take care the Custodian's head of xeno research doesn't decide you're worthy of study in the usual way. Group Leader Yarvik is a devotee of Mira Dalian, just like most of the Custodian senior leadership, and takes a literal view of our laws."

"Linc!" Atreus glowered at her colleague. "Do take care with your words."

"Or what?" A sad smile tugged at his lips. "Mira is well aware of my views, and my opposition to her nomination. The Dominion must move forward, especially now that Earth has contacted us. The days of cowering in fear of the universe have to end. Otherwise, we will continue to stagnate."

He bowed his head at Dunmoore.

"I apologize once again for airing our internal politics on this social occasion and trust you won't think too meanly of me. Do enjoy the rest of your stay, Commander."

Lam handed his glass to a passing waiter and left.

— Twenty —

The sprawling Custodian headquarters complex, nestled inside a walled-off park several kilometers north of Sanctum's city limits, matched the palace's severe architecture, but without the thin veneer of gentility that turned the latter into something less imposing. The now familiar sword and fern leaf insignia seemed to be everywhere, decorating the walls and floors in a monotonous pattern that could only appeal to what Dunmoore privately thought of as the dull mind of a secret police officer.

Senior Group Leader Yarvik, a barrel-shaped woman with a face to match, had met her at the tube station beneath the half-buried main building and led her through a maze of long corridors and staircases to an austere office that mirrored the woman's severe expression.

Dunmoore's ever-present military guards had given way to armed, gray-uniformed police troopers the moment she had stepped out of the transport pod. Judging by the brief exchange as they transferred responsibility for their guest from one to the other, there was no love lost between the two branches of Mirandan's all-encompassing security apparatus.

"Your men didn't seem too keen on the Defenders who brought me here," she remarked after sitting on a hard, leather-covered chair at her host's invitation.

Yarvik's brief laugh sounded like the bark of a rabid dog.

"The tension between Defenders and Custodians stems from time immemorial," the senior group leader replied. "We keep Miranda and its colonies safe from the inside, Chief Defender Martell's troops keep us safe from external threats. The delineation between the two isn't always obvious, as with the xeno prisoners I hope you'll be able to identify. Defenders brought down their spaceship and because of that, they wished to keep the xenos. The Protector ruled in our favor because we have so much more experience dealing with non-human species."

"Some would say competition between two services is a good thing," Dunmoore remarked, a faint smile on her lips, wondering whether the Mirandan would grasp the allusion.

"Is this what happens in your Commonwealth?"

"We have analogs to your Custodians as well as our version of the Defenders, and yes, there is competition."

"And why would this be a good thing?" Yarvik sounded genuinely puzzled. "Custodian Dalian has been trying to clarify the lines of responsibility for years so that disagreements between her and Geoff Martell no longer occur."

It apparently had not occurred to Yarvik, notwithstanding her high rank, that a prudent dictator, even one whose mandate lasted no longer than ten years, made sure the security and military services did not combine to oppose him. And he did so by fostering low-level tension, but Siobhan did not feel inclined to educate Yarvik. Internal Mirandan affairs, fascinating as they seemed, were none of their business.

"Merely an idle comment on my part and I do apologize, Senior Group Leader. I did not wish to imply that Custodian Dalian's attempts to clarify matters were inappropriate. On the contrary."

Yarvik still seemed puzzled, but inclined her head, silently accepting Dunmoore's evasive excuse.

"Perhaps I can show you these new xenos, then?"

"That's why I'm here," Siobhan smiled. "To help our Mirandan brothers and sisters."

And to see if our deadly enemies got here first, she mentally added.

The woman must have touched hidden controls because a section of wall paneling slid aside to reveal a large, matte screen.

"Custodian Dalian wishes me to show you images of the xenos first so that we don't waste your time by going down into the cell block only to find out that they're as unfamiliar to you as they are to us."

"But of course. That's very considerate of her."

Yarvik briefly stared at Dunmoore and blinked a few times, making Siobhan wonder whether her tone had conveyed disrespect.

"She is one of the finest leaders we have," the Mirandan finally said, "and I sincerely hope she becomes the next Protector."

Then, she pointed at the screen mounted to the wall.

"Is this species familiar to you?"

Dunmoore's eyes switched from the senior group leader to the image and breathed in deeply to suppress her reaction at the sight of what looked like a mutilated corpse. She slowly nodded.

"It is. They call themselves the Shrehari. My Commonwealth has been at war with them for over six years."

"Then you'll be pleased to know that we've only kept a few of them alive for further investigation. The remainder either died resisting internment or during research."

The Mirandan's matter-of-fact tone chilled Dunmoore, and then her choice of words registered.

"Research?"

"Of course. The key to defending against xenos is understanding them, no?"

Dunmoore nodded quickly, not trusting herself to speak.

"These Shrehari proved to be much tougher than the Skraeling who still infest some corners of Miranda. We certainly hope you can help us understand what kind of threat they are and how to defeat them the next time one of their spaceships invades our system."

She nodded again, desperately trying to chase the images conjured by the word 'research' from her mind.

"Are you feeling ill, Commander?" A look of genuine solicitude softened Yarvik's gray eyes. "I apologize if the discussion of your mortal enemy causes you distress."

Dunmoore waved away the Mirandan's concern.

"I'm quite alright. Perhaps a little tired after last night's reception. The members of the Two Hundred do like to talk."

"If you're sure…"

"There's no cause for concern, Senior Group Leader."

She swallowed once and focused her attention on the image of the dead Shrehari again, convinced that the marks on his body were not due to injuries suffered in battle.

"It would help if I could inspect what belongings you took from them, and perhaps even speak with the survivors. I have a particular facility with their tongue."

Yarvik brightened, all worry erased from her coarse features.

"Custodian Dalian will be so very pleased. If you'll excuse me for a moment, I shall inform her of this and then arrange matters in the xeno detention center for your visit."

"Thank you," Dunmoore murmured, "I think."

*

Bannerman Jhain led Kalivan, with Foste and Vincenzo in tow, to a conference room on a lower level where a delegation of Mirandan academics and military officers waited.

Vincenzo still fumed at Dunmoore leaving him behind for her visit to Custodian headquarters, but the invitation pointedly excluded anyone else from their landing party.

Had Chief Guthren been present, he knew there would have been a harsh exchange of words with their hosts, but the coxswain was somewhere up in orbit, aboard *Stingray*, and so, Vincenzo would sit in on the colonel's meeting, along with the bosun.

Of the dozen Mirandans sitting around a dark table, one, a white-haired civilian with a broad forehead, stood. He briefly dipped his head by way of greeting.

"Welcome, Colonel Kalivan. I'm Senior Academician Hal Yorta, attached to the Defenders."

"Pleasure." Kalivan gave Yorta his most diplomatic smile, while Jhain, behind him, pointed Foste and Vincenzo at a bench against the wall.

Once the Mirandan had introduced his colleagues, who were evenly split between military and civilian, male and female, Kalivan took the single vacant chair at the table and looked at Yorta expectantly.

"Did you have specific questions you wish to begin with, Senior Academician? Or shall I present an overview of humanity's history since *Tempest* left Earth?"

"Protector Hames kindly shared the gist of your discussion with him yesterday, as well as the copy of your historical database, so we already have a reasonable grounding when it comes to your Commonwealth."

"Specific questions then." Kalivan looked around the table at the impassive faces of the delegation. "I hope you'll be just as eager to answer my questions about your history. Although we've seen the educational videos used in your schools, there's still so much to learn. We're fascinated by the notion that your forebears were flung back in time, giving your people almost two thousand years to develop a society in isolation from humanity's mainstream."

"And yet in all that time," a thickset woman wearing the three fern leaves of a group leader said, in a raspy voice, "we've failed to develop, as you did, the technology that allows travel between the stars and harnesses enough power to make our own military might obsolete. Had we done so, we might have been spared the grief of xeno depredations. Even now, we remain at risk while savage species roam interstellar space, perhaps even the xenos your Commonwealth currently battles."

"The Shrehari, yes." Kalivan gave a half shrug and grimaced. "We co-existed peacefully with them for a long time before internal matters drove their leaders to seek war as a means to distract the population. Had the old emperor lived long enough to see his son grow up, we would still be at peace, just as we are with other non-human species. Since neither the Shrehari nor we have the will to eradicate the other, nor the strength to force a surrender, our war only keeps going. And it could have been so easily avoided."

"We were told," another of them said, "that you held distinctly strange views on relations with xenos. Perhaps the fact that you command such military power gives you the luxury to treat them as useful sentients. I'm sure our views would be amenable to change if we no longer felt surrounded by threats."

Kalivan nodded slowly, a thoughtful expression replacing his earlier smile.

"Indeed. We are all products of our own environmental pressures. I would very much like to discover how your current society came to be so far from its founder's ideals and how the xeno threat molded your outlook on the universe."

"And we would very much like to become more resistant to those environmental pressures, Colonel," Yorta replied. "Hopefully, you'll help us in that matter."

The army officer's forehead creased in puzzlement.

"I thought we'd be discussing our respective societies. Technical matters are beyond my realm of expertise."

The senior academician raised a soothing hand.

"Of course, Colonel. We are aware of that, and we will gladly share everything you wish to know about Miranda's past and present, just as we hope you'll elaborate on events in the Commonwealth over the last four centuries. But we also wish to discuss how your technical experts can impart their knowledge to ours so that we may advance to the same level as you currently enjoy. Are you not, as envoy of your people, empowered to do so?"

"Matters of military technology on this mission are decided by Commander Dunmoore, I'm afraid." He gave an apologetic smile. "I am but a diplomat without the requisite knowledge of what our government might allow us to share on our own. Once we return home and report to our superiors, I'm sure they'll be more than happy to send a full delegation of experts ready to help you catch up with us."

"We may not have the luxury of time, Colonel," the woman with group leader's insignia insisted. "A new species of xeno has found us and who knows what disasters they may bring to Miranda? I'm sure that between the experts on your vessel and your knowledge database, you can give us the elements we need to break free from our inability to produce the power to fuel faster-than-light travel."

"Surely among us humans..." Yorta said with a faint smile.

"I understand your concern about this new species but isn't it true that you haven't had a threatening xeno incursion in decades before the latest one. From what I've seen, I know the Dominion is certainly capable of defending itself for a few months longer. But as I said, this is a matter for Commander Dunmoore, senior academician." Kalivan's tone oozed diplomatic suaveness. "I shall discuss it with her when she returns from her visit with the Custodians. In the meantime, might I suggest we get better acquainted? It could help me in my conversation with her."

The thickset woman sighed, her pale eyes blazing with angry disappointment.

"Very well." Yorta gestured toward one of the other civilian men. "Academician Nestor has questions about your form of government."

*

Yarvik led Dunmoore down a winding set of stairs, deep into the bowels of the Custodian headquarters and along a harshly lit corridor, a pair of gray-uniformed guards following at a discrete distance. Compared to this part of the building, the offices above ground appeared positively luxurious in retrospect. Even the omnipresent sword and fern leaf insignia failed to make a single appearance on the gray, smooth walls.

They passed a guard station, and then entered a large airlock that would not have seemed out of place on a starship.

"To prevent contamination," the senior group leader noted when she saw Siobhan's evident surprise. "In case one of the xenos we keep for research releases something harmful."

"It must help prevent escapes as well."

A mirthless laugh shook Yarvik's heavy jowls.

"Once a xeno is in our hands, there is no chance of it ever escaping, Commander."

Strong medicinal odors assailed Dunmoore's nostrils when they stepped through the chamber's other door and into a bright white corridor.

"This is one of the finest xeno research institutes on Miranda." Yarvik's tone resembled that of a proud mother. "As you'll see, we have excellent facilities and the largest collection anywhere."

Dunmoore wanted to ask 'collection of what,' then bit her lip. She already had a good idea what Yarvik meant.

They reached another airlock-like barrier and this time, the senior group leader had to wait for someone on the other side to open the massive metal door.

"We keep live xenos in this section," she said leading the way past a stone-faced, armed guard, "though we store different species away from one another. Your Shrehari are to the left."

She pointed at an unmarked steel door, before continuing, "We keep the few live Skraeling we capture in that section. After all these years, they've given up most of their secrets, so all we do with them is verify that they haven't developed anything new."

Nothing could have prepared Siobhan for the sight that greeted her once they entered the Shrehari section. Cube upon cube with steel walls on all sides but that facing the corridor held individual members of the proud warrior race she had come to respect, be it ever so grudgingly.

However, those she saw through the thick, transparent plastic doors bore little resemblance to beings like Brakal. Emaciated, undernourished, bearing signs of injury if not outright mutilation, they appeared listless, as if drained of the soul that had kept their race going for so long. She felt her heart sink at their state. They were clearly dying.

She walked down the row of cells until she caught the eye of one who seemed to have retained some of the fire in his deep-set, dark eyes. He examined her carefully, his facial muscles working beneath the dark olive skin as if he could not believe his eyes.

Finally, his lips parted in a rictus to reveal broken yellow fangs, the Shrehari way of showing contempt.

"The uniform of the Commonwealth at last," he snarled in his tongue. "Come to judge the work of your butchers, you cowardly clod of dung?"

"Is that a way to greet a commander, even if she is one of the empire's enemies?" Dunmoore spat out the unfamiliar words, her mouth distorting around harsh syllables. She knew her accent sounded atrocious, but the prisoner in the tiny cell understood perfectly.

He rose from his crouch and unfolded to a height that forced her to look up.

"I only greet honorable enemies, little human insect, and there is no honor on this planet."

"I'm beginning to get that impression. My name is Dunmoore. I command the starship *Stingray*. We've come to this system on a voyage of exploration, just like you. We are not of the people who live here, even though we are of the same species."

His rictus turned into the Shrehari version of a smile.

"Then take care you do not join us in this prison. The entertainment and the food leave much to be desired."

She caught Yarvik's reflection on the cell door and felt a kind of dark amusement at her astonished look.

"I have named myself and my ship. Honor demands you do the same."

The Shrehari considered her statement for a few silent moments.

"You are not of these people?" He asked.

"No. Their ancestors come from the same planet as mine, but they left my people a long time ago. They are not of the Commonwealth and their warriors bear no relation to us."

"Why should I believe that you tell the truth, Dunmoore?"

"Because I'm the first to speak with you in the imperial tongue after you've been here for so long? Because I talk of honor instead of treating you like a beast?"

She locked eyes with him and held his gaze without fear or anger until he relented and touched his ridged forehead with a gnarled hand.

"I am Drang, formerly commander of the exploration vessel *Ziq Tar*, on a mission to map this sector for the Admiralty. We had no idea another species had claimed this system and did not intend to engage in hostile action. These butchers ambushed us, and those who survived are dying bit by bit ever since."

He paused, to catch his breath, head bowed in a pleading posture.

"If you end our lives now, I will commend your spirit to the Sublime Gods."

"Anything I should know before I read the log?"

Pushkin took the command chair from Devall after a sleepless watch spent worrying and wondering.

"Nothing of note," the younger officer replied, shaking his head. "Rownes' sensor ghost hasn't made a repeat appearance, and we're still half blind thanks to the Mirandans' emcon. But now that the engineers have brought our primary sensor network back online, Chief Penzara is working on something he thinks will allow us to see better, at least within a few thousand kilometers of the ship."

"And no news from the Captain or Colonel Kalivan, I gather."

"We caught a faint signal from the tracking device Kathryn planted on them once or twice, near where they landed, but that's all."

"Which means next to nothing."

Pushkin's fingers tapped the chair's arm in a rapid dance that betrayed his inner disquiet.

"Indeed," Devall replied. "If there's nothing else, I'll go do what a good acting first officer does before turning in."

"Raid the wardroom bar?"

"No. The good stuff's all gone anyway." Devall gave a half shrug. "As a substantive first officer of my acquaintance taught me, making the rounds once a day before taking my ease comes with the job."

"Good man."

Pushkin stared at the image of Miranda for a long time after the second officer's departure, before reading the log to catch up on the previous eight hours.

Clearly, Penzara and his crew had been busy. The Mirandan order of battle listing had trebled in size, as had the data on each of the ships and installations they had identified.

"I see you finally nailed the objects sitting at the L1 and L2 points, Chief," he said.

"Aye," Penzara turned to face the first officer. "Battle stations with matte black coating and almost entirely blanked out by tight emcon. First, they made the mistake of deploying gun turrets while we were within visual range and then they painted us with a targeting laser. A weak one to be sure. If I hadn't set the sensors on 'full paranoid' we might have missed it, but still..."

Something on his console screen flashed insistently.

"The computer's asking for attention, Chief."

"Ah," Penzara's seamed face brightened as he scanned the readout. "My hunch was right on the money. I think we finally have a solution to find nearby objects with Mirandan-grade stealthing. Let's see what we can see."

Pushkin sat back, schooling himself to show nothing but patience, even though his instincts screamed for answers.

"Sir," the chief finally said, "I think we may have problems."

The image of Miranda on the main screen faded away, replaced by a tactical schematic with *Stingray* at its center. Small icons began to surround the frigate in a discontinuous sphere.

"What in God's name are those?" The first officer's voice had dropped to a whisper.

"That would have to be my next trick, sir, but whatever they are, there's two dozen of them at least, and they're almost close enough to reach out an airlock and touch. We never saw them come near."

"We were looking at bigger things. Besides, if the sensor is correct about their size, those things can't be manned."

"Mines?" Petty Officer Takash asked from the helm station.

"Why not?" Pushkin's fingers started dancing again. "We've been known to use them. Why shouldn't the Mirandans? How close is the closest?"

"Ten kilometers," Penzara replied. "Now that my sensors know what to look for, I could grab one with our tractor beam and haul it in closer."

"Not if they're mines, Chief." The first officer shook his head. "I think we might send out a probe to take a closer look."

"What if that annoys our hosts?"

"Then it annoys them. They've put these things close to my ship, and I'm annoyed right now. Prepare a probe, then rig the tactical system to raise our shields automatically the moment one of those things shifts from its position relative to us or its state changes in any way at all."

"Aye, aye, sir. Consider it done."

The screen set into the command chair's arm blinked, drawing Pushkin's eyes to a brief message from Kowalski. She had completed her analysis of the Mirandan historical files and wanted a moment of his time.

— Twenty-One —

"What did it say?" Yarvik asked.

Her face and tone betrayed an eagerness at odds with her dour demeanor. However, Yarvik's use of the word 'it' to denote the Shrehari starship captain lit an angry fire deep within Siobhan's gut.

He might be the enemy, but he also came from an advanced, sentient species much older than humanity, as the now destroyed archaeological digs on Arietis had demonstrated.

Commander Drang definitely was not an 'it.' Conscious that she had stepped onto dangerous ground, she chose her words very carefully.

"*He* is an explorer, not a warrior, and came to this star system without hostile intent."

The senior group leader snorted derisively, ignoring or even completely missing Dunmoore's emphasis on the humanizing pronoun.

"No xeno comes to Miranda without a genocidal motive. Perhaps we should put it to the question again, now that we have someone who can speak its barbarous gibberish. It still has some appendages we can remove."

"What is it that you wished to know?" Dunmoore felt inordinately pleased to find her voice had remained steady and calm, even though she seethed inside.

"Everything about their species and the technology they wield, for starters."

"I can provide you with what the Commonwealth has learned about the Shrehari, and in a language you can read. Putting this being to the 'question' would be horribly counterproductive."

A soft growl in Shrehari stilled Yarvik's reply.

"What are you telling this butcher," Drang asked.

"I told her that I could provide them with all we know about the empire so that there is no need for further interrogation."

"In that case, human, you may ask the butcher to kill us now. We are dead already and would rather not suffer the dishonor of further dismemberment and mutilation. They may do as they wish with our corpses once our spirits have crossed over to join the Eternal Flames."

Dunmoore clenched her teeth, jaw muscles working as she examined Drang again, this time noting every scar, fresh or old.

"What, precisely, are these people doing to you and your crew?"

"They have been studying us from the inside out, while we still breathe." The last few words came out as a hate-filled snarl.

She felt the rage within her flare up. Never had the Shrehari treated their human prisoners or, in the case of the Commonwealth systems they had occupied, their subject populations, with the level of barbarity implied by what seemed to be, in effect, vivisection. This then, was the research Yarvik kept mentioning and the fate of Miranda's native species, the Skraeling, as well.

Dunmoore did not trust herself to speak, or even look at the senior group leader. She breathed in deeply a few times, fighting back horror and disgust, then steeled her nerves for what she knew must come next.

"I will provide you with everything known about this species," she said to the Mirandan. "That is more than you can obtain by interrogation, even with my assistance, and neither of us has the kind of time it would take to come even near the amount of data we have in my ship's memory banks."

She nodded toward Drang.

"You have nothing to fear from the Shrehari. Their sphere of influence is as far away as the Commonwealth and with their attention focused on the war, there will be no others coming this way for a long, long time. They have few explorers like this one. If you have no intention of setting them free, then killing them is the best thing to do."

"That would be Custodian Dalian's decision, Commander," Yarvik replied. "I would judge the appropriateness of such a course of action after reading the information you propose to give us. Besides, we still have much research to do over and above mere interrogation."

Siobhan had known this would be her answer and nodded, her features carefully composed in an outward show of neutrality.

"Might I see the research you're doing? We may well be able to provide you with information to assist with that as well."

"Of course." Yarvik's eyes narrowed as she studied Siobhan's face, perhaps noticing the unbearable tension beneath her outward calm. "Has talking to this xeno distressed you? If so, you have my apology, but you'll agree on the importance of seeing for yourself that our common enemy has come to Miranda."

She gestured toward the exit with her hand.

"We can do that right now."

Drang, sensing that the one human on Miranda who could speak his tongue was about to leave, perhaps forever, said, "You will ask them to kill us?"

"I already have," Dunmoore replied in her accented Shrehari, "but my request seems to have fallen on deaf ears. These people who are not of my people consider all those not of their species as no more than clever animals, you included."

"They have no honor." Drang spat. "If you would get word back to the empire about *Ziq Tar*'s fate, perhaps our shades will not stir too much in death."

"I will try, that is my promise to you and your crew."

"Then take care these butchers don't get it into their minds to see you as clever animals as well, Dunmoore of the Commonwealth, lest you and yours suffer our fate. Nothing is beyond people who would treat others with such dishonor."

"Sadly, I must agree. I wish you a good death, Drang."

"And I you."

Dunmoore felt thrown off kilter by the tragedy of two enemies conversing in this manner as if they had become allies in the face of a greater evil. A chill ran down her spine once it dawned on her that she had yet to see the worst of this place.

While part of her breathed a sigh of relief once they had returned to the sterile corridor, Drang's parting words echoed in her mind, and she felt a desperate longing to be back aboard *Stingray*.

"Would you care to see a Skraeling?" Yarvik's matter-of-fact question derailed Dunmoore's bleak train of thought, and she nodded, knowing that she could not avoid it.

The Mirandan led her through another door and stopped in front of a transparent-fronted cell in all ways identical to the one that held Commander Drang.

Inside, a small bipedal creature, no bigger than the average human ten-year-old, with long arms ending in three-fingered hands and with leathery greenish-yellow skin stared at the humans with large, dark eyes. It seemed frightened and bewildered, and Siobhan thought she heard a faint, plaintive wail.

"Long ago, before they became aggressive and threatened our survival, a significant number of them infested the planet. Now a few, like this one, survive in isolated areas."

Dunmoore felt unaccountably nauseous at the pitiful sight, unable to comprehend how this being, sentient or not, could ever be a threat to humans, to the point of its entire species having been condemned to death. Staring into those black, moist eyes convinced her that the Skraeling was indeed intelligent.

"What will happen to it?"

Yarvik shrugged.

"The usual. There are always researchers with more questions."

The Skraeling chattered softly, one hand reaching for the transparent wall and Dunmoore knew she needed to get out of this place before she lost what remained of her composure.

"Thank you." She avoided Yarvik's eyes and gestured toward the door. "I've seen enough."

"The laboratories next, then?"

Dunmoore nodded once, eyes hard, hoping that she would be able to make it to the end of the tour without grabbing Yarvik by the throat.

"How did you find matters at Custodian HQ?" Kalivan asked the moment she walked into their suite. "Did they indeed catch a few Shrehari?"

She nodded, her emotional exhaustion immediately visible to Kalivan's searching gaze.

"Bad?" A worried frown creased his forehead.

Dunmoore dropped down on the sofa and nodded again.

"Apropos of nothing at all," she met his eyes and held them, "what was the linguistic composition of the original colonist group?"

"Mostly Western European." He winked to signal that he understood her intent. "English, Spanish, German, perhaps French. The consortium that organized *Tempest* was based in London."

"Then they won't understand this?" She asked in Mandarin, a sly smile playing on her lips.

"Very doubtful," he replied in the same language, eyes brightening at her deviousness. "They might have had a few speakers in the original bunch, but I sincerely doubt they would have perpetuated it for all these centuries if their primary tongue is a Mirandan derivation of English. By the way, your accent is perfect. Most of us tend to lose a lot of our language skills after graduation from the Academy."

"Xièxiè." She bowed her head, thanking him. "And now we can talk without being overheard."

"We hope."

Dunmoore then recounted every detail of her visit to Custodian headquarters.

Kalivan stared at her in silence for almost a minute after she fell silent, confusion, and anger vying for supremacy in his eyes.

"Vivisection?" He whispered. "You're sure?"

"I'm sure. I've seen their labs and heard their so-called researchers explain in detail how they conduct their xeno studies. For them, all non-humans are no more than animals, whether or not they possess FTL technology."

"The Shrehari might be bastards," Foste said in broken Mandarin, not bothering to hide her disgust, "but they don't deserve that."

"No one here would argue the point, Chief," Kalivan replied.

"The native species, the one they call Skraeling doesn't deserve it either, Wes." Dunmoore shook her head, feeling drained of all emotion. "The one I saw struck me as clearly sentient. I'm sure it identified me as different from its captors and tried to communicate."

"Anthropomorphizing, Siobhan?"

"No. I've had contact with enough non-human species during my life to avoid that mistake."

Vincenzo handed her a glass filled with wine.

"Here you go, Captain," he said in Anglic. "It'll do you some good."

"Thanks." She smiled wanly at him. "I'll try not to down it in one sip."

"Don't hold back on our account," Kalivan said in Anglic, before, switching back to Mandarin. "After the day you had."

"Who does crap like that, sir?" Vincenzo asked, his accent even worse than Foste's.

"People who were severely scarred by their first contact with non-human space-faring species." Kalivan grimaced. "To survive, they've transformed themselves into a society that will not allow any threats whatsoever and have defined the non-human *other* as an automatic threat. Once you cross that line, the idea that the other is in any way worthy of consideration becomes heresy."

He paused to take a sip before continuing. "It's happened many times before in our history, and to societies founded on some of the noblest ideals, such as the ones that motivated the *Tempest* colonists — not as a result of first contact, but other stresses. Mind you, after deciding that non-humans were lesser beings, knowing they're able to travel between the stars when Mirandan scientists have been unable to develop the necessary technology might have exacerbated that particular societal illness."

"Well said, professor," Siobhan raised an ironic toast. "I see your training in psychological operations wasn't wasted. I trust your day went better than mine?"

"Educational. Perhaps more than yours, in a few respects. They want our technology, and they want it badly. My meeting this morning was supposed to be a getting to know you kind of event, but it turned into a high-pressure sales job on having your engineers part with the secret of antimatter power and FTL travel."

He rose and walked over to the drinks table for a refill.

"I got some very disturbing vibes from a few of the participants and now, after what you saw in their police HQ, I'm even more disturbed. These are not friendly people, Siobhan. They've developed a single-minded focus on protecting themselves and in the process lost some of what made them our kin."

"I'm not giving them anything more at this point, Wes," she replied. "In fact, I'm beginning to regret parting with a copy of our historical database. Technology? Never. These people might have a civilization of sorts, but I have a hard time considering them as being civilized."

"And if they haven't figured that out yet, I'm sure they will very soon." Kalivan sat across from her again. "This Senior Group Leader Yarvik certainly sensed your disapproval of how they deal with non-humans. Experienced police officers, especially in paranoid societies, become highly skilled at ferreting out one's innermost thoughts, even though you might have tried hard to hide them, and let's face it; you're not that good at covering your feelings."

She sighed. "Sadly all too true."

"Which means we can expect a change in tactics soon. Their reaction when I suggested we get the Fleet to send a delegation of scientists and engineers after returning home makes me think they might not let us leave until we cooperate."

"They might not let us leave at all," Dunmoore replied, remembering Drang's parting words. "After all, we're not of their people, are we?"

"Meaning?"

"Meaning they'll try to take what they want and not particularly care about how they do it. Like Linc Lam said at the reception last night, under Mirandan law, we're xenos." She shook her head.

"What makes you think they'd drop all pretense at diplomacy?"

"Anyone who does what they're doing to the Shrehari prisoners won't hesitate to help themselves to our persons if they thought it might get them the wherewithal to copy our technology. We're not Mirandans. We're intruders and can be dealt with the same way as any other intruders."

Her face hardened. "Can you imagine the Mirandans expanding across this part of the galaxy, once they get themselves modern weaponry and FTL travel? It won't be to link up with the Commonwealth, and I wouldn't wish to ally ourselves with them in any case. If the Shrehari find out what humans are doing to their prisoners, how long before our war with them turns truly ugly, even though it isn't our portion of humanity doing the deeds? My God, the fallout would be horrendous."

"Where does that leave us, then?" Kalivan gently placed his wine glass on the table and stared into its ruby depths, elbows on his knees, hands clasped together.

"Screwed." She gave him a weak smile. "With General Order Eighty-One in effect, if the Mirandans decide to extend our visit permanently and without our permission, Gregor Pushkin inherits the mantle of command, and his orders are to take *Stingray* home."

"A very pessimistic assessment, no?"

"Of these genocidal bastards? I think not. People capable of doing what I've witnessed in the belief that it's the most normal thing in the galaxy won't hesitate if it's to protect and defend Miranda."

At her heated reply, he looked up and into a mask of fury.

"What if they forcibly oppose *Stingray*'s departure?"

"Then Gregor will fight his way out of it." The steel in her voice was unmistakable. "He's actually a fine tactician beneath that quiet exterior. There's not much more I can teach him in that respect. If need be, he'll jump out of the system before reaching the hyperlimit. *Stingray*'s due for the knacker's yard anyway so one more bad transition to FTL won't matter."

Kalivan picked up his glass again and drained it in one gulp. "Let's hope your visit to their dungeons has made you more pessimistic than is warranted, Siobhan. I'm sure they recognize that taking the step of seizing us and attempting to take your ship will irretrievably sour any hope of a reconciliation with the rest of humanity."

"Perhaps." She looked at Kalivan with a grim expression on her tired face. "But what if they don't care?"

"Then we fight it out," Foste said.

"I'll drink to that, Chief."

*

The private door to Geoff Martell's office opened silently to admit his Custodian counterpart, ushered in by a discreet aide. Mira Dalian visiting the head of Miranda's armed forces might not be forbidden, but a wary Protector like Cyrus Hames would look askance at any such meeting that excluded him.

"Can I offer you a drink?" Martell asked, gesturing toward a grouping of easy chairs to one side.

"Please. If you still have some of that fine brandy, I'd gladly take a glass."

"I do."

Dalian took a seat facing the narrow, thick windows through which she could see a smattering of stars in the dark night sky. Somewhere up there orbited a starship Miranda needed and if the Two Hundred named her as Hames' successor, she would know how to use it for her people's greater glory.

Martell handed her a tulip-shaped glass, then took a facing chair. He raised his snifter.

"Cheers, Mira."

"Your health, Geoff."

Once they had taken a small sip, enjoying the alcohol's warm bite, Martell asked, "So?"

"So it might have been a mistake to let Dunmoore see the xenos."

Martell snorted.

"You mean you'll admit that Cyrus was right? Shall I decree this day to be a public celebration?"

"Laugh all you want, but it means we might have to move up the timetable, especially after that idiot Lam spoke his mind to Dunmoore at the Select Committee reception."

"Cyrus is still clinging to the notion of brotherly love. He'll not authorize us to act."

"Cyrus is done in four months. If need be, we can convince him to retire early."

"Have the Two Hundred finally named a successor?" Martell cocked an eyebrow. "Perhaps one Mira Dalian? I'm sure 'that idiot Lam' will have mobilized his entire faction to vote against your nomination."

"Mock all you want, Geoff. I won't have Cyrus let this chance slip through our fingers."

"Perhaps I should make today a national holiday. For once I agree with you."

The perfectly innocent expression on Martell's seamed face caused Dalian's eyes to narrow with suspicion.

"What have you done without the Protector's authorization?"

"I could ask you the same question, but to avoid a lengthy back and forth, I'll let you in on my little contingency plan. You see, it's a variation of the trick we played on those Shrehari a few months ago."

When he finished with his explanation, Dalian laughed.

"You sly devil. It could dovetail nicely with my own preparations, even if I have to accelerate events."

"Since I know you'll tell me about them in your own good time, why don't we go back to your original comment?" Martell took another sip. "Why was letting Dunmoore see the xenos a mistake?"

"Because she now mistrusts us. Senior Group Leader Yarvik allowed her to speak with these Shrehari in their tongue and whatever transpired upset Dunmoore, as did her visit to the Skraeling holding cells and the labs after that. These Commonwealth people have weak stomachs and soft minds, Geoff. They consider xenos to be as worthy as our own species."

"As do some members of the Two Hundred, though they're careful to keep their views quiet. Did Dunmoore tell you all of this? We knew their views differed from ours, but to that extent?" Martell's tone hinted at gentle mockery.

"Of course not. Yarvik is a seasoned interrogator. She could read Dunmoore's emotions clearly enough. Then, there's also the matter of the Earthers conversing in a tongue quite unlike any in our linguistic database the moment she returned to the Protector's Palace. I'm sure you can deduce the reasons behind that little turn of events."

"Can your experts decipher it?"

"No. It could be a non-human language for all we know."

Dalian drained her glass and gently placed it on the table between them.

"Another?"

"I'll pass, thanks. Too much of the good stuff can be addictive. How did the meeting with Kalivan go?"

"It went nowhere. He retained his insistence that any transfer of technology must be approved by Dunmoore and more likely by their superiors on Earth. We now have a lot of knowledge of their history and government institutions — quite chaotic, by the way. And he has some knowledge of ours, but if we want the secrets of their antimatter power plants, their energy weapons, and faster-than-light travel, we have to wait until their government sends a fully empowered delegation."

"We can't afford that, and we can't allow them to return to their people, Geoff."

"I know we can't wait, though I suspect Cyrus would say otherwise. As to letting them return home, I have mixed feelings." Martell's forehead furrowed with indecision. "They strike me as honorable."

"If their government decides to annex Miranda, we would be unable to resist."

"Why would their government do so?"

"Because it can." Her nostrils flared. "We are the lost colonists who must be returned to the human flock."

"Aren't you letting your paranoia take over? From what we know of their political system, they're content to live and let live."

"So the envoy says," she sneered. "Our job is to ensure the survival of the humans here on Miranda, and on Sycorax and the other off-world settlements, the survival of the Dominion we're sworn to serve. Letting them return to

Earth with all they've learned of us would threaten everything we hold dear. We need their technology. We don't need their embrace, and we certainly don't need their philosophies."

"They won't give us their technology, especially if your little slip-up with the xenos has turned Dunmoore against us."

"Then we take it, my dear Geoff. Cyrus can scream as loud as he wants. A sufficient majority of the Two Hundred will endorse any action to secure this starship and its engineers for our own use. Perhaps our researchers can even examine our cousins to see if their physiology has deviated from ours in a measurable way. After all, they're not Mirandans, and that makes them xenos under the law."

"You take too much pleasure in your work, Mira." Martell shuddered. "Besides, Cyrus would never let the law endanger these Earthers, you know that."

"And you don't take pleasure in your work? Tell me you won't feel a thrill run down your spine the day your Defenders can deploy weapons as powerful as what the Earthers have. Tell me the idea of eradicating xenos in their far away lairs doesn't fill you with a surge of patriotic feeling."

Martell raised his hands in surrender.

"You know I can't tell you any of that."

"Then you know what we have to do, even if it means going against the Protector. You said it yourself — they won't voluntarily part with what we need."

"What is Gano's position on the matter?"

"Our dear Speaker for the Two Hundred will go along with anything the two of us propose, even if it means forcing Cyrus' hand or even forcing him to step down a few months early."

"Shocking." Martell chuckled. "A Speaker who wants the Protector's mantle, be it ever so temporary."

"Be it ever so permanent, if his colleagues in the Two Hundred decide to name him after he assumes the interim between Cyrus' departure and the installation of the new Protector."

"Thus denying you a chance at the palace for ten years." A malicious smile tugged at his lips. "Gano would live dangerously if he puts himself forward after stepping into the acting role in the absence of a named successor."

"If we three tackle Cyrus together, he'll see reason and give us leave to proceed, thus obviating a constitutional crisis."

"Hah!" Martell's laughter sounded like a bark. "Now I know your reason for visiting me at this hour. To sound me out. I knew it wasn't my brandy."

She studied him with cold, emotionless eyes, waiting for his reaction. Instead of a reply, he rose and walked over to his desk, touching the comscreen.

"Yes, sir?" The aide asked.

"Contact the Protector's office and let them know the Inner Council needs to meet tomorrow morning to discuss the most recent developments."

"Immediately, sir."

Martell cut the communication and directed a grim smile at his gray-uniformed counterpart.

"And so it begins."

"Yes." The predatory gleam in her dark eyes sent a brief shiver down his spine. "The beginning of a new age for Miranda, one in which we will bestride the galaxy on our terms, not as the Earthers' poor cousins."

"One step at a time. First, we need to secure the knowledge." He sat down across from her again. "Now that I'm on board, I think it's time you told me what you have in mind that dovetails so nicely with the preparations I've made."

"In mind? My dear Geoff, I've launched the operation already. When we meet with Cyrus tomorrow, it'll be solely to obtain his imprimatur, not his permission."

"Already reaching for the levers of ultimate power, I see."

"Someone has to act," she replied, climbing to her feet. "And it appears I've inherited that responsibility, for the good of the Dominion."

"And not coincidentally also for the good of Mira Dalian." He smirked.

"Thereby joining the pleasurable to the practical."

— Twenty-Two —

"We've been invited to tour one of their agricultural facilities," Kalivan said by way of greeting when Dunmoore emerged from her room the next morning. "And the helpful sprites haunting this palace have left us an enormous breakfast again."

He pointed at the table by the door, where Foste and Vincenzo were busy loading up their plates.

"Invited, or ordered?" She replied, a sour expression on her face. "And does that order — I mean invitation — include all four of us?"

"Now, now," he gently chided her in Mandarin, "we mustn't give our hosts any reason to suspect we've come to dislike them. Unfortunately, we're still at their mercy."

Dunmoore inclined her head

"Of course."

"The invitation," he continued in Anglic, "includes all four of us. It'll be fun to get out into the country for the day and see how they've hardened their food production against off-world attackers."

"When are we leaving?" She wandered over to the buffet to examine the food offerings.

"As soon as we're ready. I'm to give the ever helpful Senior Group Leader Nan a call.

"Can you ask him to have us visit a communications facility so I can speak with my first officer?"

"I already have. He promised to arrange something like the last time for when we get back from our tour."

Siobhan helped herself to a small pile of fruit and bread, a meal that seemed meager compared to Foste's, but she had not regained her appetite after visiting Custodian headquarters. Kalivan smiled at her when she sat down across from him.

"Try not to look like your favorite pet died, Siobhan. In diplomacy, when we can't paste on a convincing smile, we make sure to be as bland as distilled water."

She snorted.

"I tend to agree with the guy who said diplomacy is the art of saying 'nice doggie' until you can find a rock."

"Let's hope it doesn't come to that."

"On that point, I wholeheartedly agree, Wes." She switched to Mandarin again. "I don't want to fight my way out of Miranda's orbit. *Stingray* might be well ahead of their ships when it comes to just about everything, but she's still only one frigate to dozens of their over-sized cruisers, plus whatever they can throw at us from the moons and other space-based platforms."

"To repeat myself, let's hope it doesn't come to that."

"From your lips to God's ear, Colonel," Foste said in a solemn tone.

After that, they ate in silence and then prepared themselves to face a day of playing tourist. For all of them save Dunmoore, it would be their first time outside the Protector's Palace since arriving.

To their surprise, an officer in Custodian gray presented himself at their suite's door, accompanied by four dour-faced men with holstered sidearms, less than thirty minutes after Kalivan spoke with Nan again. He saluted them in the Mirandan manner, fist against his chest.

"I'm Bannerman Salik, and it's my honor to accompany you on this inspection tour."

"You're most kind, Bannerman," Kalivan replied, returning his salute in the Commonwealth way. "We look forward to seeing how you've developed an agricultural system that can withstand xeno incursions."

"Of course." He gestured at the corridor. "If you'll please follow me."

"Why the large escort?" Dunmoore asked once they started walking toward the stairs, boxed in by Custodian troopers.

"Not everyone is pleased with our receiving strangers, even of our own species, Commander," Salik replied, in a tone so smooth she suspected his words had been rehearsed. "The Protector has ordered that we ensure violent dissidents don't cause you discomfort."

"This is the first we hear about violent dissidents," Kalivan remarked. "We had the impression that Mirandan society was strongly unified, albeit with some political differences."

"I wish it were so, but unfortunately, there have always been those who disagree with our laws and the decisions of our leaders to a degree that is sometimes unseemly. They often join forces with criminal elements, hence the Protector's concern for your well-being."

Dunmoore caught Kalivan's eyes and curled her lips for a fraction of a second, to convey her skepticism.

"How considerate of him," she muttered.

Salik guided them through the main lobby and up a short flight of stairs that led to an airlock-like entryway. There, a sentry in Defender black opened a massive portal, and they stepped out into the brilliant morning sunshine.

An enormous wheeled vehicle sat on a smooth concrete apron bordering an equally smooth avenue that pointed at the heart of Sanctum.

The air seemed remarkably still, without the hint of a breeze or the chirp of a bird.

At their approach, a side door, set between wheels taller than Foste's lanky frame, swung down to form a short ramp.

They climbed aboard to find a spacious, well-appointed compartment with padded seats and various screens.

The vehicle had no windows beyond those in the nose, where a driver, also in Custodian gray, sat patiently in front of a control panel. At a touch, he retracted the ramp, sealing them in, and the screens came to life with a three-hundred and sixty-degree view of their surroundings.

"The facility is thirty kilometers south of Sanctum," Salik said once they started moving to the low hum of electric motors. "We shall be passing through a zone of native plants on the way, and if you wish to know more, I can answer any questions you may have."

"Most gracious." Kalivan inclined his head but had to restrain a smile when he saw Vincenzo briefly imitate, in an exaggerated way, the man's infuriatingly bland facial expression.

*

"You did what?" Protector Hames half-rose from his chair, eyes blazing with a mixture of anger and incredulity. "Call it off, Mira. Now."

"It's too late for that," she replied, shrugging. "Besides, we weren't going to get what we need from them through persuasion. You've read the reports. Dunmoore's reluctance has likely become outright hostility by now. Her discussing matters with the others in an unknown tongue proves it."

"We might still have achieved that if you hadn't overstepped the authority I gave you to show Dunmoore the new xenos. Identification would have sufficed."

"She told Senior Group Leader Yarvik she could speak their language." Dalian sounded unrepentant. "I decided it was worth the risk. No one could tell that the Earthers were xeno-lovers. Besides, I might point out that you authorized them to meet with the Select Committee, knowing Linc Lam would take the opportunity to share his hateful views."

"And yet you achieved nothing from letting her come face-to-face with these Shrehari, which makes it a hundred times worse than the most eccentric of the Two Hundred mouthing off. Not only that, Yarvik had the lack of wits to show her a Skraeling and the research labs after getting the hint that Dunmoore disapproved of our treatment of non-humans." Hames struggled to contain his fury. "These Earthers are not like us. They've not faced what we, as a people have faced and still face."

"Precisely," Dalian retorted. "They're xenos in human form."

"No." The Protector shook his head with unusual vehemence. "You will not classify them as xenos. They are as human as you and I. Bugger letter of the law. I'm still Protector and have the final say."

"Cyrus," Geoff Martell held up a placating hand. "Kalivan made it clear we wouldn't be given access to their technology until they report back to their superiors and these, in turn, send a delegation of specialists, and if humanity's existential enemy, the Shrehari, have reached our part of the galaxy, we cannot afford to wait."

"And that's your opinion as Chief Defender?"

"It is." Martell nodded. "For the good of the Dominion, we must take that which is not offered freely."

"Thereby ruining any chance we might have at establishing relations with a kin that has spread across more than fifty star systems." Hames bit his lower lip. "You're placing me in an impossible situation."

"If the Earthers don't return home," Dalian pointed out, "they'll be presumed lost and by the time someone sends a follow-on expedition, we'll have become an interstellar power in our own right, able to deal with Earth as equals. And no one will ever know about *Stingray*'s change of ownership."

"Ah yes." The Protector slumped back in his chair and, elbows on its arms, steepled his fingers. "Your notion of founding our very own empire and eradicating the xeno threat for good, based on seizing a single FTL starship and forcing its crew into our service. Sometimes I wonder about your sanity, Mira."

"At least I have a vision," she said, smiling sweetly. "All you have is a few months left before mandatory retirement and a descent into obscurity."

"Without the approval of whoever is sitting in my chair, your vision will remain just that, unless..." His eyes swiveled toward Gano Marant, who had so far remained silent. "Are the Two Hundred proposing to appoint Custodian Dalian to the Protectorship, perchance?"

"You know that we haven't finished deliberating," Marant replied, though to Hames' ears, he sounded evasive.

"Tell me, O Speaker, do you approve of Chief Custodian Dalian's plan?"

"I approve of the notion that we take what is being unfairly withheld, Protector." Marant waved his hand at the two uniformed officers. "I leave the details of how that's done to those with more extensive experience than mine."

A sly smile crossed his lips.

"Besides, speaking as a lawyer, I cannot fault Mira's logic concerning the Earthers' xeno status. They are not of the Dominion and therefore cannot expect anything more than the treatment reserved for all intruders."

"Next, you're going to tell me that if I don't agree, you'll get the necessary number among the Two Hundred to stand with the Chief Defender and the Chief Custodian, and override my will. Or simply depose me at gunpoint if that doesn't pan out?"

"It is how our constitution works, Cyrus," Gano Marant said, sounding rather weary of the discussion. "As for deposing you at gunpoint, again, I'll defer to my uniformed colleagues and their greater sense of our history."

"Have you three thought what might happen if things go wrong? If the Earthers escape to report back? It'll be seen as an act of war by their government, and we may never meet Earth as equals. We might find their foot at our throat instead, holding us down forever."

"They're too busy fighting these Shrehari." Dalian shrugged dismissively. "But Dunmoore and her ship won't escape us."

"Is that what you wish written as your epitaph?" Acid dripped from Hames' voice.

"Would you like to go down in history as the Protector who had the chance of getting us the stars and failed?" She smirked openly now. "Or would you like to be remembered as the one who freed us from the bonds of slower than light travel?"

Hames closed his eyes and shook his head.

"I don't want to be remembered as the Protector who destroyed our chances of rejoining humanity with our heads held high."

"You won't." Dalian watched Hames through half-closed eyelids, knowing she had won the battle. The Dominion's dictator pro tem seemed to have aged by a decade in the last few moments, a sure sign that he recognized his defeat.

"Since I apparently have no choice," he finally said, pinching the bridge of his nose between thumb and forefinger, "all that remains is to pray and see it through."

"And Mira," his eyes snapped open, spearing the Custodian with a cold stare, "you will not treat the Earthers like xenos, or I shall ensure that your chances of ever calling this office your own vanish along with your last breath. I may be old and feeble in your eyes, but I spent forty years as a Defender and have lost none of my martial skills."

"Of course, Protector."

*

The intercom's chime pulled Gregor Pushkin from his contemplation of the daily status reports. He reached out to stroke the darkened screen on the corner of his desk, eyes still on the latest engineering update.

"XO here."

"It's Syten, sir. Chief Penzara reports the probe ready. He's had it rigged so that we could push it out to one of the unknown contacts without leaving an emission trace."

"Excellent." Pushkin dropped his tablet. "I'm on my way."

When he got to the bridge, Syten relinquished command chair and went to stand by Penzara's console.

"What's the story, Chief?" He asked after sitting down.

"The probe is as stealthy as my techs can make it, sir. These Mirandans might be good at hiding, but there's no reason we can't do the same. I've had it shifted to the hangar deck, and when you give permission to proceed, I'll have my lads kick it out the back door, so to speak. Then, we'll use the tractor beam on its lowest setting to bring the probe close to the target, that way there's not even the hint of a drive lighting up for a few seconds to betray it. When it's ready, it'll establish a link via laser and start reporting. After that, we just pull the beastie back on board, and no one's the wiser."

"I trust you've left the self-destruct mechanism in place?"

"Indeed I did, sir. I've even improved on it. If someone unauthorized tries to open any of the access panels, its innards will turn into a blob of molten stuff. That way, there's no chance of blowing up a Mirandan ship that might take it in too close."

"A man after my own heart. Careful in his ruthlessness. You may launch."

Moments later, the status board showed the hangar deck depressurizing, then Penzara changed one of the secondary screens to an aft view. They briefly saw the dark, elongated shape of the probe against *Stingray*'s lighter colored hull and then it vanished.

Pushkin sat back in the command chair and fought to contain his impatience at finally getting some answers. They would come in due time, and no one wanted to see a fidgety first officer.

"Sir." Rownes raised her hand.

"What is it?"

"I'm getting a clear signal from the trackers Colonel Kalivan and the captain are carrying."

"It's about time." A relieved smile tugged at his lips.

Data began to appear on the telemetry readout.

"The probe has initiated the link," Penzara reported. "And we're getting a visual on the target."

A second side screen lit up, this time showing a dense field of stars against the velvety black of space. Slowly, almost imperceptibly, stars began to vanish at the center of the image, occluded by something dark and, if the telemetry was accurate, something that barely registered against the background radiation.

"There you are, my pretty," the gunnery chief murmured, "now to get close without bumping into you."

The appearance of relative motion ceased, and Penzara sat up, a satisfied grunt escaping his lips.

"Whatever that thing is," he said after studying the readout, "the Mirandans hid it well. I can't tell whether it's a communications relay, a gravitic mine or a drinks dispenser."

"I'm pretty sure we can rule out drinks machine, Chief," Pushkin smiled. "But based on the minimally detectable emissions, even this close, I'd say it's not active right now."

"Which means we'll find out only the moment it goes active, and that might not be good at all," Syten pointed out, stating the obvious.

"Would you like me to try an active ping?" Penzara asked.

Pushkin stared at the image, rubbing his chin as he tried to decide whether to play their hand.

"If we assume the thing's inactive," he finally said, "then maybe we can get away with it. One ping, Chief."

"Might I suggest we raise shields first, sir?" Lieutenant Syten suggested.

"Absolutely." Pushkin silently cursed himself for having forgotten.

"Shields up," she reported moments later.

"Go ahead, Chief. Let's see what that object carries beneath the stylish black paint job."

*

"What are those?" Kalivan pointed at one of the screens. They had emerged from the half-buried city into a countryside dotted with rolling hills, one of which seemed carpeted by dressed stones laid out in child's jumble among low brush and short, broad trees.

"The ruins of Old Sanctum, destroyed during the first xeno incursion," Salik replied. "The site is both a shrine to those who died or vanished and a reminder that we must always be ready to fight for our race's survival."

"Can we visit it?"

The Mirandan shook his head.

"It is hallowed ground, accessible only during the Days of Sorrow."

"Days of Sorrow?" Kalivan looked at Salik with a quizzical smile.

"The three most important days of the year for all Mirandans, Colonel. When we remember those who perished or were taken, and when we renew the vow to never let our people suffer at the hands of xenos ever again. The first day is the Day of Tears, the second, the Day of Rage, and the third, the Day of Vengeance."

"It would be interesting to witness your rituals. Will they occur soon?"

"No. Not for another four months, when a new Protector takes the vow of office to keep all within the Dominion safe."

"Pity." Kalivan stared at the rapidly receding ruins, mentally adding another piece to the Miranda puzzle.

They eventually entered an area overgrown with strange-looking vegetation, the advertised strip of native flora and Kalivan nodded at the side screens.

"Would it be possible to briefly stop and take a closer look?"

Salik glanced at his timepiece.

"Sorry, not right now. Perhaps on the way back."

"We're on a tight schedule?" Dunmoore asked.

"Indeed." The Mirandan's expression remained utterly bland.

Soon, they emerged back into the bright sunshine and left the hill country behind. Then, the vehicle entered a vast expanse of golden grain surrounding a flat, regular plateau that seemed out of place in the middle of the prairie.

Salik pointed at the forward screen.

"It may look like a mesa of sorts, but that's the main agricultural station serving Sanctum. Within are the animal husbandry and hydroponics facilities. You cannot see from here, but it is heavily defended by guns able to reach high up into the atmosphere."

"Fascinating." Kalivan glanced at Dunmoore. "Don't you think so, Commander?"

"Absolutely." She managed to keep her tone free of sarcasm, but Kalivan could sense that Siobhan's opinion of their hosts had not improved. Quite the contrary, in fact.

Up close, the facility seemed immense, stretching out far into the fields on either side of the road. A large, armored door opened at their approach, revealing a white, well-lit passage that sloped downward, taking them below ground level. They emerged into a cavernous garage where their vehicle came to a stop beside two more of its kind.

"We have arrived." Salik stood and waved at the driver to release the side hatch.

"Glad he told us," Vincenzo muttered into Foste's ear. "Otherwise, I'd have never known."

The bosun made a shushing motion, but a faint smile appeared on her thin lips nonetheless.

The Mirandan led them through a small chamber with doors on each end and into air so moist, it almost felt like a sauna. A rich, earthy smell tickled Dunmoore's nostrils, and she could not help but smile at the memories it evoked, memories of her childhood on the family farm, long ago.

Salik ushered them through another room, but instead of finding row upon row of hydroponic bays, they came face-to-face with a dozen grim Custodians holding carbines at the high port. They neither spoke, nor pointed their weapons at Dunmoore and her companions, yet all four instinctively knew the Mirandan mask had finally come off.

Then a coarse, gray-uniformed figure stepped out from the shadows.

"Colonel Kalivan, Commander Dunmoore, welcome to our research station." A cruel smile tugged at the corners of Senior Group Leader Yarvik's mouth. "We do some of our best work within the Sanctum Agricultural Facility."

*

A harsh voice broke through Brakal's contemplation of his mostly empty mug.

"Commander."

"You dare interrupt me?" He snarled without turning around. "Can't you see I mourn the passing of another fine ale?"

"There will always be more ale," Urag replied, ignoring his captain's ugly temper. "But there is only one *Stingray*."

"What?" Brakal dropped the mug and faced his second-in-command. Then, his raw features lit up with savage joy. "I knew it. The flame-haired she-wolf. Speak, before I squeeze it out of you."

"We have detected an emission signature in orbit around the fourth planet that resembles the one on file for Dunmoore's ship. It's not an exact match, by any means, but after Cimmeria, it would be bound to change due to repairs."

"So she fought and won? Or fought and lost?"

"Impossible to say. We're picking up increasing evidence of technological artifacts, but so well hidden that we have to infer most of them. *Stingray*'s signature is the cleanest of all."

"Someone lives in this system." Brakal scratched his bony chin. "Perhaps Dunmoore made first contact with its inhabitants and allied with them."

"A likely situation, yes. In which case, we must take care. One on one, we can fight her. If she has new friends with space-worthy ships, we may wish to avoid a battle that could leave us damaged and unable to return home."

"And yet, if the humans found allies here, we must determine what they are and the threat they may pose. Otherwise, Hralk would have reason to chastise me in public, and I don't intend to give him that pleasure. We approach the fourth planet silently and observe, but remain ready for battle should the occasion present itself."

"And if the occasion fails to materialize?"

"Then we remain silent and wait until Dunmoore leaves this system, at which point we will stalk her and avenge the loss of *Tol Vakash*. But I will know who inhabits this place before we leave, Urag."

"Whoever that may be, they hide well," the second-in-command replied. "We can barely make out artificial structures on the fifth planet's moons, but our systems cannot detect coherent emissions. Hopefully, we will see more when we approach the fourth planet."

"Have no doubt about that." Brakal slammed his fist on the table. "We will learn all about the people who allied with Dunmoore, even if I have to stick my own hand into the *kroorath*'s nest."

*

The door to Hames' office opened unbidden, and Senior Group Leader Borik Nan stepped in, coming to attention on the threshold. Mira Dalian stopped speaking in mid-sentence as all four of the Dominion's top leaders turned to stare at the intruder.

"Sir, my apologies, but we've received a report from Defender headquarters that a new intruder has been detected approaching Sycorax on a path similar to the one the Earthers took."

"Is it another of their ships?"

"Impossible to say. It has dampened its emissions quite thoroughly, almost as efficiently as Dunmoore's frigate did. The intruder is out of range of Sycorax's defensive array, but ships are being deployed to come athwart its path."

Hames chewed on his lower lip for a few moments.

"Observe but do not act," he said, "not until it comes within range of Miranda's defensive array. I do not wish to engage in two separate actions at once, not at this critical juncture."

"As you command." Nan dipped his head once and then vanished.

"Now you see why we must act rapidly?" Dalian smiled with an air of intense self-satisfaction. "Two xeno ships in our space within a few days."

The Protector waved her words away with a tired hand.

"You made your point before this occurred, Mira." Moreover, he thought, you didn't leave me much of a choice either. Pray that it doesn't come back to haunt you.

— Twenty-Three —

"What is the meaning of this, Senior Group Leader?" Kalivan asked. "I thought we had been invited to marvel at the way you've hardened food production against off-world attack, as honored guests of your Protector. Instead, we're met by this."

He gestured at the squad of Custodian troopers. "I don't quite understand where four tourists warrant a heavily armed guard, especially one led by an officer of your exalted rank."

A grim chuckle escaped Dunmoore's lips. "The meaning is simple, Colonel. Our hosts have finally figured out that soft persuasion hasn't worked and won't ever work, so now they'll try to get their hands on our technology the hard way — through us, letting impatience ruin what could have been a mutually beneficial reunion with the rest of humanity."

"Mutually beneficial? Hardly," Yarvik said in an emotionless tone. "We might be of the same species, but the Dominion is so very different from your Commonwealth. Any reunion would mean the end of our way of life. Better that we take steps to meet the rest of humanity on an equal footing. It would be better done with your cooperation, but it will be done."

"We are xenos to you, aren't we?" Dunmoore raised an eyebrow in challenge.

"Under the strict wording of the law, yes," she admitted.

"And I've seen what you do to those you deem lesser beings." A sneer twisted Siobhan's scar.

"Please." Kalivan raised a placating hand. "I'm sure we can work things out to our mutual satisfaction."

"Wes," Dunmoore pushed his arm down, "don't bother. They want to take a shortcut to FTL capability, and they'll do whatever is needed."

"We want the knowledge, yes," Yarvik turned her expressionless eyes on Siobhan. "In fact, we deserve to share in your knowledge. You have managed to do what we have not and after abandoning us to suffer in a hostile galaxy; Earth owes us a helping hand. You owe us a helping hand."

"Is the Protector aware of this gross breach of diplomacy?" Kalivan asked.

"I'm sure he is," Dunmoore answered for the Mirandan. "It's that kind of dictatorship, Wes."

"Then I demand to speak with him." Kalivan glared at Yarvik. "As Envoy of the Commonwealth, I will not allow you to treat us in this manner."

Instead of answering, the senior group leader gestured at her men. Moments later, Dunmoore, Kalivan, and the two spacers had metal restraints around their wrists and gun barrels jammed in the kidneys.

Yarvik led them through a warren of corridors that held more than a passing resemblance to those Dunmoore remembered from her previous day's visit to Custodian headquarters until they entered a cellblock identical to the one holding the Shrehari survivors.

"If you'll excuse me," the Mirandan said, "I need to report your detention to Chief Custodian Dalian and obtain further orders."

The troopers shoved them into individual cells and removed their manacles. Then, they left.

"Commander Drang was right," Dunmoore said, staring across the aisle at Kalivan, who wore a thoroughly disgusted expression. "Nothing is beyond the Mirandans."

"In that case, we should get something," Foste joked from the next cell, "if nothing's beyond them."

"I'm sure you won't like that something, Chief."

"No." The bosun sighed. "I probably won't. Do you think Mister Pushkin is going to go medieval on their asses once he finds out?"

"The walls have ears," Dunmoore reminded her in Mandarin.

"Sorry." Foste caught Vincenzo's eye. "Keep a zip on the lip, Vince."

"Got it." He gave her thumbs up.

More than an hour elapsed before the door to the cellblock opened again.

"Good morning, my dear Earther friends." Mira Dalian beamed at them. "It's time we tried to reconcile our differences for the greater good of all, don't you think?"

"Why would you expect us to wish reconciliation after luring us here under false pretenses and then shoving us into cells?" Dunmoore stared at Dalian through half-closed eyes. "That's hardly a basis for reasonable accommodation and certainly no way to deal with diplomatic guests."

"We need your cooperation to take the leap into FTL technology, Commander, and for the sake of the Dominion and its people, we will have that cooperation. It can be easy or hard as you may choose, but the outcome is preordained."

"And what would you have us do?" Kalivan asked.

"Turn over a copy of your ship's entire database for starters," Dalian turned toward him and smiled, "then we would have your technicians and engineers work with ours to understand the principles behind your power sources, your weapons, and your ship's drives. Of course, we would also have you train our people to operate your starship so that it may protect the Dominion while we build our own."

"And then? Once my crew no longer has any use for you?" Dunmoore looked down her nose at the shorter Chief Custodian, disgust creasing her lean features.

"If you've cooperated nicely, we might grant you a settlement. If you haven't..." she shrugged, leaving the implications unvoiced.

"Why not let us go home?"

"Until Miranda has increased its power to match your Commonwealth, we'd rather no one there knows about us. We do not intend to subordinate ourselves to your government for the sake of human unity. Miranda will create its own empire and secure itself against non-human species for all times. Besides, you and yours are xeno-lovers, and on that point, we will never see eye-to-eye."

"Is that what this is about? The fact that we respect the rights of other sentient species?" Dunmoore's face twisted into a sneer. "The fact that we don't consider humanity the master race of the galaxy?"

Dalian laughed.

"You waste emotion on beings who certainly don't see humans as a species with rights. But then, you are very different from us. Our civilization has had almost sixteen centuries more than yours to understand what existence in a hostile universe means. Come now, Commander, surely your long war against the Shrehari is teaching you otherwise when it comes to xenos. Surely you can understand us."

When neither Dunmoore nor Kalivan spoke, the Mirandan shrugged.

"We could have avoided this unpleasantness if you'd cooperated from the get-go. I'm sure Protector Hames would have let you return to your Commonwealth in due course, but you chose to deny us."

"I will not go down in history as the one who unleashed another bunch of technobarbarian savages on the galaxy," Dunmoore said through clenched teeth, "and all that I've seen of your Dominion so far leads me to believe I'm taking the correct course of action."

"Technobarbarians?" Dalian tilted her head to one side as she considered Siobhan. "What do you mean?"

"A society that went from barbarism to FTL travel without the intervening development of a responsible civilization, because someone gave them technology they shouldn't have obtained. There's been all too much of that over the last few centuries, either by accident or design, and we end up spending too much time, effort and lives beating them back until they learn that piracy, raiding, and slavery aren't acceptable."

"Oh?" Dalian's eyes lit up. "So it *is* you we have to thank for the xeno raids on Miranda. All the more reason for us to build our own interstellar empire."

"I doubt that happened through human agency. This system is much too far out. Your xeno raids began at roughly the same time Earth mastered antimatter power sources, the precondition for FTL travel. However, we were not the only ones to develop it independently. The Shrehari did, for one. Others may have as well."

"Perhaps, but I do take exception to your insinuation that the Dominion is not a responsible civilization, especially when it's older than yours."

"Thanks to a space-time anomaly." Dunmoore shrugged. "Age does not imply development. As I said, I will not be the one who helps you out into the galaxy after what I have seen. If my government thinks otherwise, then they can make that call after I've turned in my mission report."

"Your government isn't going to be in a position to decide, Commander. You seem to have forgotten that we won't let you leave the Dominion."

"I'd like to see you stop my ship." A defiant smile pulled at her lips. "It'll lay waste to your orbitals and your lunar installations in a matter of minutes."

"You're hardly in a position to have it do so, but I admire your boldness. Now, if we can drop the posturing and have a serious discussion as to how you'll comply with our requests so that we may ensure no one dies needlessly, we might have you back in more comfortable quarters before the day is out."

"Screw you."

Dalian seemed nonplussed at the retort.

"I gather that's a refusal?"

"Smart girl."

"It's a shame that the current Protector refuses to deem you xenos under our laws. It would make things so much easier."

Dunmoore repressed an involuntary shiver and felt pleased that she could retain her contemptuous expression.

"We have several options open to us, you and me," Dalian continued. "For example, I could inject you with a serum designed to make you more tractable and then have you order your second-in-command to cooperate with our requests. Or we could seize your ship by force, which will most assuredly result in needless casualties among your crew."

"Really?" Siobhan snorted. "You'll seize my ship. Good luck with that."

"I don't believe in luck, only thorough preparations. We've already put in place that which is necessary, a net to keep it in place while the Defenders act. The only thing left is to issue the order. Of course, once your people fight Mirandans, you'll quickly be branded as xenos and those whose technical expertise isn't required will be disposed of in our customary manner."

"My second-in-command will destroy *Stingray* if he sees no other outcome than falling into your hands. You'll be no further ahead, and I can guarantee you that he'll make sure to cause as much damage to Miranda as he can."

"He would cause the death of all aboard?" Dalian's eyebrows shot up. "Impressive. Perhaps you do have as much steel in your spines as we of the Dominion. A pity that we cannot work toward the common good. I wonder…"

She tapped her chin with her forefinger.

"Would you become more pliable if I demonstrated our research techniques on this individual here?" Dalian pointed at Vincenzo. "He looks like a healthy specimen, able to take a lot before succumbing."

"As a matter of fact, he wouldn't."

"Why is that?"

"We, in the Armed Services have been programmed to die if subjected to torture or mind probing," Dunmoore lied, "in the case of capture."

Dalian's predatory smile returned.

"Now that might be something our researchers would like to witness. Perhaps the useless ones among your crew would find some ultimate way to serve us."

"And you wonder why I don't want to be responsible for giving your people the means to leave this star system. Even my government won't wish to enable your expansion if that's the way you operate."

"Which is precisely why we don't intend to let you return home, Commander. Now, what will it be?"

Dalian's eyes flickered from cell to cell before resting on Siobhan again.

"Shall I demonstrate my determination by making you watch as we perform live research on your two crew members? On Colonel Kalivan? After all, none of them have the power to grant our wishes and are therefore surplus to requirements."

"Don't give in, Captain," Foste growled. "Vince and I knew the score when we enlisted."

"As did I," Kalivan added.

"How very brave." Dalian chuckled. "It will be interesting to see how long that spirit lasts once my scientists begin."

"You wouldn't!" Siobhan growled.

"In a second, my dear Commander. As I said, under our laws you are xenos and therefore have no status at all, and by the time Protector Hames finds out, the deed will be done."

Dunmoore stared at Dalian for a long time, aghast, hoping she would be able to see this through. Pushkin had to get *Stingray* away from here, and the only way that would happen before things went horribly wrong was if she managed to get their predicament across without alerting Dalian and her minions. And that meant seeming to give in.

She bit her lip and then looked down at the floor.

"I can't have you practice vivisection on my friends."

"Then show some solidarity with your fellow humans." The sound of Dalian's evil chuckle was one of the most offensive things she had heard in a long time.

"Just as you're showing with us?"

"Needs must, Commander. Put yourself in my shoes. I have a Dominion to protect, just as you have a crew to protect. What's a little information exchange between like-minded folks? Or shall I see what information I can get from one of your companions?"

"Fucking monster," Vincenzo growled, earning a pointed stare from the Chief Custodian.

"I might warm up my researchers with your foul-mouthed man here." Dalian pointed at the spacer.

An agonized expression twisted Siobhan's face.

"Very well. Let me speak with my first officer."

"Siobhan! No!"

"It's okay, Wes. I don't see much in terms of a way out, and I don't want to subject my crew to — to the horrors these damned people enjoy inflicting."

"A sudden change of heart." Dalian approached the cell until she was close enough to touch Siobhan, had there been no transparent wall. "Interesting. We will, of course, prepare one of your people for our researchers, to ensure you don't stray from the approved scenario. Do as I say and he won't get hurt."

"I'd expect no less from someone like you." Dunmoore cocked a defiant eyebrow. "Well, shall we?"

"And impatient too. Try to contain yourself, Commander. We have to arrange a few things first."

Then, Dalian turned on her heel and left the cellblock without as much as a goodbye.

"I hope you know what you're doing, Siobhan," Kalivan said once they were alone again.

"So do I, Wes. So do I."

*

"The results of the scan are coming in." Chief Penzara pointed at a side screen. "A lot of electronics, what seems like a fuel cell, some shielding. I can't rightly make much of it without more analysis, and that would mean an active scan a blind Mirandan would see."

Pushkin stared at the data for a few seconds and then tapped the screen set into the command chair's arm.

"Engineering, this is the bridge."

"And what can we do for the acting captain on this beautiful day?" Lieutenant Commander Kutora's gruff voice asked almost instantly.

"I had the probe ping one of the objects surrounding the ship, and I'd like your opinion on the results." Pushkin nodded at Penzara.

Silence, then Kutora spoke again. "Got the scan. We'll give it a gander but I can tell you right off the bat that I don't see anything that could pass for a warhead, so I don't think it's a mine. Doesn't mean some of the others aren't but this one? Not likely. Give me an hour or so. Engineering, out."

"What the hell are the Mirandans playing at?" The first officer's eyes latched onto the image of the planet.

"Whatever it is," Penzara replied, "we've just started to pick up some active scans bouncing off the hull."

"Can you tell where they're coming from?"

"That would be the trick, sir. As far as I know, they're not coming from anywhere."

Pushkin's fingers began to drum absently. He tapped the screen again.

"Engineering, this is the bridge."

"Yes?" Kutora managed to sound not quite exasperated. "I'll need a little bit longer than that, Mister Pushkin."

"I've got a different request. With the beating our shield generators took thanks to the ion storm, what's our ability to keep them up for a prolonged period of time?"

"Expecting trouble?"

"Always."

"I'll have my assistant figure it out and send up the answer within a few minutes. Engineering out."

"Sir?"

Pushkin looked up at Lieutenant Syten and nodded.

"Yes?"

"Might I suggest we post armed security at all airlocks and direct more of our sensors to scan close-in around the ship?"

"Good thinking. Pass the word to make it so." He paused, and then a grim smile split his square features. "In fact, have the entire ship's company draw side arms, then go to active scanning and begin registering targets both in orbit and on the moons. They want to play silly bugger, we'll play along."

When he sat back and looked at the main screen again, he felt unaccountably relieved for having given in to his fears. Better to be prepared and have nothing happen, than the contrary. Now if he could only speak with the captain and figure things out properly.

Kutora called back fifteen minutes later with the results.

"Can't tell you what it is, Mister Pushkin. There's no visible warhead, but it's got what looks like a fuel cell and a capacitor and a whole lot of electronics, so I suppose it could still explode, but without a nuclear kick, we wouldn't even feel the thing."

The first officer sighed.

"Thank you, Mister Kutora."

"If you'd bring one on board, we could dissect it, but I suppose not knowing what the damned thing does, that would be foolish."

"And the shield generators."

"You're good to keep them up for forty-eight hours straight, as long as you don't fight anyone. If you do, your timer's on a countdown, and you would be well advised to avoid straining the aft starboard one. Engineering, out."

Pushkin glanced at Penzara.

"What's the latest count on those objects?"

"I'm up to thirty-five, sir."

"Keep scanning." He stood. "You have the bridge, Mister Syten."

The first officer went aft to the wardroom for a desperately needed cup of coffee and some quiet time to think. He would get one, but not the other.

"Mantle of command sitting uneasily?" Devall asked, looking up from his pad.

"Shouldn't you be inspecting something or someone, Mister Acting First Officer?"

"Done and done, for now. I figure I've earned a break. Anything from the Captain or Colonel Kalivan?"

"No." Pushkin shook his head. He stirred in his usual heap of sweetener and cream under Devall's fascinated stare, then sat across from him.

"Everyone with side arms, airlocks guarded?" Devall let go of his pad and sat back in the chair. "Are we having a little bout of paranoia?"

"Maybe." The first officer shrugged. "The Mirandans are up to something. I can feel it. I just can't figure out what that is. Then, there's the sensor ghost PO Rownes picked up. What are the odds of another FTL ship showing up not long after us? It's not from the Commonwealth, that's for sure."

"Shrehari?"

"Why? Their space is just as far from here as ours. Besides, if the empire has found out about this system, we'd have heard of it."

"True." Devall nodded. "And the Mirandans didn't build up this Maginot Line in space for kicks, so they must be getting unwelcome visitors on a regular basis."

"Maginot what, now?" Pushkin frowned.

"Heaviest and most intricate defensive line in Earth history. France, circa early to mid-twentieth century, all along the frontier with their hereditary enemy, Germany."

The first officer dug through his memories of distant Academy history lessons, then nodded. "If I recall correctly, the Germans simply went around one end and took it from behind or something to that effect. Interesting simile to make under the circumstances, Mister Devall."

"Another one comes to mind, seeing as how we're supposedly a diplomatic mission to our far-flung cousins."

Pushkin raised an eyebrow. "Oh?"

"Siege of the International Legations in Peking, very early twentieth century. Heard of that one?"

"No."

"The only difference being that we won't have a column of troops to come rescue us. You should look it up when you have some downtime."

"Downtime? What's that?" Pushkin drained his cup and stood. "Until the captain is back in her rightful command chair, you and I are the wicked for whom there is no rest."

*

A squad of guards led Siobhan to an office overlooking the hydroponics plantation, where she found Mira Dalian standing by a window, gazing down. The trooper holding Dunmoore's arm released her, then stepped back into the corridor and closed the door. Dalian turned around and smiled.

"I find all of this," she pointed over her shoulder at the greenery, "very relaxing. One of my predecessors must have as well, to co-locate one of our research stations with this agricultural complex."

"An excellent way to hide things as well, no?"

"Of course." Dalian waved her hand as if to indicate the matter was of little importance. "We have dissidents who sometimes command a following, and it can get awkward if we hold them near Sanctum."

"You allow protests?"

"The people need an outlet, don't you think? We've been a militarized, even militant society for several centuries and stresses will build up. Xenophobia can only take one's compliance with the state so far before questions arise, and they do, with depressing frequency, as you may have noticed at the Select Committee reception."

"So you admit that Mirandan civilization is fundamentally xenophobic?"

"Admit to an obvious fact? Please, Commander. Fear of attacks by non-humans might have radically transformed us, but by now, we've become so hardened that before your arrival, no outsider stood a chance. Yet, that fear gives us a stable form of government, much better than the quasi-anarchy and Utopian dreams that drove our forebears."

"Those same ancestors left Earth to start anew," Siobhan replied, pleased that her tone sounded conversational rather than confrontational, "without making the mistakes that turned our planet of origin into what it had become by the dawn of the twenty-second century, and yet, here you are."

Dalian shrugged, her lips briefly twisting into a sad smile.

"Their ideals didn't survive a hostile universe, Commander. I'll venture that the Commonwealth has had to discard some of its ways of thinking once your people began encountering hostile species, even if they may not have taken the path our ancestors took. The early Mirandans were lucky to have experienced an extended period of peace before the first xeno incursions, but that merely made the shock of first contact so much the greater. Many could not adapt to the new reality and still, we managed to become what we are today. Mind you, some would like us to go back to those softer, gentler times, now that we haven't had a severe xeno attack in many decades, but that would make us weak again."

"What about the Shrehari?"

"They didn't attack us." Dalian gave a half shrug. "We took care of them shortly after they blundered into our defenses, as have so many in recent years. Pity that we couldn't get anything from their vessel. Martell's people barely managed to seize three dozen captives before the brutes destroyed it. Of course, we wouldn't have been able to make heads or tails of their technology, no more than we did any of the others we seized, so it's rather fortuitous that you showed up."

"No doubt." Dunmoore raised her chin. "But what will you do once you've harnessed antimatter and built a fleet of ships like mine? You said that Miranda hasn't been subjected to a xeno attack in decades, thanks to the strength of your Defenders."

"Expand, my dear. Just as you have. This system has been our prison for almost two thousand years. I think it's time we broke out and took a greater slice of the galaxy for ourselves. Don't you? Considering how far away your Commonwealth is, I'd say we have plenty of room to spread out."

"And what of non-human races you encounter along the way?"

Another dismissive wave.

"We'll deal with them."

"As you will with us once your empire abuts the Commonwealth?"

Dalian laughed with delight.

"Now that is something I'd like to witness, but it'll be for another Protector, far in the future."

"So that's what this is all about — expansion."

"Oh," Dalian spread her hands, "it truly is for the defense of the Dominion. You see, I fear that in the absence of an existential threat, we might backslide into the civilization we once were. Weak, indecisive, and motivated by unrealistic ideals. Therein lay the seeds of our destruction and we cannot allow that to happen again. By breaking away from Miranda's star, we can give the malcontents an outlet while at the same time increasing our security perimeter. Room to grow, as it were."

"At the expense of any other civilization that may be in your path."

The Mirandan shook her head.

"Commander, your concern for non-human species is no doubt commendable where you come from, but here, we know only one law. It's them or us, and we prefer it to be us, though some might disagree with our methods."

"Even your so-called dissidents agree with that law?"

"Most recognize the need for self-preservation before everything else, yes. We have something akin to genetic memory of those horrible times, driving us to construct things like this facility." Dalian gestured toward the window again. "And to keep building up our military capabilities. But enough about Miranda and her past, present and future. It's time for you to play your part."

"After which, I die, right?" Dunmoore's expression turned to stone.

"Please, Commander!" Dalian held up her palms. "I promised you and yours a healthy life if you cooperate. That promise stands."

"But we'll be the worst dissidents you've ever had."

Dalian mouth twitched.

"I can believe that, but I'm sure you and your folks have the same survival instincts we have, so I'm confident that you'll take care to keep your views to yourselves."

She pointed at a screen on the wall by the door.

"In a moment, you'll see the young man with the mustache being prepped in our lab downstairs."

"You're a nasty piece of work, Dalian," Dunmoore growled. She folded her arms over her chest and stared at the Custodian with all the defiance she could muster.

"I thought starting with the most junior in your delegation might ensure that if you fail to cooperate, we can slowly make our way up the chain of command, so to speak. Besides, I'm told that he shows all the signs of being very protective of you. Therefore, I'm curious to see if you're as protective of him. Loyalty can be a powerful motivator."

Dunmoore's jaw muscles tightened.

"Let's get on with this, Dalian."

As if on cue, the screen lit up to show Vincenzo, naked as the day he was born, strapped to a metal examination table. He stared straight at the camera, jaw set, prepared to endure what he must.

"And now," Dalian pointed at a console facing the screen, "if you sit right there, my technicians will hail your ship."

"Remind me what I'm supposed to say."

"Really, Commander." The Custodian shook her head in mock disappointment. "An intelligent woman like you should be able to figure out what's required to initiate the transfer of your technology into our hands without awakening any suspicions among your crew. It's in everyone's interest that this goes smoothly so we can avoid any unnecessary loss of life."

Dunmoore nodded once, and then took the indicated seat. She looked up at Vincenzo again, and her jaw tightened.

He had saved her life, showing up moments before *Stingray*'s former second officer, Drax, tried to kill her. Loyalty was indeed a powerful thing.

"Connect me to my ship."

— Twenty-Four —

"Mister Pushkin."

Kowalski's shout through the open door to the bridge broke through his concentration and, with a grunt of annoyance, he dropped the datapad on Dunmoore's desk.

"What?"

"Incoming transmission from the surface. It's the captain."

Pushkin's face lit up.

"Finally. Pipe it to the ready room."

He turned to face the screen, a smile of anticipation tugging at his lips. When *Stingray*'s emblem dissolved, replaced by Dunmoore's face, he sat up straighter and leaned forward.

"Captain! I trust all is well."

She half-smiled and cocked her head to one side.

"We've had eighty-one kinds of fun so far, Gregor."

Her words, as well as her unusual facial expression quickly registered and his hands tightened into fists. His worst fears had become reality, but if they allowed her to speak with him, he had to see the game to its conclusion.

"Glad to hear it, sir. Things have been quiet as the grave up here. When are you coming back?"

"In good time," she replied.

"Understood. Is there anything we can do for you in the meantime?"

She nodded.

"Indeed there is. Our Mirandan friends are in dire need of a helping hand to make them an FTL-capable civilization, and I thought we'd do just that, among human beings."

Pushkin's smile became uncertain.

"How are you proposing we do that, sir?"

"What I'd like to do is have our technical folks, headed by Lieutenant Commander Kutora, come down and meet with Mirandan engineers to help explain the data dump we're about to give them."

"Data dump, sir?"

"Everything we have, Gregor, all eighty-one databases, right down to the medical files, viruses and all."

"Understood." He briefly chewed on his lower lip. "I think if I have Mister Kutora carry a copy of the database, it'll be better than trying to stream that much information over a comlink. Give us a few hours to get everything together, the people briefed and a clean data dump ready for the Mirandans to upload. May I ask where I should send the shuttles?"

Dunmoore turned to glance at Dalian. The Chief Custodian pointed downwards.

"Can you pinpoint the origin of this transmission, Gregor?"

His eyes slipped to one side, searching for Kowalski through the open door. She gave him thumbs up.

"We can."

"That's where you send our folks. It's a mesa-like artificial construct south of Sanctum, their capital city."

Pushkin glanced at a visual that had suddenly appeared on the desk console.

"We've got it. I assume you'll be greeting our folks?"

She looked at Dalian again. A nod, this time, the finger pointing at her."

"Yes, I will."

"Good. I'll send down the cox'n to accompany them."

He saw her eyes widen slightly when she understood the import of his words and set his lips in a thin, disapproving line.

"He wants to experience your eighty-one kinds of fun, sir and perhaps find a few more you missed. I'm afraid that he'll insist if I try to deprive him of the chance."

Dunmoore breathed in deeply, trying to keep her face expressionless, and then glanced down at her folded hands before meeting Pushkin's eyes again.

"You know your duty, Gregor. I expect you to carry out my orders."

"Aye, aye, sir." His stare remained defiant. "I will make it so."

Stingray's crest replaced Dunmoore's angry features, and Pushkin slumped back in his chair. When he looked up, Kowalski stood at the door.

"Shall I tell Mister Guthren it's a go?"

The first officer's bitter laugh echoed in the small compartment.

"You didn't think I'd obey her instructions to follow General Order Eighty-One and abandon our people, not when there's a chance? I don't know what they've done to the captain, but I can't believe it's anything good, not after we've had a glimpse at their mentality."

"Of course not, sir." The corners of her mouth twitched. "Though if she refuses to come with the cox'n on general principles, there's nothing you can do."

"Between Mister Guthren, Foste, and Vincenzo, they'll toss her in the back of a shuttle before she can say boo. Besides, with active scanning, we picked up the trackers Colonel Kalivan and the captain are carrying and they're right where she told us to land the shuttles."

Pushkin stood and yanked his tunic into place.

"Assemble the officers and chiefs in thirty minutes. I want to speak with them in person before we launch this little forlorn hope. They deserve to see my face when I issue orders that directly contravene the captain's."

"I'm sure they'll be in full agreement with you."

"And that, Kathryn, is what I fear." He gave her a tight grin. "Now off with you. I need a cleansing coffee before I commit the sin of disobedience."

*

"You see, Commander, that wasn't so difficult." Dalian's smile sent shivers down Siobhan's spine. "Continue cooperating and you'll find life on Miranda to be quite tolerable. Who knows, once we leave this system in our very own FTL starships, you might find employment as an adviser to the Defenders. Of course, your next trick will be to hand your ship over to us, but one step at a time."

Dunmoore glowered at the Mirandan and swallowed her rage with great difficulty. When she looked up at the screen above the console, it showed nothing more than an empty metallic examination table.

"He's been taken off the research subject list," Dalian said. "For now. As will you. In recognition for your willingness to help the Dominion, I've arranged better accommodations for you and your companions. It even has a view of the hydroponics field."

She pointed toward the window.

"In fact, you can see it from here if you'll look to the left. A suite, not as luxurious as the one at the Protector's Palace to be sure, but comfortable just the same. Your engineers and technicians, once they arrive, will be housed in similar accommodations in this very facility."

"How very kind of you," Dunmoore murmured, letting sarcasm drip from every word.

"Isn't it?" Dalian beamed at her. "And my continued kindness is entirely dependent on your continued cooperation."

She touched something on her desk, and the door opened.

"Take the commander to her new living quarters."

Before Dunmoore could step out into the hallway, Dalian's voice rang out again. "By the way, Commander. I've meant to ask. The language you've been speaking among yourselves to ensure we couldn't understand. What is it?"

When Dunmoore did not immediately reply, Dalian nodded toward the screen that had shown Vincenzo moments earlier.

"Cooperation, remember?"

"An Earth language called Mandarin," Dunmoore replied through clenched teeth.

"Oh?" She turned to her console and entered a command. "We have no such designation in our records. Is it non-human?"

"Quite human. One of the major languages used in the Commonwealth, in fact. It's among several taught in our military schools."

"Fascinating." Dalian's expressionless eyes rested on her for a few more seconds. "Perhaps we'll have time to explore your Commonwealth's linguistic diversity once we've taken care of technical matters."

She nodded at the guard.

"You may go."

Their new suite was literally around the corner. When Dunmoore entered, her three companions, who had been inspecting their surroundings, looked at her with questions in their eyes. However, she immediately turned her attention on Vincenzo.

"Are you okay?"

He smiled sheepishly.

"Yes, sir. I'm all right, though it wasn't the most comfortable experience I've ever had. That table was *cold!*"

She recognized bravado when she heard it and clasped his shoulder.

"Good."

"Sir, what were they going to do to me if you didn't cooperate?" He asked half fearfully as if he had already guessed the answer.

"You don't want to know. Trust me on this. I'm just glad you're back here with us."

"What's the lay of the land?" Kalivan asked in Mandarin.

"With the caveat that I had to tell our gracious hostess we're speaking Mandarin, a language she pretended to know nothing about," Dunmoore replied, "I'll just say that I gave as clear a hint as possible to my first officer that he had to obey General Order Eighty-One. His reaction, in many ways, reminded me of myself."

"Oh?" Kalivan's eyebrows shot up, indicating that he understood her meaning.

"I'll leave it at that, Wes, just in case our friends with the big ears found an Anglic-Mandarin dictionary in their archives in the last few minutes. If Gregor is going to disobey me..." Her voice trailed off.

"You don't sound particularly enthusiastic."

"Our Mister Pushkin has a sentimental streak that's a hundred parsecs wide. The idea of sailing away and leaving us here would kill him. I just hope the other officers, and maybe even the chiefs will talk some sense into him."

"Not Mister Guthren," Foste said in her broken Mandarin. "He's just as sentimental."

A sad smile tugged at Dunmoore's lips.

"And that's my problem, encapsulated by two names."

"You'll forgive me if I don't join you in wishing to be marooned here for the rest of my life." Kalivan shrugged. "Your first officer is welcome to do whatever he thinks is best."

"The ship has to come first, Wes."

"I've heard the whole 'needs of the many' crap before, Siobhan. It never sounds right to my ears. Besides, the Commonwealth Navy has a proud tradition to uphold."

"Oh? Which one would that be?"

"The one that involves saying those immortal words damn the torpedoes, full speed ahead."

*

"Atten-SHUN."

Lieutenant Devall's voice echoed across *Stingray*'s vast shuttle hangar, followed, a fraction of a second later, by the crack of two dozen left heels stomping the metal deck.

Pushkin returned the second officer's salute and then let his eyes range over the assembled officers and chief petty officers. A solemn looking bunch, with a mixture of determination and concern writ large on their somber faces.

"At ease." Once they had adopted a more relaxed posture, he continued, "If you don't know why I've called this assembly, then either something's gravely wrong with the ship's grapevine, or you haven't been paying attention. Either way, I'll be checking up on you in the next few days."

After the expected laughter had died down, he motioned at Lieutenant Kowalski.

"Play the recording."

Twenty-five pairs of eyes locked onto the screen hanging above the control room windows. It generally served to communicate with deck crew and pilots during shuttle launch and recovery operations, but on this occasion, Siobhan Dunmoore's face replaced the ship's badge.

When her image faded out again a short time later, Pushkin could feel the sudden tension that seemed to emanate from *Stingray*'s leadership like a living, writhing presence.

"You've seen Lieutenant Kowalski's precis on Mirandan history, and now you've heard my exchange with the captain. Comments?" Pushkin tried to meet as many eyes as possible while he waited for them to process what they had just heard.

"Aye." Kutora scratched his beard like a man lost in deep thought. "We're not permitted to transfer technology of any kind to societies that haven't achieved FTL travel status. At least not without explicit permission from HQ. I daresay the captain is well aware of this restriction."

"That regulation is to prevent us from creating more technobarbarian kingdoms," Devall pointed out. "The Mirandans are human colonists, even if they've been out of touch with Mother Earth for four hundred or two thousand years, depending on whose calendar you use."

"True." The chief engineer nodded. "But last I checked, the rules didn't specify species."

Pushkin fought hard to hide a grin. Trust Kutora to miss the main point and wallow in irrelevant details, although his intervention, seen from another angle, reinforced the notion that the Mirandans had taken Dunmoore and the others captive, intending to use them to get at Commonwealth technology.

Devall gracefully conceded the point, having come to the same conclusion as the first officer.

"I daresay the captain is well aware of this point, sir."

"I know she is," Pushkin added.

Kutora, chin raised defiantly, asked, "If you haven't called us here to explain why you're about to violate regulations concerning tech transfers, why are we standing around like a herd of sleeping wildebeest when there's work to be done?"

"You know the captain invoked General Order Eighty-One when she left a few days ago. Am I losing my mind or did she remind me of it several times in a veiled fashion during our chat?"

Most of them nodded.

"I can't see anyone finding eighty-one different ways of having fun around here," Chief Guthren said, "and our captain, God bless her, isn't known as a party animal when she's ashore."

"The way I see it, I've got two choices," Pushkin said. "The first one is to obey the captain by lighting up the drives and getting the hell away from Miranda. Some bright spark in their general staff might get the idea that taking *Stingray* could be the quickest way to becoming an antimatter using, FTL sailing civilization."

"If they haven't already," Chief Penzara pointed out, "what with those unidentified thingamajigs hanging around us like a bad smell."

"True." The first officer nodded in agreement. "Option one, of course, means that the captain, Colonel Kalivan, Chief Foste and Leading Spacer Vincenzo will be stuck here, perhaps for good if we can't negotiate their release."

"Or for however long they're allowed to live," Guthren growled.

"The whole point of Order Eighty-One, Mister Pushkin," Kutora crossed his arms defensively as if he knew his words wouldn't find much popularity, "is to avoid risking ship and crew for the sake of a few. The Mirandans surely know they've crossed into the territory from where there's no return. After this, our government will not consider letting the slightest bit of tech go in their direction. Since we won't cooperate, they'll try to take the ship. And that's when we're back to the whole reason for General Order Eighty-One."

"Hiding behind orders isn't my cup of tea." Guthren scowled at the chief engineer. "Sir."

"I'm not saying it's right, cox'n, I'm merely pointing out that the captain gave those orders because she wants to make sure her crew doesn't die needlessly for her sake. Then there's the matter of folks who're ready to hold a diplomatic delegation hostage getting their hands on advanced technology, something I think we all agree shouldn't happen in our lifetimes or the universe's. The longer we stick around, the more chances they'll have, as Mister Pushkin pointed out."

When no one offered agreement with his position, Kutora sighed.

"But if the first officer's called us together like this, it's not to announce he's obeying the captain."

"Indeed." Pushkin looked at the tense faces again, jaw muscles twitching. "I don't know about the rest of you, but I wouldn't be able to live with myself if we ran, leaving our people behind for good if there's even the slightest chance we could recover them."

A few nods at first, then several more, until all but Kutora had signified their agreement with the first officer's sentiments. Finally, even the first engineer assented, visibly melting under Pushkin's hard stare.

"I don't believe we'll be able to negotiate their release," he continued. "You heard the captain, saw her reactions. She knows more of what's going on than we do and she told us, if not in so many words, that we're to consider them missing in action, not to be recovered."

He paused for a few heartbeats.

"That leaves us only one option, and if it goes wrong, we will have to fight our way out of this system, or at least out of Miranda's orbit. We know where they're holding our people, and we have the perfect Trojan horse, handed to us by the Mirandans themselves. I think they have no idea who we really are and what we can do, and that gives us the element of surprise."

"If you're asking whether or not we agree," Chief Penzara said, "count me among those supporting a rescue, and I'll be glad to enter my words in the log to make it official."

"Me as well," Chief Petty Officer Weekes, the engineering chief nodded.

"And me. I'll fly one of the shuttles." Kowalski jerked her thumb at the boxy craft parked cheek-to-jowl behind them.

"If you don't need me to fight the ship, sir," Sub-Lieutenant Sanghvi came to attention, a grave expression on his youthful face, "I'll fly a shuttle as well."

One by one, the chiefs and officers gave their assent, until only the chief engineer remained. He glowered at Pushkin, arms still crossed, then nodded.

"Be on with your foolish scheme then, Mister Acting Captain. If you can spare a few hours, I'll jury-rig a shield generator for each shuttle out of the parts I pulled after the storm, so they'll not make too easy a target on the way back.

They'll likely burn out after a few shots and kill the reactors in the long run, but as long as the shuttles make it back here, they'll have served a purpose."

"Thank you." Pushkin gave Kutora a brief but grateful smile. "Chief Petty Officer Guthren will lead the rescue party on the ground. He has more experience than the rest of us put together thanks to his stint with Special Forces before joining *Stingray*. Lieutenant Kowalski, as the mission's senior officer, will be in overall command. The ship will go to battle stations the moment we launch the rescue effort. I would like to see Lieutenants Kowalski and Sanghvi, as well as Chief Guthren in the conference room afterward. If there's nothing else?"

He looked at each of them in turn one last time and when he got nothing more than a few brief head shakes, he said, "Thank you. This is one of the few times where I will gladly borrow a quote from our Marine Corps brethren. *Stingray* will leave no one behind. Carry on."

Devall called the assembly to attention again and raised his hand in a salute so crisp it would have impressed the most demanding admiral.

— Twenty-Five —

"I think having Yarvik show Dunmoore how we deal with xenos turned out to be a good idea after all," Dalian announced, sailing into the Protector's office with a triumphant smile on her face. "Earthers have no backbone."

"Really?" Martell raised a skeptical eyebrow. "Do tell, Mira."

"She had a change of heart and is ready to give us the knowledge we need."

"That was quick," Hames said.

"Motivation is a fine thing, Cyrus." Dalian dropped into an empty chair at the Protector's table. "Her second-in-command will send down their engineers and technicians, as well as a copy of their database within the next day."

"Really?" The Protector mimicked his military commander. "And how did you motivate the Earthers?"

A nasty smile tugged at the corner of Dalian's slips.

"It's merely a matter of incentives, Cyrus." She waved away his alarmed expression. "Oh, nothing like that. They're all unharmed and well, at least for now. I found Dunmoore's weak spot, that's all."

"And what if we need their help with the newest intruder? I think it's a given that they won't trip over themselves to cooperate in that respect after you applied this so-called motivation."

"I'm sure Geoff's people can handle it."

"Even if it's as powerful as the Earther's ship?" Hames furrowed his brow.

"Assuredly," Martell replied. "We didn't throw the full weight of our defenses on them once they made their origin known. In any case, we should have control over *Stingray* within a matter of days. I have no doubt we'll find members of the crew who are willing to teach my Defenders in its use. Everyone has his price, or weak spot, as Mira so successfully demonstrated."

"I don't know." The Protector shook his head, face sagging into a mask of exhaustion. "Part of me can't help thinking you moved too fast. We may find that it would have been preferable to continue wooing them for a while longer until we resolved this new intrusion. Or even wait until Earth sent a full delegation of experts."

"Perhaps." Dalian seemed unconcerned. "But it's been clear from the outset that the Earthers wouldn't share voluntarily, and Dunmoore would likely have influenced her government in that respect if we'd let them go home. Waiting for a miracle to change their minds now is futile. We've survived this long by taking forceful action to defend the Dominion. I see no need to change our policies just because the Earthers have shown up uninvited."

"And what do we do with the Earthers once we've taken everything from them?" Marant spoke for the first time.

Dalian gave a half shrug.

"Those who wish to serve the Dominion will be useful. Those who don't will still help the Dominion, but in other ways. Once my people have squeezed every last bit of information from their minds, we can do whatever the Protector wishes."

"We still have to get them, Mira," Martell warned. "The Earthers have begun active scans of our installations and the planet's surface, where previously they refrained."

"So they became curious. If nothing else, they'll get a better appreciation of the Defenders' might, and think twice before acting in a manner we might construe as hostile. Seeing how Dunmoore eventually submitted to save her companions from the fate we reserve for xenos, I doubt they have enough courage to face what they see."

"Besides," she added as an afterthought, "once we have her delegation of engineers in our hands, we'll have that much more leverage to enforce compliance. You'll have that ship of theirs soon enough."

*

"I'm picking up a standard Deep Space Fleet emergency beacon near the fourth planet." *Tol Vehar*'s senior sensor technician shook his head. "It pretends to come from the survey cruiser *Ziq Tar*."

"Hah!" Brakal's fist connected with the command chair's arm. "The damned spy was right. Command did send a *Ziq* class into this forsaken part of the galaxy. It seems Dunmoore ended its surveying career permanently. Find the damned thing. I wish to know what happened."

"I've commanded it to transmit *Ziq Tar*'s log, Commander. Finding its actual position will require a bit more time." The technician paused. "Transmission complete."

"Well?" The word came out as a harsh growl. "Let's hear what its captain had to say before he died."

"Immediately."

Commander Drang's bloodied face materialized, and he began speaking, while other images and telemetry filled the bottom part of the screen.

"I am Drang, commanding *Ziq Tar*, survey cruiser, sent by the Admiralty to chart the systems beyond the black. To my dishonor, I must report my mission unfulfilled and my ship and crew soon to join the Great Void in nothingness. The system in which you find the beacon transmitting this report is inhabited by a species that hides well and attacks without provocation or warning, even though we offered no threat of violence." Drang's head turned to the right, reacting to something off-screen.

"*Ziq Tar* is heavily damaged, and we've been boarded. Duty demands that I order it destroyed," he continued in a more urgent tone, "and I will do so..."

The voice and video portion of the transmission ended abruptly, but the other images and the telemetry continued, giving Brakal and his bridge crew a brief chance to see the survey ship invaded by armored intruders. Then, a short-lived flare cut off everything but the monotone of the beacon's call to other Shrehari who might venture near enough.

"It wasn't Dunmoore," Urag said once the screen turned black. "*Ziq Tar* and its crew died months ago, well before we headed out on her trail to find this system."

"You failed to notice something," Brakal replied in an uncharacteristically soft voice. "We will, of course, review the transmission, many times if necessary, but I believe the beings who boarded *Ziq Tar* were human or at least appeared to be so. Like Dunmoore and her crew."

"Surely you jest, Commander." Urag looked at his captain with anger burning in his dark eyes.

"I do not." Brakal stood up and pointed at the main screen. "We will find who they are and make them pay for their insolence."

"And Dunmoore?"

"By all means, Urag." A toothy smile spread across the bony face. "We will dispatch her as well, but first, we must discover who these new humans are and why they live under a star so far removed from the rest of their species. An enemy colony planted beyond the black, expanding and swallowing up system after system will become a threat to the empire."

"If they are human, why has no one heard of them before?" Regar, who had remained silent until this moment, asked. "Consider that, Commander. Perhaps they just resemble our enemy but are of a different race altogether."

"Does it matter?" Brakal turned his hands palms upwards and made the Shrehari equivalent of a shrug. "They took one of our ships, and that means they're just as much our foes as Dunmoore's people. Redouble vigilance, Urag. If they're powerful enough to destroy *Ziq Tar*, they're not to be trifled with."

"We are bigger and stronger."

"And yet, Urag, and yet."

"May I recommend we go active? If these people are demons at emissions control and dissimulation, then who knows what might have crept up on us even now. Commander Drang did say they attacked without warning."

Brakal considered the request, all the while rubbing his chin as if the repeated gesture could speed up his thought processes.

"Not yet. Let us get closer. I don't wish to alert Dunmoore while we find the inhabitants of this system."

"We'll need to make a minor course adjustment. Just a little burst."

"Then do it."

"As you command."

*

"Have you got spares for the captain and the others?" Kowalski had laid out her own suit on the deck, ready for Guthren's inspection. They would fly buttoned-up in case the Mirandans caused a shuttle to lose pressure integrity.

"Aye." The coxswain pointed at four bags neatly lined up by the door. "I got a large-sized spare from the arms locker for the colonel. If it fits me, it'll fit him. Better too loose than the opposite, right?"

He knelt and ran his hands over the joints, the electronics, and the air recycler, then plugged the suit into his sensor and checked the readout.

"It's good to go, Lieutenant."

"You've done a lot of raids like this before?" She asked.

Guthren half-smiled at her.

"One raid's never like another so it's a new experience every time, but some things remain universal, such as the truism that a plan never survives contact with the enemy, or the enemy's tendency to see what they want to see."

"In this case, they want to see two shuttle loads of engineers and technicians coming to teach them the mysteries of FTL travel."

"Right." He nodded. "As long as our people are close to where we land, the element of surprise should carry us through long enough. Me? I'm more worried about the trip back into orbit. By then, Mister Pushkin is going to be dealing with a lot of other crap and won't be able to give us covering fire if — no scratch that — when the Mirandans decide play time is over."

"And yet, you're still going down there," she replied, making conversation to cover her own nervousness.

"Someone's gotta lead the raid, Lieutenant." A grin now split his square face. "And I'm it, seeing as how I let my little side trip with Special Forces appear in my personal records. If I'd only kept that one quiet..."

He winked at her.

"As for plans not surviving contact, I figure we go in under false pretenses, wallop 'em where it hurts the most, and then run like hell. As plans go, that one's almost foolproof."

"Still, it's going to be carried out by fools." She smiled back, a measure of confidence now returning thanks to the coxswain's good humor.

"Speaking of which," he jerked his thumb over his shoulder, "you might wish to cheer young Sanghvi up. I know he volunteered but right now, he's dropping parts all over the deck, and that won't make his passengers feel any better."

Kowalski glanced across the hangar deck at the second shuttle. The junior navigator, face as serious as she had ever seen, was trying to lay out his pressure suit for inspection and fumbling badly. The petty officer first class in charge of that half of the landing party seemed torn between taking the pieces from his hands and doing the job himself, and praying the younger man got a grip on his nerves.

"PO Rakkan looks like he's about to lose patience," she said.

"Aye and he doesn't have much in the first place when it comes to officers. I've thought of transferring into that shuttle and shifting Rakkan over to you, but the juniors need to find their footing, and it won't happen if we hold their hands all the time."

"I'll wait until his suit's been checked, then take him for a coffee."

"Thanks, Lieutenant. Anyway, I could use some time alone with the hands to make sure they're all squared away and ship-shape. It's better that I do the early rehearsals without any officers around. Maybe you can talk through the flight plan a few times with the young gentleman, especially the part where we take off with an entire planet of pissed-off maniacs on our ass."

Kowalski laughed.

"I'm sure that'll help calm his nerves."

"Lieutenant, getting him scared now rather than when the shit hits the fan is just the right thing to do. He has time to think it through, get used to the idea, and then shove it aside. It's always worked for me."

"You get nervous before a mission?" She sounded surprised.

"Every single time. Those who have no fear are the ones who die before they finish the mission. I figure the day I go raiding with a smile and song while thinking about my next shore leave is going to be my last in this life."

He watched Sanghvi finally get his suit sorted, under Rakkan's disgusted gaze, and shook his head.

"I'm reminded of a saying I once saw in the Special Operations HQ mess. A hero is a man who's afraid to run away. The lad volunteered, knowing what it meant. You two aren't the only pilots among the crew. He just needs some bucking up." Guthren sighed. "Rakkan on the other hand needs to tone it down. There's no reason to show your opinion of an officer by making faces where the troops can see, not when you're preparing to go out the door shooting. More reason for you and the sub-lieutenant to go talk flying for a while."

When Kowalski walked up to her wingman and his petty officer, the latter gave her an annoyed glance but stepped away at Guthren's nod.

"If Petty Officer Rakkan is happy with your pressure suit, let's go discuss our flight parameters and leave the chief and his POs to continue the preparations."

"Yes, sir." Sanghvi's prominent Adam's apple bobbed a few times. "We're done."

Once the two officers had left the hangar deck, Guthren stood between both shuttles and shouted, "Okay, my pretties, it's time to talk about how we'll rescue the captain, Chief Foste, our buddy Vincenzo and Colonel Kalivan without leaving a drop of our blood on that damned planet. Gather around and I'll tell you the tale of how we'll kick ass and take names. It'll be a thing of beauty you'll recount to your grandchildren over and over again until they're bored to tears."

Pushkin hid his surprise at seeing Kowalski and her wingman in the wardroom, enjoying a cup of coffee, while preparations for the rescue mission had kicked into high gear. He gave her a questioning look over Sanghvi's shoulder, and she gave a minute shake of the head.

"We're reviewing the flight plan, sir," she said. "Chief Guthren is instructing the ratings on the finer points of busting into an enemy stockade to extract friendlies."

The first officer poured himself a coffee and joined the two officers.

"Are you two okay?" He looked at each of them in turn, evaluating their mood. What he read in Sanghvi's eyes told him why the mission's two shuttle pilots had taken a break away from the rest of the team.

He was about to open his mouth and offer to replace the younger man with another pilot when he caught Kowalski's warning glance.

"We're fine, sir," Sanghvi replied. "I guess I'm just a bit nervous. This is my first time flying a rescue mission, that's all."

"It'll be a first for most of the team, Martin." Pushkin clapped him on the shoulder. "Other than Chief Guthren, there's not many aboard who can boast of living through fights away from a starship."

"We were discussing the return trip, sir." Kowalski drained her cup and placed it on the table with exaggerated care. "Under the assumption that you'll have your hands full with angry Mirandans."

The first officer's brief burst of laughter sounded grim to her ears.

"Don't worry; I'll spare enough to cover for your flight. After all, there's no point in green-lighting the mission if we can't recover the landing party, complete with rescuees."

"Anything new on the objects surrounding us?"

He shook his head.

"Nothing. I've had Jeneva register them as targets for the close-in defense guns so that the moment things go sideways, we can neutralize them."

"Remind me again why we're here?" She sighed.

"Because Colonel Kalivan got a wild hair up his ass and convinced the Admiralty to pursue it. And because *Stingray*'s the most expendable starship in the Fleet."

"Is it too late to get out of this chickenshit outfit?" An ironic smile creased her face.

"You could always ask the Mirandans for asylum."

"Pass. They don't seem like my kind of people, whether or not they deliberately modeled their rank system on that unfortunate period in history."

The intercom chimed, killing Pushkin's reply.

"Bridge to the first officer. It looks like we're about to get company."

"*Yebat*," he swore in Russian as he stood up. "What now?"

Grimacing at Kowalski, he said, "I'll talk to you again before you launch."

Then, he vanished down the passageway.

— Twenty-Six —

The first officer slipped into a command chair still warm from Lieutenant Syten's posterior and studied the main screen, where Petty Officer Rownes had projected a tactical schematic of Miranda's orbitals.

"Several small ships or large shuttles," she said, "departed Ariel Base on the moon Iris and assumed an orbit close to ours, approximately thirty thousand kilometers aft. I didn't think much of it at the time, but they've gone silent and are slowly closing in on us. If the sensors hadn't spotted them lifting off, we might not have been able to keep tabs on them once they went into full stealth mode."

The first officer rubbed his jaw as he studied the three-dimensional image of Miranda's close surroundings.

"The sensors didn't spot anything coming from the hidden stations at the Lagrangian points?"

Rownes shook her head.

"No, which doesn't mean there's nothing ahead of us, slowly braking, if that was your question, sir. They wouldn't have had to boost and therefore wouldn't have left a signature we could see."

"Am I paranoid, or are the Mirandans trying to box us in?"

"If it weren't for the stealthy objects surrounding *Stingray*, and the captain invoking General Order Eighty-One in veiled speech," Syten said, "we probably wouldn't have worried much about their ships' movements."

"True. As the captain likes to say, once is happenstance, twice is coincidence but three times likely means it's enemy action. The part of me that sees threats in every ionized gas cloud has reached that fateful count of three."

"We could break orbit without requesting permission," Syten pointed out. "That would place us beyond their reach."

"And risk tipping them off before we've recovered our landing party? No. Besides, we have no idea how many over-sized cruisers are lurking nearby, their targeting systems locked onto us. Add those ships or shuttles, or whatever they are to your preregistered target list," Pushkin replied, "and scan ahead, using full power. At this point, I don't care if they pick up our emissions and decide we're less than gracious to our hosts. I'll be on the hangar deck, to see if we can't get the rescue mission going a bit earlier. My gut instinct is telling me that we might be running out of time."

"Very well, sir."

*

Pushkin, hidden from sight in the control room, watched the landing party go through its paces under Chief Guthren's sharp eyes, practicing not only the moves that would get them inside the enemy's facility but those that would get them out when everything went to crap. They did not have much more than the scans from orbit to go on, so the coxswain improvised.

Kowalski and Sanghvi had not joined them yet, both still shoring up each other's resolve by discussing everything that might go wrong during the mission, which was more or less the pilot's version of Guthren's rehearsals.

"Once you've opened your mind enough to acknowledge everything that could go wrong," a voice said behind him, "your fears are half conquered, no?"

Pushkin turned to face Devall, a tight smile briefly softening his drawn features.

"Trying to cheer me up, Trevane?"

"No. I meant our folks out on the hangar deck and the two nut cases who'll fly them down into the heart of darkness. For us, there is no cheer but that which results from getting away with a full crew roster and two functioning hyperdrives."

"Then I pray that we'll be cheerful indeed. You heard about our Mirandan friends and their stealthy ship movements?"

"Indeed. I've taken the liberty of having the airlock sentries don battle armor, and setting the bulkhead condition to 'closed.' It'll be a pain to move around the ship with all doors and hatches sealed, but I think we've pretty much reached the point where it's necessary."

"So I'm not the only paranoid aboard." A grim chuckle escaped Pushkin's lips. "Good to know."

Devall jerked his chin toward the window.

"Do you think they'll have a chance?"

"Considering the only other option is to break orbit and leave our people to who knows what fate, we don't have much of a choice."

This time, Devall let out a burst of humorless laughter.

"Wonderful non-answer, sir. I'll take that as a sign you're in no mood to speculate."

"Smart course of action." Pushkin's eyes turned back toward the figures scurrying about on the other side of the armored glass. "If we didn't have someone with Guthren's experience, I might not have chosen this course of action."

"If we didn't have Guthren," Devall replied, his sardonic smile back in its accustomed place, "we might have had a chance to obey General Order Eighty-One and leave Miranda far aft of our hyperspace wake. As it is…"

"As it is, I might have experienced a mutiny if I'd done what the captain ordered. When it comes to the rescue party's chances, I'm reminded of a saying the Marine Pathfinders like to use. If they go down, we all go down — together."

"Provided we take half of the Mirandan fleet with us, it'll have been worth it. Some days I'm not sure I want to experience the long transit back to Commonwealth space. Coming out here gave me enough boredom to last until the heat death of the universe."

*

"Ah, Trask. How are things?" Martell's eyes lit up at the sight of Ariel Base's commander on his screen.

"All is well, and everything's in place." A smile briefly relaxed the man's face. "They've not given any indication they've found our interdiction buoys and the battalion designed to board them is on its way, also without indication they've been spotted."

"Excellent. Just keep in mind that they're only to be used if we can't get the Earthers to let us aboard their ship voluntarily."

"Of course." Trask inclined his head.

"Senior Group Leader Zellig's task force is also in place, ready to cut off any attempt at escape, so I think we can safely say that we're set to act at the Protector's orders."

"Indeed. You've done well."

"Anything more on the new intruder?"

"No. He's still on a course toward Miranda. Did you intend to have him intercepted while he's still at a distance? Whoever's aboard must have detected the Commonwealth ship by now and determined this system is inhabited."

"I'm hoping we'll have the Earthers' cooperation before he comes in range. With its more powerful weapons, we needn't risk any of ours. That is if the intruder is of a higher caliber than the usual xeno riff-raff. Otherwise?" Martell shrugged.

"How much longer?"

"A day at most, I'd venture." Martell's aide appeared at the door, reminding him of his next appointment. "If there's nothing else, I've got to go. Thank you for the call, Trask, and good luck. Someone will let you know when you can expect the Earthers to begin shuttling down their engineers. It would be a shame to shoot down that precious cargo."

"No fears, sir. Goodbye."

The screen turned back to its accustomed black, and Martell glanced at his aide.

"I'll see Academician Yorta now."

*

"Disappointed?" Dunmoore sniffed the juice carafe, wondering whether their hosts had slipped some noxious substance into it.

"About what?"

"That the *Tempest* colonists failed to establish their utopia, free of violence, greed and all those nasty human characteristics we never managed to breed out of our DNA."

A sad smile appeared on Wes Kalivan's tired face.

"By all appearances, they got close enough in their earlier days, before the realization that the universe is a nasty, harsh place intruded on them."

"So they say, though we've seen scant evidence of anything other than a xenophobic, militarized society. Considering all the other lies we've been fed, I wouldn't believe the likes of Dalian if she said the sky was blue."

"More like turquoise," Kalivan replied, a small grin lifting the corners of his mouth. "I wouldn't be too harsh on them, Siobhan. We have many historical examples of civilizations taking a ninety-degree turn in their entire outlook due to overwhelming external pressures. Our branch of humanity is far from having clean hands, even compared to the Mirandans."

"At least we've managed to evolve a bit more." She sat across from him, aware that his eyes searched hers for something.

"Have we? Really?"

"Is that it, Wes? You expected to find folks who rebuilt humanity while avoiding the massacres of our two Migration Wars and the endless colonial conflicts, not to mention our periodic clashes with non-human species. Perhaps for a time they did, but then reverted to the historical mean when reality intervened. In fact, they regressed further back compared to where we are now."

"They had longer than we did to get there," Kalivan pointed out, "thanks to their little encounter with a space-time phenomenon."

Dunmoore's humorless chuckle sounded harsh to her own ears.

"Are you saying that in another fifteen centuries, we'll turn into something like them?"

"Given similar pressures? Sure. Didn't you just mention something about reverting to the mean?"

She made a face at him, and for the first time since everything went wrong, she heard genuine laughter. It lifted her own spirits for few moments.

"I did, but I'm feeling rather pessimistic right now. Dalian wants to use our technology to bootstrap the Mirandan Dominion into an interstellar empire. It makes me wonder how many back home dream of doing away with the messiness of our dear quasi-democratic, if not entirely republican Commonwealth and turn the SecGen's chair into a throne."

"More than you'd think, Siobhan." The sadness returned. "And they're using the crisis of war against a non-human enemy to consolidate their power. Sound familiar?"

"We don't treat our captives in such an inhuman way." Anger and disgust warred with indignation in her expression.

"Are you sure? We capture so few Shrehari, it's not hard to make them vanish in the SSB's dungeons unseen."

"The Fleet would never hand prisoners of war to the secret police."

He nodded. "Point taken, but you can see how slight the real differences are when we look at ourselves with more dispassionate eyes."

"So you agree that we should cooperate with the Mirandans and help unleash them on an unsuspecting galaxy?"

The warning look he gave her dampened some of the outrage she felt. Their hosts had undoubtedly placed audio and video devices throughout this suite of rooms.

"You've made that call, for reasons you deem honorable. I'm merely pointing out that the moral difficulties you may or may not experience aren't as insurmountable as you may believe."

"Did it hurt?" She asked, a crooked grin twisting her pale scar.

"Did what hurt?"

"Being trained to see three or more sides in a two-sided problem."

"The cognitive dissonance took some getting used to, but as you can judge for yourself, I'm perfectly sane now."

Dunmoore snorted.

"Sane? Perhaps in your aristocratic world, buddy."

"Actually, compared to my peers, I am something of an outsider."

"Those peers being the imperialists?"

"Some," he admitted. "But to answer your original question, yes I'm disappointed. I won't be able to show those learned beings who laughed at me that I had it right when it came to *Tempest* vanishing in time as well as space and that their log buoy really did take almost two thousand years to get home."

She shrugged, but then let a small smile emerge.

"The universe is a big place, Wes, especially when it comes to time. Maybe we will tell our people about the Mirandans in due course."

"You think?" He raised a skeptical eyebrow. "I thought the game plan called on us to stay here and teach our cousins about the mysteries of antimatter and hyperspace so they'll be able to leave their star system."

"Situations change and evolve all the time."

— Twenty-Seven —

Chief Petty Officer Second Class Guthren called the landing party to attention, then turned around and waited for Lieutenant Kowalski to take charge of the formation.

The young woman, dressed in battle armor just like the rest of them, although less heavily armed, nodded at the first officer and stepped out of the control room, Sub-Lieutenant Sanghvi on her heels, the sound of their footsteps loud on the metal deck. She came to a halt one pace in front of the chief and returned his snappy salute while her wingman took position in front of the left-most file of spacers.

"Landing party, one chief, four petty officers and twenty ratings ready for departure."

"Thank you."

Guthren saluted again, then pivoted to the right and marched off to take his place on the flank of the formation.

Kowalski turned to face the control room and waited for the acting captain. Pushkin, not wanting to drag things out any longer than they had to, marched out, and stopped in front of her, the two of them exchanging salutes.

"I'm pleased to report that the landing party, twenty-seven strong, is ready to launch at your command. Would you care to inspect the troops?"

His eyebrows shot up, and she nodded once, saying in a low voice, "I think they'll appreciate it, sir. We're all just a little tense right now."

"Very well, lead on."

Trailed by Kowalski and Guthren, Pushkin took the time to exchange a few words with each one of them, trying to sound confident and relaxed, though his gut churned at the thought that they could easily be dead within a few hours.

And all because he had chosen to ignore the captain's order to abandon the captives. Once done, he stood in front of the group and placed them at ease.

"Folks, you're some of the Navy's finest and I have confidence that you'll get the captain, Colonel Kalivan, Chief Foste, and Spacer Vincenzo back safely. I also have faith that you'll show the Mirandans the futility of taking our people hostage. I know I'm probably stepping on the coxswain's toes in saying this, but I expect you to kick ass and take names. Let 'em know that you never, ever fuck with *Stingray*. I won't wish you good luck because you don't need it. I will, however, wish you Godspeed and good hunting."

He paused for a few seconds, meeting their sober eyes while he forced himself to smile, and then barked out, "The word is given, Lieutenant Kowalski. Launch the mission."

"Aye, aye, *sir*!" She turned to face the troops. "Load up, folks. We have four of ours waiting to get home."

Pushkin retreated to the control room and watched as the duty petty officer shut the airlock separating the hangar deck from the rest of the ship, in preparation for depressurizing it. He touched a com screen.

"Bridge, first officer here. Tell the Mirandan's we're about to launch two shuttles, heading for the ground south of Sanctum, as indicated by Captain Dunmoore."

"Aye, sir," Syten replied. "PO Rownes just caught her sensor ghost again, sir. I thought you might want to know."

"Where?"

"Not far beyond Miranda's outermost moon. Rownes thinks it might be Shrehari. *Tol* class, based on the brief image she got when they fired attitudinal thrusters."

He growled a curse in his native Russian.

"Wonderful. One more clown for this fucked-up party."

"Shall I warn the Mirandans?"

"Don't bother. I'm sure they're already tracking him. They didn't have much problems finding us and our emcon is better than the Shrehari's, even with their improvements."

And if they were not tracking him, Pushkin thought, then another variable thrown into the mix would probably help, especially if the supposed *Tol* class was coming in hot.

"Get the ship to battle stations, but keep the shields down. It wouldn't do to alert them any earlier than necessary."

*

Kowalski sealed up her shuttle and then turned to look at the passenger compartment. Guthren gave her thumbs up before taking a seat on one of the benches against the bulkhead.

"Mantis Two, this is Mantis One, checking in, over."

She heard Sanghvi's voice almost immediately, sounding steadier than he had looked just before climbing aboard his craft.

"Mantis Two is go."

"Thank you, Mantis Two. Control, Mantis Flight is ready. You can depressurize and open the space doors. Confirm that our hosts have cleared the flight."

"Flight has been cleared," Syten replied from the bridge. "No change in destination. Operation Mantis is a go."

Moments later, a red light began flashing, and her control panel showed the drop in air pressure outside the small craft's hull. Then, the light died, and the space doors opened to reveal *Stingray*'s aft hull, framed by the mighty hyperdrive nacelles.

Gently, Kowalski nudged Mantis One across the deck and then through the opening, lighting her thrusters the moment she cleared the ship. Mantis Two joined her a minute or so later, taking up position to the left and slightly behind.

"*Stingray*, this is Mantis One, permission to go weapons free."

"Granted." Pushkin's voice came through loud and clear. "Go get 'em."

The two shuttles banked to starboard and aimed their blunt bows straight at Miranda's blue-green orb, position lights bright to make sure no one would mistake them for anything other than a peaceful delegation headed down as ordered, to share Earth's technological bounty with the descendants of *Tempest*'s idealistic passengers. Except, as Chief Guthren had told the landing party, they would be sharing a shipload of whup-ass instead.

Leading Spacer Demianova, one of *Stingray*'s gunners met his eyes as he looked at the dozen armored ratings sitting silently, each lost in his or her own thoughts. One of Vincenzo's cronies, she had volunteered for the mission to save him, a reason that rang even truer than one proclaiming to have a deep and abiding wish to rescue the captain, though she had become popular among the crew. He winked at Demmi, who returned a shy smile.

Chief Penzara had also volunteered. Foste was one of *his* cronies, but Pushkin had declined, accepting Petty Officer First Class Rakkan's candidacy instead, not just because the latter had more boarding party experience as one of the senior bosun's mates, but also because he wanted Penzara at his station when things inevitably went pear-shaped.

A crew of Special Forces operators, they weren't, Guthren thought, but they had guts, discipline, and something previous raiders targeting Miranda had lacked: modern weaponry, armor, and a powerful starship to ride top cover. And a seething rage at Mirandan duplicity.

*

The door to their suite opened without warning to reveal Senior Group Leader Yarvik.

"Your ship confirms that it launched the shuttles with the engineers and technicians."

Dunmoore saw a disturbing gleam of mistrust in the woman's eyes and forced herself to smile.

"Excellent. Perhaps now we can start mending bridges and setting the groundwork for a lasting friendship between the Commonwealth and the Dominion of Miranda."

Yarvik grunted, her suspicious eyes still boring into Siobhan's as if trying to find a truth she knew hid under the blank facade.

"Chief Custodian Dalian has asked me to greet them. She's been recalled to Sanctum by the Lord Protector."

"She also mentioned that I'd be part of the welcoming committee."

"Of course." The Mirandan inclined her head.

"With one of my aides."

Her eyes narrowed and snapped to the left, where Vincenzo and Foste did everything they could to look as innocent as possible.

"That would be appropriate." Then, without a further word, she turned on her heel, and the door slid shut again.

"Take Vince," the bosun said. "The colonel might need a bit more handholding. No offense, sir."

"None taken," Kalivan replied. "It's a shame there's no chessboard. We could have played a few rounds while waiting."

"I have cards," Foste said.

"Really?"

"I never leave the ship without them, Colonel. Can't tell when I might have time to kill or a pigeon to pluck."

"In that case, break out your pack, and let's stick to something that doesn't involve your picking my pocket, okay?"

Foste laughed.

"I'm sure you're just as able to pick mine, sir. You have a face that can tell a thousand stories, none of them entirely true."

"Please!" He put on a mock-wounded expression. "It's purely for entertainment purposes."

The bosun pulled a small, hard box from her pocket and flipped it open.

"There are four of us. Shall we say Hearts?"

*

"The Earthers have launched their shuttles."

"Thank you." Group Leader Trask stood and walked over to a screen dominated by *Stingray*'s image. Two small specks detached themselves from the larger vessel and banked away, the glow of their drives a dark orange. "Please advise HQ that we're tracking them."

He stared at the frigate and then turned to face his aide, a young man wearing a bannerman's silver leaf. "Otmar, please call up a tactical rendition of near space. I'd like to see the latest projections on the new intruder."

After studying the resulting schematic, he touched a communications screen. "Operations Center, this is Trask.

The most recent xeno intruder seems to have adjusted its course to bring it closer to Miranda. Please confirm with the shadowing force that they retain the ability to neutralize it."

"Yes, sir. Immediately."

The commander of Ariel Base rubbed the side of his face while he contemplated the various moving parts in this most delicate operation. He would have preferred that this new intruder had not appeared, or at least waited a few more hours. As things stood, he would be at his closest approach to Miranda near the time HQ had designated for the seizure of the Earthers' ship, if Dunmoore failed to cooperate.

"Get me a link with Chief Defender Martell."

He paced his large office for the few minutes it took to establish the connection. When Martell's face appeared, he stopped and pulled himself to attention.

"Thank you for taking my call, sir."

Martell nodded once. "What is it?"

"I would like to propose we advance the seizure. The newest xeno intruder has modified his course to come closer than first projected. I fear we might find ourselves at a confluence of events that could become difficult to control. All elements are in place."

"Not before their technical personnel has disembarked at the Sanctum Research Facility, Trask. If something goes wrong with the seizure, I'd like to make sure we have at least their most important people to draw on."

"Understood, sir. Then I modify my suggestion to trigger the seizure the moment we've detained them."

"Very well. I'll have the HQ operations center alert you once we get news from our Custodian friends."

"Thank you."

"Was there anything else?"

"No."

Martell cut the transmission without a further word, leaving Trask to contemplate the fern and sword emblem on an otherwise darkened screen. The next few hours might decide their entire future, he mused. Finally achieving the ability to travel across interstellar space and establish a Greater Dominion over all xenos, and woe betide those who dared resist.

He smiled at the thought, saddened only by the realization that he would be too old for the new expeditionary forces, conquest being a job for the young.

Then, something that had been bothering him since he saw the shuttles depart *Stingray* crystallized in his mind.

"Otmar, call up an image of the Earther shuttle that came to Ariel and project it beside a picture of the two craft that are heading for the surface."

When the aide had done so, Trask sat back in his chair and, elbows on its arms, he steepled his fingers, eyes flicking between both images.

"Tell me," he pointed at the screen, "do these craft look different to you?"

The bannerman nodded.

"The one that brought the Earthers here didn't have these additional layers on its top and bottom."

"Between them, they almost double the size of the shuttles, no?"

"Yes, sir. Perhaps a variant for longer trips? They seem like add-ons. Extra fuel maybe."

"Or additional weaponry."

Trask contemplated warning HQ of the difference, then figured that whatever it might be, Miranda's defenses could handle two insignificant spacecraft.

— Twenty-Eight —

Their Hearts tournament had inevitably morphed into seven-card stud, and Dunmoore had won many imaginary creds by the time Yarvik and a squad of guards came to fetch her and Vincenzo. When half the guards surrounded Kalivan and Foste as well, Siobhan gave the Mirandan an interrogatory stare.

"Chief Custodian Dalian has ordered that your companions be taken to the lab, to ensure your continued cooperation. She said you'd understand what she meant."

"I most certainly do." She sneered. "Your notions of hospitality leave a lot to be desired."

Yarvik shrugged.

"The needs of the Dominion take precedence over personal comforts and desires. Besides, Chief Custodian Dalian has classified you as xenos, which means any hospitality we offer is on sufferance."

Dunmoore glanced over her shoulder at Kalivan.

"Don't worry, Wes. We'll have this sorted out soon, one way or another."

"We'll be alright, sir," Foste said, drawing herself ramrod straight. "You go say hi to our folks and get things settled."

"I will." Siobhan held the bosun's eyes for a few moments, to ensure she understood the implied promise. "Remember what the Marines always say."

"Aye." Foste raised her arm in salute.

The Mirandans seemed to be growing increasingly impatient, and Dunmoore had to shake off an impertinent hand trying to steer her to the door. Vincenzo seethed with barely repressed fury and before he did something foolish, she snapped, "Take your post, spacer."

He nodded once, pivoted with parade ground precision, and took a step to place himself one pace ahead of Dunmoore. His dark eyes flung daggers at the gray-clad Custodian troopers, but they ignored him with cold indifference.

Senior Group Leader Yarvik led the procession down the corridor connecting their suite with the office Dalian had used earlier and then up a broad, winding staircase that ended in a blockhouse-like structure on top of the artificial mesa housing the facility.

A pair of guards flung metal doors open, and bright sunshine momentarily blinded them. When their eyes adjusted, Dunmoore saw a smooth surface seemingly stretching to the horizon, glinting here and there where the outer lenses of light tunnels captured the sun's rays and funneled them down onto the hydroponics gardens.

In the distance, rounded protrusions made a stark contrast against the washed-out sky, their sides festooned with antennae of all sorts.

"Your shuttles will land here," Yarvik pointed at an array of yellow symbols painted on the ground. "You will greet them enthusiastically and invite them to follow you down the stairs. There, my people will separate your engineers and technicians by specialty and they will be led to the appropriate parts of the research facility."

Dunmoore nodded once, wondering what or whom Pushkin had sent. She glanced at the dozen armed men who had taken position in an extended line on the edge of the landing zone and wondered why they had not used an entire battalion, considering it did not take a tactical genius to think about the possibility of Trojan shuttles.

On the other hand, they considered everyone not of the Dominion to be inferior species, Dunmoore, and her crew included, and they expected them to comply with orders on fear of dismemberment and death. She had to repress a smile at the thought. What was the expression again? Hoist by their own petard?

A faint rumble, far above, drew her eyes, and she raised her hand to her brow, to block the afternoon sun. One way or another, it would be over within the hour.

*

"Look sharp." Kowalski's voice crackled in Guthren's ears. "There's a reception committee of about twenty, and I count at least six weapons emplacements around the tarmac."

A projection appeared on the inside of the coxswain's helmet visor, showing the landing zone in its entirety.

"Got it, thanks."

"The captain's transponder is where I see her. Colonel Kalivan's is a few meters below the surface. I make out Vincenzo, but not Foste."

"Having all four where we could toss them into the shuttles and bugger off would have been too much to hope for."

"At least the Mirandans aren't armored."

"A small piece of good luck, I suppose."

"If life in the Navy were easy, cox'n, you'd have joined the Marines."

"God forbid, sir. I already have a brother in the Corps. Two of us would have made Momma Guthren die of despair."

Kowalski chuckled.

"Proper lady, your mother?"

"Proper enough to want at least one of her boys doing honest service."

She flipped to the tight beam link with Sanghvi's shuttle.

"Two, this is One. I'm assuming you see the reception committee and the six weapons emplacements?"

"Affirmative." His youthful voice echoed with barely repressed nervous tension.

"We'll land facing away from the personnel on the ground to give the assault force a clear run. Once on the ground, you'll target the three emplacements to starboard, and I'll take the ones to port. I have a notion that they might object to our lifting off once the chief has worked his magic."

"Roger."

"Don't bother with guns. One missile apiece should suffice."

"Would we be too close?"

"We'll only get one chance. Shields don't work too well in an atmosphere."

"Got it."

"Good. Let's try to touch down in tandem. The more of a show they get, the less they'll expect a scruffy bunch of pirates."

"I resemble that remark," Guthren said with mock outrage.

"The whole point is to confuse them, Chief."

"So you mean I should try and look like I'm friendly? I guess it's worth a try, though I don't have much practice."

He heard a muffled guffaw over the radio and smiled. Nothing like a little humor to take the edge off just before going into battle.

The shuttles banked hard to line up with the artificial mesa's long side, then shed altitude over the many kilometers of grain fields surrounding it until they flew only a few meters higher than the square structure.

"Time," Guthren said. "Link me up with Rakkan's folks, Lieutenant."

"You've got everyone," she replied moments later.

"Okay folks, this is it. Helmet visors down, check that you're linked up with the rest of the party, and put a round up the spout. Make sure you have the safety on because a negligent discharge inside a shuttle means I'm leaving you here. What are the rules of engagement, Demianova?"

"We fire only on order from you or the PO," the young woman replied, "or if we're shot at."

"Exactly. This is a rescue mission, not a search and destroy raid. If we can get away without leaving a trail of bodies, it might make things easier for us once the Mirandans realize we're not cuddly little space critters."

He paused.

"One last thing — we're twenty-seven on this mission and twenty-seven, plus four are going back to the ship. We leave no one behind. If I go..."

"We all go," twenty-six voices shouted back.

"God help the Mirandans, because I sure as hell won't."

"If we're all good," Kowalski said, "stand by. We land in sixty."

Dunmoore had no idea who sat at the controls, but both shuttles moved as one, banking in a smooth ballet, their nacelles almost touching until they dropped to eye level and slowly crept up on the Sanctum Research Facility.

She noticed the top and bottom additions, correctly identifying the former as add-on missile launchers. The latter's function, however, escaped her.

"Good pilots," Yarvik said, watching the craft through eyes narrowed against the sun. "Perhaps they can be useful."

"Flying shuttles is a secondary duty, Senior Group Leader. Whoever is at the controls has a primary job aboard *Stingray*."

"Not for much longer."

She felt Vincenzo tense beside her and reached out to grasp his forearm.

The shuttles passed no more than a few meters above their heads before they shed all forward momentum and gently dropped down until they rested side by side on their stubby landing gear.

She just had time to glimpse *Stingray*'s emblem on the rear ramps before these came down and four files of armed, armored spacers walked off, the ones on their left led by a barrel-shaped figure with a chief petty officer's starburst insignia on his chest.

Even without a rank marking and with the helmet visor down, masking his face, she would have recognized Guthren anywhere. They had been captain and coxswain at the start of the war, and it seemed like they were going to end it together.

Two of the four files, the outer ones, curved away to cover the extended line of Mirandan troops, while the remainder came straight toward the little cluster formed by Dunmoore, Yarvik, and Vincenzo. Siobhan suddenly realized she had been holding her breath while her heart pounded a mad tattoo, and she forced herself to exhale.

Guthren stomped to a perfect parade ground halt one pace in front of them, plasma carbine held high across his chest and saluted.

"Captain. Reporting as ordered."

"Who is this individual?" Yarvik asked in a querulous voice. "And why are they dressed in these suits?"

"This is my chief engineer, Lieutenant Commander Kutora," Siobhan lied, "and the suits are for safety, in case a shuttle loses pressure."

"You'll have to surrender your weapons, of course. Only Custodian personnel may be armed inside a research facility."

Yarvik had focused solely on Guthren, as the latter had hoped, and failed to notice that half his landing party now covered her guards, ready to take them down at his signal.

The armored head with the blank visor turned to face the Mirandan.

"I think not."

— Twenty-Nine —

Guthren's carbine snapped up, and the tip of its barrel touched Yarvik's chest. The remainder had waited for precisely that signal and carbine butts rose as one to strike down the Mirandan guards. In the space of a few heartbeats, they had taken the landing zone.

The Mirandan senior group leader had not twitched a muscle during that brief spasm of violence, her incredulous eyes on the weapon pointing at her heart. She had never been threatened before and seemed unable to process this new sensation.

"Kalivan and Foste are being held in labs below," Dunmoore said, "against our continued cooperation."

He nodded.

"I've got his transponder signal. And if we don't cooperate?"

She made a slicing motion across her neck.

"Rakkan, have your men tie up the bastards, including this ugly moron here," Guthren shouted. "The rest, on me. Are we weapons free, Captain?"

"Oh yes," Dunmoore nodded. Before she had the chance to say anything else, the coxswain pulled a blaster from his belt and handed it to her, butt first.

"You make sure to stay in the back, sir. Armor can take whatever these assholes are going to throw at us. Skin can't."

He yanked a spare carbine from the pack slung over his shoulder and tossed it at Vincenzo.

"And you make sure she doesn't get ahead of the suits. Otherwise, I'll make you wish you'd chosen jail instead of the Navy."

A loud siren began to wail, its mournful sound rising up the stairwell behind Dunmoore.

"Seems like the Mirandans figured out things have gone sideways," she said. "Shoot first, don't bother asking questions. We don't have much time to save Kalivan and Foste. These bastards don't fuck around."

She stepped aside, to let Guthren and a dozen spacers storm down the steps, the chief's comment about a transponder signal finally registering, but it was too late to ask.

The sound of chemically propelled weapons echoed over the stairs, answered by the deeper cough of plasma carbines. One scream, then several proved that Guthren had not only engaged the Mirandans but hit them where it hurt.

With Vincenzo hard on her heels, she took the treads two by two, one hand on the banister, the other clutching her gun. The stench of voided bowels, charred flesh, and burned cordite assaulted their nostrils, and she sneezed.

A warning shout in Commonwealth Anglic made both of them duck just as the slash of a high-powered laser beam cut through the air where her head had been. Then, several carbines fired at once, silencing the Mirandan gunner.

To her right, four spacers, tucked into doorways, kept a squad of Mirandan troops from risking a peek around the corner that led to their temporary quarters and covered the backs of the team searching for Wes and the bosun.

She risked a look down that corridor, and when nothing moved, she darted to the left and the next stairwell, where Guthren had taken his rapidly dwindling team.

Her step faltered when she saw one of hers lying on the ground, his armor scored by multiple hits, but the autodoc screen had popped out of the chest plate and showed her that he still lived, although kept alive only by the suit.

She tumbled down the steps, heart pounding, hoping they would reach the labs before Yarvik's butchers started cutting — out of spite if for no other reason.

One of her spacers intercepted them on the lower landing, his arm stretched out.

"They're fighting back like banshees, Captain. It'll take the chief a few more minutes."

And indeed, they were. The flash of lasers, the thump of chemical propellant, and the cough of plasma weaponry underscored the siren's ghostly howl.

Disembodied voices rang out from hidden speakers, alternately demanding the intruders cease firing and surrender and seeking status reports from embattled Custodians. The latter still could not comprehend that anyone would be brazen enough to invade their facility, gun in hand, without any respect for the authority of their uniforms.

The spacer tilted his head, as if listening, then nodded at Dunmoore.

"Chief's found the colonel and Foste, sir. They're in bad shape. He says he's extracting." The man turned his blank visor on Vincenzo. "He says that you're to take the skipper back to the shuttles now, Vince, and on the double, or your ass is grass."

Vincenzo gave her a pleading look and then jerked his chin toward the stairs. She clenched her jaw, fighting back the need to see what the Mirandans had done to Wes and the bosun, but nodded.

With her bodyguard in the lead, they climbed back up to find the covering party now caught between two enemy squads and their escape route cut off.

Dunmoore heard more firing from below, then the sound of armored feet pounding on the concrete steps. She stepped out of the way to let the first two spacers pass and then looked down hoping to catch a glimpse of her companions.

Instead, she saw Guthren plow his way through, a grenade in hand. One of the point men opened the door, and the coxswain's grenade sailed down the corridor at the new arrivals. It exploded with a dull thump, then the two spacers burst through, firing from the hip while they took up positions to cover the rest.

Guthren pointed his finger at Vincenzo, then at the door, before detailing two men to pick up the one who had been hit.

The corridor, so quiet and neat only a few hours earlier, now seemed like the antechamber of hell. The Mirandans stood little chance against armored troops equipped with plasma rifles in confined quarters. They scampered to the next stairwell and ran up, the pair with the wounded man hard behind them.

Up top, the six domes she had noted earlier had split open to reveal multiple gun barrels, which, fortunately, could not depress low enough to engage the shuttles, but the moment they lifted, the Mirandans would assuredly start shooting.

Vincenzo urged her to climb aboard the nearest one, but she stood rooted to the spot, waiting to see her crew withdraw in good order from the facility.

Another wounded man limped by, his leg blackened by a direct hit, then two more dragged one whose autodoc panel showed nothing but a sea of red.

Then, Foste appeared, naked as a jaybird, bleeding from multiple injuries. She gave Siobhan a tight grin before hustling into Sanghvi's shuttle, where one of the spacers was already preparing her armor.

Another spacer stepped out of the stairwell's shadows, a bleeding body slung over his shoulder. He saw her intense stare and shook his head before running a gauntleted hand over his throat.

A pit of anguish opened in Siobhan's guts, and she fought back a sudden surge of tears. Then, the remainder of the landing party emerged, with Guthren and his wingman at the tail end.

This time, she did not resist Vincenzo's tug and jogged up the ramp where someone thrust a large bag at her.

"Chief said you're to put this on, Captain." The man pointed at the other satchel. "That's yours, Vince. The ride upstairs might get hairy."

Dunmoore, head still swirling at the rapid pace of events, and the pain of Kalivan's senseless death nodded. Then, the last of her crew climbed aboard, and the ramp slammed shut.

*

"What do you mean the research facility is under attack?" Mira Dalian's voice rose to a high pitch, her basilisk stare lancing through the hapless operations officer detailed to deliver the bad news.

"It's the Earthers, Chief Custodian. Their shuttles carried an assault force rather than the expected technical personnel."

"Do we know what's going on?"

"Sorry, sir, but information is still fragmented and confused."

"Get me Senior Group Leader Yarvik, now." She snarled, fury mounting quickly at the Earthers' audacity.

"No one's able to contact her. She was with the reception party on the roof of the facility when the attack started."

Then she had better be dead, Dalian thought, because this failure will cost her everything.

"How about the facility's chief officer?"

"He's the one we're talking to, sir."

She took a deep breath, forcing her rage back down. They could still salvage this.

"Tell him to make sure the shuttles don't lift off. Now get me Chief Defender Martell."

"Immediately, Chief Custodian."

When Martell's face appeared on the screen, she saw his right eyebrow go up, and then a mocking little smile twisted his lips.

"Mira. You look like one of the Erinyes. What has earned me the task of looking into the face of an Angry One?"

"The damned Earthers sent a raiding party aboard their shuttles, to rescue the envoys. It seems they've managed to sow utter chaos among my people."

"No doubt the survivors will feel your wrath." His smile vanished. "Have they lifted off yet?"

"I can't get any answers from the facility. Everyone is running around like a Skraeling with its head cut off."

"And you'd like me to assist you how?"

"Seize their damned ship. Those with the knowledge we need are still aboard. I'll take care of the shuttles."

"As you wish." He nodded once and then cut the communication.

Dalian cursed, wishing she had a xeno on hand to serve as a punching bag. This would cost her the chance at becoming the next Protector.

Speaker Marant had supported her plan against Hames' best instincts, and he would disown her now that it had come apart. If Geoff Martell succeeded with his, then the Two Hundred would offer him the chair, and she would have a long ten years to wait until her chance came around once more. If the Two Hundred did not end her tenure as Chief Custodian permanently.

She called the operations officer again.

"Have the Earther shuttles brought down by whatever means necessary."

"Including their destruction?"

"Including their destruction."

*

"Sir, Mantis Leader reports they've recovered our people and are preparing to lift off."

"Casualties?" Pushkin asked.

"Five, including two dead, Spacer Wim and Colonel Kalivan."

"Damn." The first officer's fist slammed into the command chair's much-abused arm. "That makes it war. Guns, raise shields and go to active targeting. Commo, give me ship-wide."

When the signals petty officer gave him thumbs up, Pushkin fought to keep from clearing his throat. Instead, he took a deep breath and nodded.

"This is the first officer," he began, "as you know, we've launched a raid to rescue four of ours held prisoner by people who pretended to be friendly. The landing party has recovered the captain, Chief Foste, and Spacer Vincenzo. Colonel Kalivan and Spacer Wim however, died during the raid, while three more of ours are injured. They have yet to return to us safely, so the casualty list might not yet be closed off. In the meantime, we must treat our current position as that of a ship surrounded by hostile forces and in a state of war. You went to battle stations as a preventative. I have ordered shields raised and active targeting on Mirandan forces, in preparation for a fight. We will not fire first, but we will respond shot for shot and show them what it costs to harm us. Once we've recovered our shuttles, we will leave this system and return home. That is all."

He made a cutting motion at the signals PO.

"Do you think they'll try something, sir?" Lieutenant Syten asked.

A humorless laugh escaped the first officer's throat.

"Count on it."

"Then why not destroy the objects surrounding us right away. They're not carrying any living beings."

"Definitely an idea whose time has come. Do so."

However, before Syten could fire, Chief Penzara turned from his console, aghast.

"We're being jammed. And I don't just mean a bit. Every frequency known to humanity is being jammed. My sensors can't see a damned thing. It's almost as bad as the ion storm."

Then, he cursed.

"Mister Kutora's repairs just gave up the ghost. Our primary sensor network is down again, and the secondary is as blind as a cave fish."

"I've lost our lock on every preregistered target as well," Syten confirmed. "Attempting to regain. Searching. Negative."

Pushkin turned to the signals alcove and the petty officer nodded.

"The comms as well, sir, other than subspace, for all the good it does us out here."

"I guess we now know what those objects do."

"Aye," Penzara nodded, "turn us deaf, dumb, and blind, and that means..."

"It means they're about to attempt a boarding."

"Through our shields? Good luck." Syten waved a dismissive hand.

"We know that, but they don't." Pushkin left the command chair to stand behind the gunnery console as he went through every possible permutation. "Or if they do, they'll be opening fire to collapse the shields."

"Or wait until we have to open them aft for the shuttles."

"Whatever." The first officer shook his head. "This kind of trick must have worked on ships that didn't have our advantages, so they're obviously expecting us to freeze in place while we figure out what's going on. And all the while, their little ships box us in, latch on and board in the confusion. I'll even bet they have some big boys nearby we haven't seen, ready to make us think again about running."

"Agreed." Syten nodded.

"Since they can't jam our visual pickups, we'll navigate by sight." He grinned at Petty Officer Takash's appalled expression. "You'll do just fine. Prepare to break out of our current orbit. Let's screw with them as much as we can and head closer to the planet. I'll wager we're more maneuverable than their giant cruisers. Besides, the Mirandans know about the intricacies of orbital mechanics, and that'll slow down their reactions. They won't want to fire at us if there's a risk of the shot hitting one of the low-level platforms or the surface."

"If nothing else, it'll speed up our recovery of the landing party," the sailing master said.

"Indeed, Mister Tours. What we need now is a course that even a blind helmsman can safely sail and halve our distance with Miranda. Then, prepare to get us away from here and to the hyperlimit as fast as possible once we've recovered our shuttles. I think we've overstayed our welcome."

*

The sound of creative cursing from the sensor console pulled Brakal's wandering thoughts back to his bridge.

"What?"

"Emissions in the area of space occupied by Dunmoore's ship just spiked by several orders of magnitude."

"Impossible. Your equipment is faulty and requires investigation by our *Tai Kan* spy."

"You did hear my cursing, Commander, but the sensor gear and the computer are innocent of treason."

"Show me."

"This," the technician said, projecting an image over half the main screen, "are the emissions moments before the spike. And this," a second image joined the first, "are the emissions now."

"By all the infernal demons. Dunmoore is under attack. It cannot be anything else."

"A species hostile to us and the humans? What bad luck." Urag managed to sound thoroughly disgusted.

"Perhaps we should ask Dunmoore, no?" Brakal's predatory smile made a brief appearance. "Maybe offer our help so she can escape and meet me in open space so we may settle our differences in honorable battle."

He glanced over his shoulder at Regar. "Or would helping an enemy against a mutual enemy violate all the rules that govern our empire?"

The *Tai Kan* officer shrugged. "You know what we say back home, Commander. What happens in deep space stays in deep space."

A wave of recklessness washed over Brakal, fed by weeks of inactivity crossing the black, and before that, long months on half-pay, waiting for a ship.

"Bring all systems up and prepare us for battle. Navigator, plot a direct course toward Dunmoore's ship, best transit time. If we cannot fight, perhaps we can at least figure out what, in all that's unholy, lives in this system."

— Thirty —

"Mantis Two, this is Mantis One."

Kowalski tried hard not to shout. The adrenaline coursing through her veins seemed almost too much to bear. She knew that the hard part of the mission still lay ahead, now that the element of surprise had vanished, and it seemed like all of her senses had become hyper-focused.

"Engage the defensive emplacements. Do not, I repeat, do not lift."

"Two, roger. Firing now."

Six close-in defense missiles, taken from *Stingray*'s stocks and loaded into jury-rigged launcher pods attached to the top of each shuttle, erupted on columns of flame.

They headed up into the sky before executing a graceful parabola that aimed them back at the ground, each programmed to destroy one of the Mirandan gun emplacements.

Taken by surprise, the multiple barrel arrays remained horizontal, waiting until the spacecraft lifted into their arcs of fire until one suddenly raised its muzzles and began shooting straight up.

A missile exploded no more than a twenty meters above the gun, showering it with debris. The remaining five struck almost simultaneously, vaporizing barrels, mounts, and power cells. Miniature mushroom clouds rose over the emplacements and Sanghvi whooped with delight.

"Two, this is One, we have an incomplete," Kowalski reminded him, aiming her shuttle's Gatling at the surviving gun. A stream of plasma shot out, splashing against the armored sides of the dome, until she lifted off, giving herself a better field of fire.

The Mirandan barrels came down to lock onto the offending craft, but before it could fire, Sanghvi's own Gatling chimed in, chewing through the mount until it reached the laser's capacitor. Then, it too grew an instant mushroom cloud.

"Go, go, go!" This time, Kowalski did not bother controlling her intonation, the words echoing through cockpit and passenger compartment, and nearly deafening her wingman. She activated the surface-to-orbit radio link.

"Control, this is Mantis Flight, we have liftoff, I repeat we have liftoff."

When *Stingray* failed to reply, she tried again, also with no result.

"Two, this is One. Control's not answering me. Try them."

The research facility dwindled rapidly below them, but a sudden flash of light almost overloaded Kowalski's visual pickups.

"Someone's got a laser on us," she shouted into the radio. "Break formation and take evasive maneuvers."

Both shuttles banked hard, one to port, the other to starboard and briefly shed altitude. Another burst of laser fire passed through the spot Sanghvi's craft had occupied moments earlier.

Then, the threat sensor squealed, a high-pitched noise that turned Kowalski's guts to water.

"I've got a seeker on my tail," she said.

"Same here," Sanghvi replied.

They passed through the first layer of clouds, and another flash of light narrowly missed Kowalski's craft.

"I've got a fix on the seekers," she announced. "Four missiles fifty kilometers aft, closing at hypersonic speed. We have less than thirty seconds to impact. Firing now."

Her Gatling turned aft and began spewing plasma, joined seconds later by Sanghvi's main gun.

"Where the heck is *Stingray*," she muttered. "Control, this is Mantis Flight, over."

A bare head above battle armor appeared in her peripheral vision.

"No contact with the ship?" Dunmoore nodded at the empty co-pilot seat. "Need another pair of everything, Kathryn?"

"If you would, sir." A brief smile softened her tense features. "But put your helmet on. If we get holed at this altitude, you'll be doing your own version of the stranded goldfish dance."

The alarm fell silent, and Kowalski exhaled with relief.

"That takes care of one threat."

"And yet, the Mirandans aren't done yet," Dunmoore replied after sealing her suit. "A squadron of something just popped up on the sensors. Judging by speed and size, I'd call them fighters of some sort, ten in all."

She looked at their airspeed, then back at the readout. "Not a chance in hell of catching us, thankfully, which makes me wonder why they bothered."

They emerged from the clouds into a sky rapidly losing its cerulean blue for the lavender of high altitude.

The proximity detector chimed softly, and Kowalski said, "I think I know."

She jerked her chin toward the secondary readout.

"There's another bunch of them coming down from orbit."

*

A visual replaced the almost useless tactical schematic on the main screen, showing half a dozen small vessels, each not much bigger than an average space yacht, approaching *Stingray* on the starboard side.

"There's another six trying for our port side," Penzara said. "The buggers must have engaged their drives the moment we lost all of our sensors. They're about to bounce off our shields."

The first of the ships seemed to come to a sudden halt relative to the frigate, and a brief arc of greenish light flared up around it.

"Permission to fire, sir. They're so close my gunners could do it blind drunk over iron sights."

"Negative." Pushkin shook his head. "They're no threat at this point, and I don't want to cause more casualties than necessary for us to get away."

More energy flares lit up the starboard shield when PO Takash lit the bow thrusters to direct *Stingray* onto a new, lower orbit.

"I wonder how they like us pushing them out of the way like that."

"Probably not much, Chief."

A brighter flare suddenly erupted on the port shield, followed by two more.

"Something big has just engaged us. Shields are holding, but I'd like to get my targeting sensors back," Syten said.

"And there's your answer. The Mirandans aren't happy we decided to leave early."

"Tough shit," Penzara chuckled. The chief's laughter abruptly stopped, and he leaned forward to stare closely at his screen. "I'm getting a flicker of life in my sensors, sir. We must be nearing the outer range of those damn jammers."

"Excellent." Pushkin sat up straighter. "Mister Syten, the moment we have a lock on whoever is shooting at us, you're cleared to fire, but guns only at this stage."

No sooner had the words left his mouth that plasma streaked from the port side battery.

"That was quick."

Syten smiled shyly.

"I got a good enough fix on the jammers and couldn't resist."

"And I'm glad you didn't, sir," Penzara said. "I'm almost back at full capacity on the secondary sensor net and not a moment too soon. Rownes was right. We've got a *Tol* class Shrehari cruiser inbound."

The first officer swore under his breath.

"That's all we need. Recovering our landing party in the middle of a three-sided fight had always been a dream of mine."

"I'm sure the shrinks can help with that, sir." Penzara made a face. "Let's hope the buggers get into it with our Mirandan friends and leave us alone."

*

"Someone's shooting at the human ship, and it seems to be shooting back."

"Really?" Brakal sat back in his chair with a thoughtful smile on his face. "Let me see. Dunmoore has been in orbit around this planet for several days, and she is attacked only now? What manner of beings inhabit this system?"

"The kind that doesn't seem to like us either," the sensor tech replied. "Something has just fired missiles in our direction."

"Show me."

A tactical schematic filled the screen, identifying the incoming ordnance, but no point of origin.

"The demons are well hidden, it seems," Urag commented from his usual station to the right of Brakal's command chair. "Trace the flight path and let's see if there's a way we can make out the ship that engaged us."

"I'm already doing so, Sub-Commander."

"Good." Brakal's smile turned into a savage rictus. "Gun master, destroy those missiles, and then prepare to follow up with whatever the sensors discover."

"You may follow up whenever you wish," the technician said, pointing at the main screen. "I've used a very simple technique that consists of watching the background stars vanish, and I've found our shooter as well as four of its friends."

The tactical schematic changed to add five new icons.

"Trying to box us in with a retrograde maneuver, eh?" Brakal's thick fingers caressed his bony chin. "Open fire with all guns at the nearest one. Let's see how he reacts to that."

"Commander?"

"Yes."

"Dunmoore's ship is shifting closer to the planet. She's started to engage ships in a higher orbit that weren't apparent to our sensors a moment ago."

"The beasts uncloak."

"We've scored a hit," the gun master reported. "It's forced the demon's spawn to activate its systems."

The image of a massive spaceship, several times larger than *Tol Vehar* filled a side screen. Bright lights winked on its hull.

"It's firing lasers."

"Lasers?" Brakal's incredulous laugh echoed across the bridge. "How primitive."

"Notice that he has no nacelles for an otherspace drive system either."

"You mean we're up against a civilization that hasn't achieved FTL travel? Yet they managed to destroy *Ziq Tar*? Unbelievable."

"Given enough of them," Urag said, "even the best can be overwhelmed. See Dunmoore's ship."

He pointed at the three-dimensional rendering of Miranda and its moons.

"She's about to get pinned against the planet by five of those behemoths. What odds do you give her, Commander?"

"I don't give odds because she must have a reason to do whatever she's doing. A woman who bested me would not let herself get trapped without thinking."

"Perhaps someone other than Dunmoore is in command," Urag suggested.

Brakal shrugged.

"Perhaps. Let us blow through this screen of over-sized garbage scows and find out. It would pain me if someone else took the vengeance that is rightfully mine."

"Lasers and missiles can still hurt us if deployed in sufficient numbers. After all, they overwhelmed one of ours already."

"A survey ship."

"Based on a *Tol* class hull."

"But still a survey ship. We head for the planet. I'm not leaving until we find out who lives here, why they killed our comrades from *Ziq Tar* and why they seem to dislike Dunmoore as much as I do."

*

"We now have a full-scale battle in near orbit and another one just beyond the outermost lunar orbit," Hames snarled at his communications screen.

Martell, Dalian, and Marant stared back at him with a collective expression of stunned surprise on their faces.

"To say this plan of yours went utterly sour would be an understatement. Does anyone grasp the fact that we are now at war with our kin from the Commonwealth, as well as their foe the Shrehari Empire?"

"They cannot get away," Martell replied, fighting a sudden tendency to stutter. "One ship against many of ours."

Hames' fist came down on his desk.

"That's not what it looks like from here, Geoff. I'm getting a live feed of the damage reports and rest assured that the lives lost today are squarely on the three of you."

"Calm down, Cyrus." Dalian's cold eyes tried to dominate the Protector's hard stare but without success. "This is far from over."

"No. I'll tell you what's over, Mira. Your tenure as Chief Custodian is over."

"Only the Two Hundred can remove me."

"But I can suspend you pending a decision by the Two Hundred."

"And we wouldn't approve," Marant smoothly interjected. "Mira's done what was necessary for the Dominion. We could not have foreseen that the Earthers would be so duplicitous. No other xenos have tricked us like that in centuries."

"Therein lies the problem," Hames shouted at the Speaker. "They are human, like us, not xenos. If you'd remembered that, perhaps we might have taken the long view instead of grasping for a quick solution."

"Yelling at me won't solve anything." Marant seemed untouched by the outburst. "Let the Defenders do their duty."

"And the other intruder, who seems to be of this Shrehari species, like the previous one, based on the reports I'm seeing? He's savaging the blocking force as we sit here arguing."

"Again, the weight of our ships will wear him down." Martell raised his hand in a placating gesture. "And the Earthers' shuttles will be taken down shortly. With a squadron of fighters above them and one below, they have nowhere to go."

"At this point, your optimism seems vastly out of sync with reality."

— Thirty-One —

"Mantis Flight, this is control, come in, over."

"Finally."

Kowalski's exclamation pulled Dunmoore from her contemplation of the twin threats.

"This is Mantis Leader. You'll be happy to hear that I have Mantis Mother sitting beside me. We're at seventy klicks and rising. Bogeys above and below us trying for a sandwich."

"Roger that. We'll drop down to five hundred clicks for recovery, but we're in a running battle with the better part of the local battleship squadron so you need to hang on for a little longer."

"We'll try, but no promises."

"No need to come aboard with spare ordnance," Pushkin's voice replied. "You're still weapons free to shoot down anyone who comes near."

"A bit of a war on your hands?" Dunmoore asked.

"Just a bit." The first officer's voice seemed to brighten upon hearing hers. "Bastards tried to take us, but didn't quite count on our shields being up, that's if they understand shield technology at all. Unfortunately, we've started leaving wreckage in our wake, not ours, theirs, so I'd say we've overstayed our welcome."

"The sooner we're out of here, the better, and don't worry about the wreckage. It's no more than they deserve. Make sure we don't leave parts of *Stingray* behind."

"That bad?"

"I'll tell you once we're on board, but yeah, that bad. The Mirandans are no friends of ours."

"Speaking of friends," Pushkin replied after a brief pause, "a *Tol* class cruiser seems intent on joining the fun, and if it's any consolation, he's neither stinting on the ammo where the Mirandans are concerned, nor is he shooting at us yet."

The shuttle suddenly shook and veered off course.

"A glancing hit from a space-based laser," Kowalski said. "We don't know how long Mister Kutora's improvised shield generator will last."

Another one struck the shuttle dead center and the damage control system squawked.

"Hang tight, Mantis. We just found the shooter. He's about to have bigger problems than bad aim."

Not long after, a bright star briefly came into being above and ahead of them before winking out.

"Thanks. But we still have the inbound bogeys."

A constellation of laser bursts struck their shield almost head-on, creating a bright blue-green aurora that crackled and danced around the small craft. Their damage control system's squawk rose by both a decibel and an octave as if the shuttle itself felt outraged at the unfairness of a ten on two attack.

Sanghvi's voice crackled in their ears, distorted by the clash of energies around both crafts.

"My shields aren't going to take much more."

"Kutora did say they might not last long," Kowalski replied. "Slave your missile launcher to mine. We'll fire off our remaining birds at the bogeys ahead and keep them distracted while control finds us."

"Done."

Six missiles, three per shuttle, streaked out, headed for the oncoming Mirandan gunships. Another laser burst struck Kowalski's craft, and she swore.

"We're sitting ducks up here." She flicked back to the general frequency. "Control, if you can't get those bastards out of our faces soon, you might as well head home."

Whatever else Kowalski wanted to say died in her mouth, stillborn.

Ahead, rising over the curvature of the planet, they saw bright flash after bright flash, briefly interspersed by a green aurora, *Stingray*'s shields holding strong against the continued assaults. A miniature nova appeared, and then vanished just as quickly, marking the death of a Mirandan ship and Dunmoore cheered.

"This is the first time I've actually seen my ship fight from anywhere other than the bridge," she said, sounding awed by the sight. "Would it be wrong of me to describe this as beautiful?"

"Of course not, sir. *Stingray* is one of the grand old ladies of the star lanes."

Smaller explosions drew their attention away from the magnificent sight, and they had just enough time to see three Mirandan gunships tumble out of formation, hit by the missiles but not badly enough to explode.

The remainder fired their lasers again and once again, the shuttle's shield turned into a bluish-green hollow sphere. Then, with a loud pop of overloaded circuitry, it vanished to the screech of a siren and flashing red warnings on the control screen.

"I'm hit," Sanghvi screamed over the radio. "Shields are down and my left engine's gone. Losing pressure fast."

Dunmoore called up a side view just in time to see the other craft tumble away on a diverging course.

"God, I hope they're all strapped in," she murmured. Then, louder, "Control, this is Mantis Mother. My wingman took a bad hit. He's out of control and losing air."

Kowalski fired her attitudinal thrusters to follow Sanghvi as best she could.

"Roger, Mantis. Look sharp. We're almost there."

The Mirandan's lasers fired one last time, missing them by a wide margin thanks to the sudden course correction, and then a salvo from *Stingray* turned the remaining gunships into their constituent atoms.

"Crap!" Dunmoore pointed at her sensor readout. "A pair of Mirandans craft just uncloaked ten thousand klicks away."

Massive gigawatt lasers lanced out at the frigate, sending the hue of its shields from the preceding green into teal and then blue as they tried to bleed away the excess energy.

"They're going to have a hard time recovering us if they can't open a window in the shields and let us through."

Kowalski pointed toward the distant disk of Miranda's smallest moon, Juno, where an almost continuous light show gave testimony to the other running battle fought by their former hosts.

"Looks like our Shrehari buddy's having a grand old time as well."

"Let's hope he draws off some of the bastards."

"Mantis Flight, this is control. We're going to grab you with our tractor beams as we pass by, then break orbit. You might have guessed that recovering you properly right now isn't going to work."

"Roger," Kowalski replied, echoed by Sanghvi, who added, "I'm fully depressurized, so we're on suit air. That'll put a hard limit on how long we can last before you have to haul us in."

"Understood, Mantis Two. Stand by."

A tiny spot of color, still under constant fire by pursuing Mirandan vessels, rapidly approached and then, without warning, their view of the planet shifted radically as their stomachs tried to go sideways.

Chief Penzara's voice sounded over the radio. "We have you, Mantis Flight. Sit tight."

"Mantis Flight confirms." Kowalski slumped back, feeling utterly drained. "Well, that was fun. Remind me of this mission the next time I have the urge to volunteer."

Dunmoore patted her armored shoulder.

"Even if I did, you'd still take a step forward in a good cause, Kathryn."

"Yeah." Siobhan could picture her grin beneath the blank helmet visor. "Story of my life."

"Mantis Mother," Pushkin's voice sounded strange. "The Shrehari ship is hailing us. It's Brakal. He wants to speak with you."

For a moment, Dunmoore felt like she had stepped through the looking glass and into a surreal universe where the rules had been reversed. Then she remembered the promise she had made to Commander Drang.

"Can you patch it through?"

"Sure. Just give us a moment. We're going to pull you up against the hull, now that we have a moment between engagements. Once that's done, signals will patch you in on a secure connection."

Stingray's crest dissolved, replaced by Brakal's bony, olive-skinned face. His lips drew back to reveal yellow fangs, worn and cracked with age.

"Dunmoore," he rumbled. "An interesting place to meet again, no? We are far from our last field of battle."

As before, the Shrehari's Anglic seemed distorted, but it sounded surprisingly clear after days of listening to the Mirandans' thick accent.

"All places are interesting when it comes to a good fight. You have a new ship?"

His predatory smile widened.

"Indeed, and one with improvements you'd hardly believe us capable of making. It is named *Tol Vehar*, by the way."

"Your *Tai Kan* spy lets you speak like that to the enemy?"

"Ha!" Brakal's fist pounded his chair's much-abused arm. "My *Tai Kan* spy has some curious notions. He's a much better companion than the one foisted on me aboard *Tol Vakash*. This one might actually live to report back."

Then, his eyes narrowed as he examined what little he could see of her surroundings.

"You are not aboard your ship? Yet your ship's second had no difficulties connecting us."

"I am indeed *on* my ship if you wish to be precise."

She allowed herself a vaguely mysterious smile. Each shuttle had been safely tucked beneath one of the short pylons connecting the hyperdrive nacelles to the main hull, where they would not interfere with the guns.

"If not exactly inside. It's a long story, Commander."

"Perhaps this story is one I wish to hear," Brakal replied. "Finding an enemy of my enemy who also seems to consider *me* an enemy is a rare occasion. Since we don't appear to be fated for individual combat right now, I wish to know more about this thing we have in common."

Drang's mangled face, with its deep-set, pleading eyes appeared before her like a ghostly figure, and she nodded.

"Then you shall hear it because this story also involves members of your species."

What Dunmoore took for the Shrehari version of a surprised expression crossed Brakal's seamed face.

"The survey cruiser *Ziq Tar*."

"Just so."

"How did you..."

Dunmoore raised her hand to still his outburst.

"You'll have to let me tell this story my way, Brakal."

"Very well, but don't be all day about it. You and I are still in the midst of a fight with a species whose ships are ancient but whose numbers are vast. Even the best of us can be overcome by quantity."

"Not just any species, Brakal, but humans. My species."

She had to smile at her first glimpse of a Shrehari showing utter puzzlement.

"You dare mock me?" He growled, showing his fangs again. "You would fight your own?"

"Never. A long time ago, before we discovered the secret of traveling faster-than-light, my species' homeworld sent out a number of colony ships designed for travel to distant stars in the course of several generations, its passengers in suspended animation. Many of these ships vanished, never to be found once we began to travel interstellar distances in a matter of weeks or months, instead of decades."

"Yes." He rubbed his chin, eyes narrowed. "We also had such in the distant past, and like you, we haven't found all of them. Go on."

"One of these became entangled by a space-time phenomenon we call a wormhole and transported here, far from its intended destination, but well back in time, centuries before it even left our planet of origin. I know it sounds like madness, but all the evidence points to this being the evident truth. They established a civilization on this planet and eventually expanded to the moons and then the fifth planet. They left Earth before the time of faster-than-light travel, and so didn't have the theoretical foundations upon which to develop their own capacity. They are a purely sublight civilization."

"This would explain much about their primitive technology."

"It does. Along the way, they suffered repeated attacks by other species who were capable of crossing interstellar space, and they developed a deep-seated hatred of anyone not of their society. These species are probably ones your empire and my Commonwealth have never encountered."

"This is why they attacked you? Even though you're of the same race, you're not of their world?"

"It's a bit more complicated than that. At first, they greeted us as friends, but as it turned out, only to steal our technology so they could expand beyond this system and annex this part of the galaxy."

"And so they attacked you. Yes, that does make sense, strangely enough. Predatory, but scavengers as well."

"That's one way of putting it. They tried to take *Ziq Tar* and almost succeeded."

Again that particular Shrehari expression of surprise.

"Almost succeeded? Explain."

"These people, they call themselves Mirandans, managed to trap your survey vessel and board it, taking off some prisoners before the crew could self-destruct. They attempted the same thing with my ship. Unfortunately for them, they overplayed their hand and my ship's second was ready."

"Are you saying they hold Shrehari prisoners?" A dangerous growl emerged from Brakal's throat.

"They do. And they've practiced research experiments on their living bodies."

The growl turned into a string of shouted curses, barely understood by Dunmoore, who physically recoiled at Brakal's fury, even though hundreds of thousands of kilometers and the better part of the Mirandan fleet separated them.

"I saw Commander Drang, who led *Ziq Tar*. He asked me to arrange for his death and that of those who survived the experiments. I have a recording of my conversation with him, which I can't access just now, but if you like, I can transmit it later. Sadly, I was not able to kill him, something I regret."

"Then *I* will," the Shrehari snarled. "Where do these accursed slugs hold my people?"

Dunmoore held up a hand again.

"Mister Pushkin, I assume you're listening in on this transmission. Have the sensor watch pull up the logs from two mornings after our arrival on the surface of Miranda.

There will be a period where I'm moving from the Protector's Palace, where we spent our nights, to another well-guarded building outside Sanctum. Get a description of that building's location and transmit, with visuals, to *Tol Vehar*."

"Sir." The first officer's voice conveyed not just a little outrage. "You're going to give the enemy pointers on where best to attack other humans?"

"These humans need striking, Number One. We will discuss the matter when this is over. In the meantime, I expect you to comply."

He heard the barely suppressed anger in her tone and his reply sounded, if not contrite then less adversarial.

"As you wish, Captain."

"What I would suggest, Commander Brakal, is to use a kinetic ground penetrating strike as your first salvo. Expect a lot of air defense weaponry, meaning you may want to get in as close as you can. Once the penetrator has punched through the upper levels of the compound, a conventional warhead should ensure the Shrehari prisoners die quickly and painlessly."

The few seconds of silence she had expected before a reply dragged out into minutes, but finally, the image of a half-buried compound surrounded by green parkland appeared on the screen.

"This would be the place, Captain," Pushkin said. "Do you concur?"

"I do. Transmit to Brakal."

A few moments later, the Shrehari commander spoke again.

"We have the target indication, Dunmoore, and we will end our brothers' suffering."

"Don't worry about collateral damage on my account."

Brakal barked out a laugh.

"I wasn't about to."

Dunmoore had to smile at this unexpected evidence that their foes knew the meaning of sarcasm.

"What are your intentions?" Brakal asked.

"Go home. Our mission here failed, for more reasons than I care to discuss. If you'd like to do me a big favor in return for pointing you at where Drang and his crew are being held, then go home yourself when you're done. I'm too tired to fight you after fighting those who should have been my kin."

"In that case, Dunmoore, run like the winter wind howling over Shredar Plain during the Month of Death. I will do what I must here, and then turn my attention back onto your trail. We are still foes, even if we fight a common enemy this day."

"I wouldn't have it any other way. Just make sure you don't miss. Seeing Commander Drang's face in my nightmares for the rest of my life and hear him pleading for me to help them die isn't something I'd wish on my worst enemy."

"Nor I. Good luck, Dunmoore."

"Same to you, Brakal. I hope your *Tai Kan* spy won't cause problems."

The Shrehari held up a hand and then turned to face left. When he looked at her again, that fang-baring smile had returned.

"Lieutenant Regar, of the *Tai Kan* sends his regards and hopes you have a happy voyage home. He says finding a human colony beyond the black will impress our superiors enough that they'll ignore any indiscretions I may have committed. If you have nothing else to impart, I will turn my attention on these contemptible, dishonorable creatures. Until we meet again."

Her screen faded to black, Brakal's harsh, angular features replaced by *Stingray*'s crest.

Dunmoore let out a sigh long enough that Kowalski stared at her with alarm, wondering if her captain's body had sprung a leak.

"I'm not sure that I should have done what I just did, Kathryn," she finally said, "but I didn't see any alternative."

"And I'm sure you had some very profound reasons if I may be so bold."

"That, I did. When we finally get back aboard, I'll brief everyone on what happened during our stay on Miranda."

"Somehow, I think I can guess part of it." The younger woman, who had also removed her helmet, smiled shyly. "Something bothered me about this culture from the get-go."

"I'm not surprised." Then, Dunmoore shook her head and began laughing, at first almost silently, then with increasing gusto.

"Captain?"

"I've just realized that I'm the first starship commander in history to be stuck on the outside of her ship in the middle of a battle fought by her first officer."

"Perhaps we can make sure that little bit doesn't end up in the log, sir."

"Oh, no, Kathryn. I want our log to be as accurate as possible, and if that means future generations will read of Siobhan Dunmoore sitting in a shuttle that's attached to her ship's nacelle pylon while mortal combat rages all around, then so be it."

She sobered with surprising suddenness.

"If our log of this mission ever gets declassified, that is. I may not have a *Tai Kan* officer stuck to my ass, but I'm sure our Admiralty will be just as unimpressed as Brakal's once we send in our report."

— Thirty-Two —

Drang, former commander of the Shrehari Deep Space Fleet survey cruiser *Ziq Tar* steeled himself for another torture session while the dishonorable humans infesting this world strapped him down on a steel table, all the while jabbering in a language he could not understand.

Then, a lugubrious siren began to wail, and the jabbering turned into panicked sounds. Instruments dropped into metallic trays while masks were torn off and discarded. The humans ran from the room, leaving Drang to lie helpless while he prayed to the gods for a swift death.

This deep beneath Custodian headquarters, Drang could not hear the penetrator, essentially an anti-ship missile without a warhead, cutting through Miranda's atmosphere at hypersonic speed, too fast for what air defenses the humans could muster while a space battle still raged among the high orbitals.

All he knew of events came down to one thing: his captors had shown fear for the first time, and a spark of hope began to burn deep within his soul. Had Dunmoore finally come to see the truth and decided to act? Or did an act of the gods drive these new events?

The penetrator struck the headquarters building with such force that it reached two stories beneath the surface before its energy dissipated. The resulting shock wave destroyed most of the surface structures around the point of impact, killing all within, and sending up a cloud of dust, stone, and debris that reached high into the clear blue sky.

Drang felt its impact — how could he not — and a fierce smile transformed his dark, bony features. Around him, the laboratory began to disintegrate. Clumps of concrete fell from above while cabinets, counters, and medical equipment shook hard enough to break apart.

A chunk of ceiling struck a glancing blow on his skull, the pain mixing with a kind of exultation. Death had come to take them.

He had but a few seconds to rejoice.

An anti-ship missile, its warhead fully operational, slammed into the hole created by the penetrator and obliterated Custodian headquarters, killing Drang, the remaining Shrehari and the sole Skraeling captive still held in the basement cells.

The force of the detonation flattened all of the parkland surrounding this once imposing building. Many more Mirandans died in the resulting inferno, while others would die over the coming days and weeks from radiation burns and the sickness that would destroy their bodies.

Of course, Mira Dalian's candidacy for the office of Protector of the Dominion had been terminated by Brakal's strike, her body charred beyond recognition.

*

A brilliant flash of light flooded Cyrus Hames' office, forcing him to screw his eyes shut, even though he sat with his back to the windows.

The chatter of Mirandan's Defenders on the frequency he had been monitoring suddenly died as if the appearance of a new sun over Sanctum had frozen their very ability to form words.

When the light died down, he turned to face the shocking reality playing out over the capital of the Dominion he had sworn to protect.

There, on the other side of Sanctum, a mushroom cloud rose over what had been, moments before, the heart of Miranda's security apparatus. It had been the home of those who mercilessly persecuted xenos and human dissenters, and who propped up a centuries old dictatorship built on the simple proposition that nothing would threaten the survival of *Tempest*'s children ever again.

At that moment, Hames knew his Protectorship had failed, that the worst disaster in four hundred years had befallen Miranda and for what? A shortcut to interstellar empire? The gilding of Mira Dalian's vanity?

Senior Group Leader Nan burst into the office, dragging the sharp scent of panic with him. Hames held up a hand to forestall his aide's words.

"Tell Chief Defender Martell that it's over. He is to cease battle and allow both the Earthers and the Shrehari to withdraw. Then, get me Speaker Marant. We need to discuss a way ahead now that the entire Custodian command structure has been decapitated."

"As you command."

Nan clicked his heels together and bowed his head, having won the struggle to contain his fear.

"And Nan, pass the order to all Custodian and Defender commanders. They are to free any Skraeling held in custody and return it to where they found it. After today, the Dominion of Miranda needs to take a good, hard look at its soul because the universe has evolved without us and that," he waved toward the dissipating nuclear mushroom, "is the sign we must change as well, or perish. Perhaps paying more than lip service to our forebear's ideals would be a good start."

"Sir?" His aide seemed puzzled.

"Later, Nan. For now, contemplate the fact that two starships, from species at war with each other, have apparently been able to cooperate, be it ever so briefly, against a common enemy. Once you review the logs of today's battle, you will find two facts that should give you pause for thought. For one thing, they did not fight each other. They only fought us. And for another, the only way the Shrehari would know to strike at Custodian headquarters, and nothing else, is if Dunmoore told them about the prisoners Mira Dalian held there. Now go."

*

The shuttle's rear ramp dropped to reveal Gregor Pushkin's relieved face.

"Captain, it's good to see you back on board, safe and sound."

"Agreed." She nodded at Sanghvi's heavily damaged craft, retrieved first, once *Stingray* had sailed beyond Mirandan weapons rage. "Is everyone alright?"

"A few additional bruises and one or two broken bones. The injured are already under Doc Luttrell's tender care."

They stepped aside to let a pair of medics climb aboard.

"We're headed for the hyperlimit at best speed," he continued. "No damage to the hull but the shield generators took a severe beating. The aft starboard generator is completely gone, as is the primary sensor net, and our ammunition stocks are low. If we have to fight Brakal, it might get hairy."

She shook her head, and a weary smile tugged at the corners of her mouth.

"I don't think he'll come after us. If I recall their culture properly, giving him the coordinates he needed to end his fellow Shrehari's misery laid a debt of honor on him and from what I got, his *Tai Kan* political officer won't object if he fails to prosecute his pursuit of *Stingray* with the vigor his Admiralty would expect."

"It's a strange galaxy when we make common cause, however temporary, with our enemy so that we can fight others of our species."

"They might be humans, Gregor, but once I've told you what transpired on Miranda, you'll not be so quick to acknowledge any kinship. Suffice to say that I won't shed a tear for their losses."

"That's just as well," he replied, grim-faced. "We detected a small nuclear explosion near their capital, which means Brakal took your advice. Our Admiralty might not be so quick to overlook this temporary alliance once they find out we facilitated the one thing humanity, and indeed the Shrehari, have vowed never to do again."

"One small explosion, Gregor. Not nuclear annihilation on the scale of the Second Migration War. Besides, if you'd seen what I saw..."

"Yes," he asked, falling into step beside her, headed for Dunmoore's quarters, "what have you seen?"

She stopped and turned to face him.

"I'd like to tell the tale only once, and to all officers and chiefs, so they understand when I say to them that the records of this mission will likely be tossed into the nearest black hole, and we'll be ordered to forget everything we lived through in the last few weeks. And I'll do that once we're FTL."

"As you wish, Captain."

"When I've got this armor off, I'll visit the wounded in sickbay. Warn Viv, will you?"

"I hope you intend to take a shower and put on a fresh uniform beforehand."

"That sounded suspiciously like an order."

"Until I'm satisfied that you're ready, Captain, I will retain command of *Stingray*."

"You will, will you?" A crooked smile lit up her face, and she touched his arm. "Thank you for ignoring my orders. If not for my own sake, then for the sake of Foste and Vincenzo. And for the sake of Drang and his people. Without my being able to tell Brakal where to strike, they would still be suffering."

"As long as you won't press charges against me for disobedience, you're welcome."

"Charges?" A tired laugh escaped her bruised lips. "I intend to make sure the Admiralty understands that you've more than proved yourself ready for your own command, now that I've spent a battle as a mere spectator to my own ship's actions."

"I had a good teacher."

They stopped in front of her cabin's door.

"Take half an hour to freshen up. It'll give Doc Luttrell time to settle everyone in. I'll make sure Wim and Kalivan are cared for with all due respect and readied for burial in space when we're safely away from this place."

"What would I do without you, Gregor?"

"Break in a new first officer?" He grinned at her. "Which you'll have to do if you keep trying to get me my own command."

*

"And that, ladies and gents, is the sum total of what transpired since I left *Stingray* to make friends with the Mirandans."

Dunmoore's eyes roamed over the assembled officers and chiefs standing in the middle of the hangar deck, just as they had done when Pushkin informed them he intended to disobey her orders.

Most seemed stunned by her revelations, some seemed angry as well, but none looked like they intended to raise formal objections when it came to her pointing Brakal at Custodian HQ and the captive Shrehari spacers.

"Not only do I not expect the Admiralty to plan any follow-on expeditions, but I also expect them to tell us this mission never happened."

"So Colonel Kalivan and Spacer Wim didn't die, did they?" A bitter Foste asked, still bearing visible scars from the injuries she had incurred at Mirandan hands.

The bosun had recounted her treatment at the hands of the Mirandans in the moments before Guthren's landing party attacked and how Kalivan had died fighting off three Custodian troopers at once. Her tone and words had born witness to a newfound respect for the man whose body now lay in a stasis pod, awaiting burial and Dunmoore had felt deeply touched.

"I'm sure the Admiralty will spin a cover story," she replied. "At least their deaths have been avenged."

"By the Shrehari." She spat out the words, but Siobhan sensed no great emotion behind them as if the bosun had expended all her energy recounting her part of the tale.

"It could have been by Satan himself, for all I care. I'm sure many of you will have questions about what happened, and I'll be happy to answer them as best I can. My report on the mission will be available to all who care to read it, and it will cover everything in excruciating detail. You will pass on to your people what Chief Foste and I have told you at the first opportunity. Otherwise, we'll spend the voyage home quenching rumors."

"Seems strange, doesn't it," Guthren said, "that folks who left Earth with such noble ideals would have their descendants turn into *that*. But I guess fear will make humans do just about anything."

"Fear, greed, ambition. As a species, we've pretty much seen all of those motivate the basest actions. But in this case, your summary will do nicely, Chief. Was there anything else?"

"Funeral ceremony, sir?" Pushkin reminded her.

"Thank you, Number One. Colonel Kalivan and Spacer Wim will be buried in space when we drop out of FTL tomorrow, after a memorial service held right here at seven bells in the morning watch. I expect off-duty personnel to attend. That is all."

*

Dunmoore and two-thirds of the ship's crew, crammed shoulder to shoulder in the hangar deck, watched on the big screen as the two missiles, stripped of warheads and transformed into caskets, slowly slid into their launch tubes.

The honor guard raised and then folded the Commonwealth flags that had been draped on them during the memorial service.

Though not her first burial in space, it had been one of the most difficult, for in the absence of a chaplain, the captain led the service.

One of the gunners raised a bugle to his lips, and the mournful sounds of the Last Post echoed through the ship. When it fell silent, eight bosun's mates and Foste herself raised their silver calls to their lips and blew a sad farewell.

"Ship's company, atten-SHUN." Guthren's voice drowned out the trill of the whistles.

"We now commit the mortal remains of our brothers Andrew Wim and Wesley Kalivan to the depths of the universe," Dunmoore said. "Guns, you may fire tubes one and two."

Seconds after the last word left her mouth, Lieutenant Syten ejected the missiles into space, their drives lighting the moment they cleared *Stingray*.

Tears welled up in her eyes, and she thanked the rules of protocol that had her face the screen, her back to the ship's company.

The bugler played the Reveille, and when the last note faded away, the ceremony had run its course.

"Ship's company, dis-MISSED."

Pushkin gently touched her arm.

"Would you like a while to reflect, sir? We're ready to go FTL for the next leg."

"An order again, rather than a suggestion, Gregor?"

"I'd rather your reputation as a hard-ass doesn't suffer if the crew sees you show human emotion." His disarming smile took the sting out of his words.

"Can the officer of the watch do everything without your supervision?"

"Devall can do anything I can by now. Why?"

"I have the dregs of a brandy bottle in my quarters. I think it would be appropriate for you and me to toast the departed with the last few drops."

*

After the chiefs had watched the off-duty crew exit the hangar deck, Guthren tapped Foste on the shoulder.

"I've got a few drams of Glen Arcturus tucked inside an old duffel bag. Maybe it's time you and I checked the taste."

Their eyes locked and the bosun understood she could not refuse the invitation. This was not just the Chief of the Ship speaking; it was also the friend, who felt a duty to make sure she understood he would be there for her if she needed to talk.

Four people on the ship had private cabins: the captain, the first officer, the chief engineer, and, of course, the coxswain. Guthren's was the smallest of the four, but no less a private sanctuary for all that.

Once the door shut behind them, Guthren unfastened his dress uniform tunic and shrugged it off.

"Feel free to get comfortable, Brun. Glen Arcturus isn't a formal drink."

She opened her collar and dropped into the cabin's only chair.

"Uncle Kurt figuring it's time for the after-action talk, is it?"

He pulled a half-empty bottle and two glasses from a cabinet beneath his bunk.

"You know how it goes," he replied, straightening up. "Shit like you went through, it has to come out at some point, and that can't happen while you're running your department. Doesn't mean it has to be here and now, but I figured I'd remind you over a drink. One day you'll be doing the Aunt Brun thing too."

He poured a measure into each glass and handed her one.

"You spoke with Vince yet?"

"Yeah. He'll be okay. I saw him and Demmi having a long natter in the mess last night."

Guthren raised his glass. "To absent friends?"

"Sure." She nodded. "To absent friends."

They enjoyed the smoky taste in companionable silence for over a minute.

"You know," she said, eyes still staring into the amber liquid. "For all that the colonel could give Lieutenant Devall a run for his money when it comes to being an Earth aristo, he was a damn good officer. The thing I didn't tell the rest of you was that I owe him my life. Damn bastards were getting set to cut me open when he went berserk. If he hadn't, I'd be dead and maybe he'd still be alive. I saw his eyes when he attacked. He damn well knew he wasn't going to live long enough for the rescue to make it down to the lab, but he did it anyway. For me. Distracted them long enough so I'm here, and he's out there, in a cold missile casing, spending eternity between the stars."

Foste waved at the bulkhead while tears began to run down her cheeks. A barely repressed sob racked her lean body, then another.

"Fucking officers," she said, one hand wiping her face with savage gestures. "Never do like they're supposed to."

Guthren raised his glass again.

"Absent friends. Even if they are fucking officers who never do like they're supposed to."

"You're a right bastard, Kurt Guthren, and that's why you're the cox'n. To Colonel Wes Kalivan. One of the good guys."

She swallowed the rest of her Glen Arcturus in one shot, reveling in the warmth left by its passage.

"Make sure you tell the captain, okay?" Guthren held out the bottle for a refill. "She deserves to know."

— Thirty-Three —

"Come."

Dunmoore looked up as the door to her ready room opened and sighed softly, both glad and annoyed at Pushkin's interruption. She saved the draft report and sat back.

The last few weeks had been difficult for all aboard, not just because of the boredom or their mission's failure, or even the senseless loss of life, but because they instinctively knew their ship had started to show evidence her time had come.

The long voyage, the ion storm, and the battle of Miranda had taken a toll significant enough to make another refit unlikely.

Lieutenant Commander Kutora and his engineers tried their best, but some repairs had proved to be beyond them, and Dunmoore preferred not to take any further risks after two technicians ended up in sickbay with severe burns. They would make it home, but *Stingray* had fought her last battle.

"Mister Tours confirms that we've crossed the black as per planned course and we'll be ready to tackle the last few jumps in a few hours without any further ado."

The first officer grabbed two mugs from the sideboard and filled them, handing Siobhan her usual black, after which he turned his into the usual creamed, sugary sludge that made her grimace every time.

"And Brakal?"

He took a chair across from his captain, amused that she asked about her opposite number by name rather than asking about the Shrehari.

"Not a trace. Perhaps miracles happen and he's been as good as his word in terms of heading straight back to his own sphere, in deference to your leaving him a free hand in dealing with the Mirandans."

"Is that a strong hint of disapproval in your voice, Gregor?"

"No." He shook his head. "I agreed with you at the time, although not all of the crew was of my opinion, and I still share the sentiments that drove you to act as you did. I'm more concerned about the Admiralty's reaction. Have you decided how to tackle that particular little issue?"

She chuckled, though without much humor.

"Oh, I have, Gregor. Indeed I have. I will be accurate and honest down to the most excruciating detail. Then, I'll have Kowalski slap the highest designation allowed by regulations on the report and encode it with the strongest cipher we carry before she purges our logs, navigation records and every other data bank of anything related to Miranda and the descendants of the *Tempest* colonists. The crew will be formally warned that any mention of the mission will have the blabbermouth in question spend quality time in a penal battalion for the rest of his or her natural life."

Pushkin's eyes narrowed as he parsed her words before deciding that her proposed course of action would work.

"Meaning," he said, "that once the mighty folks with stars on their shoulders read your report, they'll classify it top secret, special access. Then, they'll file it in a database unconnected to any network and leave it there under ten layers of quantum encryption until you and I have joined the 'dearly departed' list of Academy alumni."

"I'm hoping it'll be longer than that even. Honestly, I'm also hoping Nagira and most of his own circle will be as revolted by the Mirandan social experiment and what they've become as we were. Perhaps it'll motivate them to ensure that someone with fewer scruples and no morals doesn't take my report as a 'how to' in our war against the Shrehari, rather than a 'never in any universe,' as it should be."

She shook her head in disgust, eyes staring at the star map on the far bulkhead.

"You asked me if I disapproved of your leaving Brakal to take his full revenge on the Mirandans," Pushkin began, wondering where her thoughts had gone. "After what they did to us, or at least tried to do to us, and what they did to their Shrehari captives, let alone the native sentients the original colonists found, I cannot in good conscience see them as being of the same species as we are. We might share a planet of origin, DNA and even some linguistic and cultural elements, but the Mirandans are as different from our branch of humanity as we are from the Shrehari."

"Not everyone would agree, Gregor." She turned a crooked smile on him. "Blood being thicker than water and all that; or, my people right or wrong. And history seems to be full of humans who considered other humans who differed in religion, skin color, or nation of origin to be subhuman, with rather horrifying end results."

Pushkin shrugged.

"We, and I mean Commonwealth humans, aren't the genocidal ones here, Captain. The Mirandans seem to have taken that mantle with unseemly glee."

"Part of me, the part that still clings to the blood is thicker than water philosophy, can't entirely blame them," she replied. "They spent a long time fighting back non-humans intent on taking everything from them to the point where it twisted their whole view to something that ended up being the total opposite of their earlier ideals."

"Perhaps their earlier ideals were just the flip side of what they are now. There's plenty of historical evidence for that too, the drive for a perfect society ending up in tyranny of the worst sort."

"True. What was it Wes Kalivan called the version that nearly ended us before we could expand into space a few centuries ago?" Dunmoore felt a stab of pain in her gut at his memory. He had been so enthusiastic at finding the Mirandans, only to see his spark snuffed out in a useless death.

"Communal righteousness?"

"Something like that, but not those exact words. A social thing of some sort. I'm sure Guthren would remember. He got a good chuckle out of the notion. Not a proponent of mindless political naivety, our coxswain."

"The galaxy needs more Guthrens, I think." This time, Pushkin grinned. "We might have found a way to end this war by now with a few of him knocking heads in the government precinct."

"We almost had the chance to do so," she reminded him, "if Corwin had been able to carry out his plan."

The first officer shivered theatrically.

"Thank God we made it out of that one intact."

"And right into the Mirandan expedition." Dunmoore snorted. "It's almost enough to make me think the *Stingray* is still an unlucky ship."

"Bite your tongue, Captain. We made it out of this one intact, or nearly so, as well." He paused for a few heartbeats. "We might even have made a friend, or at least a foe with a newfound respect for us. Who knows what dividends that could bring?"

"Provided Brakal can play the whole mess out to his political advantage."

"Oh, I have a feeling he might," Pushkin replied. "That *Tai Kan* man of his doesn't seem to be a big fan of the current regime."

"From your lips, Gregor." She glanced back at her pad and the draft report it held.

"You know it's funny," she said after a few moments of silence. "For all that Wes Kalivan came across as a prickly character at the outset, I feel deep sorrow that he didn't live to enjoy his vindication, even if it will end up being kept top secret. He was a good man. A good officer." And a good friend, she thought, still feeling a profound sense of loss after all these weeks. She had included Foste's detailed description of his final moments in her report, in the hopes that the Admiralty might grant him a small measure of immortality with a posthumous award for valor.

"You miss him, don't you?"

The question startled her, and she looked up into Pushkin's dark eyes, seeing unaccustomed gentleness where she expected his usual stoic gaze.

She nodded. "I do. Wes was an excellent companion down on Miranda, and during the trip there, no matter what you may have thought. I considered him a true friend."

"I've had time to reflect on that, sir," he replied in a rueful tone. "And I'm sorry that I didn't see how much good it did you to have a friend aboard, someone who wasn't a member of the ship's company. Though my tenure as acting captain proved to be mercifully short, I've gained a new appreciation of the old adage that it's lonely at the top."

"You're forgiven, Gregor." She reached out to touch his arm. "Just promise me you'll savor the few friendships a captain can enjoy once you have your own ship."

"Promised." He nodded at the tablet. "Done for the day?"

"I might as well be. And you? Slacking off?"

"I've been giving Devall a taste of my duties, to help prepare him for his next assignment."

"Ah, the joys of delegating." She leaned back and stretched her arms behind her head. "Have you delegated enough to young Trevane that the ship can run without us for a few hours?"

"I have indeed."

"Then pull out the chess board. Let's see how mentally fresh you are with a reduced workload."

*

"Are you sure you want me to read your report?" Regar of the *Tai Kan* asked, surprised at Brakal's offer.

"Perhaps it will inspire yours." The commander shrugged. "It's only for that fat leech Hralk and the gods know what he'll do with it. Certainly nothing to advance my career, what little is left."

"And so you wonder whether my more direct connections might ensure some measure of truth is transmitted to the home world." Regar nodded. "Perhaps."

The spy considered Brakal for a few silent moments, meeting his eyes without guile.

"Still, you have no idea what might occur once the truth is in Shredar, with no filters from admirals anxious to cover up the fact they have little control over your actions."

"You have suggestions, spy?"

"A few." Regar's ironic smile made an appearance. "The Admiralty needs to know of these new humans, yes. It needs to know about *Ziq Tar*'s end, yes. It does not need to know about Dunmoore. Tell them you had a wild hair up your ass and used Hralk's criminally vague orders to indulge it, saving the honor of Commander Drang's crew at the same time. No one need ever know you spoke with the flame-haired she-wolf and not only accepted her advice but declined to pursue her ship."

"You're a strange *Tai Kan* spy indeed, Regar."

"I'm a *Tai Kan* spy tired of seeing the worst our empire has to offer. Perhaps it is time to do things differently."

"Meaning?"

"Meaning there is more you can do for the empire in command of *Tol Vehar* than in *Tai Kan* custody, accused of treason."

"One ship against the might of the Ruling Council, the Admiralty and all that pollutes the Imperial Deep Space Fleet?" Brakal roared with laughter. "You entertain me, Regar."

"Sometimes it only takes one pebble to start a landslide," the spy replied with a sibylline smile. Regar raised his mug of ale. "Your health, Commander. May we see an honorable end to this war before the empire faces a new age of darkness."

*

"Not even a hello and well done," Kowalski grimaced when she read the orders from headquarters during the night watch a week later. "All we get is a patrol route and space-time coordinates to meet *Petrel* for a replenishment underway. That's it. Do they not understand we need time in dry-dock?"

"They do, but apparently, they don't care." Pushkin shook his head as he glanced at the screen over the signals officer's shoulder. "Seems like we won't even be allowed to step ashore. I think the Admiralty hasn't quite decided what to do with us after reading the captain's report. At least they've assigned us to internal security, where we're unlikely to stumble across the Shrehari. However, I'll take the replenishment, seeing as how it comes with everything we desperately need, spare parts included. Pipe it to the captain's quarters, but don't wake her. We can handle this by ourselves. Have Mister Sanghvi plot the course and get us on the first tack to our patrol area. Jump when ready."

"Aye, aye, sir."

He clapped her on the shoulder. "I'll be doing my rounds before turning in."

"Have a good night, Commander."

"Thanks." As he turned to leave the bridge, he suddenly stopped as if he'd had a thought.

"When's the last time you were ship handler for a replenishment underway?"

"Nice try, sir." She snorted with amusement. "I think it's Sanghvi's turn. Shall I tell him to start boning up once he's plotted our course?"

"Be my guest, Kathryn. Try not to enjoy yourself too much when you do so."

"No promises, sir."

The wicked smile that lit up her face somehow gave her more than a passing resemblance to Siobhan Dunmoore.

— Thirty-Four —

The intercom chimed, shattering a silence punctuated only by the subliminal humming of the sublight drives.

"Captain, this is signals. We have an incoming for your eyes only from battle group HQ."

Dunmoore looked up irritably from the chessboard.

"Is it wrong of me to suspect another imagined emergency from some put-upon shipping corporation whose flagship liner is overdue? It seems like all we've been doing since our return is reassuring civilian shippers. What I'd give for a little Shrehari action right now."

"Not wrong, Captain," the first officer replied, eyes still on the game, "just not particularly healthy. Paranoia, once it sets in, can eat at your soul until it becomes your go-to reaction."

She made a face at him.

"The voice of reason again." Then, to the intercom, "Pipe it to my pad."

Dunmoore reached over to grab the tablet in question, and when she read the message, her face turned to stone. Once done, she stared at the star map in silence for almost a minute before speaking again.

"I guess the Admiralty has finally digested my mission report and is ready for us to come home. Read this."

She handed it to Pushkin and watched his expression as the words sank in.

"We're done then."

He looked up, bitterness seeping through the usually stolid facade.

"Aye. We knew it was coming, Gregor. We've spent the last few weeks waiting for the order, whether we'll admit it or not. She's old. Kutora is reduced to manufacturing parts that aren't in stock anymore, and between the Mirandans and the ion storm, we're overdue for a refit that'll never happen. I'm surprised they left us in commission for this long. I suppose the mission to Miranda was the only thing that extended her life, for what *that* was worth."

Her gut clenched with grief at the sudden memory of Wes Kalivan. The pain of loss had never quite gone away and could still catch her unawares at odd moments. She fiercely hoped that Brakal had given them a thoroughly bloody nose for the atrocities they had visited on the Shrehari survey crew, even though the Mirandans were human — just not the kind she would acknowledge as her kin.

"Read the next message."

Pushkin thumbed the screen. His double take seemed almost comical.

"I can't believe it," he whispered. "Lieutenant Commander Gregor Pushkin is promoted to the rank of commander and appointed captain of the Commonwealth Starship *Jan Sobieski*, frigate."

"Aye, Gregor," Dunmoore almost purred, "you get the first of the new Voivode class frigates. Keep reading."

"Commander Dunmoore is promoted to post captain; assignment orders to follow." He looked at her with suspicion in his eyes. "Congratulations on the step up, sir, but why isn't your next billet on here?"

"Perhaps because they haven't yet found an admiral who would take me. It'll likely be a staff job with a fleet or at headquarters."

She called up the message on her desk console while Pushkin kept reading.

"Looks like most of the crew is either going with you to *Jan Sobieski* or headed to the next of the Reconquista class cruisers preparing for space trials, *Cimmeria*, except our engineers. Kutora and his folks are posted to one of the Reconquista cruisers currently under construction."

"Fairly standard, though I'm surprised at so few shore postings," Pushkin nodded. "I get Devall as first officer and Foste as cox'n, both promoted, of course. In fact, there are many promotions: Kowalski goes as second officer to *Cimmeria* with her lieutenant commander's stripes and Penzara as bosun. I get Syten as second and Sanghvi as sailing master. Tours is off to the Academy to teach astrogation while Luttrell is also getting another stripe to be chief surgeon aboard *Cimmeria*. Guthren gets his chief first class starbursts and goes back to special operations, which should thrill him to no end."

He chuckled gleefully.

"Now this is the kind of message from battle group I can enjoy. It's almost as if I'd chosen my share of *Stingrays* personally, although I find it curious that the other half is headed for *Cimmeria*, but not you, considering you've been promoted to the right rank for command of a cruiser."

"The mysteries of the Admiralty." She shrugged as if it didn't matter to her, but she knew that deep within, she had been hoping for another command and would have been overjoyed at taking the new cruiser since it meant keeping so many of her current crew.

"When are the promotions effective?"

"Read," she commanded with a sly smile.

"*Boze moi*," Pushkin looked up again, this time smiling broadly, "there's a bunch of people on this ship who aren't wearing their proper rank insignia, us included."

"Indeed, Commander Pushkin." She reached over to touch her console. "Bridge, this is the captain, pass the word for the sailing master. He's to set a course for Starbase 39. We're going home."

For the last time, she thought. Now, Dunmoore had to break the news to the crew.

*

The door to her ready room slid open.

"We're on final approach, Captain."

"Thank you, Commander Pushkin." Dunmoore adjusted her dress uniform tunic, with the fours stripes of a post captain on the sleeves, and glanced at her reflection in the view screen. Today was the first time she had worn her medals since taking command, and it seemed fitting that she would wear them on what would be the last day of her command. Once *Stingray* docked, she would not sail again as a rated ship of war. Siobhan grasped her sheathed naval sword and walked out onto the bridge.

The crew also wore full dress uniforms, with medals, and the officers and chiefs looked distinctly uncomfortable seated at their stations. A sword was hard to place when not on parade. It seemed anachronistic in an era of FTL travel, but tradition demanded such formality on the day a starship came into port for the last time.

Dunmoore went to stand by the helm, eyes fixed on the rapidly growing spindle shape of the station on the main screen.

"Mister Pushkin, please deploy our commissioning pennant."

The first officer, also standing, touched his console and a long, narrow streamer unfurled from the commo array on the top side of the frigate, its fabric stiffened by the nanoparticles woven into the white and blue material.

"Commissioning pennant is deployed."

"Unfurl our battle flag," she ordered with a catch in her voice, knowing that each step in the formal process took them closer to *Stingray*'s demise, "and make sure the running lights show off all of our kill marks."

"Aye, aye, Captain."

She turned to Kowalski and nodded.

"Bridge to engineering," she said once the ship-wide public announcement system came online so that all could hear.

"Kutora here, Captain." The usually dour chief engineer sounded as solemn as she had ever heard him.

"Vent the antimatter fuel."

*

"Admiral on deck."

"At ease." Rear Admiral Ryn, flag officer commanding, 39th Battle Group, returned the salute with measured precision as she entered the operations center at the heart of Starbase 39, her headquarters.

"*Stingray* is on final approach, sir."

"Thank you, Commander." She let her gaze roam over the assembled staff for a few moments, then said, "Folks, we're about to witness an event we've seen too little of in the last six years: a starship coming home to be decommissioned with all due ceremony. I want you to observe, reflect, and ultimately honor the men and women aboard that frigate for what they've accomplished, not least bringing the old girl back under her own power. Captain Dunmoore and her crew have provided sterling service to the Commonwealth, and I intend to see that service honored."

Ryn's eyes met those of the assembled officers and petty officers one by one. When she saw that they understood the importance she placed on the events about to unfold, she nodded with satisfaction.

"Can we have a visual, please?"

Stingray's image filled the large main screen dominating the ops center, just as her commissioning pennant unfurled.

"That's definitely not something you see every day," Commander Spaak, the head of battle group operations said in a quiet tone.

"No, it's not," Ryn agreed. The sight of *Stingray*'s battle flag appearing stilled any further comment she might have made.

Suddenly, a huge rooster tail of light, brighter than a thousand suns, materialized behind the oncoming frigate.

"She's venting her antimatter fuel," one of the petty officers remarked, awed by the spectacle.

"Aye, and when she's done, *Stingray* will never again sail FTL under her own power again. She'll cease to be a rated warship." Ryn's voice was soft, her tone even, but the others could hear the unmistakable sadness in her words.

"I trust you'll be assigning docking port number one."

"Of course, Admiral."

*

"Antimatter fuel has been vented," the chief engineer announced a few minutes later. "We are no longer capable of FTL travel."

"Thank you, Mister Kutora. Secure hyperdrives and start the shutdown procedures."

Dunmoore paused to repress the deep sorrow that threatened to overwhelm her now that *Stingray* had begun the process of sailing into history.

"All hands, this is the captain. The Commonwealth frigate *Stingray* has secured and shut down hyperdrives in preparation for our final docking with Starbase 39. I would like to take this occasion to tell you how proud I am to have served with all of you. I couldn't have asked for a finer crew. You're a credit to the Navy, the Commonwealth, and humanity."

She paused again to let her words sink in.

"You may be interested to know I've received word that Admiral Hoko Nagira, deputy chief of naval operations and *Stingray*'s first captain, will preside over the decommissioning ceremonies. This is as high an honor as we could have wished for and I know we will march off this ship with pride, precision and in such good order as to bring tears to the spectators' eyes." And mine, she thought. "All hands, prepare for docking. Captain, out."

When she looked around the bridge, she noticed that everyone's eyes had somehow become brighter and shinier with unexpected moisture.

"Mister Pushkin, as you'll soon be driving your own frigate, I will use my captain's privilege for one last time and take her in myself."

"But of course, sir." The first officer came to stand by the command chair, ramrod straight in a picture perfect parade rest position and locked his eyes on the main screen.

"Helm, braking thrusters on full for five seconds," she ordered.

"Braking thrusters full for five seconds, aye," Guthren replied.

"Engage."

Slowly, the last of the Type 203 frigates decelerated and entered orbit, her bow aimed at docking ring number one on the immense Starbase. The men and women of her crew were unaware that many, very many aboard the station, even now watched *Stingray*'s approach, including Rear Admiral Ryn and her staff, paying a quiet tribute to the old ship's long years of service.

*

A drum began to beat out the measure for a slow march, joined by the pipes of the local garrison's Marine band as Captain Siobhan Dunmoore and her officers walked down the gangway for the last time, in full dress uniforms with drawn swords.

To the skirl of a traditional march, they took up position on the floor of the Starbase hangar deck, facing a packed audience come to see the decommissioning. When all stood in their appointed positions, Dunmoore turned around to face the way she had come.

"Coxswain, march off the ship's company."

Her command rang echoed loud and clear in the vast compartment.

In response, a muffled male voice aboard the ship passed a series of orders, and the band struck up again, this time to the beat of several hundred pairs of heels as the petty officers and ratings followed their officers ashore.

The chiefs marched in the lead with Chief Petty Officer First Class Guthren at their head, sheathed swords at the hip, and the black rosewood canes of office tucked under their left arms. The remainder followed, formed by division under their petty officers, rifles and carbines at the shoulder, arms swinging, heads held high.

Wheeling, counter-marching, and never missing a beat, the ship's company formed three solid ranks behind their officers until the last spacer came to a halt, the signal for the band to stop playing.

Dunmoore turned back to face the reviewing stand, just in time to see Admiral Nagira march across the front of the audience and take his place on the dais.

"Ship's company, to the deputy chief of naval operations, present ARMS."

Weapons rose, then the sound of hands slapping forestocks rang out while swords arced down gracefully under the impetus of the band playing the general salute.

"Shoulder ARMS. Order ARMS."

Had this been a usual parade, Dunmoore would have invited Admiral Nagira to inspect the ranks, but this was far from an ordinary ceremony. Instead, the admiral himself spoke, as much to the formation as to the audience.

"Officers, petty officers and crew of the *Stingray*, ladies, and gentlemen. We are here today to witness the decommissioning of one of the finest frigates in the Navy, one I had the privilege of commanding many years ago. As the last act before I order Captain Dunmoore to proceed, it is my great pleasure to inform you all that the ship has been awarded the Secretary General's Commendation for her service to the Commonwealth."

A spontaneous cheer erupted from the ranks while the crew frantically tapped the butts of their rifles on the steel deck, accompanied by the enthusiastic applause of the spectators.

Nagira met Dunmoore's eyes and, unexpectedly, winked at her. The commendation would not make up for the fact that she was about to send her ship into history, but it would lessen the sting of loss somewhat. He waited until the commotion died down before continuing.

"As much as I would be proud to inspect the formation, this ceremony isn't about the crew or their reviewing officer. It is about *Stingray,* and I have no need to inspect her to know what a grand old lady she is. Captain Dunmoore, you may proceed."

Siobhan turned to face the gangway again and took a deep breath to clamp down on her emotions. Her next order would make the end of the ship's existence very real.

"March off *Stingray.*"

A muffled command answered hers from inside the ship and then, they heard the clicking of a dozen pairs of heels marching off the ship in unison.

Soon, a detail of spacers of all ranks appeared, weapons at the high port as they escorted the gleaming ship's bell, carried by Petty Officer Rownes, ashore. As soon as the first row of guards appeared, a single drum started beating, accompanied by a single bagpipe, and a strong alto voice broke over the assembly. Chief Foste began singing an old, old song of pride, loss, and duty. Soon, the entire ship's company joined in while the rest of the band struck up their instruments.

The bell and its escort marched off to the right flank in front of the formation, counter-marched, and then, when Dunmoore gave the order to present arms, started walking down the ranks in slow time. Each member of the crew got a last close-up glimpse of the bell that embodied the frigate's soul.

With their slow procession completed, the escort took position in the center of the formation, facing Dunmoore.

"As this is the final parade for *Stingray*'s company," Nagira began, "we must give remembrance to all who served and especially those who have lost their lives in her. I would ask the audience to please rise."

A single piper began to play Amazing Grace, and Dunmoore ordered the formation to present arms, and then reverse them in the mourning position.

As more and more pipes joined the first one, Admiral Nagira began reciting the names of those who had died serving aboard the ship. When he came to Lieutenant Commander Tiner, Commonwealth Medal of Honor and Able Spacer Bertram, Commonwealth Medal of Honor, Dunmoore choked back a sob. If it had not been for those two saving the ship at Cimmeria, she and the rest of the ship's company would not be alive today.

Although Colonel Kalivan, Commonwealth Army, had not been a member of the crew, strictly speaking, she had made sure he figured on the long list, so that his memory would forever be associated with *Stingray*. When Nagira read out his name, the last after Spacer Wim, a tear ran down her cheek. Then, the pipes died down one by one until the last strains faded away.

After a minute of silence that felt like an eternity, Dunmoore placed the ranks back at the shoulder arms position and looked up to the admiral on the reviewing stand.

She dreaded the next order but knew she could not avoid the duty the moment she had read the message calling them home.

"Captain Dunmoore, please ring nine bells."

She sheathed her sword, turned and marched up to the bell, grasping the braided rope that hung beneath. At an unheard command, the band began playing Auld Lang Syne and at the appropriate moments in the tune, she rang the bell that had counted out the hours until she reached eight, usually the number marking the end of a watch.

The ninth, by tradition, was the death knell, and when it rang out, *Stingray* would be no more, the formation in front of her would no longer be a ship's company, and she would be a captain without a command.

She pulled the rope, and the last peal rang out.

Her ship now belonged to history.

"Parade, to *Stingray*, present ARMS."

She raised her hand in salute while the escort slow marched out of their place in the center of the formation, wheeled to the right and left the hangar deck to the wail of the pipes, consigning the bell to a museum until such a time as a new ship of the same name came into commission.

The remainder of the ceremony passed in a blur, and she soon found herself sharing a cocktail with Admiral Nagira in an adjoining compartment that had been set up for the reception.

"You've done well, Siobhan and the promotion is well deserved." A tight smile softened his severe features.

"Thank you, sir."

She nodded, staring into her drink to keep her disappointment at not getting another ship from showing, but she could not fool the old man.

He motioned her to follow him away from the crowd and the former crewmembers lining up for farewells, as many of them would be shipping out that evening and the remainder the next day. The war did not allow any lengthy periods of idleness for anyone wearing a uniform.

"You know I never waste talent, Siobhan," he said when they had a modicum of privacy and could not be overheard.

"Yes, sir."

Nagira spoke at length in that calm, almost serene tone she had always found so soothing and when he finished, the hugs, handshakes, and adieus became much easier to bear.

By the time she slipped into her bunk in the station's transient quarters, exhausted, a little woozy from drinking and sore from the crew's many, many displays of sorrow at their parting, she nevertheless had a smile on her face. Tomorrow would be an exciting day indeed.

— Found —

"A desk job?" Pushkin shook his head at the injustice of it all. "I get a frigate. Not just any frigate but *Jan Sobieski*, the newest of the Voivode class. Everyone else aboard with a few exceptions here and there gets a billet in space, but you're beached. I knew the Navy wasn't big on fairness, but this is ridiculous."

Dunmoore shrugged.

"At least I got my step to post captain, Gregor. That's something I hadn't counted on."

Her former first officer made a disgusted face as he slumped back in his chair, eyes darting over her shoulder at the space dock beyond the thick windows, where *Stingray*, now silent and dark, hung forlornly, waiting on the tugs that would take her to the knackers yard.

"Waste of talent is what I call it. Not even a flag captain's appointment."

She snorted with barely suppressed laughter.

"As if. I'm too junior for a flag captain's billet. Besides, I don't know of any rear admiral who has an eye on me and who'd be willing to call upon my services. I've had more than my fair share of time in command of FTL warships, Gregor. The promotion is all the reward I'm going to get, and I'll just have to make the best of my new duties. Speaking of which," she glanced at the large antique clock by the wardroom's simulated fireplace, "I'm due to report aboard my ride soon. I'd better make sure all of my dunnage is at the airlock."

She rose and straightened her tunic.

"Captain Pushkin," she held out her hand and smiled, "it's been a privilege to serve with you. I know you'll make sure *Jan Sobieski* becomes the finest frigate in the Navy. With

Devall as your first officer and Foste as your cox'n, you've got one of the best command teams I can think of."

"I had a most excellent teacher," his dark eyes met hers, "and I owe you a lot. You were the best captain I've ever served under and I'll make you proud. *Jan Sobieski* won't be *Stingray*, but she'll carry on the proud traditions we made our own on the old girl. You'll see."

"I know," she replied softly. "I'm going to miss you, Gregor. We might not have started off on the most auspicious basis, but I can't think of anyone I'd rather have as my first officer."

On impulse, she hugged him, fighting back the tears.

"Take care of yourself."

"You too, Siobhan."

She stepped back, came to attention, and saluted.

"Fair winds and following seas, Captain."

"To you as well."

She winked at him and before he could do more than glimpse the moisture gathering in the corners of her eyes, she walked away, out of the wardroom and out of Commander Gregor Pushkin's life.

He would soon be the sole master aboard after God, on the bridge of his own warship with all the trials, tribulations, and rewards that implied. As for Siobhan, he need not have worried.

*

Guthren waited for her by the docking bay, a duffel bag at his feet, along with an eager leading spacer who, by all rights, should not have been there.

She returned their salutes and then cocked a questioning eyebrow at her former coxswain.

"What, pray tell, is the meaning of this, Chief? I don't recall our orders including Spacer Vincenzo."

"I still have friends in the special ops community, sir, so I pulled some very fast strings. Where we're headed, the young lad's going to be useful. Plus, it wouldn't have been right to let some other captain misuse him."

"You mean he talked you into it." She shook her head. "I thought you weren't a soft touch, Chief. How did Vincenzo find out about our new posting anyway?"

Before she could force an answer out of Guthren, a young ensign materialized on the station end of the gangway.

"Captain Dunmoore, Chief Guthren, your belongings have been stowed, the additional items required by the Admiralty are in your quarters, and we're ready to leave as soon as you're aboard." She glanced at Vincenzo. "We got word a few hours ago that there would be a third member in your party. He'll have to make do with his own kit until we've delivered you."

"Thanks." Dunmoore gave Guthren a warning glance, to indicate that she intended to continue the conversation at another time.

They followed the officer aboard the sloop and Siobhan felt right away that it did not have the aura of an ordinary warship, which was all to the good.

Special Operations Command would not be very useful if its undercover ships left a distinctly naval odor in their wake.

Once in her cabin, she opened the small package that waited for her, retrieving a set of merchant marine uniforms of the casual kind used by those whose cargo does not always conform to strict legal standards.

Dark trousers, black jacket, white, collarless shirt, a gun belt complete with non-regulation blaster and soft boots reaching almost to the knees.

She changed out of her service dress and put on the civilian clothes, down to the strap hanging from the left shoulder that identified her as a commercial ship's captain: four gold stripes without the executive curl worn by naval officers.

She dug into her duffel and pulled out a small case that contained the few items of jewelry she owned. Finding a suitably gaudy earring, she adorned her left ear in the manner favored by some of the more roguish spacers. It signaled that she was not one of those stolid masters who drove ships for large corporations. A few rings on her thumbs and fingers completed the transformation.

When she joined the sloop's captain on the bridge, he gave her an approving once over. As she had expected, the small starship's crew, now that they had undocked from the station, also looked like vaguely disreputable star lane tramps.

"If I may say so, sir, you look like a natural."

"The scar helps, no doubt." She grinned. "Every decent pirate should have one."

"We prefer to think of ourselves as pretend privateers, Captain, though *Revenge* could credibly raise the black flag."

"Not so much *Iolanthe*, I think."

"No, definitely not." He glanced at the screen embedded in his command chair's arm. "Speaking of which, she's just come out of FTL. We'll have you aboard in no time."

*

The sloop's young captain was as good as his word. Early the next day, far out on the fringes of the system, far from prying eyes, they matched velocities with a large bulk freighter outwardly resembling a less nimble, more ungainly version of the Navy's supply ships.

Siobhan had little time to examine the new arrival as she, Guthren and Vincenzo were bundled, along with their baggage, aboard a shuttle that had come from *Iolanthe*.

The two men had kept out of sight for most of the short trip and had the grace to look somewhat sheepish when they reported to the shuttle bay, dressed in moderately disreputable civilian garb, minus any sort of merchant rank insignia.

During the short flight over, the pilot, a young woman wearing the same type of clothing as Dunmoore, down to the strap hanging from the shoulder identifying her as the merchant equivalent of a sub-lieutenant, did not speak beyond identifying herself and welcoming Siobhan and Chief Guthren aboard. However, the moment, the shuttle crossed the energy barrier keeping the hanger deck's air from escaping into space she flicked on the radio.

"*Iolanthe* arriving."

Outside, a party of spacers in civilian clothing had formed up in three ranks, each carrying a short plasma carbine across the chest, held there by a combat sling.

A one-eyed man wearing the three stripes of a merchant first officer on his strap took position in front of the formation, joined by a hulking woman with a silver bosun's call hanging from a chain around her neck.

They were evidently going to do this in proper Navy style, even though they looked more like a bunch of semi-feral mercenaries, with the determinedly non-regulation hairstyles and decorations to match. At least Ezekiel Holt had resisted the temptation to grow a beard like so many of the crew standing behind him.

The moment the shuttle's rear ramp dropped a sharp command called the formation to present arms. As one, the carbines rose up while hands slapped the forestock.

The bosun's mate, who had raised the call to her lips moments before, began trilling the proper sequence marking the arrival of a warship's captain in her new command.

Ezekiel Holt's sharp salute might have seemed incongruous, but it felt quite natural to return it.

"Welcome aboard *Iolanthe*, Captain. Your ship is in all respects ready for space."

"Thank you, Mister Holt."

"Would the Captain care to inspect the side party?"

"By all means."

As she walked down the ranks, recognizing a face here and there from previous ships, she felt heartened by the sense of quiet competence the men and women of her new command exuded. She would find no *Stingray*-sized problems here. Not that the Special Operations Command would let those happen aboard their pride and joy, a ship like no other in the Fleet.

Holt dismissed the crew, and then led her toward the bridge, followed at a discreet distance by Guthren and Vincenzo. Once in the passageway she reached out and squeezed his upper arm briefly.

"When I found out you'd be my first officer in *Iolanthe*, I couldn't quite believe my ears. How did you manage that?

Last I heard you were still doing dark deeds for counter-intelligence."

"I finally got my turn in the regen tanks for my leg, and once I'd completed the course of therapy with success, I demanded a return to duties in space. Since, apparently, I've been so useful doing those dark deeds, they gave me a compromise, Number One aboard the newest Q-ship, with notice that I'd have to sail her as acting captain for a few weeks, until her permanent skipper showed up."

"That came as quite a surprise, you know. For all anyone could tell, Command was sending me to a desk job at HQ, the promotion to post rank being a consolation prize for taking away my ship. I found out about *Iolanthe* from Admiral Nagira in person after *Stingray*'s decommissioning ceremonies, said appointment to be kept a secret. My former first officer, now a frigate captain in his own right, was cursing the Navy only yesterday for the unfair way in which it had treated me."

"He turned out alright, didn't he, your Mister Pushkin."

She gave him a warm smile.

"He did at that. A very reliable officer and a good friend to boot. My luck with the first officer's union has been pretty decent over the years, seeing as how I've got you again."

"First officer's union?" Holt looked at her with amusement.

"Gregor Pushkin's quip, whenever I'd protest at his telling me something I didn't want to hear, was to remind me of the first officers' union rules."

Holt laughed with delight.

"He definitely turned out alright. I'll be remembering that, Captain. Union rules indeed."

"I think I'm going to be sorry I told you."

"I think you will."

"Still, it's good to have you at my side again. Did you keep the eye patch as an affectation or because they couldn't slot you for that kind of regen?"

"A bit of both. There's probably an eye growing somewhere with my own tissues, and when it's ready, they'll beach me for however long it takes to transplant and make sure it works."

"Considering what we are, I think the patch is appropriate for once."

"I thought so too." He stopped at a door set into the left bulkhead, a few meters ahead of the door to the bridge. "The officer of the watch has us at sublight cruising stations. We'll hold in this system until you've digested our orders. It'll give you time to familiarize yourself with *Iolanthe*."

Turning to Guthren, he nodded toward the bridge.

"Chief, you'll find the bosun taking her turn as a watchkeeper. She's been doing double duty pending your arrival, and I'm sure she'll be glad to turn things over to you now."

"Aye, aye, sir. Knowing Chief Dwyn, she's chomping at the bit to pass all of the ship's little problems on to me."

Iolanthe's new coxswain briefly snapped to attention and nodded instead of saluting, then jerked his chin back toward the way they had come as he looked at Vincenzo.

"Go make yourself familiar with the layout and see that the captain's quarters have been cleaned up. You never know with this lot. Then, report to the security division and show them you know the business end of a blaster from a hole in the deck."

While Guthren spoke, Commander Holt touched a pad set into the bulkhead, and the door slipped aside silently, revealing a large, almost luxurious office, complete with a conference table big enough for all of the department heads and then some.

At the look on Siobhan's face, he laughed.

"The one thing we're not short of on this ship is space, as you'll find out." He waved her through the opening. "Why don't you take your desk for a spin while I make us a brace of coffees? As I recall, you take yours black?"

"As black as my soul, Zeke."

"Pshaw. If you had a black soul, you'd be an admiral by now."

"Instead, I'm in command of a cruiser disguised as a freighter."

"Close, but not quite."

"Oh?" She took the proffered mug, amused to see it display a commercial logo above the ship's name. The cover identity reached down into the smallest details.

"Unlike every large Q-ship the Navy has used over the centuries, they purpose-built *Iolanthe* from the keel up, using some of the same architecture as the Warlord class battle cruisers. In other words, she carries a battleship's ordnance on an extended cruiser base wrapped in an innocuous bulk freighter's envelope. We even have cargo holds large enough to serve as proof that we're a commercial ship, or to carry mission-specific pods, ground troops, or fighters. She looks cumbersome and ungainly, and can dampen her emissions to the point of fooling anyone, even with good sensors, but in battle, you'll find her just as nimble as any good cruiser."

"Crew?"

"Not that much bigger than a frigate's for all her size. She's heavily automated and with the Q-ship envelope around her core hull, she doesn't need the kind of gunnery, systems, or damage control teams a warship of the same tonnage requires."

"Nice." She took a sip of the hot liquid and grimaced. "Navy style, Zeke? I would have thought that you'd brief the wardroom steward better than that."

He shrugged.

"It's what the officers like. If you want to change their tastes, be my guest. They consider themselves salty dogs and like their brew to be suitable. Nevertheless, they're a solid bunch, as you'll see. Veterans all and volunteers for special operations."

"Volunteers, eh? Does that mean I'm the only one who didn't raise her hand when the Admiralty fairies came flitting around asking for people keen on serving the Navy in new and innovative ways?"

"Pretty much." He chuckled. "But I can't think of a captain who's better suited to take this big girl through her paces and give the bad guys the largest and last fright of their miserable lives. You have a knack for surprising the enemy, and with a Q-ship under your command, you can run rampant along the frontier."

She snorted with derision.

"Who'd have thought the Admiralty would let me run rampant once again, after the frights I've given them."

"Admiral Nagira, no doubt, sir," Holt replied mischievously. "The old man's always got a plan, and he'll always have a soft spot in his hard heart for maverick captains like you. If you need proof, just consider that he's let you keep Guthren as your cox'n."

"At least he's got the excuse of having done time with special operations before joining *Stingray*. By the way, I still owe him a talking-to for finagling Vincenzo's transfer without permission."

Holt shrugged.

"We have plenty of spare billets and it's just as well that you have a bodyguard, considering the places we might end up visiting. I'm sure the second officer won't mind an additional pair of hands for the damage control parties either."

Siobhan glared at him with suspicious eyes.

"I see that my new first officer is already conspiring with my old cox'n to manage their captain. Well then, Mister Holt, why don't we open our orders from Admiral Nagira and see which disreputable places we'll visit first."

About the Author

Eric Thomson is the pen name of a retired Canadian Eric Thomson is the pen name of a retired Canadian soldier with thirty-one years of service, both in the Regular Army and the Army Reserve. He spent his Regular Army career in the Infantry and his Reserve service in the Armoured Corps.   He worked as an information technology specialist for a number of years before retiring to become a full-time author.

Eric has been a voracious reader of science fiction, military fiction, and history all his life. Several years ago, he put fingers to keyboard and started writing his own military sci-fi, with a definite space opera slant, using many of his own experiences as a soldier for inspiration.

When he is not writing fiction, Eric indulges in his other passions: photography, hiking, and scuba diving, all of which he shares with his wife.

Join Eric Thomson at: www.thomsonfiction.ca/

Where you will find news about upcoming books and more information about the universe in which his heroes fight for humanity's survival.

Read his blog at: www.ericthomsonblog.wordpress.com

If you enjoyed this book, please consider leaving a review on Goodreads, or with your favorite online retailer to help others discover it.

Also by Eric Thomson

Siobhan Dunmoore

No Honor in Death (Siobhan Dunmoore Book 1)
The Path of Duty (Siobhan Dunmoore Book 2)
Like Stars in Heaven (Siobhan Dunmoore Book 3)
Victory's Bright Dawn (Siobhan Dunmoore Book 4)
Without Mercy (Siobhan Dunmoore Book 5)

Decker's War

Death Comes But Once (Decker's War Book 1)
Cold Comfort (Decker's War Book 2)
Fatal Blade (Decker's War Book 3)
Howling Stars (Decker's War Book 4)
Black Sword (Decker's War Book 5)
No Remorse (Decker's War Book 6)
Hard Strike (Decker's War Book 7)

Quis Custodiet

The Warrior's Knife (Quis Custodiet No 1)

Ashes of Empire

Imperial Sunset (Ashes of Empire #1)

Printed in Great Britain
by Amazon